新编英国文学教程(修订版)

彭家海 曾 莉 卢秋平 编著

华中科技大学出版社
中国·武汉

内 容 简 介

《新编英国文学教程》(修订版)是用英语编写、文学史和作品选读相结合的高等学校英语专业本科生教材,语言规范、地道,史料翔实,可供英语专业高年级学生和英语水平相当的英语爱好者以及文学爱好者阅读,也可作为英语专业考研参考书。《新编英国文学教程》(修订版)全书共七章,按时间顺序编排,每章包括时代背景、文学流派和作家介绍、代表作故事梗概、作品选读、作品注释和生词表,以及思考题等。所选作家及其作品具有代表性和可读性,便于学生欣赏和教师授课。

图书在版编目(CIP)数据

新编英国文学教程/彭家海,曾莉,卢秋平编著.—2版(修订本).—武汉:华中科技大学出版社,2016.3(2023.7重印)
  ISBN 978-7-5680-1560-8

Ⅰ.①新… Ⅱ.①彭… ②曾… ③卢… Ⅲ.①英国文学-文学史-教材 Ⅳ.①I561.09

中国版本图书馆 CIP 数据核字(2016)第 029298 号

新编英国文学教程(修订版)　　　　　　　　　　　　彭家海　曾　莉　卢秋平　编著
Xinbian Yingguo Wenxue Jiaocheng (Xiudingban)

策划编辑:	刘　平
责任编辑:	刘　平
封面设计:	原色设计
责任校对:	曾　婷
责任监印:	周治超

出版发行:华中科技大学出版社(中国·武汉)　　电话:(027)81321913
　　　　　武汉市东湖新技术开发区华工科技园　　邮编:430223

录　排:	华中科技大学惠友文印中心
印　刷:	武汉邮科印务有限公司
开　本:	787mm×1092mm　1/16
印　张:	15
字　数:	412 千字
版　次:	2023 年 7 月第 2 版第 4 次印刷
定　价:	39.80 元

本书若有印装质量问题,请向出版社营销中心调换
全国免费服务热线:400-6679-118　竭诚为您服务
版权所有　侵权必究

前　　言

　　现在大家谈论的热点问题是素质教育。大学生应该具备的素质中最主要的是人文素质,而对英语专业的学生来说,西方文化、英美文学等是真正的专业课程,当属核心。然而,在应试教育的冲击下,目前很多学生只关心语言技能,以为只要能说一口流利的英语就足够了。这是对英语专业一种肤浅和错误的认识,因为学生的思维能力、分析能力以及对异域文化的接受能力等没有得到应有的训练。其实,学生在文化、文学方面的学习与获得语言技能不但不冲突,而且它还是语言学习的更高阶段。如何在提高人文素质的同时培养学生各种与语言有关的能力已经成了一些有识之士关注的焦点。为此,我们根据多年的实践经验,编写了一套英语专业文化、文学教材。其中《新编英国文学教程》是在收集了广大读者使用《新编美国文学教程》的情况基础上编写的。本教程的特点如下。

　　一、突出实用性。鉴于课时的限制,我们精选了部分作家、作品。所选作家均在很大程度上代表某一文学流派;所选作品能反映该作者的风格和特色。在确保作品的经典性的同时,考虑其可读性。这样可以激起学生阅读的兴趣。

　　为了便于读者阅读,除了必要的注释,本教程特地为部分生词较多、难度较大的作品提供了生词表。我们之所以这样做是因为很多学生由于作品中的生词较多而不能深入地阅读和理解,从而失去了对文学课的兴趣,使作品欣赏和课堂讨论无法进行。

　　二、考虑到英国文学的特点,我们在突出诗歌、散文和短篇小说的同时,兼顾戏剧和长篇小说等文学形式。主要选读作品是诗歌、散文和短篇小说,对戏剧和长篇小说中的名篇提供故事梗概等内容,以便让读者对作家和文学流派等有更全面的认识。作品的多样性可以保持读者对英语学习的兴趣。

　　三、坚持把作品置于首位。对作家只进行简短扼要的介绍;为了保证作品的完整性,尽量不从长篇中节选。因为对某一作家的风格和作品的主题等的了解和认识最好是通过阅读作品本身来实现而不应依靠对作家、作品的介绍。这更有利于读者自己阅读理解。

　　四、文学史和作品选读相结合。除了作家介绍,我们还对英国文学中各个时期的社会背景和文学特色进行了介绍。

　　五、注重培养读者对文化的兴趣。由于文学与文化密不可分,我们在背景及作家介绍、选材和注释等方面都把文化置于突出位置。注释主要集中在词典等工具书上难以查到的文化现象。

　　另外,为了提高读者用目的语思维和分析的能力,我们为所有选读作品都提供了思考题,供讨论时使用。我们希望通过此类活动提高读者的表达能力。

　　《新编英国文学教程》的问世是华中科技大学出版社几位编辑辛勤劳动的结晶。他们在时间紧、任务重的情况下,为本教程的出版做出了细致的工作。我在此深表谢意。

　　参加本书编写工作的都是教学一线的老师。除主编外,还有詹琍敏副教授、谢群副教授、贾勤副教授,以及卢秋平、李晶和卫华老师。全书的设计、选材、文字修改和最后的通读定稿都由主编负责。由于编者水平有限,再加上时间仓促,谬误之处,请读者指正。

彭家海

2006年元月于武昌

修订说明

为了给文学爱好者和英语学习者提供更丰富的背景知识和更好的阅读材料,我们对《新编英国文学教程》进行了全面修订,主要包括以下几个方面。

一、删除了第一版里的部分作品;修改了其中的语言错误;更新了作家、作品等的相关信息。借此机会,我们向就第一版提出各种修改意见的读者表示感谢。

二、增加了对各个时期英国文学发展演变情况的介绍,以便于读者把握相应时期文学的特点。

三、为了让读者更好地把握英国文学的全貌,修订版收进了斯宾塞、马洛、德莱顿、戈尔丁、莱辛、奈保尔等作家,使教材涵盖了二十世纪后期及二十一世纪初的英国文学,并增加了一些优秀作品。

参加本教程修订、编写工作的都是在英国文学教学和研究方面进行了多年探索的一线老师。其中,曾莉教授负责德莱顿和戈尔丁两位作家的编写,卢秋平老师负责莱辛和奈保尔两位作家的编写,其他作家及其作品注解、介绍和各章节的绪论修订以及全书的选材和最后的通读定稿都由第一作者负责。美籍教师 Daniel Churchman 对编著部分的文字进行了润色。在此深表谢意。

由于编著者水平有限,本教程中难免有谬误、疏漏之处,欢迎广大读者继续提出修改意见。

编著者

2015 年 11 月 7 日于武昌

Contents

Chapter One The Medieval Period ··· (1)
1. Introduction ··· (1)
　1.1　Historical Background ··· (1)
　1.2　Literature in the Middle Ages ··· (1)
2. Geoffrey Chaucer (ca. 1343-1400) ·· (2)
3. Selected Writings ··· (3)
　3.1　*Beowulf* (an excerpt) ·· (3)
　3.2　The Twa Corbies (a popular ballad) ······································ (4)
　3.3　The General Prologue (excerpts from *The Canterbury Tales*) ······ (5)

Chapter Two The Elizabethan Age ·· (11)
1. Introduction ··· (11)
　1.1　The Renaissance ·· (11)
　1.2　The Renaissance in England ·· (12)
　1.3　Literature of the Renaissance ··· (12)
2. Edmund Spenser (1552-1599) ·· (13)
3. Francis Bacon (1561-1626) ··· (14)
4. Christopher Marlowe (1564-1593) ·· (15)
　4.1　Life and Career ··· (15)
　4.2　*Dr Faustus* (synopsis) ·· (16)
5. William Shakespeare (1564-1616) ··· (16)
　5.1　Life and Career ··· (16)
　5.2　Major Works ··· (17)
　　5.2.1　*Hamlet* (synopsis) ·· (17)
　　5.2.2　*Macbeth* (synopsis) ·· (19)
　　5.2.3　*The Merchant of Venice* (synopsis) ································· (20)
6. John Donne (1572-1631) ·· (21)
7. Selected Writings ·· (21)
　7.1　*The Faerie Queene* by Spenser (two excerpts from Canto I, Book I) ········· (21)
　7.2　*Dr Faustus* by Marlowe (an excerpt from Scene I, Act I) ············· (22)
　7.3　*The Merchant of Venice* by Shakespeare (an excerpt from ACT IV) ········· (25)
　7.4　*Hamlet* by Shakespeare (An Excerpt from Act III) ····················· (36)
　7.5　"Sonnet 18" by Shakespeare ·· (37)
　7.6　"Sonnet 29" by Shakespeare ·· (38)
　7.7　"The Flea" by Donne ··· (38)

7.8 "The Sun Rising" by Donne ……(39)
7.9 "The Canonization" by Donne ……(40)
7.10 "Death Be Not Proud" by Donne ……(42)
7.11 "Of Studies" by Bacon ……(42)
7.12 "Of Marriage and Single Life" by Bacon ……(44)

Chapter Three   The Restoration ……(46)
1. Introduction ……(46)
   1.1 The Restoration ……(46)
   1.2 Literary Characteristics ……(46)
2. John Milton (1608-1674) ……(47)
3. John Bunyan (1628-1688) ……(48)
   3.1 Life and Career ……(48)
   3.2 *The Pilgrim's Progress* (synopsis) ……(49)
4. John Dryden (1631-1700) ……(49)
5. Selected Writings ……(50)
   5.1 *Paradise Lost* (Excerpts from Book I) by Milton ……(50)
   5.2 "When I Consider How My Light Is Spent" by Milton ……(52)
   5.3 "Methought I Saw My Late Espoused Saint" by Milton ……(53)
   5.4 *The Pilgrim's Progress* by Bunyan (An Excerpt from Part I) ……(53)
   5.5 "To the Memory of Mr. Oldham" by Dryden ……(56)
   5.6 "A Song for St. Cecilia's Day" by Dryden ……(57)

Chapter Four   The Enlightenment Period ……(61)
1. Introduction ……(61)
   1.1 Enlightenment Ideas ……(61)
   1.2 Literature during the Enlightenment Period ……(61)
2. Daniel Defoe (1660-1731) ……(63)
   2.1 Life and Career ……(63)
   2.2 *Robinson Crusoe* (synopsis) ……(63)
3. Jonathan Swift (1667-1745) ……(64)
   3.1 Life and Career ……(64)
   3.2 *Gulliver's Travels* (synopsis) ……(65)
4. Joseph Addison (1672-1719) ……(66)
5. Alexander Pope (1688-1744) ……(66)
6. Samuel Richardson (1689-1761) ……(67)
   6.1 Life and Career ……(67)
   6.2 *Clarissa*: or *The History of a Young Lady* (synopsis) ……(68)
7. Henry Fielding (1707-1754) ……(68)
   7.1 Life and Career ……(68)
   7.2 *Tom Jones* (synopsis) ……(69)

8. Samuel Johnson (1709-1784) ……………………………………………………… (69)
9. Selected Writings ……………………………………………………………………… (70)
   9.1 "A Modest Proposal" by Swift ……………………………………………… (70)
   9.2 "Sir Roger at Church" from *The Spectator* (July 9, 1711) by Addison ………… (77)
   9.3 *An Essay on Man*: *Epistle* II (an excerpt) by Alexander Pope ……………… (79)
   9.4 "To the Right Honourable the Earl of Chesterfield" by Johnson ……………… (80)

Chapter Five   The Romantic Period ……………………………………………… (83)
1. Introduction …………………………………………………………………………… (83)
   1.1 Historical Background …………………………………………………………… (83)
   1.2 Romanticism ……………………………………………………………………… (84)
   1.3 English Romanticism …………………………………………………………… (84)
2. William Blake (1757-1827) ………………………………………………………… (85)
3. Robert Burns (1759-1796) ………………………………………………………… (86)
4. William Wordsworth (1770-1850) ………………………………………………… (86)
5. Walter Scott (1771-1832) …………………………………………………………… (88)
   5.1 Life and Career …………………………………………………………………… (88)
   5.2 *Ivanhoe* (synopsis) ……………………………………………………………… (88)
6. Samuel Taylor Coleridge (1772-1834) …………………………………………… (89)
7. Jane Austen (1775-1817) …………………………………………………………… (90)
   7.1 Life and Career …………………………………………………………………… (90)
   7.2 *Pride and Prejudice* (synopsis) ……………………………………………… (90)
8. Charles Lamb (1775-1834) ………………………………………………………… (91)
9. George Gordon Byron (1788-1824) ……………………………………………… (92)
10. Percy Bysshe Shelley (1792-1822) ……………………………………………… (93)
11. John Keats (1795-1821) …………………………………………………………… (94)
12. Selected Writings …………………………………………………………………… (95)
    12.1 "London" by Blake ……………………………………………………………… (95)
    12.2 "The Tyger" by Blake …………………………………………………………… (95)
    12.3 "The Chimney Sweeper" by Blake …………………………………………… (96)
    12.4 "A Red, Red Rose" by Burns ………………………………………………… (97)
    12.5 "Auld Lang Syne" by Burns …………………………………………………… (98)
    12.6 "Robert Bruce's March to Bannockburn" by Burns ……………………… (99)
    12.7 "For a' that and a' that" by Burns ………………………………………… (100)
    12.8 "She Dwelt among the Untrodden Ways" by Wordsworth ……………… (102)
    12.9 "I Wandered Lonely As a Cloud" by Wordsworth ……………………… (102)
    12.10 "The Solitary Reaper" by Wordsworth …………………………………… (103)
    12.11 "To the Cuckoo" by Wordsworth …………………………………………… (104)
    12.12 "Composed Upon Westminster Bridge, September 3, 1802" by Wordsworth
    …………………………………………………………………………………………… (105)

12.13	"London, 1802" by Wordsworth	(106)
12.14	"Kubla Khan" by Coleridge	(107)
12.15	"Dream Children; a Reverie" by Lamb	(108)
12.16	"She Walks in Beauty" by Byron	(113)
12.17	"The Isles of Greece" (from Canto III, *Don Juan*) by Byron	(113)
12.18	"Ode to the West Wind" by Shelley	(117)
12.19	"Ozymandias" by Shelley	(120)
12.20	"To—" by Shelley	(121)
12.21	"To a Skylark" by Shelley	(122)
12.22	"Ode to a Nightingale" by Keats	(125)
12.23	"Ode on a Grecian Urn" by Keats	(128)
12.24	"On first Looking into Chapman's Homer" by Keats	(130)

Chapter Six   The Victorian Age ······ (131)

1. Introduction ······ (131)
   1.1　Historical Background ······ (131)
   1.2　Literary Characteristics ······ (131)
2. Alfred Lord Tennyson (1809-1892) ······ (133)
3. Robert Browning (1812-1889) and Elizabeth Browning (1806-1861) ······ (134)
4. Charles Dickens (1812-1870) ······ (135)
   4.1　Life and Career ······ (135)
   4.2　*David Copperfield* (synopsis) ······ (136)
5. The Brontë Sisters ······ (136)
   5.1　Literary Career ······ (136)
   5.2　Major Works ······ (137)
     5.2.1　*Wuthering Heights* (synopsis) ······ (137)
     5.2.2　*Jane Eyre* (synopsis) ······ (138)
6. George Eliot (1819-1880) ······ (140)
   6.1　Life and Career ······ (140)
   6.2　*Middlemarch* (synopsis) ······ (141)
7. Thomas Hardy (1840-1928) ······ (142)
   7.1　Life and Career ······ (142)
   7.2　*Tess of the D'Urbervilles* (synopsis) ······ (142)
8. George Bernard Shaw (1856-1950) ······ (144)
   8.1　Life and Career ······ (144)
   8.2　*Mrs. Warren's Profession* (synopsis) ······ (144)
9. Selected Writings ······ (145)
   9.1　"Ulysses" by Tennyson ······ (145)
   9.2　"Break, Break, Break" by Tennyson ······ (147)
   9.3　"My Last Duchess" by Robert Browning ······ (148)

9.4 "Home Thoughts, from the Sea" by Robert Browning ……………… (150)
9.5 "How Do I Love Thee? Let me Count the Ways." by Elizabeth Browning … (151)
9.6 "Biographical Notice of Ellis and Acton Bell" by Charlotte Bronte …………… (151)

Chapter Seven The Twentieth Century …………………………… (158)
1. Introduction …………………………………………………………… (158)
   1.1 Historical Background ………………………………………… (158)
   1.2 Modernism ……………………………………………………… (159)
   1.3 Literary Characteristics ……………………………………… (160)
2. Joseph Conrad (1857-1924) ………………………………………… (161)
   2.1 Life and Career ………………………………………………… (161)
   2.2 *Heart of Darkness* (synopsis) ……………………………… (162)
3. William Butler Yeats (1865-1939) ………………………………… (162)
4. E. M. Forster (1879-1970) ………………………………………… (163)
   4.1 Life and Career ………………………………………………… (163)
   4.2 *A Passage to India* (synopsis) ……………………………… (164)
5. James Joyce (1882-1941) …………………………………………… (165)
   5.1 Life and Career ………………………………………………… (165)
   5.2 *Ulysses* (synopsis) …………………………………………… (166)
6. Virginia Woolf (1882-1941) ………………………………………… (167)
   6.1 Life and Career ………………………………………………… (167)
   6.2 *To the Lighthouse* (synopsis) ……………………………… (168)
7. D. H. Lawrence (1885-1930) ……………………………………… (168)
   7.1 Life and Career ………………………………………………… (168)
   7.2 *Sons and Lovers* (synopsis) ………………………………… (169)
8. T. S. Eliot (1888-1965) …………………………………………… (170)
9. Samuel Beckett (1906-1989) ……………………………………… (171)
10. Wystan Hugh Auden (1907-1973) ………………………………… (172)
11. William Golding (1911-1993) …………………………………… (173)
    11.1 Life and Career ……………………………………………… (173)
    11.2 *Lord of the Flies* (synopsis) ……………………………… (174)
12. Doris Lessing (1919-2013) ……………………………………… (174)
    12.1 Life and career ……………………………………………… (174)
    12.2 *The Golden Notebook* (synopsis) ………………………… (175)
13. Sir V. S. Naipaul (1932-) …………………………………… (175)
    13.1 Life and Career ……………………………………………… (175)
    13.2 *A House for Mr. Biswas* (synopsis) ……………………… (176)
14. Selected Writings ………………………………………………… (176)
    14.1 "Down by the Salley Gardens" by Yeats …………………… (176)
    14.2 "Leda and the Swan" by Yeats ……………………………… (177)

14.3	"Sailing to Byzantium" by Yeats	(178)
14.4	"The Second Coming" by Yeats	(179)
14.5	"My Wood" by Forster	(180)
14.6	"Araby" by Joyce	(183)
14.7	"Dorothy Wordsworth" by Woolf	(189)
14.8	"The Mark on the Wall" by Woolf	(195)
14.9	"Tickets, Please" by Lawrence	(202)
14.10	"Journey of the Magi" by Eliot	(212)
14.11	"Sweeney among the Nightingales" by Eliot	(214)
14.12	*Waiting for Godot* by Beckett (An Excerpt from Act Ⅰ)	(215)
14.13	"Who's Who" by Auden	(223)
14.14	"Their Lonely Betters" by Auden	(223)
14.15	"In Memory of W. B. Yeats" by Auden	(224)

Bibliography (228)

Chapter One   The Medieval Period

1. Introduction

1.1 Historical Background

As is known to many, English Literature enjoys a long history and lasting popularity due, at least partly, to the fact that English has become the global language in many fields. It dates back to the Middle Ages which covers the period from the 5th century A. D. to the end of the 15th century in European history, although the Middle Ages is sometimes restricted to the period from the 11th to the 15th centuries. Known as the Medieval period, it saw the rise of Christianity, followed by Catholicism which is one of its two branches, and the Roman Catholic Church became so powerful that it came to dominate the whole of Western Europe. In Britain, the Middle Ages includes the Anglo-Saxon period (446 A. D. -1066) and the first four centuries after the Norman Conquest which took place in 1066.

The Angles and Saxons came to Britain several decades after the Roman legions withdrew from it. They and the earlier arriving Jutes established seven kingdoms—Kent, Essex, Sussex, Wessex, East Anglia, Mercia and Northumbria. The Anglo-Saxons were from what is now Germany and after they established themselves in England they developed Anglo-Saxon, a language which is known today as Old English. The Anglo-Saxons also brought their culture, including folk tales, to the island country.

In 597 Pope Gregory I sent St. Augustine, the prior of St. Andrew's Monastery in Rome, to England to convert the English, many of whom had been converted to Christianity during the Roman occupation, back to Christianity. Ethelbert, King of Kent, soon became a Christian. He provided accommodation for St. Augustine and his followers, and in the same year St. Augustine became the archbishop of Canterbury. Faced with the attacks by the Vikings and Danes in the early 9th century, Alfred (849-899), the Wessex king, managed to preserve the country, with the Danes controlling the north and east of England.

After William the Conqueror (William I) took over England, a feudal system was established. After much contact with the Danes, Old English took in many words from Danish and from Norman-French, and became simpler, evolving into Middle English in the 12th century. At the same time, mainland European cultures such as the French civilization were introduced into Britain by the Normans.

1.2 Literature in the Middle Ages

With complicated inflections, Anglo-Saxon is difficult to understand for the modern reader. This is the reason why the literature at that time, which is represented by *Beowulf*, the first great English literary work and the national epic of the Anglo-Saxons, can not be appreciated today unless translated into modern English. Composed in the 8th or 9th century and handed down orally and finally transcribed during the 10th century, it is the story of Beowulf, a hero among the ancient Scandinavians, who was considered a protector of the people for fighting against a monster named Grendel, his revengeful mother and a fire-breathing dragon, representatives of evil forces in society and human life.

With Britain opened to mainland Europe after the Norman Conquest, the writings of the period, known as Middle English literature, dealt with a wider range of subjects. The medieval romance, a popular literary form at that time, is filled with stories of conquerors of the classical world like Alexander the Great and legends of great figures such as Charlemagne of France and King Arthur of Britain and the like. A narrative verse form, medieval romance appeared in France in the 12th century. In the following centuries it spread to Germany and England. In the 13th century a romance was almost any sort of adventure story, be it of chivalry or of love. It is usually concerned with characters who live in a royal court rather than those from the everyday. *Sir Gawain and the Green Knight* (c. 1375) is the most well-known in medieval English literature. The romance records a chivalric age during which knights played an important role in court life as well as in society at large.

Middle English literature also saw the flourishing of ballads. Originally a song intended as a musical accompaniment to a dance, a ballad might be a light, simple song of any kind, or a popular song. Originating usually in rural areas, ballads are composed in simple language. In the relatively recent sense, a ballad is taken to be a single, spirited poem in short stanzas, in which some popular story is graphically narrated, and in this sense, the oral tradition is an essential element. Traditional ballads deal with the pagan supernatural, with tragic love, or with historical or semi-historical events, e. g. the English-Scottish border ballads, or the Robin Hood ballads. A folk ballad is anonymous and handed down orally. In later centuries, the ballad has been imitated, adapted and greatly developed by a number of writers, which is shown in the writings of Romantics and Modernists. Consequently, the literary ballad, as opposed to folk or popular ballad, came into being.

Middle English literature was, to a great extent, chained by religious considerations with stress laid on the Christian doctrines as well as personal salvation. The Book of Kells, illustrated versions of the *Bible* produced by Anglo-Saxons in the late 7th century, is a case in point.

Middle English literature reached its height with the writings of Geoffrey Chaucer, the greatest English writer during the Medieval period.

2. Geoffrey Chaucer (ca. 1343-1400)

The son of a well-off London vintner, Geoffrey Chaucer had various experiences: a page in the royal household, soldier, emissary, controller of customs, justice of the peace, Member of Parliament for Kent, Clerk of the King's Works, and so on. In 1359 he was taken prisoner while he was in France with Edward Ⅲ's invading army. After having been ransomed he married Philippa in 1366, and subsequently he got a patron—John of Gaunt, a friend of John Wycliffe, who, with the Lollards, translated the *Bible* into English. In 1367, he entered the service of King Edward Ⅲ and was sent to France and Italy, an experience which provided him exposure to Renaissance ideas and the works of French poets and Italian writers like Dante, Petrarch and Boccaccio. The influence of these writers can be found in some of his writings such as *The House of Fame* (an unfinished dream-poem, 1370s), a romance entitled *Troilus and Criseyde* (1385), and *The Canterbury Tales* (1386-1400), his masterpiece. He died in 1400 and was the first to be buried in the Poets' Corner in Westminster Abbey.

Geoffrey Chaucer

Chaucer contributed greatly to the development of the English language. Primarily through the influence of his poems, the dialect of London became the most-used literary language, and this helped to form Modern English in the middle 15th century. Chaucer is regarded as the father of English poetry. He introduced from France the rhymed stanzas into English poetry. He is considered to be the first realistic writer in English literary history. His works presented us an array of characters from all walks of life and a panoramic view of the English society at that time. He is looked upon as a messenger of humanism. In his writings, Chaucer affirmed man's right to earthly happiness. For example, his female characters, like the prioress in *The Canterbury Tales*, tend to show readily their charm in public, regardless of the convention of monasteries. This indicates they long to love and to be loved.

3. Selected Writings

3.1 *Beowulf* (an excerpt)

                        ... The dragon
Coiled and uncoiled, its heart urging it
Into battle. Beowulf's ancient sword
Was waiting, unsheathed, his sharp and gleaming
5   Blade. The beast came closer; both of them
Were ready, each set on slaughter. The Geats'
Great prince stood firm, unmoving, prepared
Behind his high shield, waiting in his shining
Armor. The monster came quickly toward him,
10 Pouring out fire and smoke, hurrying
To its fate. Flames beat at the iron
Shield, and for a time it held, protected
Beowulf as he'd planned; then it began to melt,

And for the first time in his life that famous prince
15 Fought with fate against him, with glory
Denied him. He knew it, but he raised his sword
And struck at the dragon's scaly hide.
The ancient blade broke, bit into
The monster's skin, drew blood, but cracked
20 And failed him before it went deep enough, helped him
Less than he needed. The dragon leaped
With pain, thrashed and beat at him, spouting
Murderous flames, spreading them everywhere.
And the Geats' ring-giver① did not boast of glorious
25 Victories in other wars: his weapon
Had failed him, deserted him, now when he needed it
Most, that excellent sword Edgetho's②
Famous son stared at death,
Unwilling to leave this world, to exchange it
30 For a dwelling in some distant place—a journey
Into darkness that all men must make, a death
Ends their few brief hours on earth.

Quickly, the dragon came at him, encouraged
As Beowulf fell back; its breath flared,
35 And he suffered, wrapped around in swirling
Flames—a king, before, but now
A beaten warrior. None of his comrades
Came to him, helped him, his brave and noble
Followers; they ran for their lives, fled
40 Deep in a wood. And only one of them
Remained, stood there, miserable, remembering,
As good man must, what kinship should mean.
(translated by Burton Raffel)

Questions

1. What can we learn about the characteristics of epic from this excerpt?
2. What might be the author's view of human life and human nature?

3.2 The Twa Corbies (a popular ballad)

As I was walking all alane,

---

① Referring to Beowulf, who, as king, would reward his followers with rings.
② Edgetho is the name of Beowulf's father.

I heard twa corbies making a mane;
The tane unto the t'other say,
"Where sall we gang and dine to-day?"

"In behint yon auld fail dyke,
I wot there lies a new-slain knight;
And naebody kens that he lies there,
But his hawk, his hound and his lady fair.

"His hound is to the hunting gane,
His hawk, to fetch the wild-fowl hame,
His lady's ta'en another mate,
So we may mak our dinner sweet.

"Ye'll sit on his white hause-bane,
And I'll pike out his bonny blue een.
Wi'ae lock o' his gowden hair,
We'll theek our nest when it grows bare.

"Mony a one for him makes mane,
But nane sall ken where he is gane;
O'er his white banes, when they are bare,
The wind sall blaw for evermair."

Questions

1. What can we learn about the scope of subject matter of popular ballads from this one?
2. Do you think this ballad is a fable? Why or why not?

3.3 The General Prologue (excerpts from *The Canterbury Tales*)

    When the sweet showers of April fall and shoot
    Down through the drought of March to pierce the root,
    Bathing every vein in liquid power
    From which there springs the engendering of the flower,
5   When also Zephyrus① with his sweet breath
    Exhales an air in every grove and heath
    Upon the tender shoots, and the young sun
    His half-course in the sign of the Ram② has run,
    And the small fowls are making melody

---

① **Zephyrus**: westerly (the west wind).
② **ram**: one sign of the Zodiac (The sun is in the ram from March 21 to April 21 every year).

10　That sleep away the night with open eye
　　（So nature pricks them and their heart engages）
　　Then people long to go on pilgrimages
　　And palmers① long to seek the stranger strands
　　Of far-off saints, hallowed in sundry lands,
15　And specially, from every shire's end
　　In England, down to Canterbury they wend
　　To seek the holy blissful martyr②, quick
　　In giving help to them when they were sick.
　　　It happened in that season that one day
20　In Southwark③, at The Tabard④, as I lay
　　Ready to go on pilgrimage and start
　　For Canterbury, most devout at heart,
　　At night there came into that hostelry
　　Some nine and twenty in a company
25　Of sundry folk happening then to fall
　　In fellowship, and they were pilgrims all
　　That towards Canterbury meant to ride.
　　The rooms and stables of the inn were wide,
　　They made us easy, all was of the best.
30　And shortly, when the sun had gone to rest,
　　By speaking to them all upon the trip
　　I was admitted to their fellowship
　　And promised to rise early and take the way
　　To Canterbury, as you heard me say.
35　　But none the less, while I have time and space,
　　Before my story takes a further pace,
　　It seems a reasonable thing to say
　　What their condition was, the full array
　　Of each of them, as it appeared to me,
40　According to profession and degree,
　　And what apparel they were riding in;
　　And at a Knight I therefore will begin...

---

① **palmer**: pilgrim.
② **martyr**: refers to St Thomas à Becket (1118-1170), Chancellor of England under Henry Ⅱ (1154-1189). He became archbishop of Canterbury and defended the rights of the Church against the King and quarreled with him. In 1170 Becket was killed by King Henry Ⅱ's knights in Canterbury Cathedral. In 1173, Becket was canonized and his shrine was a popular place of pilgrimage until the Reformation.
③ **Southwark**: name of a place near London.
④ **The Tabard**: name of an inn at Southwark.

　　　　There also was a Nun, a Prioress;
　　Simple her way of smiling was and coy.
45　Her greatest oath was only "By St. Loy①!"
　　And she was known as Madam Eglantyne,
　　And well she sang a service, with a fine
　　Intoning through her nose, as was most seemly,
　　And she spoke daintily in French, extremely,
50　After the school of Stratford-atte-Bowe②;
　　French in the Paris style she did not know.
　　At meat her manners were well taught withal;
　　No morsel from her lips did she let fall,
　　Nor dipped her fingers in the sauce too deep;
55　But she could carry a morsel up and keep
　　The smallest drop from falling on her breast.
　　For courtliness she had a special zest.
　　And she would wipe her upper lip so clean
　　That not a trace of grease was to be seen
60　Upon the cup when she had drunk; to eat,
　　She reached a hand sedately for the meat.
　　She certainly was very entertaining,
　　Pleasant and friendly in her ways, and straining
　　To counterfeit a courtly kind of grace,
65　A stately bearing fitting to her place,
　　And to seem dignified in all her dealings.
　　As for her sympathies and tender feelings,
　　She was so charitably solicitous
　　She used to weep if she but saw a mouse
70　Caught in a trap, if it were dead or bleeding.
　　And she had little dogs she would be feeding
　　With roasted flesh, or milk, or fine white bread.
　　Sorely she wept if one of them were dead
　　Or someone took a stick and made it smart;
75　She was all sentiment and tender heart.
　　Her veil was gathered in a seemly way,
　　Her nose was elegant, her eyes glass-grey;
　　Her mouth was very small, but soft and red,
　　And certainly she had a well-shaped head,
80　Almost a span across the brows, I own:

---

① **St. Loy**: name of a famous French goldsmith in the 6th century.
② **Stratford-atte-Bowe**: name of a monastery near London.

She was indeed by no means undergrown.
Her cloak, I noticed, had a graceful charm.
She wore a coral trinket on her arm,
A set of beads, the gaudies tricked in green,
85 Whence hung a golden brooch of brightest sheen
On which there first was graven a crowned A,
And lower, *Amor vincit omnia*①...

    A worthy woman from beside Bath city②
Was with us, somewhat deaf, which was a pity.
90 In making cloth she showed so great a bent
She bettered those of Ypres and of Ghent③
In all the parish not a dame dared stir
Towards the altar steps in front of her
And if indeed they did, so wrath was she
95 As to be quite put out of charity.
Her kerchiefs were of finely woven ground;
I dared have sworn they weighed a good ten pound,
The ones she wore on Sunday, on her head.
Her hose were of the finest scarlet red
100 And gartered tight; her shoes were soft and new.
Bold was her face, handsome, and red in hue.
A worthy woman all her life, what's more
She'd had five husbands, all at the church door,
Apart from other company in youth;
105 No need just now to speak of that, forsooth.
And she had thrice been to Jerusalem,
Seen many strange rivers and passed over them;
She'd been to Rome and also to Boulogne④,
St. James of Compostella⑤ and Cologne⑥,
110 And she was skilled in wandering by the way.
She had gap-teeth, set widely, truth to say.
Easily on an ambling horse she sat
Well wimpled up, and on her head a hat

---

① **Amor vincit omnia** (Latin): Love conquers all.
② **Bath city**: a city (district) in Avon, England, famous for its natural hot springs, where the Roman bathing pool still exists.
③ **Ypres and Ghent**: names of Belgian cities famous for cloth-making at that time.
④ **Boulogne**: name of a city in northern France.
⑤ **Compostella**: name of a city in Spain, where there was a shrine of St James.
⑥ **Cologne**: name of a city in what is now Germany.

As broad as is a buckler or a shield;
115 She had a flowing mantle that concealed
Large hips, her heels spurred sharply under that.
In company she liked to laugh and chat
And knew the remedies for love's mischances,
An art in which she knew the oldest dances...

120   He and a gentle Pardoner rode together,
A bird from Charing Cross① of the same feather,
Just back from visiting the Court of Rome.
He loudly sang *"Come hither, love, come home!"*
The Summoner sang deep seconds to this song,
125 No trumpet ever sounded half so strong.
This Pardoner had hair as yellow as wax
Hanging down smoothly like a hank of flax.
In driblets fell his locks behind his head
Down to his shoulders which they overspread;
130 Thinly they fell, like rat-tails, one by one.
He wore no hood upon his head, for fun;
The hood inside his wallet had been stowed,
He aimed at riding in the latest mode;
But for a little cap his head was bare
135 And he had bulging eye-balls, like a hare.
He'd sewed a holy relic on his cap;
His wallet lay before him on his lap,
Brimful of pardons come from Rome all hot.
He had the same small voice a goat has got.
140 His chin no beard had harbored, nor would harbor,
Smoother than ever chin was left by barber.
I judge he was a gelding, or a mare.
As to his trade, from Berwick② down to Ware③
There was no pardoner of equal grace,
145 For in his trunk he had a pillow-case
Which he asserted was Our Lady④'s veil.
He said he had a gobbet of the sail

---

① **Charing Cross**: name of a convent in London.
② **Berwick**: a place in northeastern England.
③ **Ware**: a place in southeastern England.
④ **Our Lady**: St Mary.

　　　　Saint Peter① had the time when he made bold
　　　　To walk the waves, till Jesus Christ took hold.
150　He had a cross of metal set with stones
　　　　And, in a glass, a rubble of pigs' bones.
　　　　And with these relics, any time he found
　　　　Some poor up-country parson to astound,
　　　　On one short day, in money down, he drew
155　More than the parson in a month or two,
　　　　And by his flatteries and prevarication
　　　　Made monkeys of the priest and congregation.
　　　　But still to do him justice first and last
　　　　In church he was a noble ecclesiast.
160　How well he read a lesson or told a story!
　　　　But best of all he sang an Offertory②,
　　　　For well he knew that when that song was sung
　　　　He'd have to preach and tune his honey-tongue
　　　　And (well he could) win silver from the crowd.
165　That's why he sang so merrily and loud. (translated by Nevill Coghill)

Questions

1. What can we learn from the first eleven lines of "The Prologue"?
2. Why did the palmers go to Canterbury?
3. In your opinion, how should a nun behave and dress? What is the writer's purpose in describing the appearance, features and table manners of the prioress in great detail? What can we learn about the monastery in medieval Europe from the author's mentioning of the food the prioress gave to her dogs?
4. Does the letter "A" stand for secular love or divine love? What is your understanding of "Amor vincit omnia"?
5. Why does the author mention the trips to those holy places taken by the woman from Bath city? What can we learn about her attitude towards love and marriage?
6. What did a Pardoner do? Why did the Pardoner in this poem sing an offertory best of all?
7. Why did the Pardoner visit the Court of Rome? What can we learn about people's religious belief at that time from this part?

---

① **St Peter**: a character in the Bible and disciple of Jesus Christ.
② **Offertory**: the verse sung when offerings of money are being made.

Chapter Two　The Elizabethan Age

1. Introduction

The Elizabethan age corresponds roughly with the reign of Queen Elizabeth I, that is, the years from 1558 to 1603.

1.1 The Renaissance

With economic growth and the development of capitalism in the late Middle Ages, Renaissance served as a reaction against the ideology of the Medieval period. The word "Renaissance" comes from the French language, meaning "revival" or "rebirth". As an artistic movement, Renaissance refers to a period in European history between the 14th and 17th centuries during which the discovering and reading of ancient Greek and Roman classics led to the flowering of painting, sculpture, architecture and so on. It first started in Florence and Venice, Italy, and was typified by the universal genius of Leonardo Da Vinci (1452-1519). Tired of the complex writing style of Scholasticists, people like Petrarch (1304-1374) tried to find the manuscripts of ancient Greeks and Romans to improve themselves. In the libraries of monasteries in Italy and southern France, the humanists—scholars who were interested in literature, history and moral philosophy—found many copies of Latin literature. More Greek and Latin classics were available in the 15th century when the Italian humanists developed contact with Byzantine scholars who escaped to Italy after the fall of Constantinople in 1453. From the Mediterranean coast Renaissance spread northwards to other European countries. It coincided with the discoveries made in geography and astronomy and the Religious Reformation in Europe. As a result, people began to learn more about themselves and the world around them, began to lift the restrictions placed by the Roman Catholic Church and to get rid of ignorance and superstition. The appearance of the Renaissance shows the acceptance by Christians of the pagan classical culture.

The Renaissance brought with it new ideas and a new outlook on life, such as humanism which means a shift from the divine element to the human element. Humanists like Thomas More (1478-1533), Montaigne (1533-1592) and Shakespeare believed man has dignity and is noble and he has the ability to realize his potential. People from all walks of life became the subjects of art which tried to show their interests and dignity and to justify their pursuit of happiness in this life rather than show the promised future of the afterlife.

The Renaissance marked a transition from the Medieval period to the modern age in European history.

1.2 The Renaissance in England

The Renaissance appeared much later in England than in mainland Europe. It was usually thought of as beginning with the accession of the House of Tudor to the throne in 1485.

From 1337 to 1453 a long war went on and off between England and France and it was followed at home by the War of the Roses which ended with the victory of Henry Tudor who later became Henry Ⅶ (1485-1509). Henry Ⅷ (1509-1547), his son, succeeded him and is remembered for initiating the religious reformation in England which led to the establishment of the independent Church of England around 1530. Monasticism disappeared as abbeys were deprived of their property and abbots were removed from the House of Lords. The reformation was carried on by his son Edward Ⅵ (1547-1553), but when Mary Tudor (1553-1558), Henry Ⅷ's daughter, became the Queen after Edward she brought England back to Catholicism and many Protestants were persecuted. When Elizabeth (1558-1603) became the Queen, she restored the independent Church of England but kept to Catholic doctrines and practices while remaining free of the Papal control. The compromise, however, didn't win any support from the radical Protestants, known as Puritans who had been influenced by the teachings of John Calvin (1509-1564), or from ardent Catholics. For many years Elizabeth Ⅰ had to fight against Catholic attempts to convert the heretic English to Catholicism, which led to the invasion by the Spanish Armada in 1588. The English navy won a great victory and England has been Protestant ever since.

1.3 Literature of the Renaissance

While the Renaissance in some European countries is characterized by the blossoming of painting, sculpture and architecture, it is represented by great achievements in drama in England.

The earliest drama came from ancient Greece and it had much to do with primitive religion—the worshipping of gods in classical mythology. With no actors at first but with increasing numbers of them later plus a chorus, the aim of the plays by Eeschylus, Sophocles, Euripides, Aristophanes and their predecessors as well as contemporaries is to cleanse the human soul with tragedies and to satirize the ruling class and human nature as well as to entertain the audience with comedies. Roman dramatists such as Plautus, Terence, and Seneca modeled their plays on Greek ones, but their comedies, more than the Greek originals, have tremendous influences on later European dramatists though the influence didn't come immediately, but rather, more than a millennium later.

After Christianity was established, drama was staged to spread the Gospels at many places in Europe. Owing to the basic human need for fun, drama became more and more secularized later. But because of the constant wars such as those against the invading Muslims, drama seemed to have disappeared in Europe in the first few centuries of the Middle Ages. Monasticism is, most probably, another important factor. When it finally reappeared, medieval drama, practiced during the ritual of the Christian Church, was used to strengthen religious beliefs, which can be found in Mysteries or Miracles. Staged till the Religious

Reformation, they are stories about Jesus and saints. Common folk in England were able to watch the performances beginning around 1350. In the 15th century Morality plays, stories about men who represent virtues, sins, or good and evil, arose out of sermons by church priests and those plays were aimed to provide the audience with moral lessons. Examples are *The Castell of Perseverance* (c. 1425), *Mind, Will and Understanding* (c. 1460), *Everyman* (c. 1509), and *Magnificence* (1516). Early medieval drama was performed in Latin, the official language of the Christian Church then. In late 15th-century England, plays were written and printed in English. By the way, the Latin Bible had been translated into English by John Wycliffe (1320-1384) and his followers. Prose, together with doggerel, was initially used in English drama, but verse became popular gradually, and *Gorboduc* (1562) by Thomas Sackville and Thomas Norton is the earliest play to have been written in blank verse and it is the first Elizabethan tragedy. Drama was used more to amuse and to entertain the audience than to give people religious instructions in the following decades.

The naval triumph, the Religious Reformation, together with the compromise in religion, left the English intellectuals free from the restriction of the Roman Catholic Church and religious persecution. Some even felt high-spirited. The subsequent social stability enabled them to devote their time and energy to artistic creation.

The English Renaissance was largely literary, and it achieved its finest expression in the Elizabethan drama created mainly by William Shakespeare, the greatest writer in the English language, Christopher Marlowe, who perfected the art of blank verse in plays, and Ben Johnson (1572-1637). Writers at that time started to move gradually away from religious subjects that characterized previous writings and they ventured into other realms of social as well as personal life.

2. Edmund Spenser (1552-1599)

The son of a poor tailor, Edmund Spenser was born in London. After attending Merchant Taylors' School he entered Pembroke College, Cambridge, and stayed there until 1576 for his M. A. degree. While in college, Spenser translated some sonnets by Petrarch and an anti-Catholic tract. In 1578 he became the secretary to the Bishop of Rochester, and in the next year he received an appointment to the house of the Earl of Leicester, where he later met Philip Sidney (1554-1586), a poet. By imitating Virgil, Spenser wrote *The Shepheardes Calender* (1579), which includes 12 eclogues, one for each month of the year and one of them a panegyric to Eliza, the queen of shepherds, apparently representing Elizabeth Ⅰ. In 1580 he became secretary to Lord Grey de Wilton, Lord Deputy of Ireland, a colony of England since 1541 (Henry Ⅷ declared himself king of Ireland that year). Spenser held various offices in Ireland

Edmund Spenser

under Grey and in 1586 he was granted an estate with a castle at Kilcolman in Cork, where he received Sir Walter Raleigh (1552-1618), a courtier, statesman and man of letters. In 1590 at Raleigh's suggestion, Spenser published the first three books of *The Faerie Queene*, dedicated to Queen Elizabeth I with the intention of winning royal favor. In 1591 Spenser wrote the elegy *Daphnaida*. Three years later Spenser married Elizabeth Boyle, which inspired him to write his sonnet sequence *Amoretti* (1595), and *Epithalamion* (1595), a marriage poem with 24 stanzas which represent the hours of Midsummer's Day. In 1595 Spenser went back to England, and *Astrophil*, an elegy on Sir Philip Sidney, and *A View of the Present State of Ireland*, a prose dialogue, appeared. The next year saw the appearance of *Fowre Hymnes*, and *Prothalamion*, another marriage poem, and the next three books of *The Faerie Queene*.

After returning to Ireland Spenser became Sheriff of Cork in September, 1598, but in October Tyrone's Rebellion broke out. His castle was burnt down and he fled with his wife and children back to London, where he died the next year after his health failed following these terrors, leaving *The Faerie Queene* unfinished.

The Faerie Queene, Spenser's masterwork, was intended to fill 12 books, each with a knight who, through the test of adventures and battling with giants, monsters, dragons, lions, serpents, sorceresses, represents one of the following virtues: holiness, temperance, chastity, friendship, justice, courtesy, and constancy. In all the books a unifying figure, Arthur (King Arthur), who represents all virtues, is engaged in a great mission—the search for the Fairy Queen (Gloriana), the object of his love. A master of meter and language, Spenser wrote this great epic in the form of a nine-line stanza, the first 8 lines in iambic pentameter, rhyming ababbcbcc. It is now known as the Spenserian stanza. A simulation of Chaucerian English with antique spellings, the language in his poetry serves as an example of early modern English. Spenser, reputed as the poets' poet, has tremendous influence on later poets such as Milton, Shelley, Byron, Keats and Tennyson.

3. Francis Bacon (1561-1626)

Francis Bacon

The son of the lord keeper in Queen Elizabeth's court and a Puritan mother, Francis Bacon was born in London. At 12 he started to study scholasticism at Trinity College, Cambridge, and then at Gray's Inn to study law. At 23 he entered Parliament, thus beginning his political career. In 1597 he published his first group of essays. *The Advancement of Learning*, which was dedicated to the new king, came out in 1605. Two years later he was appointed Solicitor-General and then Attorney-General. In 1617 he became lord keeper and in the next year lord chancellor of England under King James I (1603-1625). He was made a peer, with the titles of Baron Verulam and Viscount St Albans. At the height of his politic life Bacon was imprisoned in the Tower for taking bribes as a judge. After his release from prison he retired to his estate of Cornhambry and spent his last five years in writing.

Bacon is believed to be the first to write essays in English. His works cover a wide range of subjects: philosophy, science, history, literature, and so on. *The Advancement of Learning* (1605), *Novum Organum* (The New Instrument, 1620), *Essays* (1625), and *The New Atlantis* (1627) are his major works.

4. Christopher Marlowe (1564-1593)

4.1 Life and Career

The son of a shoemaker, Christopher Marlowe was born in Canterbury in 1564. Though his parents were not well-off, Marlowe had a good education: first at the local King's School and then Corpus Christi College, Cambridge, where he obtained his MA in 1587. He visited London early in 1584 and was influenced by Renaissance ideas, and during later visits he befriended actors from the Admiral's Men. The year 1587 also saw the performance of his first play *Dido, Queen of Carthage* (1594), a joint work with Thomas Nashe (both being among the University Wits). Marlowe was believed to be also working as a government agent at that time. Marlowe's first performed play, *Tamburlaine the*

Christopher Marlowe

Great (1590), which brought him some fame, is the story of Timur, a Scythian shepherd chieftain who became the Tartar king of the 14th-century Central Asia. In the play Timur is portrayed as a great warrior who overthrows the king of Persia (Mycetes), Mycetes' brother (Cosroe) who later seizes the throne, and then the Turkish emperor (Bajazet). He also takes over Damascus from the Sultan of Egypt. The play came at a time when British nationalism and heroism were greatly aroused after their navy defeated the Spanish Armada and the play was so popular that Marlowe added a second part to it.

In the late 1580s Marlowe visited the continent and turned out to be a troublemaker: once involved in a street fight causing one death, and in 1592 he was arrested in the Netherlands for counterfeiting coins. In 1589 Marlowe composed *The Tragical History of Doctor Faustus* (1604), his most famous play. Marlowe and his colleague Thomas Kyd (another figure of the University Wits) worked mainly for their patron Ferdinando Stanley, Lord Strange. *Edward II* (1594) and *The Jew of Malta* (1633) were both staged in the same year. In 1592 Marlowe wrote *The Massacre at Paris* (1593), a play about the massacre of Protestants in Paris in 1572. Marlowe was killed in a fight in a tavern the next year, caused maybe by his homosexuality or a quarrel over a bill.

Besides the above-mentioned plays, Marlowe also wrote a narrative poem *Hero and Leander* (1598, completed by George Chapman) and a collection of poems *The Passionate*

Shepherd (1599).

Containing classical learning and rejection of established order, limits and morals, Marlowe's plays such as *Dr. Faustus* and *Tamburlaine the Great* show the characters' wish to realize the full human potential. The speech in earlier blank-verse tragedies is stilted, monotonous, stately and heavy, and it is Marlowe who perfected the art. He had great influence on his contemporaries, most notably on William Shakespeare.

4.2 *Dr Faustus* (synopsis)

Faustus, a brilliant scholar, is tired of the limits of the academic curriculum of his day, and so turns to the study of magic by incantations, and calls up Mephistophilis, the devil's servant. With the intention of getting more knowledge and power, he makes a compact with the devil—Lucifer: He will surrender his soul to the latter in return for 24 years of life during which he will have everything he desires. After Mephistophilis becomes Faustus' servant, the new master makes a tour in the universe by riding a dragon and has his desires: see the Pope, conjure the spirit of Alexander the Great, bid Mephistophilis give Helen of Troy ("Was this the face that launch a thousand ships?") to him in marriage, and so on. Faustus experiences great anguish when the 24-year period is coming to an end, and finally he is carried away by the Devil.

5. William Shakespeare (1564-1616)

5.1 Life and Career

William Shakespeare

Though one of the most influential writers in world literary history, William Shakespeare is a person about whom we know so little. Naturally his life story and career are, to a considerable extent, based on speculation.

One son out of eight children of a prominent local glover and dealer of various commodities, William Shakespeare was born in the market town of Stratford-upon-Avon on April 23, 1564. When he was seven, he entered the local grammar school where the principal subject taught was Latin. In 1582 Shakespeare married Anne Hathaway, a country girl eight years his senior. They had three children, one son with the name Hamnet. In 1585, he left Stratford and his family for London where he was without money or friends. He earned a little by taking care of the horses of the gentlemen who attended plays at the playhouses. Gradually, due to his quick wit and humour, the actors befriended him and invited him to join their company. By 1592 Shakespeare had become one of the three leading members of a company of actors called the Lord Chamberlain's Men. The company traveled about the country, giving performances in different towns, and also performed plays at Court. In addition to acting, Shakespeare wrote plays as well as poems. He became rich and famous, and in 1597 he bought a large property in Stratford. Shakespeare tried to win royal favour by writing such plays as *Merry Wives of Windsor* for the Queen, but his efforts went neglected. In 1599 the Lord Chamberlain's Men built the Globe Theatre, and many of Shakespeare's plays were later produced there. Around 1610, Shakespeare left London and retired permanently to his hometown, though he continued to write. He died on April 23, 1616.

With much knowledge of Greek and Roman mythology and with Catholic sympathies, Shakespeare began his literary career by writing history plays and comedies, such as *Henry VI* (1590?), *Richard III* (1592?), *The Comedy of Errors* (1592?), and *The Taming of the Shrew* (1593?). Then he wrote more comedies and history plays like *Love's Labour Is Lost* (1594), *A Midsummer Night's Dream* (1595), *Richard II* (1595), *The Merchant of Venice* (1596), *Henry IV* (1596-1597), *Henry V* (1598?), *As You Like it* (1599), *Much Ado about Nothing* (1599), *Julius Caesar* (1599?), and *Twelfth Night* (1600). For the inexperienced, optimistic playwright, life is full of laughter and hope.

Then Shakespeare turned to the writing of tragedies—he had already written one—*Romeo and Juliet* (with strongly comic elements)—in 1595. The four great tragedies were created: *Hamlet* (1601), *Othello* (1604), *King Lear* (1605), and *Macbeth* (1605), besides *Anthony and Cleopatra* (1606?), *Timon of Athens* (1608?), and some dark comedies like *All's Well That Ends Well* (1602?). With bitter experiences in career, life and with improved understanding of human nature and the society around him, the dramatist saw no future for the world.

Finally, when, as a celebrity, Shakespeare began to enjoy his fame and prestige, he must have found that life was not made up of misery, bitterness or failure only, or realized that life could still be enjoyable even if it is a tragedy. Thus in the last few years of his life, Shakespeare wrote some romantic tragicomedies such as *Cymbeline* (1610?), *The Winter's Tale* (1610?), *The Tempest* (1611?), and *The Two Noble Kinsmen* (1613), and he had written *Measure for Measure* early in 1604. *Henry VIII* (1613?), a history play, is one of his last works.

Besides his 38 plays, William Shakespeare also published two long poems—*Venus and Adonis* (dedicated to the Earl of Southampton, 1593) and *The Rape of Lucrece* (1594) as well as 154 sonnets. In 1623, thanks to the efforts made by two friends in his acting company, the First Folio, a collection of Shakespeare's plays, came out.

Shakespeare has contributed greatly to world literature and the English language. His plays represent the summit of Western literature and exercise tremendous influences on later writers all over the world. Many of Shakespeare's sonnets are masterpieces and have come to represent English sonnet in meter, structure, rhyme scheme, and so on.

5.2 Major Works

5.2.1 *Hamlet* (synopsis)

Old Hamlet, the king of Denmark, dies unexpectedly while sleeping in his orchard one day, and his wife, Gertrude, remarries shortly after his death. Now Hamlet, the prince, seems unable to find any meaning or purpose in life. Claudius, his uncle, becomes the new king and his stepfather.

Then a strange thing occurs. Horatio, Hamlet's friend, tells him that the guard of soldiers who keep watch by night on the platform of the castle where the king and the queen stay, see, for several nights in succession, a ghost hovering in the sky and it looks like old Hamlet. When Hamlet himself comes and sits up there, the ghost appears again and beckons to him to follow it. Then the ghost tells Hamlet that he has been murdered by his brother Claudius. It asks Hamlet to revenge his murder.

Hamlet doesn't know whether the ghost has told him the truth, and he is puzzled and meditates a lot all by himself. The young prince pretends to be mad so that Claudius will not suspect him of planning revenge. Polonius, a courtier, has a daughter—Ophelia, and he attributes Hamlet's madness to his frustrating love for her, and Polonius tells this to Claudius and Gertrude.

It so happens that a party of wandering actors have come to the palace and Hamlet asks them to put on a play with a murder similar to the one which his father' ghost has described to him. He invites Claudius and his mother to watch it. When the actors are acting out the killing, Hamlet finds that Claudius gets uneasy and frightened. The king and queen leave in great confusion before the play ends. Finding Claudius really guilty, Hamlet decides to take action against him. Just then a messenger informs Hamlet that his mother wants to speak to him at once. On his way he sees the king on his knees, trying to pray. For religious reasons, Hamlet holds back his impulse to kill the murderer there and then, and proceeds on his way to his mother's room and upon arrival his mother blames him for offending the king. But Hamlet accuses her of being unfaithful to his father and he intends to make her confess the murder by seizing her by the wrists. She is frightened into crying out "Help", meaning to get help from Polonius who has been asked to hide behind the curtains. Instead of coming out to help the queen, Polonius also calls out "Help". Thinking that it must be Claudius Hamlet runs his sword through it, and Polonius is killed.

When the king learns this he urges Hamlet to leave Denmark immediately for England to escape the revenge of the courtier's son—Laertes, who is a famous fencer. Before Hamlet sets off, the king writes a letter telling the king of England to kill Hamlet upon his arrival there and he gives the letter to Rosencrantz and Guildenstern, two of Hamlet's former schoolmates who have tried to befriend Hamlet in order to spy on him and who will accompany Hamlet to England. During the Journey the prince, however, discovers the letter and he changes the name. On the sea, they are chased by some pirates and they part company with each other. Hamlet manages to get back to Denmark while his two "friends" go on with their trip to England, only to be killed in accordance with what is instructed in the letter.

On his way back to the castle Hamlet finds himself before the funeral of Ophelia who has drowned herself after her lover has killed her father and deserted her. Among the mourners present are the king, the queen and Laertes who, overcharged with grief, jumps into the grave. Rushing out from among the bushes, Hamlet follows suit. Laertes, believing that Hamlet is responsible for all that has happened, starts a fight with him in the grave.

Attendants have much difficulty in separating them.

In order to get rid of Hamlet, Claudius arranges a fence match between Hamlet and Laertes, making it clear to the prince that Laertes has misunderstood him and now wants to make friends with him. Before the match Claudius tells Laertes to use a pointed sword (not allowed in a match) and makes Laertes poison it and he himself has prepared a cup of poisoned wine for Hamlet, who, he thinks, will without doubt die even if he wins the match. Thus in either case, the prince's life is doomed. In the match Hamlet is wounded by Laertes's sword. Infuriated, Hamlet seizes Laertes's sword and injured him with it. Realizing that he will soon die, Laertes tells Hamlet that his sword has been poisoned and the king is to blame. Just at that time Gertrude, after having absentmindedly taken and swallowed the cup of wine prepared for Hamlet, dies immediately, crying out that she has been poisoned. Seeing the king's foul plot, Hamlet uses all his might and kills Claudius before he himself dies.

5.2.2 *Macbeth* (synopsis)

Macbeth, Thane of Glamis, is a great general of Scottish King Duncan. He, together with Banquo, has defeated two separate invading armies. On their way returning to a military camp, they encounter three witches who prophesy that Macbeth will be made thane of Cawdor and eventually king of Scotland. They also prophesy that Banquo will be the father of Scottish kings to come, although Banquo will never be king himself. Then the witches vanish. Macbeth and Banquo treat their prophecies skeptically until Macbeth is informed by some of King Duncan's men that he has indeed been given the title of Thane of Cawdor.

Intrigued by the prophecies, Macbeth writes to his wife, Lady Macbeth, to tell her what has happened. In contrast with his uncertainty, Lady Macbeth determines to push her husband to the throne. When King Duncan decides to visit Macbeth's castle and spend a night there, Lady Macbeth thinks that the opportunity is too good to be ignored. Pressed on by his ambitious wife, Macbeth plots Duncan's death. Instantly after the murder, Macbeth feels the shame and guilt, and Lady Macbeth is also haunted by the bloody crime.

Discovering the death of their father, Duncan's sons Malcolm and Donalbain flee to England and Ireland to secure their lives. They are assumed to be the conspirators. Macbeth succeeds to the throne. Fearful of the witches' prophecy that Banquo's heirs will seize the throne, Macbeth hires a group of murderers to kill Banquo and his son Fleance. Banquo is dead while Fleance escapes. At the feast that night, Banquo's bloody ghost visits Macbeth, and he is lost in despair. Lady Macbeth tries to neutralize the damage, but Macbeth's kingship incites increasing resistance from his nobles. Macduff, who suspects Macbeth's foul play of kingship, flees to England. Macbeth butchers all of Macduff's family in anger.

Frightened, Macbeth goes to visit the witches in their cavern. He is given further prophecies: he is incapable of being harmed by any man born of woman; and he will be safe until Birnam Wood comes to Dunsinane Castle. Macbeth is relieved and feels confident of his victory, as he is sure that all men are born of women and that forests cannot move.

Prince Malcolm, Duncan's son, has succeeded in raising an army in England, and vengeful Macduff joins him. They are supported by the Scottish nobles, who are frightened by Macbeth's tyrannical and murderous behavior. When the English army is approaching, Lady

Macbeth commits suicide after long suffering from guilt. Upon her death, Macbeth sinks into a deep despair. The messenger reports that the English army is advancing on Dunsinane shielded with boughs cut from Birnam Wood. It seems that Birnam Wood is coming to Dunsinane, fulfilling half of the witches' prophecy. Macbeth desperately sets to battle.

In the battle, nobody can bring Macbeth down. At last, he is challenged by Macduff, who declares that he is not "of woman born" but is instead "untimely ripped" from his mother's womb (birth by cesarean section). Macduff kills Macbeth, and Malcolm becomes the king of Scotland.

5.2.3 *The Merchant of Venice* (synopsis)

The story begins with Antonio's (a Christian merchant in the city state of Venice) wondering of the cause for his recent low spirit. One reason given by his friends is his excessive worry about his new investment which costs all his money. This is the reason why he has to go, together with his playboy friend Bassanio, to Shylock, a Jew, to borrow money when Bassanio needs much to travel to Belmont to win the love of Portia, a beautiful lady who has recently inherited a large sum of money after the death of her father. Although Shylock bears much hatred for Antonio who has denounced him publicly for charging interests when lending money to others, he agrees to lend 3000 ducats to Antonio on condition that he will be entitled to cut one pound of flesh from any part of the merchant's body if Antonio can't repay the money in three months. Sure of the success of his investment, Antonio signs his name, against Bassanio's objection, on the bond with the above-mentioned terms drawn up by Shylock. After getting the money Bassanio, with Gratiano and others, makes his way to Belmont to try his fortune. Like all the other suitors, some of them princes, Bassanio is presented with three caskets for him to choose, in one of which Portia's portrait is laid. After much reasoning and with some hints dropped by Portia who has previously met Bassanio once and has cherished good impressions of him, Bassanio makes the right choice and they soon get engaged, his companion Gratiano also falling in love and getting engaged with Nerissa, Portia's maid.

The lovers' happiness is suddenly interrupted by the arrival of words that Antonio, whose cargoes are said to have been lost in the sea, will have to face in a court of justice the revenge of Shylock who has been maddened by the elopement of his daughter Jessica with Lorenzo, a Christian. The young lovers have taken all of Shylock's money with them. Bassanio hurries back to Venice, but at the court, since the time is due, Shylock doesn't accept any money, no matter how much is offered him. Instead he is determined to put the merchant to death. The duke of Venice entreats Shylock to show mercy but is turned down, and has to ask a famous doctor of law to come to Venice to be the judge. The doctor, being ill at the moment, asks another lawyer to go to the court of Venice instead of him. Portia, who happens to be also a learned woman, and who has disguised herself as a man, appears at the trial to serve as the judge. With her quick wit and cleverness she turns the tables on Shylock and saves the life of Antonio. The play ends, after the trial, with the reunion of the three young couples at Belmont. Antonio, a guest among them, declares that his ships have safely arrived at the harbour.

6. John Donne (1572-1631)

John Donne

Born into a merchant family, John Donne received good education: first taught by a tutor, and then went to Oxford and to Trinity College, Cambridge, but left without taking a degree because of his Roman Catholic background. At the age of 20, Donne began his legal studies at the Inns of Court in London. He wrote some love poems over the next ten years. Circulating in manuscript, they had an immense influence on younger poets like George Herbert (1593-1633) and Andrew Marvell (1621-1678). In those poems Donne gives nearly every theme a verse and stanza form peculiar to itself; and instead of decorating his theme by conventional comparisons, he illumines or emphasizes his thought by fantastic metaphors and extravagant hyperboles.

Donne was a great traveler. After a naval expedition against Spain he became private secretary to Sir Thomas Egerton, lord keeper of the Great Seal. In 1601, he fell in love with Ann More, niece of the lord keeper, married her secretly and was imprisoned for some time by his father-in-law. The next decade was a hard time for Donne and his growing family. The "holy sonnets" he wrote during the period reflect his dark sense of despair. He entered the Anglican Church in 1615 and then devoted all his time and energy to his priestly duties and the writing of sermons and religious poems. In 1621 Donne became the Dean of St. Paul's. He died in 1631.

John Donne is remembered today as the leading figure of the metaphysical poets.

7. Selected Writings

7.1 *The Faerie Queene* by Spenser (two excerpts from Canto I, Book I)

A gentle Knight was pricking on the plaine,
Y cladd in mightie armes and siluer shielde,
Wherein old dints of deepe woundes did remaine,
The cruell markes of many a bloudy fielde;
Yet armes till that time did he neuer wield.
His angry steede did chide his foming bitt,
As much disdayning to the curbe to yield:
Full iolly knight he seemd, and faire did sitt,
As one for knightly giusts and fierce encounters fitt.

...

A lovely Ladie rode him faire beside,

Upon a lowly Asse more white then snow,
Yet she much whiter; but the same did hide
Under a vele, that whimpled was full low;
And over all a blacke stole shee did thraw:
As one that inly mournd, so was she sad,
And heavie sate upon her palfrey slow;
Seemed in heart some hidden care she had,
And by her, in a line, a milkewhite lambe she lad.

Questions

1. Are there any differences between a Spenserian stanza and that of previous English poems?
2. What influence does a Spenserian stanza have on later English poetry?

7.2 *Dr Faustus* by Marlowe (an excerpt from Scene I, Act I)

[FAUSTUS *in his Study*]

FAUST. Settle thy studies, Faustus, and begin
To sound the depth of that thou wilt profess.
Having commenc'd, be a divine in show—
Yet level① at the end of every art,
And live and die in Aristotle's works.
Sweet Analytics② 'tis thou hast ravish'd me,   [Reads.]
*Bene disserere est finis logices*③.
Is to dispute well logic's chiefest end?
Affords this art no greater miracle?
Then read no more; thou hast attain'd the end.
A greater subject fitteth Faustus' wit.
Bid *on kai me on*④ farewell, and Galen⑤ come,
Seeing *ubi desinit philosophus, ibi incipit medicus*⑥,
Be a physician, Faustus, heap up gold,
And be eternis'd for some wondrous cure.   [Reads.]
*Summum bonum medicinae sanitas*⑦—
The end of physic is our body's health.
Why, Faustus, hast thou not attain'd that end!

---

① **level**: aim.
② **Analytics**: title of a treatise on logic by Aristotle.
③ **Bene ... logices**: The end of logic is to argue well. (Latin)
④ **on kai me on**: being and not being. (Greek)
⑤ **Galen**: Greek authority on medicine (129 A. D.-199 A. D.)
⑥ **ubi ... medicus**: Where the philosopher leaves off, the doctor begins.
⑦ **Summum ... sanitas**: Health is the greatest good of medicine (Latin, translated from Aristotle's Nichomachean Ethics).

Is not thy common talk sound aphorisms?
Are not thy bills hung up as monuments
Whereby whole cities have escap'd the plague
And thousand desperate maladies been eas'd?
Yet art thou still but Faustus and a man.
Couldst thou make men to live eternally,
Or, being dead, raise them to life again,
Then this profession were to be esteem'd.
Physic, farewell. Where is Justinian①　　　　　　　　　　[Reads.]
*Si una eademque res legatur duobus,
Alter rem, alter valorem rei, et cetera.*②—
A pretty case of paltry legacies!　　　　　　　　　　　　[Reads.]
*Exhaereditare filium non potest pater nisi*③—
Such is the subject of the Institute
And universal body of the law.
This study fits a mercenary drudge
Who aims at nothing but external trash,
Too servile and illiberal for me.
When all is done, divinity is best.
Jerome's *Bible*④, Faustus, view it well.　　　　　　　　[Reads.]
Stipendium peccati mors est. ⑤ Ha! *Stipendium*, et cetera.
The reward of sin is death? That's hard.　　　　　　　　[Reads.]
*Si peccasse negamus, fallimur, et nulla est in nobis veritas*⑥—
If we say that we have no sin
We deceive ourselves, and there's no truth in us.
Why then belike
We must sin and so consequently die.
Aye, we must die an everlasting death.
What doctrine call you this, *Che sera sera*⑦:
What will be, shall be? Divinity, adieu!
These metaphysics of magicians
And necromantic books are heavenly;
Lines, circles, signs, letters, and characters—

---

① **Justinian**: emperor of Eastern Roman Empire and authority on law, author of the Institute.
② ***Si ... et cetera***: If one thing is willed to two persons, one of them shall have the thing itself, the other the value of the thing, and so forth. (Latin)
③ ***Exhaereditare ... nisi***: A father cannot disinherit his son unless. (Latin)
④ **Jerome's Bible**: the Vulgate, which was completed by St. Jerome (340-420) in 405.
⑤ ***Stipendium ... est***: The wages of sin is death. (Romans 6: 23)
⑥ ***Si ... veritas***: to be translated in the next two lines. (John 1: 8)
⑦ ***Che sera sera***: to be translated in the first half of the next line.

Aye, these are those that Faustus most desires.
O what a world of profit and delight,
Of power, of honour, of omnipotence
Is promised to the studious artisan!
All things that move between the quiet poles
Shall be at my command. Emperor and kings
Are but obeyed in their several provinces,
Nor can they raise the wind or rend the clouds;
But his dominion that exceeds in this
Stretcheth as far as doth the mind of man.
A sound magician is a demi-god:
Here tire my brains to gain a deity!
Wagner!

 [Enter WAGNER]

Commend me to my dearest friends,
The German Valdes and Cornelius;
Request them earnestly to visit me.
WAGNER I will, sir. [Exit.]
FAUST Their conference will be a greater help to me
Than all my labours, plod I ne'er so fast.

 [Enter GOOD ANGEL and EVIL ANGEL]

GOOD ANGEL O Faustus, lay that damned book aside,
And gaze not upon it lest it tempt thy soul
And heap God's heavy wrath upon thy head.
Read, read the Scriptures! That is blasphemy.
EVIL ANGEL Go forward, Faustus, in that famous art
Wherein all Nature's treasure is contain'd:
Be thou on earth as Jove is in the sky,
Lord and commander of these elements. [Exeunt Angels.]

Questions

1. What do the two angels ask Faustus to do respectively?
2. What can we learn about the education of Faustus from this excerpt?
3. What might be the reason that Faustus' life story has inspired several important writers in Europe?

7.3 *The Merchant of Venice* by Shakespeare (an excerpt from ACT IV)

Scene 1 Venice. A court of justice

Enter the DUKE, the MAGNIFICOES, ANTONIO①, BASSANIO②, GRATIANO, SALERIO③, and others.

DUKE OF VENICE	What, is Antonio here?
ANTONIO	Ready, so please your Grace.
DUKE OF VENICE	I am sorry for thee: Thou art come to answer
	A stony adversary, an inhuman wretch,
	Uncapable of pity, void and empty
	From any dram of mercy.
ANTONIO	I have heard
	Your Grace hath ta'en great pains to qualify
	His rigorous course; but since he stands obdurate,
	And that no lawful means can carry me
	Out of his envy's reach, I do oppose
	My patience to his fury, and am armed
	To suffer with a quietness of spirit
	The very tyranny and rage of his.
DUKE OF VENICE	Go one, and call the Jew into the court.
SALERIO	He is ready at the door; he comes, my lord.

Enter SHYLOCK

DUKE OF VENICE	Make room, and let him stand before our face.
	Shylock, the world thinks, and I think so too,
	That thou but leadest this fashion of thy malice
	To the last hour of act; and then, 'tis thought
	Thou'lt show thy mercy and remorse more strange
	Than is thy strange apparent cruelty;
	And where thou now exacts the penalty,
	Which is a pound of this poor merchant's flesh,
	Thou wilt not only loose the forfeiture,
	But, touched with human gentleness and love,
	Forgive a moiety of the principal,
	Glancing an eye of pity on his losses,
	That have of late so huddled on his back—
	Enow to press a royal merchant down,
	And pluck commiseration of his state

---

① **Antonio**: a merchant in Venice, a city state at that time.
② **Bassanio**: Antonio's friend.
③ **Gratiano and Salerio**: Bassanio's friends.

	From brassy bosoms and rough hearts of flint,
	From stubborn Turks and Tartars①, never trained
	To offices of tender courtesy.
	We all expect a gentle② answer, Jew.
SHYLOCK	I have possessed your Grace of what I purpose,
	And by our holy Sabbath③ have I sworn
	To have the due and forfeit of my bond.
	If you deny it, let the danger light
	Upon your charter and your city's freedom.
	You'll ask me why I rather choose to have
	A weight of carrion flesh than to receive
	Three thousand ducats. I'll not answer that,
	But say it is my humor. Is it answered?
	What if my house be troubled with a rat,
	And I be pleased to give ten thousand ducats
	To have it baned? What, are you answered yet?
	Some men there are love not a gaping pig;
	Some that are mad if they behold a cat;
	And others, when the bagpipe sings i' th' nose,
	Cannot contain their urine; for affection,
	Master of passion, sways it to the mood
	Of what it likes or loathes. Now, for your answer:
	As there is no firm reason to be rendered
	Why he cannot abide a gaping pig;
	Why he, a harmless necessary cat;
	Why he, a woolen bagpipe, but of force
	Must yield to such inevitable shame
	As to offend, himself being offended;
	So can I give no reason, nor I will not,
	More than a lodged hate and a certain loathing
	I bear Antonio, that I follow thus
	A losing suit against him. Are you answered?
BASSANIO	This is no answer, thou unfeeling man,
	To excuse the current of thy cruelty.
SHYLOCK	I am not bound to please thee with my answers.
BASSANIO	Do all men kill the things they do not love?
SHYLOCK	Hates any man the thing he would not kill?

---

① **Turks and Tartars**: The Europeans used to regard Turks and Tartars as savages.
② **gentle**: a pun. In Shakespeare's time, it also meant "Gentile".
③ **by our holy Sabbath**: an oath.

BASSANIO	Every offence is not a hate at first.
SHYLOCK	What, wouldst thou have a serpent sting thee twice?
ANTONIO	I pray you, think you question with the Jew.
	You may as well go stand upon the beach
	And bid the main flood bate his usual height;
	You may as well use question with the wolf,
	Why he hath made the ewe bleat for the lamb;
	You may as well forbid the mountain pines
	To wag their high tops and to make no noise
	When they are fretten with the gusts of heaven;
	You may as well do anything most hard
	As seek to soften that—than which what's harder? —
	His Jewish heart. Therefore, I do beseech you,
	Make no more offers, use no farther means,
	But with all brief and plain conveniency,
	Let me have judgment, and the Jew his will.
BASSANIO	For thy three thousand ducats here is six.
SHYLOCK	If every ducat in six thousand ducats
	Were in six parts, and every part a ducat,
	I would not draw them. I would have my bond.
DUKE OF VENICE	How shalt thou hope for mercy, rendering none?
SHYLOCK	What judgment shall I dread, doing no wrong?
	You have among you many a purchased slave,
	Which, like your asses and your dogs and mules,
	You use in abject and in slavish parts,
	Because you bought them. Shall I say to you
	"Let them be free, marry them to your heirs—
	Why sweat they under burdens? Let their beds
	Be made as soft as yours, and let their palates
	Be seasoned with such viands?" You will answer
	"The slaves are ours." So do I answer you:
	The pound of flesh which I demand of him
	Is dearly bought. 'Tis mine, and I will have it.
	If you deny me, fie upon your law!
	There is no force in the decrees of Venice.
	I stand for judgment. Answer: shall I have it?
DUKE OF VENICE	Upon my power I may dismiss this court,
	Unless Bellario①, a learned doctor,

---

① **Bellario**: Portia's cousin. "Take this same letter, / And use thou all th' endeavour of a man/In speed to Padua. See thou render this/Into my cousin's hands, Doctor Bellario;" (Scene 4, Act Ⅲ)

	Whom I have sent for to determine this,
	Come here to-day.
SALERIO	My lord, here stays without
	A messenger with letters from the doctor,
	New come from Padua①.
DUKE OF VENICE	Bring us the letters; call the messenger.
BASSANIO	Good cheer, Antonio! What, man, courage yet!
	The Jew shall have my flesh, blood, bones, and all,
	Ere thou shalt lose for me one drop of blood.
ANTONIO	I am a tainted wether of the flock,
	Meetest for death; the weakest kind of fruit
	Drops earliest to the ground, and so let me.
	You cannot better be employed, Bassanio,
	Than to live still, and write mine epitaph.

Enter NERISSA dressed like a lawyer's clerk

DUKE OF VENICE	Came you from Padua, from Bellario?
NERISSA	From both, my lord. Bellario greets your Grace. [*Presents a letter*]
BASSANIO	Why dost thou whet thy knife so earnestly?
SHYLOCK	To cut the forfeiture from that bankrupt there.
GRATIANO	Not on thy sole, but on thy soul, harsh Jew,
	Thou mak'st thy knife keen; but no metal can,
	No, not the hangman's axe, bear half the keenness
	Of thy sharp envy. Can no prayers pierce thee?
SHYLOCK	No, none that thou hast wit enough to make.
GRATIANO	O, be thou damned, inexorable dog!
	And for thy life let justice be accused.
	Thou almost mak'st me waver in my faith,
	To hold opinion with Pythagoras②
	That souls of animals infuse themselves
	Into the trunks of men. Thy currish spirit
	Governed a wolf who, hanged for human slaughter,
	Even from the gallows did his fell soul fleet,
	And, whilst thou layest in thy unhallowed dam,
	Infused itself in thee; for thy desires
	Are wolfish, bloody, starved and ravenous.
SHYLOCK	Till thou canst rail the seal from off my bond,
	Thou but offend'st thy lungs to speak so loud;

---

① **Padua**: name of a city in the north of Italy. It was a research center in civil law at that time.

② **Pythaporas**: an ancient Greek philosopher who believed that souls of some human beings pass after death into animals and vice versa.

	Repair thy wit, good youth, or it will fall
	To cureless ruin. I stand here for law.
DUKE OF VENICE	This letter from Bellario doth commend
	A young and learned doctor to our court.
	Where is he?
NERISSA	He attendeth here hard by
	To know your answer, whether you'll admit him.
DUKE OF VENICE	With all my heart. Some three or four of you
	Go give him courteous conduct to this place.
	Meantime, the court shall hear Bellario's letter.
CLERK	[*Reads*] "Your Grace shall understand that at the receipt of your letter I am very sick; but in the instant that your messenger came, in loving visitation was with me a young doctor of Rome. His name is Balthasar. I acquainted him with the cause in controversy between the Jew and Antonio the merchant; we turned o'er many books together; he is furnished with my opinion which, bettered with his own learning—the greatness whereof I cannot enough commend—comes with him at my importunity to fill up your Grace's request in my stead. I beseech you let his lack of years be no impediment to let him lack a reverend estimation, for I never knew so young a body with so old a head. I leave him to your gracious acceptance, whose trial shall better publish his commendation."

Enter PORTIA for BALTHASAR, dressed like a Doctor of Laws.

DUKE OF VENICE	You hear the learned Bellario, what he writes;
	And here, I take it, is the doctor come.
	Give me your hand; come you from old Bellario?
PORTIA	I did, my lord.
DUKE OF VENICE	You are welcome; take your place.
	Are you acquainted with the difference
	That holds this present question in the court?
PORTIA	I am informed thoroughly of the cause.
	Which is the merchant here, and which the Jew?
DUKE OF VENICE	Antonio and old Shylock, both stand forth.
PORTIA	Is your name Shylock?
SHYLOCK	Shylock is my name.
PORTIA	Of a strange nature is the suit you follow;
	Yet in such rule that the Venetian law
	Cannot impugn you as you do proceed.
	You stand within his danger, do you not?
ANTONIO	Ay, so he says.

PORTIA	Do you confess the bond?
ANTONIO	I do.
PORTIA	Then must the Jew be merciful.
SHYLOCK	On what compulsion must I? Tell me that.
PORTIA	The quality of mercy is not strained;
	It droppeth as the gentle rain from heaven
	Upon the place beneath. It is twice blest:
	It blesseth him that gives and him that takes.
	'Tis mightiest in the mightiest; it becomes
	The throned monarch better than his crown;
	His sceptre shows the force of temporal power,
	The attribute to awe and majesty,
	Wherein doth sit the dread and fear of kings;
	But mercy is above this sceptred sway,
	It is enthroned in the hearts of kings,
	It is an attribute to God himself;
	And earthly power doth then show likest God's
	When mercy seasons justice. Therefore, Jew,
	Though justice be thy plea, consider this—
	That in the course of justice none of us
	Should see salvation; we do pray for mercy,
	And that same prayer doth teach us all to render
	The deeds of mercy. I have spoke thus much
	To mitigate the justice of thy plea,
	Which if thou follow, this strict court of Venice
	Must needs give sentence' gainst the merchant there.
SHYLOCK	My deeds upon my head! I crave the law,
	The penalty and forfeit of my bond.
BASSANIO	Yes; here I tender it for him in the court;
	Yea, twice the sum; if that will not suffice,
	I will be bound to pay it ten times o'er
	On forfeit of my hands, my head, my heart;
	If this will not suffice, it must appear
	That malice bears down truth. And, I beseech you,
	Wrest once the law to your authority;
	To do a great right do a little wrong,
	And curb this cruel devil of his will.
PORTIA	It must not be; there is no power in Venice
	Can alter a decree established;
	'Twill be recorded for a precedent,
	And many an error, by the same example,

	Will rush into the state. It cannot be.
SHYLOCK	A Daniel① come to judgment! Yea, a Daniel!
	O wise young judge, how I do honor thee!
PORTIA	I pray you, let me look upon the bond.
SHYLOCK	Here 'tis, most reverend Doctor; here it is.
PORTIA	Shylock, there's thrice thy money offered thee.
SHYLOCK	An oath, an oath! I have an oath in heaven.
	Shall I lay perjury upon my soul?
	No, not for Venice.
PORTIA	Why, this bond is forfeit;
	And lawfully by this the Jew may claim
	A pound of flesh, to be by him cut off
	Nearest the merchant's heart. Be merciful.
	Take thrice thy money; bid me tear the bond.
SHYLOCK	When it is paid according to the tenor.
	It doth appear you are a worthy judge;
	You know the law; your exposition
	Hath been most sound; I charge you by the law,
	Whereof you are a well-deserving pillar,
	Proceed to judgment. By my soul I swear
	There is no power in the tongue of man
	To alter me. I stay here on my bond.
ANTONIO	Most heartily I do beseech the court
	To give the judgment.
PORTIA	Why then, thus it is:
	You must prepare your bosom for his knife.
SHYLOCK	O noble judge! O excellent young man!
PORTIA	For the intent and purpose of the law
	Hath full relation to the penalty,
	Which here appeareth due upon the bond.
SHYLOCK	'Tis very true. O wise and upright judge!
	How much more elder art thou than thy looks!
PORTIA	Therefore, lay bare your bosom.
SHYLOCK	Ay, his breast—
	So says the bond; doth it not, noble judge?
	"Nearest his heart." Those are the very words.
PORTIA	It is so. Are there balance here to weigh the flesh?
SHYLOCK	I have them ready.
PORTIA	Have by some surgeon, Shylock, on your charge,

---

① **Daniel**: a prophet and upright judge in the Bible.

	To stop his wounds, lest he do bleed to death.
SHYLOCK	Is it so nominated in the bond?
PORTIA	It is not so expressed, but what of that?
	'Twere good you do so much for charity.
SHYLOCK	I cannot find it; 'tis not in the bond.
PORTIA	You, merchant, have you anything to say?
ANTONIO	But little; I am armed and well prepared.
	Give me your hand, Bassanio; fare you well.
	Grieve not that I am fall'n to this for you,
	For herein Fortune shows herself more kind
	Than is her custom. It is still her use
	To let the wretched man outlive his wealth,
	To view with hollow eye and wrinkled brow
	An age of poverty; from which lingering penance
	Of such misery doth she cut me off.
	Commend me to your honourable wife;
	Tell her the process of Antonio's end;
	Say how I loved you; speak me fair in death;
	And, when the tale is told, bid her be judge
	Whether Bassanio had not once a love.
	Repent but you that you shall lose your friend,
	And he repents not that he pays your debt;
	For if the Jew do cut but deep enough,
	I'll pay it instantly with all my heart.
BASSANIO	Antonio, I am married to a wife
	Which is as dear to me as life itself;
	But life itself, my wife, and all the world,
	Are not with me esteemed above thy life;
	I would lose all, ay, sacrifice them all
	Here to this devil, to deliver you.
PORTIA	Your wife would give you little thanks for that,
	If she were by to hear you make the offer.
GRATIANO	I have a wife who I protest I love;
	I would she were in heaven, so she could
	Entreat some power to change this currish Jew.
NERISSA	'Tis well you offer it behind her back;
	The wish would make else an unquiet house.
SHYLOCK	[*Aside*] These be the Christian husbands! I have a daughter;
	Would any of the stock of Barrabas[①]

---

① **Barrabas**: a Jewish bandit and contemporary of Jesus.

	Had been her husband, rather than a Christian!
	We trifle time; I pray thee pursue sentence.
PORTIA	A pound of that same merchant's flesh is thine.
	The court awards it and the law doth give it.
SHYLOCK	Most rightful judge!
PORTIA	And you must cut this flesh from off his breast.
	The law allows it and the court awards it.
SHYLOCK	Most learned judge! A sentence! Come, prepare.
PORTIA	Tarry a little; there is something else.
	This bond doth give thee here no jot of blood:
	The words expressly are "a pound of flesh".
	Take then thy bond, take thou thy pound of flesh;
	But, in the cutting it, if thou dost shed
	One drop of Christian blood, thy lands and goods
	Are, by the laws of Venice, confiscate
	Unto the state of Venice.
GRATIANO	O upright judge! Mark, Jew. O learned judge!
SHYLOCK	Is that the law?
PORTIA	Thyself shalt see the act:
	For, as thou urgest justice, be assured
	Thou shalt have justice more than thou desir'st.
GRATIANO	O learned judge! Mark, Jew. A learned judge!
SHYLOCK	I take this offer then: pay the bond thrice,
	And let the Christian go.
BASSANIO	Here is the money.
PORTIA	Soft!
	The Jew shall have all justice. Soft! No haste.
	He shall have nothing but the penalty.
GRATIANO	O Jew! An upright judge, a learned judge!
PORTIA	Therefore prepare thee to cut off the flesh.
	Shed thou no blood, nor cut thou less nor more
	But just a pound of flesh; if thou tak'st more
	Or less than a just pound—be it but so much
	As makes it light or heavy in the substance,
	Or the division of the twentieth part
	Of one poor scruple; nay, if the scale do turn
	But in the estimation of a hair—
	Thou diest, and all thy goods are confiscate.
GRATIANO	A second Daniel, a Daniel, Jew!
	Now, infidel, I have you on the hip.
PORTIA	Why doth the Jew pause? Take thy forfeiture.

SHYLOCK	Give me my principal, and let me go.
BASSANIO	I have it ready for thee; here it is.
PORTIA	He hath refused it in the open court;
	He shall have merely justice, and his bond.
GRATIANO	A Daniel still say I, a second Daniel!
	I thank thee, Jew, for teaching me that word.
SHYLOCK	Shall I not have barely my principal?
PORTIA	Thou shalt have nothing but the forfeiture
	To be so taken at thy peril, Jew.
SHYLOCK	Why, then the devil give him good of it!
	I'll stay no longer question.
PORTIA	Tarry, Jew.
	The law hath yet another hold on you.
	It is enacted in the laws of Venice,
	If it be proved against an alien
	That by direct or indirect attempts
	He seek the life of any citizen,
	The party'gainst the which he doth contrive
	Shall seize one half his goods; the other half
	Comes to the privy coffer of the state;
	And the offender's life lies in the mercy
	Of the Duke only, 'gainst all other voice.
	In which predicament, I say, thou stand'st;
	For it appears by manifest proceeding
	That indirectly, and directly too,
	Thou hast contrived against the very life
	Of the defendant; and thou hast incurred
	The danger formerly by me rehearsed.
	Down, therefore, and beg mercy of the Duke.
GRATIANO	Beg that thou mayst have leave to hang thyself;
	And yet, thy wealth being forfeit to the state,
	Thou hast not left the value of a cord;
	Therefore thou must be hanged at the state's charge.
DUKE OF VENICE	That thou shalt see the difference of our spirit,
	I pardon thee thy life before thou ask it.
	For half thy wealth, it is Antonio's;
	The other half comes to the general state,
	Which humbleness may drive unto a fine.
PORTIA	Ay, for the state, not for Antonio.
SHYLOCK	Nay, take my life and all, pardon not that.
	You take my house when you do take the prop

	That doth sustain my house; you take my life
	When you do take the means whereby I live.
PORTIA	What mercy can you render him, Antonio?
GRATIANO	A halter gratis; nothing else, for God's sake!
ANTONIO	So please my lord the Duke and all the court
	To quit the fine for one half of his goods;
	I am content, so he will let me have
	The other half in use, to render it
	Upon his death unto the gentleman
	That lately stole his daughter—
	Two things provided more; that, for this favor,
	He presently become a Christian;
	The other, that he do record a gift,
	Here in the court, of all he dies possessed
	Unto his son Lorenzo and his daughter.
DUKE OF VENICE	He shall do this, or else I do recant
	The pardon that I late pronounced here.
PORTIA	Art thou contented, Jew? What dost thou say?
SHYLOCK	I am content.
PORTIA	Clerk, draw a deed of gift.
SHYLOCK	I pray you, give me leave to go from hence;
	I am not well; send the deed after me
	And I will sign it.
DUKE OF VENICE	Get thee gone, but do it.
GRATIANO	In christ'ning shalt thou have two god-fathers.
	Had I been judge, thou shouldst have had ten more[①]—
	To bring thee to the gallows, not to the font.
	Exit SHYLOCK.
DUKE OF VENICE	Sir, I entreat you home with me to dinner.
PORTIA	I humbly do desire your Grace of pardon;
	I must away this night toward Padua,
	And it is meet I presently set forth.
DUKE OF VENICE	I am sorry that your leisure serves you not.
	Antonio, gratify this gentleman,
	For in my mind you are much bound to him.
	Exeunt DUKE and his train.

---

① **ten more**: A jury in Britain is made up of 12 people. The meaning is that Shylock should have been sentenced to death, rather than being baptized, at birth.

Questions

1. What role do you think the Duke plays in the court of justice? If he is the judge, do you think he is biased even before the trial? Does he stand for mercy judging from the excerpt? How do you understand "How shalt thou hope for mercy, rendering none"? What can we learn about the practice of showing mercy to the merciful in a court of law at that time?
2. Do you think Shylock is mean or greedy or both? Do you think Shylock just wants to cut a pound of flesh from Antonio's body? What does he intend to do? And why?
3. Comment on the effect of comic elements in this part of the play.
4. Do you think the conflict in this play is caused by the difference in religious belief between the Christians and Jews or by human nature? Do you think the writer has made that clear in the play?
5. What kind of society do they live in according to what Shylock says about slaves?
6. What do you think of Portia's remark concerning mercy? Do you think justice should go together with mercy in a court of law?
7. What can we learn about the law and justice of Venice at that time according to the sentence "There is no power in Venice can alter a decree established"?
8. Do you think Portia or rather the author Shakespeare is clever or learned? Which one is more important in a court of law?
9. Do you think friendship is important in a person's life after reading the play? Do you think Antonio stupid in signing such a bond?

7.4 *Hamlet* by Shakespeare (An Excerpt from Act Ⅲ)

Scene Ⅰ A room in the castle

Enter Hamlet

HAMLET
    To be, or not to be—that is the question:
    Whether'tis nobler in the mind to suffer
    The slings and arrows of outrageous fortune,
    Or to take arms against a sea of troubles,
    And by opposing end them. To die, to sleep—
    No more—and by a sleep to say we end
    The heartache, and the thousand natural shocks
    That flesh is heir to. 'Tis a consummation
    Devoutly to be wished. To die, to sleep—
    To sleep—perchance to dream: ay, there's the rub①.
    For in that sleep of death what dreams may come
    When we have shuffled off this mortal coil,
    Must give us pause. There's the respect

---

① **rub**: (in bowling game) an obstacle (which diverts the course of a bowl).

That makes calamity of so long life.
For who would bear the whips and scorns of time,
Th' oppressor's wrong, the proud man's contumely,
The pangs of despised love, the law's delay,
The insolence of office, and the spurns
That patient merit of th' unworthy takes,
When he himself might his quietus make
With a bare bodkin? Who would fardels bear,
To grunt and sweat under a weary life,
But that the dread of something after death,
The undiscovered country①, from whose bourn
No traveller returns, puzzles the will,
And makes us rather bear those ills we have
Than fly to others that we know not of?
Thus conscience② does make cowards of us all,
And thus the native hue of resolution
Is sicklied o'er with the pale cast of thought,
And enterprises of great pitch and moment
With this regard their currents turn awry
And lose the name of action. —Soft you now,
The fair Ophelia! —Nymph, in thy orisons
Be all my sins remembered.

Questions

1. How do you understand the phrase "To be, or not to be"?
2. Do you think Hamlet is a coward? If you think he is, which one is the major reason, conscience or fear of the unknown? If you don't think he is, why not?
3. Have you read the whole play? Do you think Hamlet has arrived at a conclusion whether it is nobler to suffer in the mind or to take arms against a sea of troubles?

7.5 "Sonnet 18" by Shakespeare

Shall I compare thee to a summer's day?
Thou art more lovely and more temperate:
Rough winds do shake the darling buds of May,
And summer's lease hath all too short a date.
Sometime too hot the eye of heaven shines,
And often is his gold complexion dimmed;
And every fair from fair sometimes declines,

---

① **the undiscovered country**: the underworld.
② **conscience**: thinking.

By chance or nature's changing course untrimmed;
But thy eternal summer shall not fade,
Nor lose possession of that fair thou ow'st;
Nor shall death brag thou wander'st in his shade,
When in eternal lines to time thou grow'st:
 So long as men can breathe, or eyes can see,
 So long lives this, and this gives life to thee.

Questions

1. Why does the writer compare his friend to a summer's day? What is the similarity between them?
2. What does the author think of artistic creation?
3. What can we learn about the author's attitude towards friendship?

7.6 "Sonnet 29" by Shakespeare

When, in disgrace with fortune and men's eyes,
I all alone beweep my outcast state,
And trouble deaf heaven with my bootless cries,
And look upon myself and curse my fate,
Wishing me like to one more rich in hope,
Featured like him, like him with friends possessed,
Desiring this man's art, and that man's scope,
With what I most enjoy contented least;
Yet in these thoughts myself almost despising,
Haply I think on thee, and then my state,
Like to the lark at break of day arising
From sullen earth, sings hymns at heaven's gate;
For thy sweet love remembered such wealth brings
That then I scorn to change my state with kings.

Questions

1. What can we learn from the first four lines?
2. What does the writer most enjoy doing?
3. What can we learn about the author's attitude towards power and social position?

7.7 "The Flea" by Donne

Mark but this flea, and mark in this,
How little that which thou deniest me is;
Me it sucked first, and now sucks thee,
And in this flea our two bloods mingled be;
Thou know'st that this cannot be said

A sin, or shame, or loss of maidenhead,
   Yet this enjoys before it woo,
   And pampered swells with one blood made of two,
   And this, alas, is more than we would do.

O stay, three lives in one flea spare,
Where we almost, nay, more than married are.
This flea is you and I, and this
Our marriage bed and marriage temple is;
Though parents grudge, and you, we are met,
And cloistered in these living walls of jet.
   Though use make you apt to kill me,
   Let not to that, self-murder added be,
   And sacrilege, three sins in killing three.

Cruel and sudden, hast thou since
Purpled thy nail in blood of innocence?
Wherein could this flea guilty be,
Except in that drop which it sucked from thee?
Yet thou triumph'st, and say'st that thou
Find'st not thyself nor me the weaker now;
   'Tis true; then learn how false fears be:
   Just so much honour, when thou yield'st to me,
   Will waste, as this flea's death took life from thee.

Questions

1. Judging from the first stanza, do you think the narrator's love has been returned?
2. Is there any difference of social position between him and the person he loves according to the poem?
3. Can you find any reference to religious belief in the poem?

7.8 "The Sun Rising" by Donne

   Busy old fool, unruly sun,
   Why dost thou thus,
Through windows and through curtains call on us?
Must to thy motions lovers' seasons run?
Saucy pedantic wretch, go chide
Late school-boys and sour prentices,
Go tell court-huntsmen that the king will ride,
Call country ants to harvest offices;
Love, all alike, no season knows nor clime,

Nor hours, days, months, which are the rags of time.

Thy beams so reverend, and strong
Why shouldst thou think?
I could eclipse and cloud them with a wink,
But that I would not lose her sight so long.
If her eyes have not blinded thine,
Look, and tomorrow late, tell me,
Whether both th' Indias of spice and mine
Be where thou left'st them, or lie here with me.
Ask for those kings whom thou saw'st yesterday,
And thou shalt hear, "All here in one bed lay."

She's all states, and all princes I;
Nothing else is;
Princes do but play us; compared to this,
All honour's mimic, all wealth alchemy.
Thou, sun, art half as happy as we,
In that the world's contracted thus;
Thine age asks ease, and since thy duties be
To warm the world, that's done in warming us.
Shine here to us, and thou art everywhere;
This bed thy center is, these walls thy sphere.

Questions

1. What is the lovers' attitude towards time, wealth and honor according to this poem?
2. Comment on the use of figurative language such as metaphor in this poem. Do you think it effective?
3. What can we learn about Donne's metaphysical poetry from the meter and stanza used in this poem?

7.9 "The Canonization" by Donne

For God's sake hold your tongue, and let me love,
   Or chide my palsy, or my gout,
My five gray hairs, or ruined fortune, flout,
    With wealth your state, your mind with arts improve,
      Take you a course, get you a place,
      Observe His Honour, or His Grace,
Or the King's real, or his stamped face
   Contemplate; what you will, approve,
   So you will let me love.

Alas, alas, who's injured by my love?
   What merchant's ships have my sighs drowned?
Who says my tears have overflowed his ground?
   When did my colds a forward spring remove?
      When did the heats which my veins fill
      Add one man to the plaguy bill?
Soldiers find wars, and lawyers find out still
   Litigious men, which quarrels move,
   Though she and I do love.

Call us what you will, we are made such by love;
   Call her one, me another fly,
We're tapers too, and at our own cost die,
   And we in us find the eagle and the dove.
      The phoenix riddle hath more wit
      By us: we two being one, are it.
So, to one neutral thing both sexes fit.
   We die and rise the same, and prove
   Mysterious by this love.

We can die by it, if not live by love,
   And if unfit for tomb or hearse
Our legend be, it will be fit for verse;
   And if no piece of chronicle we prove,
      We'll build in sonnets pretty rooms;
      As well a well-wrought urn becomes
The greatest ashes, as half-acre tombs,
   And by these hymns, all shall approve
   Us canonized for love;

And thus invoke us: You whom reverend love
   Made one another's hermitage;
You, to whom love was peace, that now is rage;
   Who did the whole world's soul contract, and drove
      Into the glasses of your eyes
      (So made such mirrors, and such spies,
That they did all to you epitomize)
   Countries, towns, courts: Beg from above
   A pattern of your love!

Questions

1. Do you think the narrator's love has undergone any frustration?
2. Do you think the narrator is making some complaints to those who are interfering with his love?
3. How do you understand the title of the poem?

7.10 "Death Be Not Proud" by Donne

> Death, be not proud, though some have called thee
> Mighty and dreadful, for thou art not so;
> For those whom thou think'st thou dost overthrow
> Die not, poor death, nor yet canst thou kill me.
> From rest and sleep, which but thy pictures be,
> Much pleasure; then from thee, much more must flow,
> And soonest our best men with thee do go,
> Rest of their bones, and soul's delivery.
> Thou art slave to fate, chance, kings, and desperate men,
> And dost with poison, war, and sickness dwell,
> And poppy, or charms can make us sleep as well,
> And better than thy stroke; why swell'st thou then?
> One short sleep past, we wake eternally,
> And death shall be no more; death, thou shalt die.

Questions

1. Is the rhyme scheme of this poem of Petrarchan style or Shakespearen?
2. What is the writer's attitude toward death according to this poem?
3. In his prose Donne wrote: "No man is an island, entire of itself; every man is a piece of the continent, a part of the main; ... any man's death diminishes me, because I am involved in mankind; and therefore never send to know for whom the bell tolls; it tolls for thee." How do you understand his remark?

7.11 "Of Studies" by Bacon

Studies serve for delight, for ornament, and for ability. Their chief use for delight, is in privateness and retiring; for ornament, is in discourse; and for ability, is in the judgment and disposition of business. For expert men can execute, and perhaps judge of particulars, one by one; but the general counsels, and the plots and marshalling of affairs come best from those that are learned. To spend too much time in studies is sloth; to use them too much for ornament is affectation; to make judgment wholly by their rules is the humor of a scholar. They perfect nature, and are perfected by experience: For natural abilities are like natural plants that need pruning by study; and studies themselves do give forth directions too much at large, except they be bounded in by experience. Crafty men contemn studies, simple men admire them, and wise men use them; for they teach not their own use; but that is a wisdom without them, and above them, won by observation. Read not to contradict and confute; nor to believe and take for granted; nor to find talk and discourse; but to weigh and consider. Some books are to be tasted, others to be swallowed, and some few to be chewed and digested; that is, some books are to be read only in parts; others to be read, but not curiously; and some few to be read wholly, and with diligence and attention. Some books also may be read by deputy, and extracts made of them by others; but that would be only in the less important arguments, and the meaner sort of books, else distilled books are like common distilled waters, flashy things. Reading maketh a full man, conference a ready man, and writing an exact man. And therefore, if a man write little, he had need have a great memory; if he confer little, he had need have a present wit; and if he read little, he had need have much cunning, to seem to know that① he doth not. Histories make men wise; poets, witty; the mathematics, subtle; natural philosophy②, deep; moral, grave; logic and rhetoric, able to contend. *Abeunt studia in mores*③. Nay, there is no stond or impediment in the wit but may be wrought out by fit studies; like as diseases of the body may have appropriate exercises. Bowling is good for the stone and reins, shooting for the lungs and breast, gentle walking for the stomach, riding for the head, and the like. So if a man's wit be wandering, let him study the mathematics; for in demonstrations, if his wit be called away never④ so little, he must begin again. If his wit be not apt to distinguish or find differences, let him study the Schoolmen; for they are *cumini sectores*⑤. If he be not apt to beat over matters, and to call up one thing to prove and illustrate another, let him study the lawyers' cases. So every defect of the mind may have a special receipt.

Vocabulary

ornament 修饰	bound 限制	had need 应该，必须
retiring 隐退，隐居	contemn 谴责	confer 交换意见，协商
discourse 话语	confute 驳倒（人、证据等）	subtle 细微的
disposition 处理	swallow 吞，咽下	grave 严肃，认真
expert 老练的	chew 咀嚼	contend 争辩
execute 执行，实施	digest 消化	stond 障碍
particular 细节	curiously 仔细地	impediment 妨碍，障碍
counsel 见解，忠告	deputy 代理人	appropriate 合适
marshal 列举，排列	extract 摘录，抽出物，精华	stone 胆囊
sloth 懒散，懒惰	mean 次要的	rein 肾
affection 矫揉造作	distill 蒸馏	shooting 射箭
humor 惯用的格调，癖好	flashy 无味道的	demonstration 论证，证明
prune 修剪	conference 当面交谈	distinguish 区分

① **that**: that which.
② **natural philosophy**: science.
③ **Abeunt studia in mores**: Studies go to make up a man's character. (Ovid, *Heroides*)
④ **never**: ever.
⑤ **cumini sectores**: hairsplitters.

Schoolmen 经院哲学家，琐碎哲学家　　　　defect 缺陷　　　　　　　receipt 疗法

Questions

1. What is your definition of "essay" after reading the passage?
2. Give examples to show the use of figurative language in the passage. Do you think they help to illustrate the author's ideas?
3. Do you agree with the author when he says "Some books are to be tasted, others to be swallowed, and some few to be chewed and digested"? Why or why not?

7.12 "Of Marriage and Single Life" by Bacon

He that hath wife and children hath given hostages to fortune; for they are impediments to great enterprises, either of virtue or mischief. Certainly the best works, and of greatest merit for the public, have proceeded from the unmarried or childless men, which both in affection and means have married and endowed the public. Yet it were great reason that those that have children should have greatest care of future times, unto which they know they must transmit their dearest pledges. Some there are, who though they lead a single life, yet their thoughts do end with themselves, and account future times impertinences. Nay, there are some other that account wife and children but as bills of charges. Nay more, there are some foolish rich covetous men that take a pride in having no children, because they may be thought so much the richer. For perhaps they have heard some talk, "Such an one is a great rich man," and another except to it, "Yea, but he hath a great charge of children;" as if it were an abatement to his riches. But the most ordinary cause of a single life is liberty, especially in certain self-pleasing and humorous minds, which are so sensible of every restraint, as they will go near to think their girdles and garters to be bonds and shackles. Unmarried men are best friends, best masters, best servants; but not always best subjects, for they are light to run away, and almost all fugitives, are of that condition. A single life doth well with churchmen, for charity will hardly water the ground, where it must first fill a pool. It is indifferent for judges and magistrates, for if they be facile and corrupt, you shall have a servant five times worse than a wife. For soldiers, I find the generals commonly in their hortatives put men in mind of their wives and children; and I think the despising of marriage amongst the Turks maketh the vulgar soldier more base. Certainly wife and children are a kind of discipline of humanity; and single men, though they may be many times more charitable, because their means are less exhaust, yet, on the other side, they are more cruel and hardhearted (good to make severe inquisitors), because their tenderness is not so oft called upon. Grave natures, led by custom, and therefore constant, are commonly loving husbands, as was said of Ulysses[①], *vetulam suam praetulit*

[①] **Ulysses**: King of Ithaca and commander of Greek troops at the siege of Troy. On his way home after the fall of Troy he is detained by the goddess Calypso, who falls in love with him and gives him a choice: either stays with her and becomes a god or returns to his wife in Ithaca and remains human.

*immortalitati*①. Chaste women are often proud and froward, as presuming upon the merit of their chastity. It is one of the best bonds, both of chastity and obedience, in the wife, if she think her husband wise, which she will never do if she find him jealous. Wives are young men's mistresses, companions for middle age, and old men's nurses, so as a man may have a quarrel to marry when he will. But yet he was reputed one of the wise men that made answer to the question when a man should marry: "A young man not yet, an elder man not at all." It is often seen that bad husbands have very good wives; whether it be that it raiseth the price of their husband's kindness, when it comes, or that the wives take a pride in their patience. But this never fails, if the bad husbands were of their own choosing, against their friends' consent; for then they will be sure to make good their own folly.

Questions

1. What does the author want to tell us in the first sentence? Do you think the author is trying to persuade us to lead a single life?
2. Do you agree with the author when he says "It's often seen that bad husbands have very good wives"?
3. Judging from the whole passage, what is the author's attitude towards marriage?

Vocabulary

hostage 人质
enterprise 事业；实业
mischief 恶行
proceed 出（自）
transmit 转移
pledge 保证；誓言
impertinence 无关
nay 不；不仅
covetous 贪心的
abatement 减少
restraint 限制
girdle 紧身衣
garter 袜带

bond 相似处；结合；(pl.) 镣；铐；监禁
shackle 手铐
fugitive 逃跑者；逃避者
charity 慈善
biased 不公正的
corrupt 腐败的
hortative 劝告；规劝
despise 轻视
vulgar 粗俗
discipline 训练
humanity 仁慈；人性
charitable 仁慈的，大方的

exhaust 枯竭的
severe 严厉的
inquisitor 审讯者
grave 严肃的；认真的
chaste 贞洁的
froward 不易控制的
jealous 嫉妒的
mistress 情妇；情人
companion 同伴
quarrel 原因；借口
consent 同意
folly 愚蠢

---

① **vetulam suam praetulit immortalitati**: He preferred his old wife to immortality.

Chapter Three　The Restoration

1. Introduction

1.1　The Restoration

Puritans were radical members of the Protestant movement in England in the 16th century. In 1603, Queen Elizabeth died without an heir, and James Ⅵ of Scotland was invited to take the English throne and he became James Ⅰ. English Puritans were happy to have James as king at first because the Scottish Church was a pure Protestant Church with democratically elected officials. James, however, refused all their proposals for change the next year. Politically James Ⅰ didn't like to be chained by the Parliament because he thought of his right to rule as God-given, a belief he passed to Charles Ⅰ, his son and successor. This led to the confrontation with the Parliament whose members had become increasingly Puritan in sympathy. For several times Charles dissolved the Parliament, but in 1640, in order to get money, he called the Parliament, the members of which introduced, to his disappointment, a series of measures to limit the power of the crown. In 1642, Charles Ⅰ led a group of swordsmen and marched to Parliament to arrest the leading members, which led to a civil war. In 1648, the king was captured, tried, and was executed in the following year. Oliver Cromwell became Lord Protector of the Commonwealth of England.

The English Civil War, also known as the Puritan Revolution, is generally regarded as the beginning of modern world history.

After Cromwell's death in 1658, the regime began to collapse. In 1660 the Parliament asked the late king's son to return from his long exile in France as King Charles Ⅱ. After the Restoration, which went smoothly, the Parliament passed a number of laws against the Puritans, who left the Established Church and from then on became known as Dissenters or Nonconformists.

1.2　Literary Characteristics

Being opposed to the corruption in and complicated rituals of the Roman Catholic Church, the Puritans are noted for their high moral standard as well as for their sternness. They regarded pleasure-seeking as symptoms of sin: Maypole dancing was forbidden; theaters were shut down; Christmas celebrations were banned as evidences of anti-religious behaviour. Strong in religious belief, they tried to read and understand the Bible by themselves and they worked very hard in order to please God. Their life was disciplined and simple.

Because of the influence of Puritanism, poetry and prose in English literature around the Restoration are largely religious and instructive. John Milton and John Bunyan created two great masterpieces in the literary history of the world, *Paradise Lost*, an epic poem, and *The Pilgrim's Progress*, a fiction prose. In addition, John Dryden (1631-1700), in his writings like *An Essay of Dramatic Poesy*, set the example of a modern English prose style: informal and persuasive. Poets like Robert Herrick (1591-1674), who sided with Charles I and his son during the Civil War and became known as the cavaliers, wrote about the courtly themes of loyalty and love.

When the theatres reopened after Restoration, actresses, like Nell Gwyn (mistress of Charles II, 1650-1687), appeared on stage. There were only three types of play: operas, heroic tragedies and comedies. Rewriting of Shakespeare's plays became common. For example, *Romeo and Juliet* was given a happy ending. Under the influence of French drama, wit, a new element, was introduced into English drama; Moliere's comedies were also adapted. Besides Dryden, George Etherege (1635-1691), William Wycherley (1640-1715), William Congreve (1670-1729), and Aphra Behn (1640-1689) are the major playwrights. Since hardly anything great was written for the stage, English drama at that time never reached the altitude enjoyed by Shakespeare.

2. John Milton (1608-1674)

The son of a scrivener and composer of music, John Milton was born in London on December 9, 1608, into a Puritan family. He grew up in the atmosphere of a sociable home full of music, charity and respect for learning. When he was twelve, his father sent him to St Paul's School to provide him an excellent day school education with additional private tutoring in Italian, French music and other similar subjects. In 1625, he entered Christ's College, Cambridge, and stayed there for seven years for an M. A. degree, acquiring a sound knowledge of Latin.

John Milton

Milton had intended to be a clergyman of the Church of England, the normal course for a young man intending to devote his life to serious literary pursuits. But he was disgusted with the corruption in the Established Church. For over 5 years Milton lived in his father's country home near London, writing poems such as "L'Allegro" (The Cheerful Man, 1632), "Il Penseroso" (The Pensive Man, 1632), an elegy *Lycidas* (1637), and two masques—*Arcades* (1633) and *Comus* (1634) besides reading literature, science, theology and music. In 1639 when he learned that a civil war was inevitable at home, he ended his traveling in mainland Europe and, back in London, he wrote a lot of pamphlets defending the revolution and, years later, justifying the execution of Charles I. In 1642 he married Mary Powell, who soon left him to join her royalist family but returned to him three years later. In 1649 he was appointed Latin secretary to the Council of State by the government of the Commonwealth, and he worked very hard, doing all kinds of paper work. Soon his eyesight began to fail and in 1652 he became totally blind. Mary died in the same year after the birth of their third daughter. In 1656 Milton married Katherine Woodcock, who died in the next year after giving birth to a daughter.

After the Restoration Milton was imprisoned, but after some time the new king pardoned him. Now he could find time to complete poems he started earlier—dictate to his daughters and friends. After seven years' labour, *Paradise Lost*, one of the greatest epics in British literature, was finished in 1665 and published two years later. In 1666 he began his *Paradise Regained*, which was published in 1671. *Samson Agonistes*, a verse drama, was published in the same year. Milton died in 1674.

3. John Bunyan (1628-1688)

3.1 Life and Career

John Bunyan

Bunyan was born in the village of Elstow in central England. After very slight schooling and some practice at his father's trade of tinker, he was drafted for two and a half years into the Parliamentary army. After the Civil War, he got married and worked at his family trade. Influenced by his wife he read several religious works besides the Bible and the Prayer Book. In his childhood he was occasionally tormented by dreams, fears of devils and hell-fire, and when he grew up, he entered on a long and agonizing struggle between his religious instinct and his obstinate self-will.

After the death of his wife he moved his family of four children to the nearby town of Bedford, became a member of the Baptist Church in the town, and began acting as a lay preacher, at a time when various dissenting denominations or preaching laymen sprang up. In his conflict with the Quakers, he wrote and published his first writings. After Restoration the authorities forbad preaching by persons outside the communion of the Church of England and he was arrested and imprisoned in Bedford jail. Consistently refusing to give up preaching after release from the jail, he continued in prison for twelve years, working for the support of his family by making shoes-laces. During this time he wrote many books including his spiritual autobiography *Grace Abounding to the Chief of Sinners* (1666). At last, in 1672, the authorities abandoned the ineffective requirement of conformity, and he was released and became pastor of the same church. Three years later, however, he was again imprisoned for six months, and it was at that time that he composed the first part of *The Pilgrim's Progress* (1684), a prose work modeled on King James *Bible*. The rest of his life is spent in preaching and writing. Other books by Bunyan include *The Life and Death of Mr. Badman* (1680) and *The Holy War* (1682).

3.2 *The Pilgrim's Progress* (synopsis)

In the form of a dream, *The Pilgrim's Progress* consists of two parts, the first an account of the pilgrimage of a person named Christian and the second that of his wife and children. The book recounts in allegorical form the experience of Christian, from his first awareness of his sinfulness and spiritual need to his personal conversion to Christ, to his walk as a believer. He is shown as a pilgrim in this world, fleeing from the "City of Destruction", on his way to the "Celestial City", which will be his true home forever. Christian encounters many personages during the pilgrimage: Mr Worldly Wiseman, Faithful, Hopeful, Giant Despair, the foul fiend Apollyon, among others. It is the intensely sincere presentation by a man of tremendous moral energy of what he believed to be the most important subject in life, the personal salvation. It is an allegory, but one which seems inherent in the human mind and hence more natural than the most direct narrative. For all men, life is indeed a journey, and Slough of Despond, Doubting Castle, Vanity Fair, and the Valley of Humiliation are places where in one sense or another every human soul has often struggled and suffered, so that every reader goes hand in hand with Christian and his friends, fears for them in their dangers and rejoices in their escapes.

4. John Dryden (1631-1700)

Born in a well-to-do Puritan family, John Dryden graduated from Cambridge University in 1654. Dryden's earliest successful poem, *Heroic Stanzas* (1659), extolled the virtues of Oliver Cromwell. An enthusiastic supporter of the revolution, he wrote an elegy on the death of Cromwell in 1659. After the Restoration, however, Dryden became a Royalist and celebrated the return of King Charles II in *Astraea Redux* (1660) and *Panegyric* on the coronation (1661). In 1682 he wrote *Religio Laici* to defend Anglicanism. When James II came to the throne, Dryden converted to Catholicism. The move to Catholicism produced his longest poem *The Hind and the Panther*. Although he

John Dryden

often changed his stand, the clearness of his thought, the direct energy of expression, the smooth movement and the subtle argumentative skill make his works eminent expressions of his genius. Dryden was appointed Poet Laureate in 1668 and conferred the post of Historiographer Royal in 1669. But when James was deposed, Dryden lost his posts as Poet Laureate and Historiographer Royal.

From the 1660s to the 1670s Dryden devoted largely to drama. He wrote a large number of plays, including the semi-opera *The Indian Queen* written with Sir Robert Howard in 1664, the comedy *Marriage A-la-Mode* in 1671, the tragedy *All for Love* in 1677, the tragicomedy *The Spanish Friar* in 1680, and the heroic play *Aureng-Zebe* in 1675.

Dryden's greatest achievements were in his satirical and argumentative verse. He established the heroic couplet as the standard meter of English poetry. By writing successful satires, religious pieces, fables, epigrams, compliments, prologues, and plays in it, he also introduced the alexandrine and triplet into the form. His most outstanding contribution to English literature is his literary criticism. His critical writings established cannons of taste and theoretical principles that determined the character of neoclassic literature. *An Essay of Dramatic Poesy* (1668), a delightful dialogue, is the most well-known.

5. Selected Writings

5.1 *Paradise Lost* (Excerpts from Book Ⅰ) by Milton

    Of Man's first disobedience, and the fruit
    Of that forbidden tree, whose mortal taste
    Brought death into the world, and all our woe,
    With loss of Eden, till one greater Man①
5 Restore us, and regain the blissful seat,
    Sing, Heavenly Muse, that, on the secret top
    Of Oreb②, or of Sinai, didst inspire
    That shepherd who first taught the chosen seed
    In the beginning how the Heavens and Earth
10 Rose out of Chaos; or, if Sion hill③
    Delight thee more, and Siloa's brook④ that flowed
    Fast by the oracle of God, I thence
    Invoke thy aid to my adventurous song,
    That with no middle flight⑤ intends to soar
15 Above th' Aonian mount⑥, while it pursues
    Things unattempted yet in prose or rhyme.
    And chiefly thou, O Spirit⑦, that dost prefer
    Before all temples th' upright heart and pure,
    Instruct me, for thou know'st; thou from the first
20 Wast present, and, with mighty wings outspread,

---

① **one greater Man**: refers to Jesus Christ.

② **Oreb** (or **Sinai**): a mountain in the holy land where Moses ("that shepherd" in the next line) gives the Ten Commandments to the Israelites ("the chosen seed" in the next line).

③ **Sion**: Zion, a hill in Jerusalem on which stood the Temple ("the oracle of God" in the following lines).

④ **Siloa's brook**: a stream near Jerusalem.

⑤ **middle flight**: In the time of Milton, it was believed that the earth consisted of three regions, among which the middle region leads to Heaven, while all gods and goddesses in Greek mythology lived in Olympus (middle air).

⑥ **Aonian mount**: Mount Helicon in Greek mythology, home of the Muses and source of Hippocrene. The water in the spring can, in classical mythology, produce poetic inspiration.

⑦ **Spitit**: Holy spirit.

Dove-like sat'st brooding on the vast abyss,
And mad'st it pregnant: what in me is dark
Illumine; what is low, raise and support;
That, to the height of this great argument,
25 I may assert Eternal Providence,
And justify the ways of God to men.
    Say first, (for Heaven hides nothing from thy view,
Nor the deep tract of Hell), say first what cause
Moved our grand parents, in that happy state,
30 Favoured of Heaven so highly, to fall off
From their Creator, and transgress his will
For one restraint, lords of the world besides.
Who first seduced them to that foul revolt?
    Th' infernal Serpent①; he it was, whose guile,
35 Stirred up with envy and revenge, deceived
The mother of mankind, what time his pride
Had cast him out from Heaven, with all his host
Of rebel angels, by whose aid aspiring
To set himself in glory above his peers,
40 He trusted to have equaled the Most High,
If he opposed; and with ambitious aim
Against the throne and monarchy of God
Raised impious war in Heaven and battle proud
With vain attempt. Him the Almighty Power
45 Hurled headlong flaming from th' ethereal sky,
With hideous ruin and combustion down
To bottomless perdition, there to dwell
In adamantine chains and penal fire,
Who durst defy th' Omnipotent to arms ...

50   "What though the field② be lost?
All is not lost—the unconquerable will,
And study of revenge, immortal hate,
And courage never to submit or yield:
And what is else not to be overcome?
55 That glory never shall his wrath or might
Extort from me. To bow and sue for grace
With suppliant knee, and deify his power

---

① **Serpent**: Lucifer (Satan).
② **field**: war staged by Satan against God.

Who, from the terror of this arm, so late
　　　Doubted his empire—that were low indeed;
60　That were an ignominy and shame beneath
　　　This downfall; since by fate the strength of gods,
　　　And this empyreal substance cannot fail;
　　　Since, through experience of this great event,
　　　In arms not worse, in foresight much advanced,
65　We may with more successful hope resolve
　　　To wage by force or guile eternal war,
　　　Irreconcilable to our grand Foe①,
　　　Who now triumphs, and in th' excess of joy
　　　Sole reigning holds the tyranny of Heaven."

Questions

1. What can we learn from lines 9-10? Are they allusions to Genesis or the creation story in Greek mythology?
2. Why does the author mention "Siloa's brook" in line 11? Do you think it has anything to do with Hippocrene?
3. What is the consequence of "impious war in Heaven and battle proud"? Find in this part one or two words to answer it.
4. What can we learn about the writer's attitude towards religious belief, or man from this part of *Paradise Lost*?
5. What do lines 28-33 tell us? Which line in the excerpts tells us the theme of the whole poem?

5.2 "When I Consider How My Light Is Spent" by Milton

　　When I consider how my light is spent
　　　　Ere half my days in this dark world and wide,
　　　　And that one talent which is death to hide
　　　　Lodg'd with me useless, though my soul more bent
　　To serve therewith my Maker, and present
　　　　My true account, lest he returning chide,
　　　　"Doth God exact day-labour, light denied?"
　　　　I fondly ask. But Patience, to prevent
　　That murmur, soon replies: "God doth not need
　　　　Either man's work or his own gifts. Who best
　　　　Bear His mild yoke, they serve Him best. His state
　　Is kingly: thousands at His bidding speed,
　　　　And post o'er land and ocean without rest;

---

①　**our grand Foe**: God.

They also serve who only stand and wait."

Questions

1. What does the poet want to express in the first two lines?
2. What can we learn about the author's religious belief from this poem?
3. Is the rhyme scheme of this sonnet Shakespearean or Petrarchan?

5.3 "Methought I Saw My Late Espoused Saint" by Milton

> Methought I saw my late espoused saint
> Brought to me like Alcestis① from the grave,
> Whom Jove's great son to her glad husband gave,
> Rescued from death by force though pale and faint.
> Mine, as whom washed from spot of childbed taint,
> Purification in the old law② did save,
> And such, as yet once more I trust to have
> Full sight of her in heaven without restraint,
> Came vested all in white, pure as her mind.
> Her face was veiled, yet to my fancied sight
> Love, sweetness, goodness, in her person shined
> So clear, as in no face with more delight.
> But O, as to embrace me she inclined,
> I waked, she fled, and day brought back my night.

Questions

1. This poem was written in 1658. Is this sonnet a love poem? Do you think it is dedicated to the author's second wife?
2. What is the function of the last line in the whole poem?

5.4 *The Pilgrim's Progress*③ by Bunyan (An Excerpt from Part Ⅰ)

Vanity Fair④

Now when they were got almost quite out of this wilderness, Faithful chanced to cast his eye back, and espied one coming after them, and he knew him. Oh! said Faithful to his brother, who comes yonder? Then Christian looked, and said, It is my good friend Evangelist. Aye, and my good friend too, said Faithful, for 't was he that set me on the way to the gate.

---

① **Alcestis**: According to Euripides' *Alcestis*, Hercules ("Jove's great son" in the next line) rescues from the underworld Alcestis, wife of Admetus, who is filled with joy when he lifts the veil from her head.

② **The old law**: See Leviticus 12. 2-8.

③ *The Pilgrim's Progress* is written in the form of allegory—story or description in which ideas such as patience, purity and truth are symbolized by persons who are characters in the story.

④ *The Pilgrim's Progress* comprises two parts, the first part with ten stages, and the second part, eight stages. This selection is from the sixth stage of the First Part.

Now was Evangelist come up unto them, and thus saluted them.

EVANGELIST: Peace be with you, dearly beloved, and peace be to your helpers.

CHRISTIAN: Welcome, welcome, my good Evangelist; the sight of thy countenance brings to my remembrance thy ancient kindness and unwearied labors for my eternal good.

FAITHFUL: And a thousand times welcome, said good Faithful, thy company, O sweet Evangelist; how desirable is it to us poor pilgrims!

EVANGELIST: Then said Evangelist, How hath it fared with you, my friends, since the time of our last parting? What have you met with, and how have you behaved yourselves?

Then Christian and Faithful told him of all things that had happened to them in the way; and how, and with what difficulty, they had arrived to that place.

Right glad am I, said Evangelist, not that you have met with trials, but that you have been victors, and for that you have, notwithstanding many weaknesses, continued in the way to this very day.

I say, right glad am I of this thing, and that for mine own sake and yours: I have sowed, and you have reaped; and the day is coming, when "both he that soweth, and they that reap, shall rejoice together, " (John 4: 36) that is, if you hold out: "for in due season ye shall reap, if ye faint not." (Gal. 6: 9) The crown is before you, and it is an incorruptible one; "so run that ye may obtain it." (Cor. 9: 24-27) Some there be that set out for this crown, and after they have gone far for it, another comes in and takes it from them: "hold fast, therefore, that you have; let no man take your crown." (Rev. 3: 11) You are not yet out of the gunshot of the devil; "you have not resisted unto blood, striving against sin". Let the kingdom be always before you, and believe steadfastly concerning the things that are invisible. Let nothing that is on this side the other world get within you. And, above all, look well to your own hearts and to the lusts thereof; for they are "deceitful above all things, and desperately wicked". Set your faces like a flint; you have all power in heaven and earth on your side.

CHRISTIAN: Then Christian thanked him for his exhortations; but told him withal, that they would have him speak farther to them for their help the rest of the way; and the rather, for that they well knew that he was a prophet, and could tell them of things that might happen unto them, and also how they might resist and overcome them. To which request Faithful also consented. So Evangelist began as followeth.

EVANGELIST: My sons, you have heard in the word of the truth of the Gospel①, that you must "through many tribulations enter into the kingdom of heaven"; and again, that "in every city, bonds and afflictions abide you"; and therefore you cannot expect that you should go long on your pilgrimage without them, in some sort or other. You have found something of the truth of these testimonies upon you already, and more will immediately follow: for now, as you see, you are almost out of this wilderness, and therefore you will soon come into a town that you will by and by see before you; and in that town you will be hardly beset with enemies, who will strain hard but they will kill you; and be you sure that one or both of you must seal

---

① **Gospel**: the proclamation of the redemption preached by Jesus and the Apostles, which is the central content of Christian revelation.

the testimony which you hold, with blood; but "be you faithful unto death, and the King① will give you a crown of life". He that shall die there, although his death will be unnatural, and his pain, perhaps, great, he will yet have the better of his fellow; not only because he will be arrived at the Celestial City soonest, but because he will escape many miseries that the other will meet with in the rest of his journey. But when you are come to the town, and shall find fulfilled what I have here related, then remember your friend, and quit yourselves like men, and "commit the keeping of your souls to God in well doing, as unto a faithful Creator".

Then I saw in my dream, that when they were got out of the wilderness, they presently saw a town before them, and the name of that town is Vanity; and at the town there is a fair kept, called Vanity Fair. It is kept all the year long. It beareth the name of Vanity Fair, because the town where it is kept is lighter than vanity, (Psa. 62: 9) and also because all that is there sold, or that cometh thither, is vanity; as is the saying of the wise, "All that cometh is vanity." (Eccl. 11: 8. See also 1: 2-14; 2: 11-17; Isa. 40: 17)

This fair is no new-erected business but a thing of ancient standing. I will show you the original of it.

Almost five thousand years ago there were pilgrims walking to the Celestial City, as these two honest persons are; and Beelzebub, Apollyon, and Legion②, with their companions, perceiving by the path that the pilgrims made, that their way to the city lay through this town of Vanity, they contrived here to set up a fair; a fair wherein should be sold all sorts of vanity, and that it should last all the year long. Therefore, at this fair are all such merchandise sold as houses, lands, trades, places, honors, preferments, titles, countries, kingdoms, lusts, pleasures; and delights of all sorts, as harlots, wives, husbands, children, masters, servants, lives, blood, bodies, souls, silver, gold, pearls, precious stones, and what not.

And moreover, at this fair there is at all times to be seen jugglings, cheats, games, plays, fools, apes, knaves, and rogues, and that of every kind.

Here are to be seen, too, and that for nothing, thefts, murders, adulteries, false-swearers, and that of a blood-red color.

And, as in other fairs of less moment, there are the several rows and streets under their proper names, where such and such wares are vended; so here, likewise, you have the proper places, rows, streets, (namely, countries and kingdoms) where the wares of this fair are soonest to be found. Here is the Britain Row, the French Row, the Italian Row, the Spanish Row, the German Row, where several sorts of vanities are to be sold. But, as in other fairs, some one commodity is as the chief of all the fair; so the ware of Rome and her merchandise is greatly promoted in this fair; only our English nation, with some others, have taken a dislike thereat.

Now, as I said, the way to the Celestial City lies just through this town, where this lusty fair is kept; and he that will go to the city, and yet not go through this town, "must needs go

---

① **King:** God.

② **Beelzebub, Apollyon, Legion:** Beelzebub refers to the Devil; Apollyon alludes to a destroyer; Legion is the major unit of the Roman army.

out of the world". (Cor. 4: 10) The Prince of princes himself, when here, went through this town to his own country, and that upon a fair-day too; yea, and, as I think, it was Beelzebub, the chief lord of this fair, that invited him to buy of his vanities, yea, would have made him lord of the fair, would he but have done him reverence as he went through the town. Yea, because he was such a person of honor, Beelzebub had him from street to street, and showed him all the kingdoms of the world in a little time, that he might, if possible, allure that blessed One to cheapen and buy some of his vanities; but he had no mind to the merchandise, and therefore left the town, without laying out so much as one farthing upon these vanities. (Matt. 4: 8, 9; Luke 4: 5-7) This fair, therefore, is an ancient thing, of long standing, and a very great fair.

Questions

1. In what way is *The Pilgrim's Progress* an allegory?
2. Comment on the religious conflict in the 17th Century through the life experiences of Bunyan.
3. Compare the style of *The Pilgrim's Progress* with that of the *Bible*.

5.5 "To the Memory of Mr. Oldham[①]" by Dryden

    Fare will, too little and too lately known,
    Whom I began to think and call my own:
    For sure our souls were near allied, and thine
    Cast in the same poetic mold with mine.
5   One common note on either lyre did strike,
    And knaves and fools we both abhorred alike.
    To the same goal did both our studies drive;
    The last set out the soonest did arrive.
    Thus Nisus[②] fell upon the slippery place,
10 Whilst his young friend performed and won the race.
    O early ripe! To thy abundant store
    What could advancing age have added more?
    It might (what nature never gives the young)
    Have taught the numbers of thy native tongue.
15 But satire needs not those, and wit will shine
    Through the harsh cadence of a rugged line[③].

---

    ① **Mr. Oldham**: John Oldham (1653-1683), a promising young poet who died at thirty, best remembered for his Satires upon the Jesuits (1681) which won Dryden's admiration.

    ② Nisus and his young friend, Euryalus, ran a race for the prize of an olive crown, and Nisus, on the point of winning, slipped in a pool of blood of a slain steer and thus helped his young friend win the race. (*Aeneid* by Virgil, V. 315-339)

    ③ **The harsh cadence of rugged line**: Here Dryden repeats the Renaissance idea that the satirist should avoid smoothness and affect rough metres ("harsh cadence").

A noble error, and but seldom made,
When poets are by too much force betrayed.
Thy gen' rous fruits, though gathered ere their prime,
20 Still showed a quickness①; and maturing time
But mellows what we write to the dull sweets or rhyme.
Once more, hail, and farewell②! Farewell, thou young,
But ah! Too short, Marcellus③ of our tongue!
Thy brows with ivy, and with laurels bound④;
25 But fate and gloomy night encompass thee around.

Questions

1. Point out examples of paradox, allusion and irony, and explain their functions.
2. What is the basic meter of the poem? Which lines contain the most dramatic variations of meter? Which variations of meter are for emphasis? Which indicate structural break? Which imitate actions or qualities being described?

5.6 "A Song for St. Cecilia's Day⑤" by Dryden

[1]

From harmony, from heavenly harmony
This universal frame began:
When Nature underneath a heap
   Of jarring atoms lay⑥,
And could not heave her head,
The tuneful voice was heard from high:
   "Arise, ye more than dead."
Then cold, and hot, and moist, and dry,
In order to their stations leap,
   And Music's power obey.

---

① **quickness**: sharpness of flavor.

② **hail, and farewell**: Dryden echoes the famous words that conclude Catullus' elegy to his brother "And forever, brother, hail and farewell!"

③ **Marcellus**: nephew of Augustus, adopted by him as his successor. Marcellus died at the age of 20 after winning military fame. Virgil celebrated him in the *Aeneid*. (VI. 854-886)

④ **Laurels bound**: the poet's wreath.

⑤ St. Cecilia, a Roman lady, was martyred for her Christian faith in Rome in 230. She is regarded as the patron Saint of music, and inventor of the organ (Chaucer tells her story in "The Second Nun's Tale" in *The Canterbury Tales*). In 1683 a musical society was founded in London to celebrate this. From that year on to 1703 annual celebrations were held to commemorate it with a religious service and a public concert which always included an ode written and set to music for the occasion, of which the two by Dryden (*A Song for St. Cecilia's Day*, 1687, and *Alexander's Feast*, 1697) are the most distinguished.

⑥ According to Genesis, God created Nature and ordered it out of chaos. Here Dryden describes nature as composed of the warring and discordant ("jarring") atoms of the four elements: earth, fire, water, air ("cold", "hot", "moist", "dry").

From harmony, from heavenly harmony
This universal frame began:
From harmony to harmony
Through all the compass of the notes it ran,
The diapason① closing full in man.

[2]
What passion cannot Music raise and quell!
　　When Jubal struck the corded shell②,
His listening brethren stood around,
And, wondering, on their faces fell
To worship that celestial sound.
Less than a god they thought there could not dwell
　　Within the hollow of that shell
　　That spoke so sweetly and so well.
What passion cannot Music raise and quell!

[3]
　　The trumpet's loud clangor
　　　　Excites us to arms,
　　With shrill notes of anger,
　　　　And mortal alarms.
　　The double double double beat
　　　　Of the thundering drum
Cries: "Hark! The foes come;
Charge, charge, 'tis too late to retreat."

[4]
　　The soft complaining flute
　　　　In dying notes discovers
　　　　The woes of hopeless lovers,
Whose dirge is whispered by the warbling lute.

[5]
　　Sharp violins③ proclaim

---

① **diapason**: The whole range of notes in the scale (音域). Dryden is thinking of the Chain of Being, the ordered creation from inanimate to man. The just gradations of notes in a scale are analogous to the equally just gradations in the ascending scale of created beings. Both are the result of harmony.

② **Jubal**: the inventor of the lyre and the pipe (Genesis 4. 21). In Greek mythology the lyre is said to have been made of a tortoise shell ("corded shell").

③ The modern violin, with its bright tone, was introduced into England at the Restoration.

Their jealous pangs, and desperation,
Fury, frantic indignation,
Depth of pains, and height of passion,
　For the fair, disdainful dame.

[6]
　But O! what art can teach,
　What human voice can reach,
The sacred organ's praise?
　Notes inspiring holy love,
Notes that wing their heavenly ways
　To mend the choirs above.

[7]
Orpheus① could lead the savage race,
And trees unrooted left their place,
　Sequacious of the lyre;
But bright Cecilia raised the wonder higher:
When to her organ vocal breath was given,
And angel heard, and straight appeared,
　Mistaking earth for heaven.

GRAND CHORUS

As from the power of sacred lays
　The spheres began to move,
And sung the great Creator's praise
　To all the blest above;
So, when the last and dreadful hour
This crumbling pageant② shall devour,
The trumpet shall be heard on high,
The dead shall live, the living die,
And Music shall untune the sky.

---

　① **Orpheus**: in Greek mythology a son of one of Muses, who played so wonderfully on the lyre that wild beasts ("the savage race") grew tame and followed the sound of his music, as did even rocks and trees.
　② **pageant**: the stage on which the drama of man's salvation is acted on; here "the universe".

Questions

1. What characteristic sound and passion, according to the poem, can be evoked by the musical instruments of trumpet, drum, flute, violin, organ and lyre?
2. This ode is a high praise to music. Give examples to show the great paradoxical power of music.
3. What does the poet mean by "The dead shall live, the living die / And music shall untune the sky" in the last stanza?

Chapter Four   The Enlightenment Period

1. Introduction

1.1 Enlightenment Ideas

With the development of education in the late 17th century, more and more people in Europe became literate. In the early 18th century magazines and newspapers appeared, for example, *The Review* (1704) by Defoe and *The Tatler* (1709) by Steele (1672-1729) in Britain. The European intellectuals at that time believed that the world was an object of study and that people could understand and control nature by means of reason and empirical research. With the advancement of scientific research, a lot of discoveries and inventions were made in the 17th and 18th centuries. The findings of Copernicus, Galileo, Kepler and Newton were significant: They rejected the idea of man as an evil creature; they saw man as capable. As a result, people began to learn more about themselves and the world around them.

In the late 17th century Enlightenment appeared in Europe and it lasted until the French Revolution in 1789. The movement was characterized by the philosophic, scientific and rational spirit, the freedom from superstition, and skepticism. Consequently the emphasis began to shift from one's duties toward God to rights, from in-born evil to in-born good. In their writings Enlightenment thinkers such as Voltaire, Montesquieu, Locke, Descartes, Condorcet and Rousseau showed their resentment against tyranny in government and against ignorance and inequality in society. For example, in his *Two Treatises on Government* (1690), John Locke, the English political philosopher, defended the natural rights of man against the power of government.

Thus, the Enlightenment movement was closely associated with some new ideas such as liberty, democracy and rights of individuals which embodied the ideology of the rising middle class in Europe at that time. Britain was no exception. With the coming of the Glorious Revolution of 1688, the age of constitutional monarchy, a monarchy with powers limited by Parliament, began in the island country.

1.2 Literature during the Enlightenment Period

With prolonged social stability and economic growth, people began to pay more attention to education and a large reading public grew. More people began to exercise their literary talents. This, in turn, gave rise to reading materials of various kinds. In addition to the popular forms of drama and pamphlets, newspapers and periodicals all made their appearance in Britain during the Enlightenment period. In 1709 the Copyright Act was passed in Parliament. Gradually writing became a profession and the patronage lost its popularity.

Meanwhile in Britain a literary movement—neoclassicism—became popular. Also known as classicism, it is a tendency in art and literature that stressed the importance of classical works as models. As a movement it began in France in the late 17th century, and then spread to other European countries and to the other side of the Atlantic Ocean. Neoclassicism flourished in the late 18th century and then declined after the fall of the First Empire in France in 1815.

Neoclassicists had a deep respect for the rules of their art. Reason and judgment became the most important faculties for them. In short, neoclassicists wanted to achieve proportion, harmony, balance, idealization, rationality, and order in their works by following what was advocated by classical thinkers. As far as literature is concerned, neoclassicists advocated that literary theory and practice should follow the models established by the major Greek and Latin writers such as Homer, Plato, Virgil, Horace and Ovid. A lot of 17th-and-18th-century writers wrote epic, eclogue, elegy, ode, satire, tragedy, comedy and epigram by imitating classical writers. In verse the use of the heroic couplet serves as a good case in point, and in drama observing unities of time, place and action became a must.

In Britain Johnson, Dryden, Pope, Swift, Fielding, Steele, Addison, Lord Chesterfield (1694-1773), and Oliver Goldsmith (1730-1774) are representatives of the movement.

Last but by no means least, modern realistic novels appeared in Britain in the early 18th century. The history of the novel can be traced back to 12th-century-BC Egypt, whereas in Europe the early form of the novel, or to be more exact, medieval romance, appeared in the 14th century. After three centuries of development the romance grew more like the novel and *Don Quixote* (1605, 1615) by Cervantes (1547-1616) serves as a landmark in the literary history of the world. In England the early form of the novel—prose narrative, or prose romance, appeared in the late 16th century with the publication of *Euphues* (1578, 1580) by John Lyly (1554-1606) and *The Arcadia* (1590) by Philip Sidney (1554-1586). The novel evolved gradually in the following centuries. *The Pilgrim's Progress* can be regarded as an allegorical novel, and *Oroonoko* (1688) by Aphra Behn is very similar to the novel in several ways. Though *Incognita: or, Love and Duty Reconciled* (1713) was presented to the public as a novel by its author William Congreve, it's generally accepted that *Robinson Crusoe* (1719) by Daniel Defoe is the first novel.

Previous literary forms, like poetry and drama, were either for the ruling and noble class who were better educated or for an audience as a group at a public place. The appearance of novels changed the situation. They became a form of entertainment and education for individuals, the middle class in particular, at home. Daniel Defoe, Jonathan Swift, Samuel Richardson, and Henry Fielding are the forerunners in the art.

As a result of the emphasis laid on education, British literature during the Enlightenment period is characteristically didactic and moralizing.

2. Daniel Defoe (1660-1731)

2.1 Life and Career

The son of a butcher named Foe, Daniel Defoe added the aristocratic prefix when he was forty years old. When he was young, Defoe attended Morton's Academy, with the intention of becoming a minister, but he changed his mind and became a hosiery merchant instead.

Daniel Defoe

An enthusiastic supporter of "the Glorious Revolution", Defoe wrote quite a number of pamphlets to support the new government, which won the favor of King William Ⅲ. In 1702 Defoe wrote his famous pamphlet *The Shortest Way with the Dissenters*. It enraged the Tories government which supported the Dissenters, and Defoe was put into prison. His poem *Hymn to the Pillory* aroused the immediate sympathy of many people. When he came out the prison, Defoe kept changing his attitude towards Tories and Whigs. During his imprisonment Defoe's business had been ruined, so he turned to journalism for his livelihood. From 1704 to 1713 he issued a triweekly news journal entitled *The Review*. He is considered to be the founder of British journalism.

Defoe was one of the first writers who started to write stories about believable characters in realistic situations using simple prose. He achieved literary immortality when he published *Robinson Crusoe* (1719). With the unexpectedly financial success of this novel, Defoe produced the second and the third book of the novel: *The Further Adventures of Robinson Crusoe*; *The Serious Reflections during the Life and Surprising Adventures of Robinson Crusoe*. From then on Defoe turned to writing fiction: *Captain Singleton* (1720), *Journal of the Plague Year* (1722), *Captain Jack* (1722), *Moll Flanders* (1722), and *Roxanda* (1724). These novels were extremely influential and showed a journalist's interest in realistic description. Defoe's simple but effective prose style ensured him widespread popularity and he is regarded as the father of the English Novel. He died in 1731.

2.2 *Robinson Crusoe* (synopsis)

Robinson Crusoe is born into a middle-class family and he often dreams of going on sea voyages. Although his father wants him to be a lawyer, he insists on going to sea and has some minor adventures before the voyage during which he meets with a series of violent storms. Finally, a terrible shipwreck occurs and Crusoe, being the only survivor, succeeds in swimming to the shore of an island.

Crusoe remains on the island for twenty-seven years. At first, to survive, he carries out plans for getting food and shelter as well as protecting himself from wild animals. He brings as many things as possible from the wrecked ship to the island, things that will be useful to him later. He gradually learns how to cook, and raise goats and crops. But, being lonely, he is very miserable, so he turns to religion for his unhappiness. To keep his sanity and to entertain himself, he begins writing a journal in which he records every task that he performs each day since he has been marooned. As time passes, Crusoe becomes a skilled craftsman, able to construct many useful things.

After about fifteen years on the island, Crusoe finds a man's footprint one day and observes cannibalistic savages eating prisoners. He is plagued with fears and resolves to save the prisoners the next time. Years later the cannibals land on the island again. Using his gun, Crusoe saves one prisoner, names him Friday, and teaches him English. Friday soon becomes Crusoe's humble and devoted slave.

For some years the two live happily together. One day another ship of savages arrives with three prisoners. Together with Friday, Crusoe is able to save two of them: One is a white man, Spaniard, and the other is Friday's father. Their reunion is joyous. After a few months, they leave to bring back the rest of the Spaniard's men. After they have gone, an English ship comes ashore. Crusoe quickly learns that there has been a mutiny on board. By devious means, Crusoe and Friday rescue the captain and two other men, and after much scheming, regain control of the ship. The grateful captain gives Crusoe many gifts and takes him and Friday back to England.

Crusoe returns to England and finds himself a wealthy man after the prolonged absence. Later, Crusoe sells his plantation for a good price, gets married, and has three children. Finally, however, he is persuaded to go on another voyage, and he visits his old island, where there are promises of new adventures to be found in a later account.

3. Jonathan Swift (1667-1745)

3.1 Life and Career

Jonathan Swift

A posthumous child of poor Englishmen, Jonathan Swift was born in Dublin, Ireland. After his graduation from Trinity College, Dublin, he became the private secretary of Sir William Temple, a remote kinsman in England. In 1694 he began to work at different clerical posts, and three years later, he started to write *The Battle of the Books*, a satire of a literary controversy concerning the relative merits of the classics and contemporary literature around the turn of the century. In 1704 he published *A Tale of a Tub* together with *The Battle of the Books*. These two books made him famous as a satirist. In 1710 he became the editor of *The Examiner*, a Tory periodical. In 1713 Swift was appointed dean of St Patrick's Cathedral in Dublin where he became a supporter for the Irish resistance to the English oppression. In 1724 Swift published *The Drapier's Letters*, and two years later he published *Gulliver's Travels*, his greatest satiric work in which he advocates the supremacy of reason over passion.

Despite his popularity and fame, Swift gradually lost his "sanity", perhaps partly caused by Meniere's disease, but also due to bitterness and loneliness in his later life as well as his desperate love for Esther Johnson, the daughter of a servant or companion of Temple's sister, for whom he wrote *Journal to Stella*. He died in 1745.

Jonathan Swift wrote many tracts, poems, letters (one to Sir Robert Walpole) in addition to those mentioned above. In his works Swift satirized not only the English who brought misery to the Irish people but also human nature as well as social institutions.

3.2 *Gulliver's Travels* (synopsis)

The story is divided into four parts:

In the first part, Lemuel Gulliver, a surgeon, is traveling on a merchant ship in the East Indies. After a shipwreck, he manages to get to the island of Lilliput, the inhabitants of which are only six inches tall. He finds that the chief ministers there are given their jobs in accordance with their skill in dancing on a rope or in leaping over a stick or creeping under it backwards and forwards. Among the Lilliputians there are civil strifes and arguments, for example, between two parties distinguished one from the other by the high heels and low heels on their shoes, between Big Endians and Small Endians due to a quarrel between the ways of breaking eggs—one at the big end and the other at the small end, and between Catholics and Protestants. Besides, there is a war between Lilliputians and their neighbours, and with the help of the giant Lilliput turns out winner. The emperor confers upon him the highest military rank, which causes envy among the high-ranking officials who conspire against him. Gulliver escapes in a boat.

In the 2nd part Gulliver is accidentally left ashore on Brobdingnag, where the inhabitants are all giants compared with Gulliver and his fellow human beings. Captured, Gulliver becomes their plaything. The streets of the capital in Brobdingnag are crowded with beggars, but they seem to have an enlightened monarch who asks Gulliver to give him an exact account of the government of England. Gulliver's proud descriptions meets with the following remark from the king: "... By what I have gathered from your own relation ... I cannot but conclude the bulk of your natives to be the most pernicious race of little odious vermin that nature ever suffered to crawl upon the surface of the earth." Gulliver tries to create a favourable impression upon the king by offering to teach him the arts of war he has learned in Europe, but the king is struck with horror and reproves "so impotent and grovelling an insect as" Gulliver for maintaining such "inhuman ideas".

The 3rd part is about a visit by Gulliver to the floating island of Laputa, which has been devised not for the benefits of people, but against them. The scientists there are engaged in projects for extracting sunshine out of cucumber, turning ice into gunpowder and making cloth from cobweb. Gulliver finds the wise men there so wrapped up in their speculations as to be dotards in practical affairs.

The fourth part is a description of the country of the Houyhnhnms, horses endowed with reason and intelligence. Their rational, clean, and simple society is contrasted with that of the Yahoos, beasts in human shape, who do vices and evil things like stealing and lying. The Yahoos are also malicious, spiteful, envious, and greedy. These remind him of the people in the English society. So alienated is Gulliver from his own species that when he finally returns home he recoils from his own family in disgust and, being miserable and lonely, he has to talk to his horse.

4. Joseph Addison (1672-1719)

Joseph Addison

The son of a clergyman, Joseph Addison was born in a village in Wiltshire. He was sent to the Charterhouse Primary School in London where he met and made friends with Richard Steele, a boy of the same age. At fifteen, they went to Oxford together where Addison took his MA while Steele went to join the army without taking any degree. *The Campaign* (1705), a poem in heroic couplets in celebration of the victory of Blenheim, where the English forces won a battle (1704) in the War of the Spanish Succession, brought Addison great fame. In 1708 he became a Member of Parliament and the next year was appointed as chief secretary for Ireland.

While Addison was in Ireland, Steele started a paper called *The Tatler* in 1709, two years later renamed *The Spectator*, a collaborative undertaking of the two friends. Addison became a great contributor, which made the paper a great success. Because of his writings Addison became the most persuasive instructor of the age. In 1713 his neo-classical tragedy *Cato* was produced with much success. In 1716 Addison married the Countess of Warwick. He died three years later.

5. Alexander Pope (1688-1744)

The son of a linen draper in London, Alexander Pope inherited a deformed and dwarfed body and an incurably sickly constitution. Until he was 12 years old, he was educated largely by priests; his Roman Catholic background barred him from England's Protestant universities; primarily self-taught afterward, he read widely in English letters, as well as in French, Italian, Latin, and Greek.

Pope's literary career began in 1704, when the playwright William Wycherley (1641-1715), pleased by Pope's verse, introduced him into the circle of fashionable London wits and writers. He first attracted public attention in 1709 with his "Pastorals". Two years later *An Essay on Criticism* was published. With its terse and epigrammatic expressions of the neoclassical principles of poetic composition and criticism, the *Essay* is amazingly brilliant and it caught the attention of Addison. "Messiah" came out in the *Spectator* the next year. *The Rape of the Lock* (1712-1714), a fanciful and ingenious mock-heroic work based on a true story, secured his reputation. *Windsor Forest* (1713), a pastoral poem, shows his support for the Tories.

Alexander Pope

In the next dozen years Pope translated *Iliad* and *Odyssey*. In 1725, Pope's edition of *Shakespeare's Works* was published. Pope and his friend Swift had for years written scornful and very successful critical reviews of those whom they considered poor writers. The adversaries hurled insults at Swift and Pope in return, and in 1728 Pope lampooned them in one of his best-known works, *The Dunciad*, a satire celebrating dullness.

While during his early career Pope imitated classical writers, it was during his last fifteen years that his original work was done. *Moral Essays* (1731-1735) deals comprehensively with human nature and institutions while *Essay on Man* (1733-1734) is intended to form "a temperate system of ethics". Pope's physical disabilities brought him to premature old age, and he died in 1744.

The subject of many of Pope's works is didactic; the substance is a restatement of the ideas of the Greek Aristotle, the Roman Horace, especially of the French critic Boileau, and of various other critical authorities. But Pope, to a great extent, represents his time in literary fashion: Most of his writings are satirical.

6. Samuel Richardson (1689-1761)

6.1 Life and Career

Samuel Richardson

Samuel Richardson was born near Derby. When still a boy he read widely and by the age of thirteen was employed writing letters for young lovers. In 1706 he was apprenticed to a printer and then started his own business in 1721, the year when he married the daughter of his former master. Like all other printers at that time, he combined printing and publishing, which enabled him to publish in 1733 his *The Apprentice's Vade Mecum*, a book of advice on morals and conduct. In 1739 he published his own version of *Aesop's Fables*. Meanwhile his friends encouraged him to write some "familiar letters" on the problems and concerns of everyday life. He set out to do it and in 1741 *Pamela, or Virtue Rewarded*, came out. It was a great success. In 1747 *Clarissa*, his masterpiece, appeared and it was followed by *Sir Charles Grandison* (1753-1754). Richardson died in 1761.

All Richardson's novels were in epistolary form with its immediacy and psychological penetration, and he is now considered to be one of the chief founders of the modern novel.

6.2 *Clarissa:* or *The History of a Young Lady* (synopsis)

About one-third of the work consists of the letters of Clarissa and Lovelace, mainly written to Anna Howe and John Belford respectively.

Looked upon as the apple of the eye, Clarissa Harlowe is a beautiful and noble-minded young lady of an acquisitive and ambitious family. Lovelace, who is courting Arabella, the elder sister of Clarissa, is a handsome rake. When he later transfers his affections to Clarissa, her family are opposed to it and decide that she must marry the wealthy Roger Soames whom she detests. When Clarissa refuses her family lock her up. Lovelace, cleverly representing himself as her deliverer, persuades her to escape under his protection and they get to London where she is taken to a brothel which she at first supposes to be respectable lodgings. She is fascinated by his charm and wit, but distrusts him and refuses his proposals for marriage. Irritated, Lovelace interferes with her letters, violently assaults her, and cunningly ensnaring her after her frustrated attempts to escape. As Clarissa stubbornly resists, he becomes more obsessive in his determination to conquer her, and encouraged by the women in the brothel, drugs and rapes her. Gradually Clarissa loses her sanity, and she manages to escape eventually, but only to find herself trapped in a debtor's prison. Although she is rescued by Belford and recovers her sanity, Clarissa dies soon. In a duel Lovelace is killed by Colonel Morden, Clarissa's cousin. This, however, doesn't help to relieve the Harlowe family from remorse and pain.

7. Henry Fielding (1707-1754)

7.1 Life and Career

Henry Fielding

The son of a lieutenant-general, Henry Fielding was born in 1707. At eleven his mother died and when his father remarried Henry was sent to Eton. At nineteen he attempted to elope with a beautiful heiress. When it failed, he settled in London and began his literary career by writing poems and plays. In order to achieve great success, Henry Fielding attended Leyden where he enlarged his knowledge of classical literature. Between 1729 and 1737 he wrote some twenty-five dramas, largely in the form of farce and satire. In 1734 Fielding married Charlotte Cradock, an admirable woman who became his model for Sophia in *Tom Jones* (1749) and for the heroine of *Amelia* (1751). His dramatic career ended in 1737 when one of his plays offended the Whig government led by Walpole that passed the Licensing Act in that year.

Forced to abandon the stage, Fielding entered the Middle Temple and began to read for the bar. From 1739 to 1740 he wrote most of the columns of *The Champion*, an opposition journal. Meanwhile he did some hack work to support his family. Suffering from gout, he was unable to pursue his legal career. When Richardson's *Pamela* was applauded, Fielding expressed his contempt in his pseudonymous parody, *An Apology for the Life of Mrs. Shamela Andrews* (1741). The year 1742 saw the publication of his first novel, *Joseph Andrews*, also a parody of *Pamela*. In the following year he published *The Life and Death of Jonathan Wild the Great*.

In 1748 Fielding was appointed justice of the peace for Westminster and he struggled determinedly against corruption and lawlessness. In 1749 *The History of Tom Jones, a Foundling* appeared and it was well received. Two years later he published *The History of Amelia*, which sold the best of all his novels. Fielding died in 1754 in Lisben, Portugal.

7.2 *Tom Jones* (synopsis)

Tom Jones, a foundling, is brought up together with an orphan—young Blifil—in the home of Squire Allworthy, Blifil's uncle. Now Tom has grown up to be a jolly and handsome young man who finds that his childhood affection for Sophia Western, the beautiful and sweet-natured daughter of a neighboring squire, has grown into adult love. Sophia's father, however, wants her, against her will, to marry Blifil even after learning about her attachment to Tom. Meanwhile by clever misrepresentation the scheming Blifil converts Allworthy's affection for Tom into anger and has Tom expelled from the house. Abandoned by his foster-father, Tom decides to join the army, but he loses his way and, instead of going to Bristol, is actually heading for London. Sophia, disgusted by Blifil's courtship, runs away with her maid Honour, hoping to find her kinswoman Lady Bellaston in London. She catches up with Tom and, not knowing where Tom is, passes him at an inn. Tom, learning that Sophia is going to London, begins to chase her. Blifil, accompanied by his uncle, also hastens to London in search of Sophia. Squire Western, too, follows his daughter to London where Sophia is in danger of being raped by an old aristocrat. Luckily she is saved by her father. Tom has a lot of adventures and love affairs on the way to and in London where his identity is disclosed: the son of Allworthy's sister Bridget before marriage. Some time later, however, he is arrested after a fight. What's more, Sophia cannot forgive him after all that has happened. But finally Blifil's villainy and his involvement in the imprisonment of Tom are disclosed. Tom is reinstated in his repentant uncle's affection and made the heir. When he meets Sophia again at last, she tells him that she loves him. Her father, accordingly, has changed his idea and gives his blessing to them. Being very generous, Tom forgives all who have wronged him, even the disgusting Blifil.

8. Samuel Johnson (1709-1784)

The son of a bookseller, Samuel Johnson was born in Richfield. He attended the local grammar school and then Oxford University. The death of his father made him quit the

Samuel Johnson

university in 1731 before he could get a degree. Several years later he married a widow, considerably older than himself. Then for over two decades Johnson tried to make a fortune as well as a name by writing, translating, running a school, editing magazines, writing parliamentary debates and so on. During this time he published some poems such as "London" (1738) and "The Vanity of Human Wishes" (1749), started *The Rambler*, a periodical written almost entirely by himself. For all his hard work, he got almost nowhere. The publication of *A Dictionary of the English Language* (1755), the first English dictionary, brought him some reputation as well as improvement in his economic condition. Then Johnson wrote altogether several hundred essays for both *The Rambler* and *The Idler*, and a series of papers contributed to the *Universal Chronicle*; or *Weekly Gazette* (1758-1760). In 1759 he published *Rasselas, Prince of Abyssinia*, a romance, and three years later he began to enjoy a crown pension. From this period onwards he was regarded as one of the most eminent literary figures of his day. At the request of a number of booksellers, Johnson wrote *The Lives of Poets* (1779-1781), the crowning work of his old age.

A poet, dramatist, prose romancer, biographer, essayist, critic and lexicographer, Johnson is regarded as a versatile writer. He died in 1784 and was buried in Westminster Abbey.

9. Selected Writings

9.1 "A Modest Proposal" by Swift

A Proposal for Preventing the Children of Poor People in Ireland from Being a Burden on Their Parents or Country, and for Making Them Beneficial to the Public.

It is a melancholy object to those who walk through this great town① or travel in the country, when they see the streets, the roads, and cabin-doors, crowded with beggars of the female sex, followed by three, four, or six children, all in rags and importuning every passenger for an alms. These mothers, instead of being able to work for their honest livelihood, are forced to employ all their time in strolling to beg sustenance for their helpless infants who, as they grow up, either turn thieves for want of work, or leave their dear native country to fight for the Pretender② in Spain, or sell themselves to the Barbadoes③.

I think it is agreed by all parties that this prodigious number of children in the arms, or on

---

① **this great town**: Dublin.
② **the Pretender**: James Edward Stuart (1688-1766), descendant of King James Ⅱ of England.
③ **Barbadoes**: Because of the poverty in Ireland, many Irishmen emigrated to the West Indies and other British colonies in America; they paid their passage by binding themselves to work for a stated period for one of the planters.

the backs, or at the heels of their mothers, and frequently of their fathers, is in the present deplorable state of the kingdom a very great additional grievance; and therefore whoever could find out a fair, cheap and easy method of making these children sound, useful members of the commonwealth would deserve so well of the public as to have his statue set up for a preserver of the nation.

But my intention is very far from being confined to provide only for the children of professed beggars; it is of a much greater extent, and shall take in the whole number of infants at a certain age, who are born of parents in effect as little able to support them as those who demand our charity in the streets.

As to my own part, having turned my thoughts for many years upon this important subject, and maturely weighed the several schemes of other projectors, I have always found them grossly mistaken in their computation. It is true, a child just dropped from its dam may be supported by her milk for a solar year, with little other nourishment; at most not above the value of two shillings, which the mother may certainly get, or the value in scraps, by her lawful occupation of begging; and it is exactly at one year old that I propose to provide for them in such a manner as instead of being a charge upon their parents or the parish, or wanting food and raiment for the rest of their lives, they shall, on the contrary, contribute to the feeding, and partly to the clothing, of many thousands.

There is likewise another great advantage in my scheme, that it will prevent those voluntary abortions, and that horrid practice of women murdering their bastard children, alas, too frequent among us, sacrificing the poor innocent babes, I doubt, more to avoid the expense than the shame, which would move tears and pity in the most savage and inhuman breast.

The number of souls in this kingdom being usually reckoned one million and a half, of these I calculate there may be about two hundred thousand couples whose wives are breeders; from which number I subtract thirty thousand couples, who are able to maintain their own children, although I apprehend there cannot be so many under the present distresses of the kingdom; but this being granted, there will remain an hundred and seventy thousand breeders. I again subtract fifty thousand, for those women who miscarry, or whose children die by accident or disease within the year. There only remain an hundred and twenty thousand children of poor parents annually born. The question therefore is, how this number shall be reared, and provided for, which, as I have already said, under the present situation of affairs, is utterly impossible by all the methods hitherto proposed. For we can neither employ them in handicraft or agriculture; we neither build houses, (I mean in the country) nor cultivate land. They can very seldom pick up a livelihood by stealing till they arrive at six years old, except where they are of towardly parts[①]; although I confess they learn the rudiments much earlier, during which time they can however be looked upon only as probationers, as I have been informed by a principal gentleman in the county of Cavan, who protested to me, that he never knew above one or two instances under the age of six, even in a part of the kingdom so renowned for the quickest proficiency in that art.

---

① **towardly parts**: ready abilities.

I am assured by our merchants, that a boy or a girl before twelve years old, is no saleable commodity; and even when they come to this age, they will not yield above three pounds, or three pounds and half a crown at most, on the Exchange; which cannot turn to account either to the parents or the kingdom, the charge of nutriment and rags having been at least four times that value.

I shall now therefore humbly propose my own thoughts, which I hope will not be liable to the least objection.

I have been assured by a very knowing American of my acquaintance in London, that a young healthy child well nursed is, at a year old, a most delicious, nourishing, and wholesome food, whether stewed, roasted, baked, or boiled; and I make no doubt that it will equally serve in a fricassee or a ragout①.

I do therefore humbly offer it to public consideration, that of the hundred and twenty thousand children, already computed, twenty thousand may be reserved for breed, whereof only one fourth part to be males, which is more than we allow to sheep, black cattle, or swine, and my reason is that these children are seldom the fruits of marriage, a circumstance not much regarded by our savages, therefore, one male will be sufficient to serve four females. That the remaining hundred thousand may, at a year old, be offered in sale to the persons of quality and fortune, through the kingdom, always advising the mother to let them suck plentifully in the last month, so as to render them plump, and fat for a good table. A child will make two dishes at an entertainment for friends, and when the family dines alone, the fore or hind quarter will make a reasonable dish, and seasoned with a little pepper or salt, will be very good boiled on the fourth day, especially in winter.

I have reckoned upon a medium that a child just born will weigh 12 pounds, and in a solar year, if tolerably nursed, increaseth to 28 pounds.

I grant this food will be somewhat dear, and therefore very proper for landlords, who, as they have already devoured most of the parents, seem to have the best title to the children.

Infant's flesh will be in season throughout the year, but more plentiful in March, and a little before and after; for we are told by a grave author, an eminent French physician②, that fish being a prolific diet, there are more children born in Roman Catholic countries about nine months after Lent than at any other season; therefore, reckoning a year after Lent, the markets will be more glutted than usual, because the number of popish infants, is at least three to one in this kingdom, and therefore it will have one other collateral advantage, by lessening the number of Papists among us.

I have already computed the charge of nursing a beggar's child (in which list I reckon all cottagers, labourers, and four-fifths of the farmers) to be about two shillings per annum, rags included; and I believe no gentleman would repine to give ten shillings for the carcass of a good fat child, which, as I have said, will make four dishes of excellent nutritive meat, when he

---

① **a fricassee**: "a dish made by cutting chickens or other small things in pieces, and dressing them with strong sauce"; **a ragout**: "meat stewed and highly seasoned". (Johnson)

② **an eminent French physician**: François Rabelais (ca. 1494-1553), a humorist and satirist.

hath only some particular friend, or his own family to dine with him. Thus the squire will learn to be a good landlord, and grow popular among his tenants, the mother will have eight shillings neat profit, and be fit for the work till she produces another child. Those who are more thrifty (as I must confess the times require) may flay the carcass; the skin of which, artificially dressed, will make admirable gloves for ladies, and summer boots for fine gentlemen.

As to our city of Dublin, shambles may be appointed for this purpose, in the most convenient parts of it, and butchers, we may be assured, will not be wanting; although I rather recommend buying the children alive, and dressing them hot from the knife, as we do roasting pigs.

A very worthy person, a true lover of his country, and whose virtues I highly esteem, was lately pleased in discoursing on this matter to offer a refinement upon my scheme. He said that many gentlemen of this kingdom, having of late destroyed their deer, he conceived that the want of venison might be well supplied by the bodies of young lads and maidens, not exceeding fourteen years of age, nor under twelve; so great a number of both sexes in every country being now ready to starve for want of work and service; and these to be disposed of by their parents, if alive, or otherwise by their nearest relations. But with due deference to so excellent a friend, and so deserving a patriot, I cannot be altogether in his sentiments; for as to the males, my American acquaintance assured me from frequent experience that their flesh was generally tough and lean, like that of our school-boys, by continual exercise, and their taste disagreeable, and to fatten them would not answer the charge. Then as to the females, it would, I think, with humble submission, be a loss to the public, because they soon would become breeders themselves; and besides, it is not improbable that some scrupulous people might be apt to censure such a practice, (although indeed very unjustly) as a little bordering upon cruelty, which, I confess, hath always been with me the strongest objection against any project, how well soever intended.

But in order to justify my friend, he confessed that this expedient was put into his head by the famous Psalmanazar[①], a native of the island Formosa, who came from thence to London above twenty years ago, and in conversation told my friend that in his country, when any young person happened to be put to death, the executioner sold the carcass to persons of quality, as a prime dainty; and that, in his time, the body of a plump girl of fifteen, who was crucified for an attempt to poison the emperor, was sold to his Imperial Majesty's prime minister of state, and other great mandarins of the court in joints from the gibbet, at four hundred crowns. Neither indeed can I deny that if the same use were made of several plump young girls in this town, who without one single groat to their fortunes cannot stir abroad without a chair, and appear at a play-house and assemblies in foreign fineries which they never will pay for, the kingdom would not be the worse.

Some persons of a desponding spirit are in great concern about that vast number of poor

---

[①] **Psalmanazar**: George Psalmanazar (ca. 1679-1763), a French imposter who imposed himself on English bishops, noblemen, and scientists as a Formosan practicing human sacrifice and cannibalism.

people, who are aged, diseased, or maimed, and I have been desired to employ my thoughts what course may be taken to ease the nation of so grievous an encumbrance. But I am not in the least pain upon that matter, because it is very well known that they are every day dying and rotting by cold and famine, and filth and vermin, as fast as can be reasonably expected. And as to the young labourers, they are now in almost as hopeful a condition. They cannot get work, and consequently pine away from want of nourishment to a degree that if at any time they are accidentally hired to common labour, they have not strength to perform it, and thus the country and themselves are happily delivered from the evils to come. I have too long digressed, and therefore shall return to my subject. I think the advantages by the proposal which I have made are obvious and many, as well as of the highest importance.

For first, as I have already observed, it would greatly lessen the number of Papists, with whom we are yearly over-run, being the principal breeders of the nation as well as our most dangerous enemies, and who stay at home on purpose to deliver the kingdom to the Pretender, hoping to take their advantage by the absence of so many good Protestants, who have chosen rather to leave their country than stay at home and pay tithes against their conscience to an Episcopal curate.

Secondly, the poorer tenants will have something valuable of their own, which by law may be made liable to a distress, and help to pay their landlord's rent, their corn and cattle being already seized and money a thing unknown.

Thirdly, whereas the maintenance of an hundred thousand children, from two years old and upwards, cannot be computed at less than ten shillings a piece per annum, the nation's stock will be thereby increased fifty thousand pounds per annum, besides the profit of a new dish introduced to the tables of all gentlemen of fortune in the kingdom who have any refinement in taste. And the money will circulate among ourselves, the goods being entirely of our own growth and manufacture.

Fourthly, the constant breeders, besides the gain of eight shillings sterling per annum by the sale of their children, will be rid of the charge of maintaining them after the first year.

Fifthly, this food would likewise bring great custom to taverns, where the vintners will certainly be so prudent as to procure the best receipts for dressing it to perfection, and consequently have their houses frequented by all the fine gentlemen, who justly value themselves upon their knowledge in good eating; and a skilful cook, who understands how to oblige his guests, will contrive to make it as expensive as they please.

Sixthly, this would be a great inducement to marriage, which all wise nations have either encouraged by rewards, or enforced by laws and penalties. It would increase the care and tenderness of mothers towards their children, when they were sure of a settlement for life to the poor babes, provided in some sort by the public, to their annual profit instead of expense. We should soon see an honest emulation among the married women, which of them could bring the fattest child to the market. Men would become as fond of their wives, during the time of their pregnancy as they are now of their mares in foal, their cows in calf, their sows when they are ready to farrow; nor offer to beat or kick them (as is too frequent a practice) for fear of a miscarriage.

Many other advantages might be enumerated. For instance, the addition of some thousand carcasses in our exportation of barreled beef, the propagation of swine's flesh, and improvement in the art of making good bacon, so much wanted among us by the great destruction of pigs, too frequent at our tables, which are no way comparable in taste or magnificence to a well grown, fat yearling child, which roasted whole will make a considerable figure at a lordmayor's feast or any other public entertainment. But this and many others I omit, being studious of brevity.

Supposing that one thousand families in this city, would be constant customers for infants flesh, besides others who might have it at merry meetings, particularly at weddings and christenings, I compute that Dublin would take off annually about twenty thousand carcasses; and the rest of the kingdom (where probably they will be sold somewhat cheaper) the remaining eighty thousand.

I can think of no one objection that will possibly be raised against this proposal, unless it should be urged, that the number of people will be thereby much lessened in the kingdom. This I freely own, and it was indeed one principal design in offering it to the world. I desire the reader will observe, that I calculate my remedy for this one individual Kingdom of Ireland and for no other that ever was, is, or, I think, ever can be upon earth. Therefore let no man talk to me of other expedients: of taxing our absentees at five shillings a pound: of using neither cloths, nor household furniture, except what is of our own growth and manufacture: of utterly rejecting the materials and instruments that promote foreign luxury: of curing the expensiveness of pride, vanity, idleness, and gaming in our women: of introducing a vein of parsimony, prudence and temperance: of learning to love our country, in the want of which we differ even from Laplanders, and the inhabitants of Topinamboo①: of quitting our animosities and factions, nor acting any longer like the Jews, who were murdering one another at the very moment their city was taken②: of being a little cautious not to sell our country and consciences for nothing: of teaching landlords to have at least one degree of mercy towards their tenants; lastly, of putting a spirit of honesty, industry, and skill into our shop-keepers, who, if a resolution could now be taken to buy only our native goods, would immediately unite to cheat and exact upon us in the price, the measure, and the goodness, nor could ever yet be brought to make one fair proposal of just dealing, though often and earnestly invited to it.

Therefore I repeat, let no man talk to me of these and the like expedients, till he hath at least some glimpse of hope that there will ever be some hearty and sincere attempt to put them into practice.

But as to myself, having been wearied out for many years with offering vain, idle, visionary thoughts, and at length utterly despairing of success, I fortunately fell upon this proposal, which, as it is wholly new, so it hath something solid and real, of no expense and little trouble, full in our own power, and whereby we can incur no danger in disobliging

---

① **Topinamboo**: the savage tribes in Brazil.
② **nor acting ... city was taken**: Even before Jerusalem was destroyed by the Roman legions, the city had been torn by bloody fights among factions of Jewish fanatics.

England. For this kind of commodity will not bear exportation, the flesh being of too tender a consistence to admit a long continuance in salt, although perhaps I could name a country which would be glad to eat up our whole nation without it.

After all, I am not so violently bent upon my own opinion as to reject any offer proposed by wise men, which shall be found equally innocent, cheap, easy, and effectual. But before something of that kind shall be advanced in contradiction to my scheme, and offering a better, I desire the author or authors will be pleased maturely to consider two points. First, as things now stand, how they will be able to find food and raiment for an hundred thousand useless mouths and backs. And secondly, there being a round million of creatures in human figure throughout this kingdom, whose whole subsistence put into a common stock would leave them in debt two millions of pounds sterling, adding those who are beggars by profession to the bulk of farmers, cottagers and labourers, with their wives and children who are beggars in effect; I desire those politicians who dislike my overture, and may perhaps be so bold as to attempt an answer, that they will first ask the parents of these mortals whether they would not at this day think it a great happiness to have been sold for food at a year old, in the manner I prescribe, and thereby have avoided such a perpetual scene of misfortunes as they have since gone through by the oppression of landlords, the impossibility of paying rent without money or trade, the want of common sustenance, with neither house nor clothes to cover them from the inclemencies of the weather, and the most inevitable prospect of entailing the like or greater miseries upon their breed for ever.

I profess, in the sincerity of my heart, that I have not the least personal interest in endeavouring to promote this necessary work, having no other motive than the public good of my country, by advancing our trade, providing for infants, relieving the poor, and giving some pleasure to the rich. I have no children, by which I can propose to get a single penny; the youngest being nine years old, and my wife past childbearing. (1729)

Vocabulary

rags 破旧衣物
importune 向……强求
alms 施舍
christening 洗礼仪式
stroll 漫步,溜达
sustenance 食物,粮食
prodigious 巨大的,惊人的
deplorable 可叹的,悲惨的
grievance 委屈,冤情,抱怨
commonwealth 国家
profess 表示,声称,自称,以……为业
mature 成熟的
scheme 计划,方案
projector 制订计划者

gross 显著的,严重的
computation 计算
dam 母亲
nourishment 食物
scrap 碎片,(fig.) 少许
parish 教区
raiment 服装
abortion 流产,堕胎
bastard 私生子
reckon 计算,估计
breeder 繁殖的动物
subtract 减去
apprehend 理解,认识
miscarry 小产,流产
rear 抚养,栽种

hitherto 迄今
towardly 有指望的,顺利发展的
rudiment 基础,入门
probationer 见习生
crown 克朗,五先令硬币
stew 炖,焖
prolific 多产的,富饶的
glut 吃的过饱
popish (贬)天主教的
collateral 并排的,附属的
flay 剥皮
shambles 屠宰场,肉店
venison 野味,鹿肉
lean 瘦的,贫乏的
censure 指责,责备

dainty 美味精致的食物
crucify 把……钉死在十字架上
mandarin 官僚
groat 四便士银币
maim 使损伤,使残废
filth 污秽
vermin 害虫
over-run (草)蔓延于,侵扰
deliver 交付,解救
tith 农产品什一税
Episcopal 国教的
curate 助理牧师

tenant 佃户
liable 易患……的,易于……
distress 贫困,危难,扣押财物
annum 一年
sterling 英国货币
tavern 酒菜馆
vintner 酒商
procure 设法获得
inducement 引诱
emulation 竞争,仿效
mare 母马

sow 大母猪
farrow 一窝仔猪
parsimony 节俭,吝啬
Laplander 拉普兰人(北欧人)
animosity 憎恶,仇恨
faction 派系斗争,内讧
subsistence 生存,口粮
overture 提议
inclemency 严寒,狂风暴雨
entail 必需,使承担
propagation 繁殖

Questions

1. What problem does the writer mention in Paragraph One? What is the proposal made by Jonathan Swift? What are the advantages of the proposal?
2. How do you understand the title of this passage?
3. In this piece of writing the author digressed in the middle part. What is his intention?

9.2 "Sir Roger[①] at Church" from *The Spectator* (July 9, 1711) by Addison

I am always very well pleased with a country Sunday, and think, if keeping holy the seventh day were only a human institution, it would be the best method that could have been thought of for the polishing and civilizing of mankind. It is certain the country people would soon degenerate into a kind of savages and barbarians, were there not such frequent returns of a stated time, in which the whole village meet together with their best faces, and in their cleanliest habits, to converse with one another upon indifferent subjects, hear their duties explained to them, and join together in adoration of the Supreme Being. Sunday clears away the rust of the whole week, not only as it refreshes in their minds the notions of religion, but as it puts both the sexes upon appearing in their most agreeable forms, and exerting all such qualities as are apt to give them a figure in the eye of the village. A country fellow distinguishes himself as much in the churchyard as a citizen[②] does upon the Change, the whole parish politics being generally discussed in that place either after sermon or before the bell rings.

My friend Sir Roger, being a good church-man, has beautified the inside of his church with several texts of his own choosing: he has likewise given a handsome pulpit cloth, and railed in the communion table at his own expense. He has often told me, that at his coming to his estate he found his parishioners very irregular; and that in order to make them kneel and join in the responses, he gave every one of them a hassock and a Common Prayer Book; and at the same time employed an itinerant singing master, who goes about the country for that purpose, to

---

① **Sir Roger**: Sir Roger de Coverley, a character created by Addison and Steele.
② **a citizen**: a citizen of London.

instruct them rightly in the tunes of the psalms; upon which they now very much value themselves, and indeed outdo most of the country churches that I have ever met.

As Sir Roger is landlord to the whole congregation, he keeps them in very good order, and will suffer nobody to sleep in it besides himself; for if by chance he has been surprised into a short nap at sermon, upon recovering out of it he stands up and looks about him, and if he sees anybody else nodding, either wakes them himself, or sends his servant to them. Several other of the old knight's particularities break out upon these occasions: sometimes he will be lengthening out a verse in the Singing-Psalms, half a minute after the rest of the congregation have done with it; sometimes, when he is pleased with the matter of his devotion, he pronounces "Amen" three or four times to the same prayer; and sometimes stands up when everybody else is upon their knees, to count the congregation, or see if any of his tenants are missing.

I was yesterday very much surprised to hear my old friend, in the midst of the service, calling out to one John Matthews to mind what he was about, and not disturb the congregation. This John Matthews, it seems, is remarkable for being an idle fellow, and at that time was kicking his heels for his diversion. This authority of the knight, though exerted in that odd manner which accompanies him in all circumstances of life, has a very good effect upon the parish, who are not polite enough to see anything ridiculous in his behaviour; besides that the general good sense and worthiness of his character, make his friends observe these little singularities as foils that rather set off than blemish his good qualities.

As soon as the sermon is finished, nobody presumes to stir till Sir Roger is gone out of the church. The knight walks down from his seat in the chancel between a double row of his tenants, that stand bowing to him on each side; and every now and then he inquires how such an one's wife, or mother, or son, or father do, whom he does not see at church—which is understood as a secret reprimand to the person that is absent.

The chaplain has often told me that upon a catechizing day, when Sir Roger has been pleased with a boy that answers well, he has ordered a Bible to be given him next day for his encouragement; and sometimes accompanies it with a flitch of bacon to his mother. Sir Roger has likewise added five pounds a year to the clerk's place; and that he may encourage the young fellows to make themselves perfect in the church service, has promised, upon the death of the present incumbent, who is very old, to bestow it according to merit.

The fair understanding between Sir Roger and his chaplain, and their mutual concurrence in doing good, is the more remarkable, because the very next village is famous for the differences and contentions that rise between the parson and the squire, who live in a perpetual state of war. The parson is always preaching at the squire, and the squire, to be revenged on the parson, never comes to church. The squire has made all his tenants atheists and tithe-stealers; while the parson instructs them every Sunday in the dignity of his order, and insinuates to them, almost in every sermon, that he is a better man than his patron. In short, matters are come to such an extremity that the squire has not said his prayers either in public or private this half year; and that the parson threatens him, if he does not mend his manners, to pray for him in the face of the whole congregation.

Feuds of this nature, though too frequent in the country, are very fatal to the ordinary people; who are so used to be dazzled with riches, that they pay as much deference to the understanding of a man of an estate, as of a man of learning; and are very hardly brought to regard any truth, how important soever it may be, that is preached to them, when they know there are several men of five hundred a year who do not believe it.

Questions

1. What does the author think of church going for country people every Sunday? What can we learn from the passage about people's attitudes toward religious service in the church?
2. Can you spot in the passage the artistic devices used in depicting Sir Roger?
3. What does the author want to tell us in the last paragraph? Do you think it has something to do with the central point?

Vocabulary

holy 神圣的	hassock 膝垫	incumbent 在职牧师
polish 使更完美	itinerant 巡回的，流动的	bestow 给予，赐赠
degenerate 堕落	Psalms 赞美诗	merit 功绩
savage 凶残或粗野之人	outdo 优于，胜过	concurrence 一致，同僚
barbarian 野蛮人	knight 爵士,（对事业）忠实的拥护者	contention 竞争，争论
converse 谈话，交谈		parson 牧师
adoration 崇拜，敬慕	diversion 分心	squire 乡绅，大地主
supreme 至高无上的	foil 衬托物，陪观者	atheist 无神论者
exert 运用，施加	blemish 损害	tithing 十户区
churchman 教士，牧师，国教教徒	presume 放肆，擅作主张	tithe-stealer 什一税的偷税者
parish 教区	chancel 圣坛	insinuate 暗示
likewise 同样，另外	tenant 佃户，承租人	patron 顾客，守护神
pulpit 布道坛，讲坛	bow 鞠躬，俯首	feud（两人）不和，宿怨
rail 用栏杆围起来，隔开	reprimand 训诫，谴责	dazzle 迷惑
communion 圣餐	chaplain 牧师	deference 顺从，尊重
estate 地产，财产，庄园	catechize 以问答法教（基督教义）	soever 无论……
parishioner 教区居民，礼拜者	flitch 腌肉，腊肉	

9.3 *An Essay on Man: Epistle* II (an excerpt) by Alexander Pope

  Know then thyself, presume not God to scan;
  The proper study of mankind is man.
  Plac'd on this isthmus of a middle state,
  A being darkly wise, and rudely great:
5 With too much knowledge for the sceptic① side,

---

① **sceptic**: deriving from the word "Skepticism", the philosophical doctrine that absolute knowledge is impossible and that inquiry must be a process of doubting in order to acquire approximate or relative certainty.

With too much weakness for the stoic①'s pride,
He hangs between; in doubt to act, or rest;
In doubt to deem himself a god, or beast;
In doubt his mind or body to prefer;
10 Born but to die, and reas'ning but to err;
Alike in ignorance, his reason such,
Whether he thinks too little, or too much:
Chaos of thought and passion, all confus'd;
Still by himself abus'd, or disabus'd;
15 Created half to rise, and half to fall;
Great lord of all things, yet a prey to all;
Sole judge of truth, in endless error hurl'd:
The glory, jest, and riddle of the world!
Go, wondrous creature! mount where science guides,
20 Go, measure earth, weigh air, and state the tides;
Instruct the planets in what orbs to run,
Correct old time, and regulate the sun;
Go, soar with Plato th' empyreal sphere,
To the first good, first perfect, and first fair ...

Questions

1. What poetic form is used in this poem?
2. What are man's powers and frailties, according to Pope?
3. Discuss the role of Pope as a representative of the English Enlightenment authors.

9.4 "To the Right Honourable the Earl of Chesterfield" by Johnson

February 7, 1755

My Lord,

I have been lately informed by the proprietor of *The World*② that two papers in which my *Dictionary* is recommended to the public were written by your Lordship. To be so distinguished is an honour which, being very little accustomed to favours from the great, I know not well how to receive, or in what terms to acknowledge.

When upon some slight encouragement I first visited yourLordship, I was overpowered like the rest of mankind by the enchantment of your address, and could not forbear to wish that I might boast myself "*le vainqueur du vainqueur de la terre*" ③; that I might obtain that regard for which I saw the world contending; but I found my attendance so little encouraged that

---

① **stoic**: deriving from Stoic, a member of a Greek school of philosophy holding that men should be free from passion and calmly accept all occurrences as the unavoidable result of divine will.

② **The World**: a newspaper in which Chesterfield recommended Johnson's Dictionary to the public.

③ *Le vainqueur du vainqueur de la terre*: French, meaning "the conqueror of the conqueror of the world".

neither pride nor modesty would suffer me to continue it. When I had once addressed your Lordship in public, I had exhausted all the art of pleasing which a retired and uncourtly scholar can possess. I had done all that I could; and no man is well pleased to have his all neglected, be it ever so little.

Seven years, my lord, have now passed since I waited in your outward rooms or was repulsed from your door, during which time I have been pushing on my work through difficulties of which it is useless to complain, and have brought it at last to the verge of publication, without one act of assistance, one word of encouragement, or one smile of favour. Such treatment I did not expect, for I never had a patron before.

The shepherd in Virgil grew at last acquainted with Love, and found him a native of the rocks. ①

Is not a patron, my Lord, one who looks with unconcern on a man struggling for life in the water and, when he has reached ground, encumbers him with help? The notice which you have been pleased to take of my labours, had it been early, had been kind; but it has been delayed till I am indifferent and cannot enjoy it; till I am solitary, and cannot impart it; till I am known, and do not want it. I hope it is no very cynical asperity not to confess obligations where no benefit has been received, or to be unwilling that the public should consider me as owing that to a patron, which providence has enabled me to do for myself.

Having carried on my work thus far with so little obligation to any favorer of learning, I shall not be disappointed though I should conclude it, if less be possible, with less; for I have been long wakened from that dream of hope, in which I once boasted myself with so much exultation, my Lord,

Your lordship's most humble,
most obedient servant,
Sam: Johnson

Vocabulary

honourable 可尊敬的
earl 伯爵
proprietor 所有者
recommend 推荐
lordship 贵族的身份
distinguish 使扬名
acknowledge 答谢
overpower 制服
enchantment 施魔法,着魔
address 谈吐

forbear 自制
boast 自夸,夸耀
contend 竞争
attendance 到访
suffer 允许
exhaust 竭尽
retire 退休
uncourtly 不是来自宫廷的
neglect 忽略

repulse 拒绝
verge 边(缘)
patron 赞助人,恩人
shepherd 牧羊人,牧师
encumber 妨碍,拖累
solitary 离群的人,隐居者
asperity 粗鲁
Providence 神,上帝
exultation 狂喜,欢欣

---

① **The shepherd ... native of the rocks**: In *Ecloque* by Virgil (70 B.C.-19 B.C.), an ancient Roman poet, a shepherd who is suffering from failure in love complains that Love is born among jagged rocks (which have no feeling).

Questions

1. What does the author mean by "I, being very little accustomed to favors from the great"?
2. What do you know about the literary patronage in Britain? What is the implied meaning of "for I never had a patron before"?
3. What can we learn about Johnson's personality from this letter?

Chapter Five The Romantic Period

1. Introduction

1.1 Historical Background

Britain is recognized as the first country to have undergone industrialization in the whole world. In the first half of the 18th century, most industries in Britain were done in the home with simple hand-operated machines. Later new techniques, and water-powered machines were introduced. In 1765, the Scottish inventor James Watt (1736-1819) improved the steam engine first devised by Thomas Newcomen (1663-1729). Several years later powered machinery was introduced in the textile industry. Similar changes occurred in other trades, like hardware, pottery, and chemicals. Advancing side by side with industrialization was the building of roads and canals. By 1830 Britain had become "the workshop of the world".

Industrialization gradually spread to other European countries, and to America. Industrialized centers appeared, and as population grew, cities became bigger and more crowded. Some craftsmen, merchants, and factory owners became rich and were regarded as the first members of the bourgeois class. Conflicts appeared between the rising middle class and the aristocracy. At the same time, industrial growth didn't bring about any change in the economic condition of the working class, which led to protest and clash, such as the Luddite riots in 1811. Theoretically the Scottish philosopher Adam Smith (1723-1790) justified the development of capitalism in his *Wealth of Nations* (1776), stating that individual's pursuit of economic interests would bring social prosperity. Besides, the French economist Francois Quesnay (1694-1774) developed in his writings the idea of laissez-faire from the Chinese Taoist term *Wu Wei*, and capitalists began to prosper in society.

In 1789, the epoch-marking French Revolution broke out. The Parisians, who had lived under oppression and in misery, stormed the Bastille, a feudal institution. Inspired by the ideas of Rousseau, they could no longer endure the tyrannical rule in their country. The revolution in France created immense enthusiasm and hope among the British liberal intellectuals, mostly young poets and essayists who were almost the first of their kind to struggle for a living in the open market and found that a literary career was by no means easy. They wrote poems, pamphlets, and so on, exalting "liberty, equality and fraternity". The early success of the Revolution made them believe that the golden age of mankind had arrived. William Blake, Thomas Paine (1737-1809), William Godwin (1756-1836), William Wordsworth, Samuel Taylor Coleridge, Robert Southey (1774-1843), William Hazlitt (1778-1830), and a few others made clear their revolutionary ideas in various writings and refuted the British historian Edmund Burke (1729-1797), the author of *Reflections on the Revolution in France* (1790), the

Bishop of Llandoff, and a few others who were against rebellious spirit and revolution. When the surrounding countries, including Britain, united in an effort to put an end to the revolution in France, the intellectuals began to condemn the British government.

1.2 Romanticism

As an approach to writing, romantic literature appeared as early as the sixth century B. C. in ancient Greece, and then again and again in world literary history. As a movement, however, it started in Germany around the French Revolution. From Germany literary Romanticism spread quickly to other European countries. The appearance of literary Romanticism was triggered by the negative attitude of the European intellectuals at that time towards the social and political conditions that came with industrialization and the growing importance of the bourgeoisie. Being active participants in social life and keen observers of the society around them, Romantics saw both the corruption and injustice of the feudal societies and the fundamental inhumanity of capitalism, and they challenged the fundamental thesis of religion.

Neoclassicism during the Enlightenment period failed to express man's emotional nature and neglected his profound inner forces. The Romantics saw and felt things brilliantly afresh, and had a new intuition for the primal power of the wild landscape, the spiritual correspondence between man and nature. With the development of industry, many people gathered in towns and cities, thus getting further and further away from the natural world. The separateness man felt from nature drove poets and writers to recover the wholeness of life, and with it faith and vitality. Sources of spiritual vitality had to be sought elsewhere in the realm of the instinctive, the spontaneous, and the deeply emotional. In the eyes of Romantics, their society was not a good place. Thus men of letters in Europe and America tried to find comfort in nature and they also turned to the idealized world. Imagination became very important for writers who tried to incorporate it with experience. With the individual at the very center of literary creation, Romantics placed increasing value on the free expression of emotion and paid more attention to the psychic states of their characters. The tone of Romanticism was shaped by the exotic legends and mythology found in Oriental and Homeric literatures. Remembered childhood, unrequited love, and the exiled hero were constant themes.

In short, Romanticism is the artistic expression of the feelings of those artists and writers who experienced both hope and the succeeding disappointment in the process of Industrial Revolution.

1.3 English Romanticism

It's generally accepted that Romanticism in Britain began in 1798 with the publication of *Lyrical Ballads* by William Wordsworth and Samuel Taylor Coleridge, although a new current in literature had already appeared in the writings of a number of writers like William Blake and Robert Burns, who rebelled against the rigid rationalism, and the increasing materialism in their society as well as the conventions in literary creation at that time. Cold rationalism made men hunger for the childlike, the primitive, the superstitious, the magical, and even the gloomy. In a rationalistic world, some writers indulged in the irrational and romantic for protest, others for aesthetic thrill, still others for spiritual fulfillment. Blake's prophetic books were written in a sort of semi-religious arbitrary mythology, increasingly obscure in form and "metaphysical" in content. Burns is famous for the Scottish ballads, the style of which was adopted later by Wordsworth and Coleridge, who thought that the language of poetry should not be chained by the laws and rules of neoclassicism. Instead, poetry, in their opinion, should be "the spontaneous overflow of powerful feelings" and should be expressed in the everyday language of the common people. Thus they started a rebellion in poetry. The spirit of rebellion was carried on by later Romantics such as Byron and Shelley who attacked violently the old ideas and social conventions of their society. Poetry, naturally, became the best choice for them to express strong feelings.

The Romantic period in Britain also saw the appearance of several outstanding novelists and essayists. Both Jane Austen and Walter Scott created great novels in this romantic age, but their writings lack romantic elements. On the contrary, they showed some typical realistic traits.

2. William Blake (1757-1827)

William Blake was born in Soho, London, on Nov. 28, 1757. At ten he was sent to a drawing school and then the school of Royal Academy of Arts, where he showed great aptitude and ability in drawing. At fourteen, however, he chose to be apprenticed to an engraver, and at twenty-one began to work at the trade of engraving on his own. In 1782 he married Catherine Boucher, an illiterate, and he taught her not only to read and write but also to paint, and eventually she could assist him in his engraving and printing. Blake wrote some poems before his marriage, and in 1783 *Poetical Sketches* was published. In the late 1780s he tried relief etching, and most of his later poems, with

William Blake

illustrations drawn by the poet himself, were produced this way. In 1789 he engraved and published his *Songs of Innocence* and *The Book of Thel*, both manifesting the early phases of his highly distinctive mystic vision. His major prose work, *The Marriage of Heaven and Hell*, a book of paradoxical aphorisms, was engraved in 1790. After the French Revolution, he wrote some "prophetic books": *The French Revolution* (1791), and *America: A Prophecy* (1793), both celebrating the revolution in France. *Visions of the Daughters of Albion* (1793) expressed his attitude of revolt against authority, combining political fervour and visionary ecstasy. In 1794, after the addition of some poems, *Songs of Innocence and of Experience* appeared, together with *The Book of Urizen*, and *Europe, A Prophecy*. In the following year he produced *The Song of Los* (Los is a mythical character created by Blake), and in 1797 published *Vala*, which was renamed *The Four Zoas* after substantial revision. In 1804 Blake began to engrave his final works and his major prophetic books: *Milton*, and *Jerusalem*.

With no children, the Blakes mostly lived a life of isolation and poverty, although Blake's achievements continued to attract the interest and admiration of a group of young painters. He cherished a true sense of religion, but hated the church. It was believed that Blake, although gifted, had become insane in his final years. An unknown poet, he died in 1827. It was not until one century later that his genius was recognized. As an original writer with a powerful imagination, his influences can be found in the writings of William Butler Yeats, Allen Ginsberg, and a few others.

3. Robert Burns (1759-1796)

Robert Burns

The eldest son among seven children, Robert Burns was born in Ayrshire, Scotland. His father, who valued learning as part of both religion and patriotism and who moved the family from one unprofitable farm to another, managed with four neighbours to raise a small salary for a teacher who taught all their children. Young Robert's spare time was almost fully employed on the farm as labourer and ploughman, but he loved reading, and occasionally wrote some verses. He was interested by the remnants of the old Scottish songs and ballads still current in the countryside. In 1786, because of financial and domestic problems, he was about to emigrate to Jamaica when he learned his *Poems, Chiefly in the Scottish Dialect* had been published. It became very successful and brought some fame for the writer, who was later asked to help to collect old Scottish songs. After years of hard work, he collected, amended, and wrote over 200 songs, which include many of his best-known lyrics, such as "Auld Lang Syne", "A Red Red Rose", "The Twa Dogs", and "The Cotters Saturday Night". In 1788 he married Jean Armour, and in the next year he received a government post. After the French Revolution, Burns was greatly inspired, and once, on passing the ancient battle site of Bannockburn where the Scottish revolution of 1314 against England took place, he produced "Scots Wha Hae". In 1791 he finally gave up his farming life. Because of the arduous farm work and undernourishment in his youth, Burns suffered for many years from some form of arthritis or rheumatic fever. He died in 1796.

4. William Wordsworth (1770-1850)

The second son of an attorney, William Wordsworth was born in Cockermouth, a small town in the north of England. After the death of his mother in 1778, he was sent to a grammar school in the nearby village of Hawkshead, where he developed a deep love for nature. In 1783 his father died, and the boys in the family, including William, and one sister, Dorothy, went to separate places. At seventeen he entered St John's College, Cambridge. After the French Revolution he showed his sympathy and support for the French people, and in the following summer he made a walking tour in France, Switzerland, and Italy, and, after taking a bachelor's degree, returned to France late in 1791 to spend a year there to learn the French language. While he was in France, he fell in love with Annette Vallon, a French lady, and came to understand the real meaning of the Revolution. Back in England, he wrote in 1793 "A Letter to the Bishop of Llandoff," condemning the bishop who was against the Revolution. Wordsworth also denounced the British government when it waged a war against France, which,

William Wordsworth

unfortunately, separated him from his lover and daughter in France. This year also saw the publication of one of his first volumes of poems, *Descriptive Sketches*.

In 1795 Wordsworth received a legacy from a friend, which made it possible for him to be reunited with his sister Dorothy, who later kept a journal that sheds much light on the meaning of Wordsworth's poetry. Together they settled at Racedown in Dorset, growing their own vegetables, reading, and writing. In the same year he met Samuel Taylor Coleridge, also a supporter of the French Revolution. They developed a close friendship, which led to the publication in 1798 of *Lyrical Ballads*, a landmark in the history of English literature, its preface serving as the manifesto of British Romantic poetry. After their trip to Germany in the winter of 1798-1799, Wordsworth and Dorothy settled in Dove Cottage, Grasmere, Westmorland, in the Lake District. The poet Robert Southey and Coleridge lived also nearby, and the three men became known collectively as the "Lake Poets". In 1802 Wordsworth, after a settlement with Annette, married Mary Hutchinson, a long time acquaintance of his. In 1807 *Poems, in Two Volumes*, which contains some of his finest lyrics, was published.

With the changing situation in France, his enjoyment of nature, and the responsibility of a growing family, Wordsworth gradually lost his enthusiasm for the French Revolution, and gave up his idealism. In 1813 he was offered a government post, and in the following year *The Excursion* was published. As his popularity gradually increased, he succeeded Southey in 1843 as poet laureate of Great Britain. Seven years later he died at Rydal Mount, and *The Prelude*, first written in the 1790s, was published posthumously in 1850.

Although later referred to as "the Lost Leader" by Robert Browning, Wordsworth, by describing the beauty of plants, birds, lakes, rivers, and so on, tried to illustrate the interaction between the inner mind of human beings and the power of surrounding nature.

5. Walter Scott (1771-1832)

5.1 Life and Career

Walter Scott

Walter Scott, the son of an attorney and descendant from an ancient Border fighting clan, was born in Edinburgh. In his childhood he spent much time in roaming about the Scottish Border country where he grew up, picking up old ballads and folklore concerning the border conflict. Loyalty to his father led him to study the law, and in 1799 to work at it.

In 1796 he translated "Lenore", a ballad, based on a Scottish one, by Gottfried August Burger (1747-1794), a German Romantic poet. In 1802-1803 he collected Scottish ballads and songs, and, consequently, *Minstrelsy of the Scottish Border* came out. In 1805, his first original verse-romance, *The Lay of the Last Minstrel* was published, followed by *Marmion* (1808), *The Lady of the Lake* (1810), both being narrative poems about medieval chivalry, and they greatly increased both his reputation and income.

In 1812 and 1813 Byron's *Childe Harold* and "Eastern tales" captured public fancy, which made Scott turn from poetry to prose fiction. *Waverley*, which deals with the Jacobite defeat in 1745, was published in 1814. Its popularity inspired him to write *Old Mortality* (1816), *Rob Roy* (1817), *The Heart of Midlothian* (1818), and *Ivanhoe*, his masterwork (1819). In 1820 Scott was conferred the title of baronet.

In 1826 the London publisher Constable, of which Scott was a partner, went bankrupt, and this left him with huge debts. An immensely proud man, Scott determined to pay off the debt by his pen. But excessive writing made him a very sick man, and after a trip to Italy to improve his health, he returned home and died in 1832, a few weeks after Goethe's death.

Altogether Scott wrote 25 novels and he became known as the father of the historical novel.

5.2 *Ivanhoe* (synopsis)

It is believed Scott bases the story on the continued hostility between the Saxons and Normans, upon which. Wilfred of Ivanhoe becomes a favoured subject of Richard I (1189-1199), the Norman king, during the crusade. Ivanhoe's father, Cedric the Saxon, banishes his son after he finds Ivanhoe is in love with Lady Rowena, descendant of the ancient Saxon princes. King Richard's brother, John, plans to depose the king, and he is assisted by Sir Brian de Bois-Guilbert, a Templar knight, as well as immoral Norman noblemen such as Maurice de Bracy and Reginald Front de Boeuf. In the battle at Ashby de la Zouche King

Richard, with the assistance of Ivanhoe, defeats the knights of John; during the siege of the castle of Torquilstone, where the beautiful Jewish girl Rebecca has been imprisoned by Bois-Guilbert, Locksley (Robin Hood) with his group of outlaws comes to aid the King. Subsequently, with Rebecca still hostage to Bois-Guilbert, Ivanhoe, who faints from loss of blood due to injuries sustained in the previous battle, has to show courage and nobility in confronting the Norman enemy. Rebecca is rescued and finally gets away with her father. Eventually, Ivanhoe and his sweetheart Rowena are brought together by King Richard.

6. Samuel Taylor Coleridge (1772-1834)

The youngest of thirteen children of the vicar of Ottery St Mary, Devon, Samuel Taylor Coleridge was born in 1772. A precocious boy, he read widely when still very young. His father died when he was nine, and he was sent to Christ's Hospital School in London where he made a lifelong friend, Charles Lamb. He won a scholarship upon his graduation in 1791, which enabled him to enter Jesus College, Cambridge. In 1794 he met Robert Southey, a student at Oxford then, and they became very good friends. Inspired by the radical intellectuals under the influence of the revolution in France, they invented Pantisocracy, a scheme to set up a commune in New England. His first poems, including "Religious Musings", were published around this time. In 1795, he married Sara Fricker, sister of Southey's fiancee. In the same year he met Wordsworth, and at the latter's suggestion, wrote "The Rime of the Ancient Mariner", the first poem in *Lyrical Ballads*. While in Germany the following winter, Coleridge spent much time studying German philosophy, especially the 18th century idealism of Immanuel Kant (1724-1804). Gradually his use of opium to ease the pain of rheumatism as well as depression led to addiction, and his health suffered, but his popularity grew. In 1808 he began to give a series of lectures on poetry and drama which covered the works of William Shakespeare. In 1813 his tragic drama *Remorse* was produced and well received. Four years later *Biographia Literaria*, his major prose work, appeared. It contains a series of autobiographical notes and some dissertations on philosophy as well as the poetic creation of Wordsworth. Coleridge died in 1834.

Samuel Taylor Coleridge

Other writings by Coleridge include *Christabel and Other Poems* (1816) and *Zapolya* (1817), a drama.

7. Jane Austen (1775-1817)

7.1 Life and Career

Jane Austen

The second daughter of a rector, Jane Austen was born in Steventon, Hampshire. Her father, a cultivated man with a good library, taught his children at home. When still a young girl, Jane read widely, including the writings of the 18th century English novelists and poets. Encouraged by her father, she began to write. But his death in 1805 seemed to have given her a heavy blow, and she didn't write much for quite a few years. Being a woman writer, she was not successful with the publishers. Finally in 1811 her first novel, *Sense and Sensibility*, was published. Her masterwork, *Pride and Prejudice*, which was originally entitled *First Impressions* and had been refused at first by a publisher, came out in 1813 after some revision, and it was followed by *Mansfield Park* (1814) and *Emma* (1815). Jane Austen died in 1817. She never married. *Northanger Abbey* and *Persuasion* were published posthumously in 1818.

Austen's novels were generally well-received from publication onwards. Sir Walter Scott became her admirer, and Thomas De Quincey (1785-1859) said of her: "We should have to turn to the prose of the cultivated gentlewoman for English uncorrupted by the slang and cant of the world." Writing about the problems in love and marriage of middle class women, with which she was so familiar, Jane Austen became increasingly popular worldwide in the 20th century, and all the above-mentioned novels are now ranked as classics.

7.2 *Pride and Prejudice* (synopsis)

With five grown-up daughters and no son, Mr and Mrs Bennet live near Meryton, a small town. One day Bingley, a young man of large fortune from London, together with his sister Miss Caroline and his friend Darcy, moves to Netherfield Park in the neighbourhood. At a local dancing party, Bingley falls in love with Jane, the eldest daughter of the Bennets. During the party Darcy, looking cold and proud, refuses to dance with Elizabeth, the second daughter of the Bennets, whom he thinks has been slighted by other men. Later, however, he falls in love with her in spite of himself. At a later party he invites her to dance with him, and the latter has the satisfaction of refusing him a dance. When aware of his increasing admiration for Elizabeth, Miss Caroline, who is eager to marry Darcy herself, goes out of her way to tease Jane and Elizabeth. In the eyes of Caroline, Mrs Bennet is vulgar and garrulous, and Elizabeth's two youngest sisters, Kitty and Lydia, are foolish enough to be fascinated by two charming officers. Elizabeth learns from Wickham, one of the officers whom Lydia loves, that Darcy is a selfish and cruel man who has cheated him out of his inheritance. Fascinated by the handsome young officer herself, she takes what he says as true.

Elizabeth now acquires a new admirer, Mr Collins, a conceited clergyman and distant cousin of the Bennets', who will some day, according to the custom of the day, inherit the Bennets' property. Urged by his patroness, Lady Catherine de Bourgh, Mr Collins proposes to Elizabeth. When turned down, he transfers his affection to Charlotte Lucas, Elizabeth's best friend, who readily accepts it.

One day the whole Bingley party suddenly leaves the neighbourhood with no intention of returning. Elizabeth believes that Darcy and Miss Caroline are responsible for what has happened, and she assures Jane of Bingley's affection for her.

As time moves on, Charlotte plans to get married and she invites Elizabeth to visit her in Kent. Although she pities Charlotte for marrying simply for the sake of an establishment, Elizabeth pays the visit. The three are honored by a dinner invitation from Lady Catherine de Bourgh, who happens to be Darcy's aunt. During their stay there, Darcy comes to visit his aunt and cousin, Lady Catherine's daughter, a thin, sickly, and shy girl. Meeting Elizabeth there, he proposes marriage, but is turned down by Elizabeth who accuses him of separating Jane and Bingley and of treating Wickham unfairly. Disappointed and angry, Darcy leaves, but writes a letter the next day answering all her charges against him: He believes that Jane doesn't really love Bingley the person, but his money; Wickham is a wicked fellow who tells lies, and who returns his generous and kind treatment with an attempt to elope with his young sister.

Before long Mrs Gardiner, Mrs Bennet's sister, asks Elizabeth to accompany her on a tour to Derbyshire, which happens to be Darcy's home county. There an embarrassing encounter takes place between Elizabeth and Darcy who is now very polite to her and asks permission for his sister to call upon her. The call is duly paid and returned, but the pleasant exchange of visits is suddenly cut short when a letter arrives from Jane informing Elizabeth that Lydia has eloped with Wickham. After telling Darcy what has happened, Elizabeth and her aunt hurry away. A few days later the runaway couple return unexpectedly home. Mrs Gardiner tells the Bennets later that Darcy has given a sum of money to Wickham and has arranged the marriage.

Soon afterwards Bingley and Darcy come back to Netherfield Park. Immediately Bingley and Jane become engaged. One day Lady Catherine pays an unexpected visit to the Bennets and tries to make Elizabeth promise her not to accept Darcy's proposal if he makes one because a marriage has been arranged between Darcy and her own daughter. Elizabeth defies her order by saying definitely "No". When Darcy learns this, he proposes marriage again to Elizabeth and it is gladly accepted.

8. Charles Lamb (1775-1834)

Born in London, Charles Lamb attended Christ's Hospital where he met Samuel Taylor Coleridge, with whom he maintained a lifelong friendship. After graduation he worked for the South Sea House before he got an appointment in the East India House at the age of seventeen. In 1795 he began suffering from a mental disorder and was occasionally on the verge of insanity. His sister, Mary, suffered from a similar mental illness and in 1796 she killed their

Charles Lamb

mother. From that time on, Lamb undertook the charge of his sister and even went so far as giving up a marriage he was expecting. Lamb began to write poems round 1795, and "The Old Familiar Faces" was published in 1798. He wrote with Mary *Tales from Shakespeare* (1807), a book for children. They also collaborated on several other books for the young: *The Adventures of Ulysses* (1808), *Poetry for Children* (1809), and *Mrs Leicester's School* (1809), a book of stories. In 1808 he also published *Specimens of English Dramatic Poets Who Lived about the Time of Shakespeare*, which made him one of the celebrated literary critics at that time. *Essays of Elia*, his masterpiece, was published in 1823. Lamb died in 1834, and his sister outlived him and died in 1847.

With the efforts of Charles Lamb the essay became a means of intimate self-expression, which made him the leading essayist among his contemporaries like William Hazlitt (1778-1830), Thomas De Quincey, and Leigh Hunt (1784-1859).

9. George Gordon Byron (1788-1824)

The son of a captain, Byron was born in 1788. He was only three when his father died, and he grew up in poverty in Aberdeen, where he attended the Presbyterian Church. Though born with a club-foot, he was strong-minded and passionate as well as handsome. At ten Byron inherited the title of a baron and an estate, the dilapidated Gothic Newstead Abbey. After attending Harrow School he entered Cambridge in 1805. Two years later his first published collection of poems, *Hours of Idleness*, appeared. It was bitterly attacked in a review. In reply Byron wrote in 1809 a satire "English Bards and Scotch Reviewers", showing his contempt for the "Lake Poets". After he earned an MA upon his graduation in 1808 Byron took his seat in the House of

George Gordon Byron

Lords. Soon he began a long tour of Europe, visiting Portugal, Spain, Malta, Greece, and so on, which led to the writing of the first two cantos of *Childe Harold's Pilgrimage* (1812-1817). In 1813 he wrote *The Bride of Abydos*, which was followed by *The Corsair* (1813) and *The Giaour* (1813). In 1815 Byron married Annabella Milbanke. In the same year *Hebrew Melodies* appeared (which contains "She Walks in Beauty"). A year later his wife left him and refused to come back: He was believed to be insane and to have committed incest with his half-sister Augusta Leigh, whom he hadn't known was related to him prior to this scandal. These events, together with his earlier liaisons with men, estranged him from his friends. Embittered, Byron left England, never to return. He went first to Geneva, Switzerland, where he met Shelley and where he wrote the third canto of *Childe Harold* as well as *The Prisoner of Chillon* (1816). Then he went to Italy, where, inspired by the success of Goethe's *Faust*, he became deeply interested in drama and finished the verse drama *Manfred* (1817), the fourth and final canto of *Childe Harold*, and the first two cantos of *Don Juan* (1818-1819). While in Italy Byron wrote two more verse dramas—*The Two Foscari* (1821) and *Cain* (1821). *The Vision of Judgment* (1821) is an attack on Southey, the poet laureate then. Meanwhile, he continued with *Don Juan*, his masterpiece. In 1823 he published the *The Age of Bronze* and *The Island*.

When he heard the news of the Greek revolt against the occupying Ottoman Empire, Byron sailed to Greece and joined the Greek insurgents. There he died of fever at the age of thirty-six.

Considered to be a perverted man and the satanic poet in his home country, Byron was hailed as the champion of liberty and a poet of the people on the Continent. A rebel figure himself, Byron has created similar ones—the Byronic Hero—in his major poems like *Childe Harold's Pilgrimage*, the "Oriental Tale" (including *The Corsair* and *The Giaour*), *Manfred*, and *Don Juan*. Byron's poetry and drama have exerted great influence on European writers like Pushkin, Goethe, Melville, Balzac (1799-1850), and Dostoyevsky (1821-1881), to name just a few.

10. Percy Bysshe Shelley (1792-1822)

The eldest son of a wealthy, conservative MP, Percy Bysshe Shelley was born in Sussex. He was educated first at Eton and then at University College, Oxford, where he was influenced by the writings of radical authors like William Godwin and Thomas Paine, and where he wrote and circulated a pamphlet, *The Necessity of Atheism* (1811), repudiating the existence of God. This event led to his expulsion from the University and being disinherited by his father. Shortly after this, Shelley eloped with 16-year-old Harriet Westbrook to Edinburgh. Two years later his first long serious work, *Queen Mab*, appeared. The next year, after the collapse of his marriage, Shelley ran off abroad with Mary Godwin, William Godwin's daughter (her mother

Percy Bysshe Shelley

being Mary Wollstonecraft, the author of *A Vindication of the Rights of Woman* published in 1792). Then he returned to London, and wrote *Alastor* (1816), which first brought him general notice and reviews. He spent the summer of 1816 on Lake Geneva with Mary, who began to write *Frankenstein* (1818) while there. In Geneva he met Byron, and they began a great friendship. Shelley married Mary immediately after Harriet drowned herself. In 1818 he wrote *The Revolt of Islam*. Owing to his ill health and bad repute as an "immoralist", Shelley took his household permanently abroad, and spent his last four years in various places in Italy, where his major works were produced: *Julian and Maddalo* (1818), which was based on his friendship with Byron, *Prometheus Unbound* (1819), *The Cenci* (1819), a verse melodrama, *Adonais* (1821), an elegy on the death of John Keats, *A Defence of Poetry* (1821), his major prose essay, and *Hellas* (1822), his last completed verse drama which was inspired by the Greek War of Independence. Shelley was drowned in August 1822, on a return trip from visiting Byron and Hunt at Livorno.

In addition to his longer works, Shelley wrote many lyrics, among them, "Ode to the West Wind", "The Cloud", and "To a Skylark". The poet of volcanic hope for a better world, Shelley is regarded as a major figure among the English romantics.

11. John Keats (1795-1821)

John Keats

The eldest son of a livery-stable owner, John Keats was born in London. Immediately after his father's death in 1804, Keats's mother remarried and left the children with their grandmother. After the collapse of the marriage four years later, she joined the children (John and his sister Fanny and brothers George and Tom), and lived with her mother at Edmonton, near London. She died there of tuberculosis in 1810. Keats was educated at the Reverend John Clarke's school, Enfield, and after his grandmother's death he was taken out of school by their guardian and was apprenticed to a surgeon apothecary at Edmonton; but he was preoccupied with poetry. Deeply impressed by Edmund Spenser's writings, he wrote his first poem in 1814. He moved to London in 1815 as a student at Guy's Hospital, studying medicine. In the next year he was licensed to practice as an apothecary surgeon, but he abandoned the profession for poetry. In London he had met Leigh Hunt, the editor of the leading liberal magazine of the day, *The Examiner*, who introduced him to Hazlitt, Lamb and Shelley. Keats' first volume of poems, which contains "Sleep and Poetry", was published in 1817, but sales were poor. *Endymion*, Keats' first long poem, appeared in 1818. With 4,000 lines, it is about the love of the moon goddess Cynthia for the young and handsome shepherd Endymion. With his anti-classicism, it was attacked mercilessly by Tory reviewers, but Keats was not discouraged. After a walking tour of the Lakes, Scotland, and Northern Ireland during the summer, he returned to London and attended his brother Tom, who was seriously ill with tuberculosis. After Tom's death, Keats moved to Hampstead to live with Charles Brown, his friend. Soon he fell in love with Fanny Brawne, to whom he later got engaged. In the winter of 1818-1819 he worked on the first version of *Hyperion*, "The Eve of St. Agnes", "Ode to Psyche", "Ode to a Nightingale", "Ode on a Grecian Urn", "Ode on Melancholy", and "To Autumn". In 1819 Keats finished *Lamia*, and wrote another version of *Hyperion*, called *The Fall of Hyperion*. In 1820 appeared the second volume of Keats' poems, *Lamia*, *Isabella*, *The Eve of*

St. Agnes, and Other Poems. It gained a huge critical success. Suffering also from tuberculosis, he sailed for Italy, and died in Rome in February, 1821, and was buried in the Protestant Cemetery.

In spite of early harsh criticism, Keats's reputation grew after his death. Original in several ways his works have influenced, among others, the Pre-Raphaelite Brotherhood, Oscar Wilde, and Alfred Tennyson.

12. Selected Writings

12.1 "London" by Blake

I wander thro' each chartered street,
Near where the chartered Thames does flow,
And mark in every face I meet
Marks of weakness, marks of woe.

In every cry of every Man,
In every Infant's cry of fear,
In every voice, in every ban,
The mind-forged manacles I hear.

How the Chimney-sweeper's cry
Every blackening Church appalls;
And the hapless Soldier's sigh
Runs in blood down palace walls.

But most thro' midnight streets I hear
How the youthful Harlot's curse
Blasts the new born Infant's tear,
And blights with plagues the marriage hearse.

Questions

1. We know that there were chartered companies at the time when Blake wrote this poem, but why was the river Thames chartered?
2. What is the tone of this poem? How did the author achieve it?
3. Comment on the use of figurative language in the poem and the effect.

12.2 "The Tyger" by Blake

Tyger! Tyger! burning bright
In the forests of the night,
What immortal hand or eye

Could frame thy fearful symmetry?

In what distant deeps or skies
Burnt the fire of thine eyes?
On what wings dare he aspire?
What the hand dare seize the fire?

And what shoulder, and what art,
Could twist the sinews of thy heart,
And when thy heart began to beat,
What dread hand? and what dread feet?

What the hammer? what the chain?
In what furnace was thy brain?
What the anvil? what dread grasp
Dare its deadly terrors clasp?

When the stars threw down their spears,
And water'd heaven with their tears,
Did he smile his work to see?
Did he who made the Lamb make thee?

Tyger! Tyger! burning bright
In the forests of the night,
What immortal hand or eye,
Dare frame thy fearful symmetry?

Questions

1. What is the symbolic meaning of the word "tyger"?
2. How do you understand the last line of the fifth stanza?
3. Who has created the tyger according to the poem?

12.3 "The Chimney Sweeper" ① by Blake

When my mother died I was very young,
And my father sold me while yet my tongue
Could scarcely cry "'weep! 'weep! 'weep! 'weep② ! "
So your chimneys I sweep, and in soot I sleep.

---

① This poem is taken from *The Songs of Innocence*. There is another poem by the same title in *The Songs of Innocence and Experience*.

② 'weep: sweep.

There's little Tom Dacre, who cried when his head,
That curled like a lamb's back, was shaved, so I said
"Hush, Tom! never mind it, for when your head's bare
You know that the soot cannot spoil your white hair."

And so he was quiet, and that very night
As Tom was a-sleeping, he had such a sight!
That thousands of sweepers, Dick, Joe, Ned, and Jack,
Were all of them locked up in coffins of black.

And by came an angel who had a bright key,
And he opened the coffins and set them all free;
Then down a green plain leaping, laughing, they run,
And wash in a river, and shine in the sun.

Then naked and white, all their bags left behind,
They rise upon clouds and sport in the wind;
And the Angel told Tom, if he'd be a good boy,
He'd have God for his father, and never want joy.

And so Tom awoke, and we rose in the dark,
And got with our bags and our brushes to work.
Though the morning was cold, Tom was happy and warm;
So if all do their duty they need not fear harm.

Questions

1. Tom, a chimney sweeper, is obviously a child. For what purpose did the author use "white hair" to describe him?
2. What is meant by "locked in coffins of black"?
3. What can we learn about the author's religious ideas from the poem?

12.4 "A Red, Red Rose" by Burns

O my Luve's like a red, red rose,
That's newly sprung in June;
O my Luve's like the melodie,
That's sweetly play'd in tune.

As fair art thou, my bonie lass,
So deep in luve am I;
And I will luve thee still, my Dear,

Till a'① the seas gang dry.

Till a' the seas gang dry, my Dear,
And the rocks melt wi'② the sun;
I will luve thee still my Dear,
While the sands o' life shall run.

And fare thee weel, my only Luve,
And fare the weel, a while!
And I will come again, my Luve,
Tho' it were ten thousand mile!

Questions

1. What are the characteristics of an English ballad?
2. Is this ballad a love poem? Can you find similar ones in Chinese?
3. Burns used Lowland Scots Dialect in his ballads. In what way is it different from the King's English?

12.5 "Auld Lang Syne" by Burns

Should auld acquaintance be forgot
And never brought to min'?
Should auld acquaintance be forgot
And days o' lang syne?

(chorus)

For auld lang syne, my dear,
For auld lang syne,
We'll tak' a cup of kindness yet,
For auld lang syne.

And surely ye'll be your pint stowp!③
And surely I'll be mine!
And we'll tak a cup o' kindness yet,
For auld lang syne.

(chorus)

We twa hae run about the braes,
And pu'd the gowans fine.
But we've wander'd mony a weary foot,

---

① **a'**: all.
② **wi'**: with.
③ **stowp**: cup.

Sin' auld lang syne.

                   (*chorus*)

We twa hae paidl'd i' the burn [1],
Frae morning sun till dine[2];
But seas between us braid[3] hae roar'd,
Sin' auld lang syne.

                   (*chorus*)

And there's a hand, my trusty fiere[4],
And gie's a hand o' thine!
And we'll tak a right gude-willie-waught[5],
For auld lang syne.

Questions

1. What element(s) has/have made this ballad a universal parting song?
2. What is the style of Burns' poetry?

12.6 "Robert Bruce's March to Bannockburn[6]" by Burns

Scots, wha hae wi' Wallace[7] bled,
Scots, wham Bruce has aften led;
Welcome to your gory bed,
 Or to victory!

Now's the day, and now's the hour;
See the front o' battle lour[8];
See approach proud Edward's power—
 Chains and slaverie!

Wha will be a traitor knave?
Wha can fill a coward's grave!
Wha sae[9] base as be a slave?

---

① **paidl'd i' the burn**: waded in the stream.
② **dine**: dinner.
③ **braid**: broad.
④ **fiere**: friend.
⑤ **gude-willie-waught**: cordial drink.
⑥ **the title**: a marching song. Robert Bruce (1274-1329), king of Scotland from 1306 to 1329. He fought Edward I (1239-1307) and Edward II (1287-1327) of England, and defeated the English at Bannockburn in 1314. England recognized Scottish independence in 1328. This poem is sometimes entitled "Scots, Wha Hae".
⑦ **Wallace**: Sir William Wallace (1272-1305), Scottish warrior, who led a revolt against Edward I in 1297 and won a victory at Stirling (1297).
⑧ **lour**: lower, meaning "appear dark and threatening".
⑨ **sae**: so.

Let him turn and flee!

Wha for Scotland's king and law
Freedom's sword will strongly draw,
Freeman stand, or freeman fa'①,
   Let him follow me!

By oppression's woes and pains!
By your sons in servile chains!
We will drain our dearest veins,
   But they shall be free!

Lay the proud usurpers low!
Tyrants fall in every foe!
Liberty's in every blow! —
   Let us do or die!

Questions

1. What has caused the border conflicts between England and Scotland?
2. What can we learn about the poet's nationality from this poem?
3. Do you think this poem is one of the border ballads?

12.7 "For a' that and a' that" by Burns

   Is there, for honest poverty
   That hings② his head, an' a' that;
   The coward-slave, we pass him by,
   We dare be poor for a' that!
   For a' that, an' a' that,
   Our toils obscure, an' a' that,
   The rank is but the guinea's stamp,
   The Man's the gowd③ for a' that.

   What though on hamely④ fare we dine,
   Wear hodden⑤ grey, an' a that.
   Gie fools their silks, and knaves their wine,

---

① **fa'**: fall.
② **hings**: hangs.
③ **gowd**: gold.
④ **hamely**: homely.
⑤ **hodden**: a coarse cloth.

A Man's a Man for a' that.
For a' that, and a' that,
Their tinsel show, an' a' that;
The honest man, tho' e'er sae poor,
Is king o' men for a' that.

Ye see yon birkie, ca'd a lord,
Wha struts, an' stares, an' a' that,
Tho' hundreds worship at his word,
He's but a coof for a' that:
For a' that, an' a' that,
His ribband, star an' a' that:
The man o' independent mind,
He looks an' laughs at a' that.

A prince can mak a belted knight,
A marquis, duke, an' a' that;
But an honest man's aboon① his might,
Guid faith he mauna fa' that②!
For a' that, an' a' that,
Their dignities, an' a' that,
The pith o' sense, an' pride o' worth,
Are higher rank than a' that.

Then let us pray that come it may,
As come it will for a' that,
That Sense and Worth, o'er a' the earth,
Shall bear the gree③, an' a' that.
For a' that, an' a' that,
It's coming yet for a' that,
That man to man the world o'er,
Shall brothers be for a' that.

Questions

1. What can we learn from this poem about the author's attitude toward wealth, power and social position? Do you know anything about the author's origin and the economic condition of his family? Is there any connection between his attitude and his family background?

---

① **aboon**: above.
② **maunna fa' that**: must not claim that.
③ **bear the gree**: win the prize.

2. How do you understand phrases like "independent mind", "the pith o' sense" and "pride o' worth"?
3. What is the meaning of the last three lines of the poem? Do you think the writer is optimistic?

12.8 "She Dwelt among the Untrodden Ways" by Wordsworth

  She dwelt among the untrodden ways
    Beside the springs of Dove.
  A maid whom there were none to praise
    And very few to love;

  A violet by a mossy stone
    Half hidden from the eye!
  —fair as a star, when only one
    Is shining in the sky.

  She lived unknown, and few could know
    When Lucy ceased to be;
  But she is in her grave, and, oh,
    The difference to me!

Questions

1. Is ballad meter adopted in this poem?
2. Comment on the use of figurative language in this poem.
3. Who is Lucy in your opinion? Do you think Lucy is the name of a specific person?

12.9 "I Wandered Lonely As a Cloud"[①] by Wordsworth

  I wandered lonely as a cloud
  That floats on high o'er vales and hills,
  When all at once I saw a crowd,
  A host, of golden daffodils;
  Beside the lake, beneath the trees,
  Fluttering and dancing in the breeze.

  Continuous as the stars that shine
  And twinkle on the milky way,
  They stretched in never-ending line
  Along the margin of a bay:

---

① According to what Dorothy Wordsworth wrote in her journal, Wordsworth wrote this poem two years after the experience.

Ten thousand saw I at a glance,
Tossing their heads in sprightly dance.

The waves beside them danced; but they
Out-did the sparkling waves in glee:
A poet could not but be gay,
In such a jocund company:
I gazed—and gazed—but little thought
What wealth the show to me had brought:

For oft, when on my couch I lie
In vacant or in pensive mood,
They flash upon that inward eye
Which is the bliss of solitude;
And then my heart with pleasure fills,
And dances with the daffodils.

Questions

1. What's the tone of this poem? Explain the author's purpose in using repetition (like "dance") and reiteration.
2. What is the meaning of the title?
3. In this poem the author used words and phrases like "a host of", "never-ending line", "ten thousand", "company", and "solitude." Do you think he intended to make a contrast between human life and plant life? Is there any difference between them?

12.10 "The Solitary Reaper" by Wordsworth

Behold her, single in the field,
Yon solitary Highland Lass!
Reaping and singing by herself;
Stop here, or gently pass!
Alone she cuts and binds the grain,
And sings a melancholy strain;
O listen! For the Vale profound
Is overflowing with the sound.

No nightingale did ever chaunt
More welcome notes to weary bands
Of travellers in some shady haunt,
Among Arabian sands:
A voice so thrilling ne'er was heard
In spring-time from the Cuckoo-bird,

Breaking the silence of the seas
Among the farthest Hebrides①.

Will no one tell me what she sings? —
Perhaps the plaintive numbers flow
For old, unhappy, far-off things,
And battles long ago:
Or is it some more humble lay,
Familiar matter of to-day?
Some natural sorrow, loss, or pain,
That has been, and may be again?

Whate'er the theme, the maiden sang
As if her song could have no ending;
I saw her singing at her work,
And o'er the sickle bending;—
I listened, motionless and still;
And, as I mounted up the hill,
The music in my heart I bore,
Long after it was heard no more.

Questions

1. Did the author intend to show sympathy to the reaper, or did he simply want to show his respect for the labourer by writing such a poem?
2. What is the author's intention in mentioning the notes of the nightingale and the voice of the cuckoo?
3. What can we learn from this poem about the author's view of human society?

12.11 "To the Cuckoo" by Wordsworth

O blithe New-comer! I have heard,
I hear thee and rejoice.
O Cuckoo! Shall I call thee Bird,
Or but a wandering Voice?

While I am lying on the grass
Thy twofold shout I hear;
From hill to hill it seems to pass,
At once far off, and near.

---

① **Hebrides**: name of a group of isles northwest off the coast of Scotland.

Though babbling only to the Vale
Of sunshine and of flowers,
Thou bringest unto me a tale
Of visionary hours.

Thrice welcome, darling of the Spring!
Even yet thou art to me
No bird, but an invisible thing,
A voice, a mystery;

The same whom in my school-boy days
I listened to; that Cry
Which made me look a thousand ways
In bush, and tree, and sky.

To seek thee did I often rove
Through woods and on the green;
And thou wert still a hope, a love;
Still longed for, never seen.

And I can listen to thee yet;
Can lie upon the plain
And listen, till I do beget
That golden time again.

O blessed Bird! The earth we pace
Again appears to be
An unsubstantial, faery place;
That is fit home for Thee!

Questions

1. In this poem the substantial bird has been shown later as something insubstantial. What does the cuckoo represent in the author's eye?
2. Do you think the poet was satisfied with his current condition? Do you think he was making a contrast between childhood and adulthood?
3. What is your understanding of the last stanza?

12.12 "Composed Upon Westminster Bridge, September 3, 1802" by Wordsworth

Earth has not anything to show more fair:
Dull would he be of soul who could pass by
A sight so touching in its majesty;

This city now doth, like a garment, wear
The beauty of the morning; silent, bare,
Ships, towers, domes, theaters, and temples lie
Open unto the fields, and to the sky;
All bright and glittering in the smokeless air.
Never did sun more beautifully steep
In his first splendor, valley, rock, or hill;
Ne'er saw I, never felt, a calm so deep!
The river glideth at his own sweet will:
Dear God! The very houses seem asleep;
And all that mighty heart is lying still!

Questions

1. Spot in the poem examples of the use of figurative language and make comments on the effect.
2. What can we learn about London at that time from this poem?
3. Being one of the "Lake Poets", Wordsworth is famous for those poems that sing high praise of natural beauty. What do you think he wants to praise in this sonnet? Do you think he is making a contrast between the natural world and the man-made world?

12.13 "London, 1802" ① by Wordsworth

Milton! Thou shouldst be living at this hour:
England hath need of thee: she is a fen
Of stagnant waters: altar, sword, and pen,
Fireside, the heroic wealth of hall and bower,
Have forfeited their ancient English dower
Of inward happiness. We are selfish men;
Oh! Raise us up, return to us again;
And give us manners, virtue, freedom, power.
Thy soul was like a Star, and dwelt apart:
Thou hadst a voice whose sound was like the sea:
Pure as the naked heavens, majestic, free,
So didst thou travel on life's common way,
In cheerful godliness; and yet thy heart
The lowliest duties on herself did lay.

---

① This poem is one of a series "written immediately after my return from France to London, when I could not but be stuck, as here described, with the vanity and parade of our own country as contrasted with the quiet, and I may say the desolation, that the revolution had produced in France" (Wordsworth).

Questions

1. Why does England have need of Milton according to this poem?
2. What figurative language has been used in the poem?
3. What is the rhyme scheme of this sonnet?

12.14 "Kubla Khan" ① by Coleridge

    In Xanadu did Kubla Khan
    A stately pleasure-dome decree:
    Where Alph, the sacred river, ran
    Through caverns measureless to man
5   Down to a sunless sea.
    So twice five miles of fertile ground
    With walls and towers were girdled round:
    And there were gardens bright with sinuous rills,
    Where blossomed many an incense-bearing tree;
10 And here were forests ancient as the hills,
    Enfolding sunny spots of greenery.

    But oh! That deep romantic chasm which slanted
    Down the green hill athwart a cedarn cover!
    A savage place! As holy and enchanted
15 As e'er beneath a waning moon was haunted
    By woman wailing for her demon-lover!
    And from this chasm, with ceaseless turmoil seething,
    As if this earth in fast thick pants were breathing,
    A mighty fountain momently was forced:
20 Amid whose swift half-intermitted burst
    Huge fragments vaulted like rebounding hail,
    Or chaffy grain beneath the thresher's flail:
    And'mid these dancing rocks at once and ever
    It flung up momently the sacred river.
25 Five miles meandering with a mazy motion
    Through wood and dale the sacred river ran,
    Then reached the caverns measureless to man,
    And sank in tumult to a lifeless ocean:
    And'mid this tumult Kubla heard from far
30 Ancestral voices prophesying war!

---

① **Kubla Khan**: Coleridge's inspiration may have come from books like Purchas his Pilgrimage (1613), a book of travelers' tales by Samuel Purchas. The title is the name of a Mongol emperor, founder of Yuan (1206-1368).

    The shadow of the dome of pleasure
    Floated midway on the waves;
    Where was heard the mingled measure
    From the fountain and the caves.
35 It was a miracle of rare device,
    A sunny pleasure-dome with caves of ice!

    A damsel with a dulcimer
    In a vision once I saw:
    It was an Abyssinian① maid,
40   And on her dulcimer she played,
    Singing of Mount Abora②.
    Could I revive within me
    Her symphony and song,
    To such a deep delight't would win me,
45 That with music loud and long,
    I would build that dome in air,
    That sunny dome! Those caves of ice!
    And all who heard should see them there,
    And all should cry, Beware! Beware!
50 His flashing eyes, his floating hair!
    Weave a circle round him thrice,
    And close your eyes with holy dread③,
    For he on honey-dew hath fed,
    And drunk the milk of Paradise.

Questions

1. Being Chinese, what do you know about Kubla Khan? Why do you think the poet wrote a poem about his pleasure dome? Does this have anything to do with the general tendency of Romantic literature?
2. What role, in your opinion, does imagination play in literary creation?
3. It's said that the poet composed the whole poem in a dream. It is intended to be over 300 lines and only the beginning has been written. Judging from this part, can you make a guess as to what the author wanted to talk about in the forgotten part of the poem?

12.15 "Dream Children; a Reverie" by Lamb

    Children love to listen to stories about their elders, when they were children; to stretch

---

① **Abyssinian**: name of a place in the east of Africa, near the Red Sea, now Ethiopia.
② **Mount Abora**: refers to, possibly, Mount Amara in Milton's *Paradise Lost* into which Abyssinian kings sent their children to avoid the outside disturbance.
③ **Weave a ... thrice**: a magic ritual, to protect the inspired poet from intrusion.

their imagination to the conception of a traditionary great-uncle or granddame, whom they never saw. It was in this spirit that my little ones① crept about me the other evening to hear about their great-grandmother Field②, who lived in a great house in Norfolk③(a hundred times bigger than that in which they and papa lived) which had been the scene—so at least it was generally believed in that part of the country—of the tragic incidents which they had lately become familiar with from the ballad of the Children in the Wood④. Certain it is that the whole story of the children and their cruel uncle was to be seen fairly carved out in wood upon the chimney-piece of the great hall, the whole story down to the Robin Redbreasts, till a foolish rich person pulled it down to set up a marble one of modern invention in its stead, with no story upon it. Here Alice⑤ put out one of her dear mother's looks, too tender to be called upbraiding. Then I went on to say, how religious and how good their great-grandmother Field was, how beloved and respected by everybody, though she was not indeed the mistress of this great house, but had only the charge of it (and yet in some respects she might be said to be the mistress of it too) committed to her by the owner, who preferred living in a newer and more fashionable mansion which he had purchased somewhere in the adjoining county; but still she lived in it in a manner as if it had been her own, and kept up the dignity of the great house in a sort while she lived, which afterward came to decay, and was nearly pulled down, and all its old ornaments stripped and carried away to the owner's other house⑥, where they were set up, and looked as awkward as if some one were to carry away the old tombs they had seen lately at the Abbey⑦, and stick them up in Lady C.'s tawdry gilt drawing-room. Here John smiled, as much as to say, "that would be foolish indeed." And then I told how, when she came to die, her funeral was attended by a concourse of all the poor, and some of the gentry too, of the neighborhood for many miles round, to show their respect for her memory, because she had been such a good and religious woman; so good indeed that she knew all the Psaltery⑧ by

---

① **my little ones**: dream children (children in a dream, who are created by the writer's imagination).

② **Field**: Mary Field, name of a real person, i.e. Lamb's grandmother, who served as housekeeper for over fifty years at Blakesware in Hertfordshire, the seat of the Plumers (See the following Note).

③ **a great house in Norfolk**: Norfolkshire, a county in the east of England; "a great house" refers to Blakesware which was actually in Hertfordshire. Lamb deliberately changed the name of the locale so that it would be thought to have had something to do with the ballad of "The Babes in the Wood" which originated in Norfolkshire. Another possible reason is that William Plumer, the owner of Blakesware, was still alive when "Dream Children" was written. Having dismantled Blakesware, he lived in another family seat which was also in Hertfordshire.

④ **the ballad of the Children in the Wood**: a ballad popularly known as "The Babes in the Wood" which is taken from Bishop Percy's (1729-1811) *Reliques of Ancient English Poetry* (1765). It's the story of the tragic death of two children: A dying Norfolk gentleman leaves his property to his infant son and daughter and gives the children into his brother's charge; the uncle plans to acquire the property by having the children killed. He hires two men to slay them in a wood. One of these, more tender-hearted than the other, changes his mind, kills his fellow instead, and then abandons the children in the wood. The children perish, and a robin-redbreast covers them with leaves. The tender-hearted man confesses, and the wicked uncle dies miserably.

⑤ **Alice**: one of the dream children, a daughter; John (in the following lines), a boy.

⑥ **the owner's other house**: Gilston, the principal seat of the Plumers.

⑦ **the Abbey**: Westminster Abbey, which includes a cemetery for famous as well as important people.

⑧ **Psaltery**: the Book of Psalms.

heart, aye, and a great part of the Testament besides. Here little Alice spread her hands. Then I told what a tall, upright, graceful person their great-grandmother Field once was; and how in her youth she was esteemed the best dancer—here Alice's little right foot played an involuntary movement, till upon my looking grave, it desisted—the best dancer, I was saying, in the county, till a cruel disease, called a cancer, came, and bowed her down with pain; but it could never bend her good spirits, or make them stoop, but they were still upright, because she was so good and religious. Then I told how she was used to sleep by herself in a lone chamber of the great lone house; and how she believed that an apparition of two infants① was to be seen at midnight gliding up and down the great staircase near where she slept, but she said "those innocents would do her no harm"; and how frightened I used to be, though in those days I had my maid to sleep with me, because I was never half so good or religious as she—and yet I never saw the infants. Here John expanded all his eyebrows and tried to look courageous. Then I told how good she was to all her grand-children, having us to the great house in the holidays, where I in particular used to spend many hours by myself, in gazing upon the old busts of the Twelve Caesars②, that had been Emperors of Rome, till the old marble heads would seem to live again, or I to be turned into marble with them; how I never could be tired with roaming about that huge mansion, with its vast empty rooms, with their worn-out hangings, fluttering tapestry, and carved oaken panels, with the gilding almost rubbed out—sometimes in the spacious old-fashioned gardens, which I had almost to myself, unless when now and then a solitary gardening man would cross me—and how the nectarines and peaches hung upon the walls, without my ever offering to pluck them, because they were forbidden fruit, unless now and then,—and because I had more pleasure in strolling about among the old melancholy-looking yew trees, or the firs, and picking up the red berries, and the fir apples, which were good for nothing but to look at—or in lying about upon the fresh grass, with all the fine garden smells around me—or basking in the orangery, till I could almost fancy myself ripening, too, along with the oranges and the limes in that grateful warmth—or in watching the dace that darted to and fro in the fish pond, at the bottom of the garden, with here and there a great sulky pike hanging midway down the water in silent state, as if it mocked at their impertinent friskings,—I had more pleasure in these busy-idle diversions than in all the sweet flavors of peaches, nectarines, oranges, and such-like common baits of children. Here John slyly deposited back upon the plate a bunch of grapes, which, not unobserved by Alice, he had mediated dividing with her, and both seemed willing to relinquish them for the present as irrelevant. Then, in somewhat a more heightened tone, I told how, though their great-grandmother Field loved all her grand-children, yet in an especial manner she might be said to love their uncle, John L—③, because he was so handsome and spirited a youth, and a king to the rest of us; and, instead of moping about in solitary corners, like some of us, he would

---

① **an apparition of two infants**: a reference to the mysterious disappearance of two children of the Plumers which occurred in the seventeenth century.
② **the Twelve Caesars**: the first twelve emperors of the Roman Empire.
③ **John L-**: John Lamb, the elder brother of Charles, who worked at the South Sea House. He died in Oct. 1821.

mount the most mettlesome horse he could get, when but an imp no bigger than themselves, and make it carry him half over the county in a morning, and join the hunters when there were any out—and yet he loved the old great house and gardens too, but had too much spirit to be always pent up within their boundaries—and how their uncle grew up to man's estate as brave as he was handsome, to the admiration of everybody, but of their great-grandmother Field most especially; and how he used to carry me upon his back when I was a lame-footed boy—for he was a good bit older than me—many a mile when I could not walk for pain;—and how in after life he became lame-footed too, and I did not always (I fear) make allowances enough for him when he was impatient, and in pain, nor remember sufficiently how considerate he had been to me when I was lame-footed; and how when he died, though he had not been dead an hour, it seemed as if he had died a great while ago, such a distance there is betwixt life and death; and how I bore his death as I thought pretty well at first, but afterward it haunted and haunted me; and though I did not cry or take it to heart as some do, and as I think he would have done if I had died, yet I missed him all day long, and knew not till then how much I had loved him. I missed his kindness, and I missed his crossness, and wished him to be alive again, to be quarreling with him (for we quarreled sometimes), rather than not have him again, and was as uneasy without him, as he, their poor uncle, must have been when the doctor took off his limb. Here the children fell a crying, and asked if their little mourning which they had on was not for uncle John, and they looked up and prayed me not to go on about their uncle, but to tell them some stories about their pretty, dead mother. Then I told them how for seven long years, in hope sometimes, sometimes in despair, yet persisting ever, I courted the fair Alice W—n[1]; and, as much as children could understand, I explained to them what coyness, and difficulty, and denial meant in maidens—when suddenly, turning to Alice, the soul of the first Alice[2] looked out at her eyes with such a reality of re-presentment, that I became in doubt which of them stood there before me, or whose that bright hair was; and while I stood gazing, both the children gradually grew fainter to my view, receding, and still receding till nothing at last but two mournful features were seen in the uttermost distance, which, without speech, strangely impressed upon me the effects of speech: "We are not of Alice, nor of thee, nor are we children at all. The children of Alice call Bartrum[3] father. We are nothing; less than nothing, and dreams. We are only what might have been, and must wait upon the tedious shores of Lethe[4] millions of ages before we have existence, and a name"—and immediately awaking, I found myself quietly seated in my bachelor armchair, where I had fallen asleep, with the faithful Bridget[5] unchanged by my side—but John L. (or James Elia[6]) was gone

---

    [1] **Alice W—n**: Alice Winterton, not the name of a real person although some people tend to think it refers to Ann Simmon, Lamb's sweetheart. She probably lived in one of the cottages near Blakesware and married William Bartrum, a London pawnbroker, which throws light on the meaning of the sentence "The children of Alice call Bartrum father."
    [2] **the first Alice**: Alice Winterton.
    [3] **Bartrum**: William Bartrum.
    [4] **Lethe**: river in Hades, which makes those who drink from it forget their past life.
    [5] **Bridget**: Mary Lamb, Charles Lamb's elder sister.
    [6] **James Elia**: John Lamb.

forever.

Vocabulary

reverie 幻想，白日梦
creep 攀附
scene 场景
tragic 悲惨的
incident 事情
ballad 民谣，叙事曲
chimney-piece 壁炉架
marble 大理石
stead 代替
tender 善良的
upbraid 责骂
mistress 女主人
commit 把……交托给
mansion 宅第
adjoin 邻近
manner 方式，态度
decay 腐烂，变坏
ornament 装饰品
strip 搬
set up（常被动）供给
awkward 别扭的
tomb 坟墓
abbey 修道院
tawdry 俗丽的
gilt 薄层的金
funeral 葬礼
concourse 集合
gentry 绅士
Psaltery《圣经》中的诗篇
ay/aye 是，对
esteem 尊重，认为
desist 停业，结束
bow 压弯

stoop 弯腰
chamber 房间
apparition 幽灵
infant 婴儿，未成年人
glide 滑
innocent 无辜
courageous 勇敢的
bust 半身雕塑像
Caesar 恺撒
roam 漫步
flutter 飘动
hanging 挂在墙上的东西（尤指窗帷）
tapestry 绣帷，壁毯
panel 镶板
solitary 独居的
nectarine 油桃
pluck 采，摘
stroll 漫步
melancholy 沮丧的
yew 紫杉
berry 浆果
fir 冷杉
orangery 柑橘园
bask 取暖
lime 酸橙
grateful 使人舒服
dace 鲦鱼
dart 猛冲，突进
to and fro 来回，往复
sulky（爱）生闷气的
pike 狗头

mock 取笑
impertinent 不礼貌
frisking 活蹦乱跳的
idle 闲散的
diversion 转向
such-like 这种的，类似的
bait 鱼饵，诱惑物
slyly 狡猾的
deposite 放下某物
meditate 考虑
relinquish 放弃
irrelevant 不相关的
spirited 精神饱满的
mope 无精打采，徘徊
mount 骑上
mettlesome 勇猛的
imp 小魔鬼，小淘气
pent 被关起来的
estate 人生阶段
make allowances for 考虑到
betwixt 在……之间
haunt 使人常想起
crossness 易怒
mourning 丧服
court 讨好，求婚
coyness 忸怩作态
denial 自我克制
faint 模糊
recede 后退
mournful 悲哀的
uttermost 最远的
thee（古）你

Questions

1. Is this passage an essay or a story?
2. In this passage Lamb succeeded in weaving a story around a popular ballad ("The Children in the Wood") and historical facts (Mary Field, his grandmother, and the Plumers). What role does imagination play in the writing of this passage?
3. Do you think this passage autobiographical? Why or why not?

12.16 "She Walks in Beauty" ① by Byron

She walks in beauty, like the night
Of cloudless climes and starry skies;
And all that's best of dark and bright
Meet in her aspect and her eyes:
Thus mellowed to that tender light
Which heaven to gaudy day denies.

One shade the more, one ray the less,
Had half impaired the nameless grace
Which waves in every raven tress,
Or softly lightens o'er her face;
Where thoughts serenely sweet express
How pure, how dear their dwelling place.

And on that cheek, and o'er that brow,
So soft, so calm, yet eloquent,
The smiles that win, the tints that glow,
But tell of days in goodness spent,
A mind at peace with all below,
A heart whose love is innocent!

Questions

1. How do you understand the word "eloquent" in the third stanza?
2. What is the responsibility of poets according to this poem?
3. What can we learn from the third stanza about the poet's opinion of the relationship between outward beauty and goodness or innocence?

12.17 "The Isles of Greece" (from Canto III, *Don Juan*) by Byron

The isles of Greece, the isles of Greece!
Where burning Sappho② loved and sung,
Where grew the arts of war and peace,
Where Delos③ rose and Phoebus sprung!
Eternal summer gilds them yet,
But all, except their sun, is set.

---

① Byron wrote this poem after he met for the first time at a ball Anne Wilmot, his young cousin by marriage, who wore a black mourning gown with spangles.
② **Sappho**: an ancient Greek poetess (ca. 600 B.C.-?) famous for her passionate love poems.
③ **Delos**: name of an island in the Aegean Sea, the birthplace of Phoebus, Apollo (sungod) in Greek mythology.

The Scian and the Teian① muse,
The hero's harp, the lover's lute,
Have found the fame your shores refuse:
Their place of birth alone is mute
To sounds which echo further west
Than your sires' "Islands of the Blest."②

The mountains look on Marathon③—
And Marathon looks on to sea;
And musing there an hour alone,
I dreamed that Greece might still be free;
For standing on the Persians' grave,
I could not deem myself a slave.

A king④ sate on the rocky brow
Which looks o'er the sea-born Salamis⑤;
And ships, by thousands, lay below,
And men in nations;—all were his!
He counted them at break of day—
And when the sun set where were they?

And where are they? and where art thou,
My country? On thy voiceless shore
The heroic lay is tuneless now—
The heroic bosom beats no more!
And must thy lyre, so long devine,
Degenerate into hands like mine?

'Tis something, in the dearth of fame,
Though linked among a fettered race,
To feel at least a patriot's shame,
Even as I sing, suffuse my face;

---

① **Scian**: of Scio, name of an island which is said to be the birthplace of Homer, the ancient Greek epic poet and the author of *Iliad* and *Odyssey*. **Teian**: of Teos, name of an ancient Ionian city where Anacreon (563 B.C.-478 B.C.), a famous Greek lyric poet, was born.

② **Islands of the Blest**: the Cape Verde islands or the Cannaries on which those who were favorites of the gods would live after death. (Greek myth)

③ **Marathon**: name of a plain in Greece where the invading Persians were defeated by the Greeks in 490 B.C.

④ **king**: Xerxes (reign 486 B.C.-465 B.C.), king of Persia.

⑤ **Salamis**: name of an island where the Greeks, with their 380 warships, defeated the outnumbered Persian fleet of 2000 vessels.

For what is left the poet here?
For Greeks a blush—for Greece a tear.

Must we but weep o'er days more blest?
Must we but blush? —Our fathers bled.
Earth! render back from out thy breast
A remnant of our Spartan dead!
Of the three hundred grant but three,
To make a new Thermopylae①!

What, silent still? and silent all?
Ah! no;—the voices of the dead
Sound like a distant torrent's fall,
And answer, "Let one living head,
But one arise,—we come, we come!"
'Tis but the living who are dumb.

In vain—in vain: strike other chords;
Fill high the cup with Samian wine②!
Leave battles to the Turkish hordes,
And shed the blood of Scio's vine③!
Hark! rising to the ignoble call—
How answers each bold Bacchanal④!

You have the Pyrrhic⑤ dance as yet;
Where is the Pyrrhic phalanx gone?
Of two such lessons, why forget
The nobler and the manlier one?
You have the letters Cadmus⑥ gave—
Think ye he meant them for a slave?

Fill high the bowl with Samian wine!

---

① **Phermopylae**: name of a mountain pass in Greece where 300 Spartan warriors fought to death against an invading Persian army in 480 B. C.
② **Samian wine**: wine produced on the island of Samos, Greece.
③ **Scio's vine**: the grapes grown on the island of Scio, which are used to produce wine.
④ **Bacchanal**: drunken reveler who worships Bacchus, the god of wine in Roman mythology.
⑤ **Pyrrhic**: of Pyrrhus (318 B. C.-272 B. C.), king of Epirus, who was famous for his bravery. It's said that the Pyrrhic dance—a mimic war dance—and the Pyrrhic phalanx—a military formation—originated with him.
⑥ **Cadmus**: the founder of Thebes, a city state in ancient Greece. He was believed to have introduced into Greece from Phoenicia an alphabet of 16 letters.

We will not think of themes like these!
It made Anacreon's song devine;
He served—but served Polycrates①—
A tyrant; but our masters then
Were still, at least, our countrymen.

The tyrant of the Chersonese②
Was freedom's best and bravest friend;
That tyrant was Miltiades③!
Oh! that the present hour would lend
Another despot of the kind!
Such chains as his were sure to bind.

Fill high the bowl with Samian wine!
On Suli's rock, and Parga's shore④,
Exists the remnant of a line
Such as the Doric mothers⑤ bore;
And there, perhaps, some seed is sown,
The Heracleidan⑥ blood might own.

Trust not for freedom to the Franks⑦—
They have a king who buys and sells;
In native swords, and native ranks,
The only hope of courage dwells:
But Turkish force, and Latin fraud,
Would break your shield, however broad.

Fill high the bowl with Samian wine!
Our virgins dance beneath the shade—
I see their glorious black eyes shine;
But gazing on each glowing maid,

---

① **Polycrates**: the ruler of Samos in the 6th century B. C. A dictator, he admired Anacreon's muse and became his friend and patron.
② **Chersonese**: name of a place in ancient Greece, now Gallipoli.
③ **Miltiades**: a tyrant of the Chersonese who lived around 500 B. C.
④ **Suli's rock**: a mountainous area near Epirus, Greece; **Parga's shore**: a seaport in Greece.
⑤ **Doric mothers**: the mothers of the Dorians, one of the four divisions of ancient Greeks. The Spartans, who were renowned for their bravery, were the chief representatives of the Dorians.
⑥ **Heracleidan**: of Hercules, the son of Zeus. Hercules, who has accomplished twelve labours, is famous for his great strength. The Spartans claimed to be his descendants.
⑦ **Franks**: western European countries.

My own the burning tear-drop laves,
To think such breasts must suckle slaves.

Place me on Sunium's marbled steep①,
Where nothing, saves the waves and I,
May hear our mutual murmurs sweep;
There, swan-like②, let me sing and die:
A land of slaves shall ne'er be mine—
Dash down yon cup of Samian wine.

Questions

1. Why did the author mention "Sappho" and "Phoebus" in the first stanza?
2. What did the author mean by "The hero's harp, the lover's lute"?
3. What did the author want to express in the last three lines of the 2nd stanza?
4. What is the author's purpose in using the reflexive pronoun "himself" in the last line of the third stanza?
5. How do you understand the question in stanza No. 6? Taking Byron's other poems into consideration, can you define the word "poet"? What role does a poet play in society? Make a comparison between Byron and Keats.
6. How do you understand "bold Bacchanal"?
7. Byron's last days were spent in Greece. Do you think the poet had achieved his purpose in arousing the Greek's emotions by writing this part and by joining in the revolt personally? Do you think there is a kind of connection between the poet's efforts and the revolt?

12.18 "Ode to the West Wind" ③ by Shelley

I

O wild West Wind, thou breath of Autumn's being,
Thou, from whose unseen presence the leaves dead
Are driven, like ghosts from an enchanter fleeing,

Yellow, and black, and pale, and hectic red,
Pestilence-stricken multitudes: O thou,
Who chariotest to their dark wintry bed

The winged seeds, where they lie cold and low,

---

① **Sunium's marbled steep**: a rocky promontory (now Cape Colonna) on which stands an ancient temple to Poseidon with marble columns.

② **swan-like**: just like a swan that sings before it dies.

③ "This poem was conceived and chiefly written in a wood that skirts the Arno, near Florence, and on a day when that tempestuous wind, whose temperature is at once mild and animating, was collecting the vapors which pour down the autumnal rains." (Shelley's note)

Each like a corpse within its grave, until
Thine azure sister① of the Spring shall blow

Her clarion o'er the dreaming earth, and fill
(Driving sweet buds like flocks to feed in air)
With living hues and odours plain and hill:

Wild Spirit, which art moving everywhere;
Ddestroyer and preserver②; hear, oh, hear!

II

Thou on whose stream, mid the steep sky's commotion,
Loose clouds like earth's decaying leaves are shed,
Shook from the tangled boughs of Heaven and Ocean③,

Angels of rain and lightning: there are spread
On the blue surface of thine aery surge,
Like the bright hair uplifted from the head

Of some fierce Maenad④, even from the dim verge
Of the horizon to the zenith's height,
The locks of the approaching storm. Thou dirge

Of the dying year, to which this closing night
Will be the dome of a vast sepulchre,
Vaulted with all thy congregated might

Of vapours, from whose solid atmosphere
Black rain, and fire, and hail will burst: oh hear!

III

Thou who didst waken from his summer dreams
The blue Mediterranean, where he lay,
Lulled by the coil of his crystalline streams,

Beside a pumice isle in Baiae's bay⑤,

---

① **azure sister**: west wind in the spring time.
② **destroyer and preserver**: Among the Hindu gods, Siva is the Destroyer while Vishnu is the Preserver.
③ **tangled boughs of Heaven and Ocean**: clouds which are torn by the west wind.
④ **Maenad**: a female worshiper dancing frenziedly in worship of Bacchus (Dionysus), the god of vegetation in classical mythology who is said to die in autumn and to be reborn in spring.
⑤ **Baiae's bay**: West of Naples, Italy, it is the locale of a resort of Julius Caesar, emperor of the Roman Empire, who had villas built there.

And saw in sleep old palaces and towers
Quivering within the wave's intenser day,

All overgrown with azure moss and flowers
So sweet, the sense faints picturing them! Thou
For whose path the Atlantic's level powers

Cleave themselves into chasms, while far below
The sea-blooms and the oozy woods which wear
The sapless foliage of the ocean, know

Thy voice, and suddenly grow gray with fear,
And tremble and despoil themselves: O hear!

IV

If I were a dead leaf thou mightest bear;
If I were a swift cloud to fly with thee;
A wave to pant beneath thy power, and share

The impulse of thy strength, only less free
Than thou, O uncontrollable! If even
I were as in my boyhood, and could be

The comrade of thy wanderings over Heaven,
As then, when to outstrip thy skiey speed
Scarce seemed a vision; I would ne'er have striven

As thus with thee in prayer in my sore need.
Oh, lift me as a wave, a leaf, a cloud!
I fall upon the thorns of life! I bleed!

A heavy weight of hours has chained and bowed
One too like thee: tameless, and swift, and proud.

V

Make me thy lyre, even as the forest is:
What if my leaves are falling like its own!
The tumult of thy mighty harmonies

Will take from both a deep, autumnal tone,
Sweet though in sadness. Be thou, Spirit fierce,
My spirit! Be thou me, impetuous one!

Drive my dead thoughts over the universe
Like withered leaves to quicken a new birth!
And, by the incantation of this verse,

Scatter, as from an unextinguished hearth
Ashes and sparks, my words among mankind!
Be through my lips to unawakened earth

The trumpet of a prophecy! O Wind,
If Winter comes, can Spring be far behind?

Questions

1. How do you understand the first line of the poem?
2. What can we learn about the west wind from lines 2-4 of the poem? How do you understand the word "destroyer" in line fourteen of the poem?
3. What can we learn about the west wind from lines 5-12? How do you understand the word "preserver" in line fourteen?
4. What time of the year does the poem describe?
5. Do you think the poet wanted to show the power of the west wind in the first three parts of the poem?
6. What did the poet want to express in lines 47-52? How do you understand lines 53-54?
7. What can we learn about the author's condition at that time from lines 55-56?
8. What does "unawakened earth" mean?
9. What does the last line of the poem mean? What did the poet want to express by writing such a poem?

12.19 "Ozymandias"[①] by Shelley

I met a traveller from an antique land,
Who said—"two vast and trunkless legs of stone
Stand in the desert... near them, on the sand,
Half sunk a shattered visage lies, whose frown,
And wrinkled lips, and sneer of cold command,
Tell that its sculptor well those passions read
Which yet survive, stamped on these lifeless things,
The hand that mocked them, and the heart that fed;
And on the pedestal these words appear:

---

① **Ozymandias**: the Greek name for Ramses II, a powerful ruler of Egypt in the 13th century B.C. His rule lasted for 60 years and brought great prosperity to Egypt. The Sphinx is his tomb.

My name is Ozymandias, King of Kings, ①
Look on my Works ye Mighty, and despair!
Nothing beside remains. Round the decay
Of that colossal Wreck, boundless and bare
The lone and level sands stretch far away."—

Questions

1. This poem of 14 lines doesn't follow strictly the conventional rhyme scheme of the sonnet. What might be the reason?
2. Which of the following two, in your opinion, is more important to the author: power or art?
3. What does "sand" represent in this poem? What does the poem tell us about time?

12.20 "To—" by Shelley

One word is too often profaned
    For me to profane it,
One feeling too falsely disdained
    For thee to disdain it;
One hope is too like despair
    For prudence to smother,
And pity from thee more dear
    Than that from another.

I can give not what men call love,
    But wilt thou accept not
The worship the heart lifts above
    And the Heavens reject not,—
The desire of the moth for the star,
    Of the night for the morrow,
The devotion to something afar
    From the sphere of our sorrow?

Questions

1. What did the poet want to express in the first two lines of the poem? In lines 3-4? In lines 5-6?
2. How do you understand "pity from thee more dear than that from another"?
3. What can we learn from the last four lines of the poem? Do you think the author wanted to show the inaccessibility of love in this poem?

---

① **My name is Ozymandias, King of Kings**: According to Diodorus Siculus, a Greek historian of the first century B. C., the largest statue in Egypt had the inscription: "I am Ozymandias, king of kings; if anyone wishes to know what I am and where I lie, let him surpass me in some of my exploit."

12.21 "To a Skylark" by Shelley

    Hail to thee, blithe Spirit!
      Bird thou never wert,
    That from Heaven, or near it,
      Pourest thy full heart
In profuse strains of unpremeditated art.

    Higher still and higher
      From the earth thou springest
    Like a cloud of fire;
      The blue deep thou wingest,
And singing still dost soar, and soaring ever singest.

    In the golden lightning
      Of the sunken sun,
    O'er which clouds are bright'ning,
      Thou dost float and run;
Like an unbodied joy whose race is just begun.

    The pale purple even
      Melts around thy flight;
    Like a star of Heaven,
      In the broad day-light
Thou art unseen, but yet I hear thy shrill delight,

    Keen as are the arrows
      Of that silver sphere,
    Whose intense lamp narrows
      In the white dawn clear
Until we hardly see, we feel that it is there.

    All the earth and air
      With thy voice is loud,
    As, when night is bare,
      From one lonely cloud
The moon rains out her beams, and Heaven is overflow'd.

    What thou art we know not;
      What is most like thee?
    From rainbow clouds there flow not

Drops so bright to see
As from thy presence showers a rain of melody.

   Like a Poet hidden
      In the light of thought,
   Singing hymns unbidden,
      Till the world is wrought
To sympathy with hopes and fears it heeded not:

   Like a high-born maiden
      In a palace-tower,
   Soothing her love-laden
      Soul in secret hour
With music sweet as love, which overflows her bower:

   Like a glow-worm golden
      In a dell of dew,
   Scattering unbeholden
      Its aerial hue
Among the flowers and grass, which screen it from the view:

   Like a rose embower'd
      In its own green leaves,
   By warm winds deflower'd,
      Till the scent it gives
Makes faint with too much sweet those heavy-winged thieves:

   Sound of vernal showers
      On the twinkling grass,
   Rain-awaken'd flowers,
      All that ever was
Joyous, and clear, and fresh, thy music doth surpass.

   Teach us, Sprite or Bird,
      What sweet thoughts are thine:
   I have never heard
      Praise of love or wine
That panted forth a flood of rapture so divine.

   Chorus Hymeneal,
      Or triumphal chant,

  Match'd with thine would be all
    But an empty vaunt,
A thing wherein we feel there is some hidden want.

  What objects are the fountains
    Of thy happy strain?
  What fields, or waves, or mountains?
    What shapes of sky or plain?
What love of thine own kind? what ignorance of pain?

  With thy clear keen joyance
    Languor cannot be:
  Shadow of annoyance
    Never came near thee:
Thou lovest: but ne'er knew love's sad satiety.

  Waking or asleep,
    Thou of death must deem
  Things more true and deep
    Than we mortals dream,
Or how could thy notes flow in such a crystal stream?

  We look before and after,
    And pine for what is not:
  Our sincerest laughter
    With some pain is fraught;
Our sweetest songs are those that tell of saddest thought.

  Yet if we could scorn
    Hate, and pride, and fear;
  If we were things born
    Not to shed a tear,
I know not how thy joy we ever should come near.

  Better than all measures
    Of delightful sound,
  Better than all treasures
    That in books are found,
Thy skill to poet were, thou scorner of the ground!

  Teach me half the gladness

> That thy brain must know,
> Such harmonious madness
> From my lips would flow
> The world should listen then, as I am listening now.

Questions

1. What metaphor is used in the 5th stanza?
2. What did the poet say about the role of a poet in stanza No. 8? Compare it with that of Byron.
3. Do you agree with what the author says in stanza No. 14?
4. Do you think ignorance of pain is one source of happiness? How do you understand stanza No. 17?
5. How much do you know about Shelley's life? Do you think he had suffered from "love's sad satiety" personally?
6. Comment on the verse "Our sweetest songs are those that tell of saddest thoughts".
7. Do you think the poet wanted to express in the 19th stanza the idea that the human world is a place where only hate, pride, fear, sorrow, and the like can be found? Do you think the skylark stands for the natural world?

12.22 "Ode to a Nightingale" by Keats

> My heart aches, and a drowsy numbness pains
>   My sense, as though of hemlock I had drunk,
> Or emptied some dull opiate to the drains
>   One minute past, and Lethe-wards[①] had sunk:
> 'Tis not through envy of thy happy lot,
>   But being too happy in thine happiness,—
>   That thou, light-winged Dryad[②] of the trees
>   In some melodious plot
> Of beechen green, and shadows numberless,
>   Singest of summer in full-throated ease.
>
> O, for a draught of vintage! that hath been
>   Cool'd a long age in the deep-delved earth,
> Tasting of Flora[③] and the country green,
>   Dance, and Provencal[④] song, and sunburnt mirth!

---

① **Lethe-wards**: See the notes in "Dream Children; a Reverie" by Lamb.
② **Dryad**: a nymph of the woods.
③ **Flora**: Roman goddess of flower. Here it simply refers to flowers.
④ **Provencal**: of Provence, an area in southern France, famous for chivalry and poetry during the Middle Ages. Provencal song: poetry of the troubadour in Provence.

O for a beaker full of the warm South,
　　Full of the true, the blushful Hippocrene①,
　　　　With beaded bubbles winking at the brim,
　　　　　　And purple-stained mouth;
That I might drink, and leave the world unseen,
　　And with thee fade away into the forest dim:

Fade far away, dissolve, and quite forget
　　What thou among the leaves hast never known,
The weariness, the fever, and the fret
　　Here, where men sit and hear each other groan;
Where palsy shakes a few, sad, last gray hairs,
　　Where youth grows pale, and spectre-thin, and dies②;
　　　　Where but to think is to be full of sorrow
　　　　　　And leaden-eyed despairs,
Where Beauty cannot keep her lustrous eyes,
　　Or new Love pine at them beyond to-morrow.

Away! away! for I will fly to thee,
　　Not charioted by Bacchus and his pards③,
But on the viewless wings of Poesy,
　　Though the dull brain perplexes and retards:
Already with thee! tender is the night,
　　And haply the Queen-Moon is on her throne,
　　　　Cluster'd around by all her starry Fays;
　　　　　　But here there is no light,
Save what from heaven is with the breezes blown
　　Through verdurous glooms and winding mossy ways.

I cannot see what flowers are at my feet,
　　Nor what soft incense hangs upon the boughs,
But, in embalmed darkness, guess each sweet
　　Wherewith the seasonable month endows
The grass, the thicket, and the fruit-tree wild;
　　White hawthorn, and the pastoral eglantine;
　　　　Fast fading violets cover'd up in leaves;

---

① **Hippocrene**: a fountain on Mt. Helicon which is sacred to the Muses. Drinking from the fountain would arouse poetic inspiration.
② **youth grows ... and dies**: Tom, Keats's brother, suffered from tuberculosis and died in the previous winter.
③ **Bacchus and his pards**: In classical mythology, the god of wine is commonly portrayed in a chariot drawn by leopards.

    And mid-May's eldest child,
The coming musk-rose, full of dewy wine,
  The murmurous haunt of flies on summer eves.

Darkling I listen; and, for many a time
 I have been half in love with easeful Death,
Call'd him soft names in many a mused rhyme,
 To take into the air my quiet breath;
Now more than ever seems it rich to die,
 To cease upon the midnight with no pain,
  While thou art pouring forth thy soul abroad
   In such an ecstasy!
Still wouldst thou sing, and I have ears in vain—
 To thy high requiem become a sod.

Thou wast not born for death, immortal Bird!
 No hungry generations tread thee down;
The voice I hear this passing night was heard
 In ancient days by emperor and clown:
Perhaps the self-same song that found a path
  Through the sad heart of Ruth[①], when, sick for home,
   She stood in tears amid the alien corn;
    The same that oft-times hath
Charm'd magic casements, opening on the foam
 Of perilous seas, in faery lands forlorn.

Forlorn! the very word is like a bell
 To toll me back from thee to my sole self!
Adieu! the fancy cannot cheat so well
 As she is fam'd to do, deceiving elf.
Adieu! adieu! thy plaintive anthem fades
 Past the near meadows, over the still stream,
  Up the hill-side; and now'tis buried deep
   In the next valley-glades:
Was it a vision, or a waking dream?
 Fled is that music:—Do I wake or sleep?

---

 ① **Ruth**: widow in "The Book of Ruth" in the Old Testament. After her husband's death, Ruth left her own people and went with her mother-in-law to work in the fields of Judah.

Questions

1. How does the narrator feel at the beginning of the poem? What change occurs to them later?
2. What did the poet want to express in the first eight lines of the 2nd stanza?
3. Judging from the 3rd stanza, what is human society like in the eyes of the poet? Compare it with the opinion of Shelley.
4. Why does the melody of the nightingale remind the poet of death?
5. As we all know, human beings are different from each other in social position, economic condition, and so on. But what do they have in common according to this poem? Why did the poet call the nightingale "immortal bird"?
6. Why is Ruth in tears when hearing the nightingale's song?
7. Compare Keats's "Ode to a Nightingale" with Wordsworth's "To the Cuckoo" and Shelley's "To a Skylark." How much do they share with one another? What difference exists between them?

12.23 "Ode on a Grecian Urn①" by Keats

    Thou still unravished bride of quietness,
        Thou foster-child of silence and slow time,
    Sylvan② historian, who canst thus express
        A flowery tale more sweetly than our rhyme:
    What leaf-fringed legend haunts about thy shape
        Of deities or mortals, or of both,
            In Tempe or the dales of Arcady③?
    What men or gods are these? What maidens loth?
    What mad pursuit? What struggle to escape?
        What pipes and timbrels? What wild ecstasy?

    Heard melodies are sweet, but those unheard
        Are sweeter; therefore, ye soft pipes, play on;
    Not to the sensual ear, but, more endeared,
        Pipe to the spirit ditties of no tone:
    Fair youth, beneath the trees, thou canst not leave
        Thy song, nor ever can those trees be bare;
           Bold Lover, never, never canst thou kiss,
    Though winning near the goal—yet, do not grieve;

---

    ① **urn**: This urn is the creation of Keats's imagination. In the urn—which captures moments of intense experience in attitudes of grace and freezes them into marble immobility—Keats found the perfect correlative for his persistent concern with the longing for permanence in a world of change.
    ② **Sylvan**: rustic, representing a woodland scene.
    ③ **Tempe**: a beautiful valley in Greece; the dales of Arcady: the valleys of Arcadia, a place in ancient Greece which was often used as a symbol of the pastoral ideal.

She cannot fade, though thou hast not thy bliss,
　For ever wilt thou love, and she be fair!

Ah, happy, happy boughs! that cannot shed
　Your leaves, nor ever bid the Spring adieu;
And, happy melodist, unwearied,
　For ever piping songs for ever new;
More happy love! more happy, happy love!
　For ever warm and still to be enjoyed,
　　For ever panting, and for ever young;
All breathing human passion far above,
That leaves a heart high-sorrowful and cloyed,
　A burning forehead, and a parching tongue.

Who are these coming to the sacrifice?
　To what green altar, O mysterious priest,
Lead'st thou that heifer lowing at the skies,
　And all her silken flanks with garlands drest?
What little town by river or sea shore,
　Or mountain-built with peaceful citadel,
　　Is emptied of this folk, this pious morn?
And, little town, thy streets for evermore
Will silent be; and not a soul to tell
　Why thou art desolate, can e'er return.

O Attic shape①! Fair attitude! with brede
　Of marble men and maidens overwrought,
With forest branches and the trodden weed;
　Thou, silent form, dost tease us out of thought
As doth eternity: Cold Pastoral!
　When old age shall this generation waste,
　　Thou shalt remain, in midst of other woe
Than ours, a friend to man, to whom thou say'st,
"Beauty is truth, truth beauty," ②—that is all
　Ye know on earth, and all ye need to know.

---

① **Attic shape**: The urn has a style characteristic of Athens (Attica is the name of a region in which Athens is located).
② **"Beauty is truth, truth beauty"**: The quotation marks around this phrase are found in the volume of poems Keats published in 1820; but there are no quotation marks in the version printed in *Annals of the Fine Arts* that same year or in the four transcripts of the poem made by Keats's friends. This discrepancy has encouraged the diversity of critical interpretations of the last two lines.

Questions

1. In the 1st stanza, the poet used some questions to "describe" what was on the urn. What is his purpose in doing this?
2. Now that you are familiar with the poet's life. Do you think the author was comforting himself in the 2nd stanza since he never married?
3. Do you think the author was talking about himself or the human society at large in the third stanza?
4. How do you understand "Beauty is truth, truth beauty"?

12.24 "On first Looking into Chapman's Homer" ① by Keats

Much have I traveled in the realms of gold,
  And many goodly states and kingdoms seem;
  Round many western islands have I been
Which bards in fealty to Apollo② hold
Oft of one wide expanse had I been told
  That deep-browed Homer ruled as his demesne;
  Yet did I never breathe its pure serene
Till I heard Chapman speak out loud and bold:
Then felt I like some watcher of the skies
  When a new plant swims into his ken;
Or like stout Cortez③ when with eagle eyes
  He stared at the Pacific—and all his men
Looked at each other with a wild surmise—
  Silent, upon a peak in Darien④.

Questions

1. What's the meaning of the first line of the poem? Why did the author use the word "gold"?
2. What's the similarity between reading great classics and discovering an ocean or planet?
3. Judging from the fact that the poet used mythological figures like "Apollo" in this poem and in his earlier ones, how much did Keats already know about Greek mythology when he first read Homer?

---

① Keats's mentor, Charles Cowden Clarke introduced him to George Chapman's Homer. They read through the night, and Keats walked home at dawn. This sonnet reached Clarke by the ten o'clock mail that same morning. Chapman (1559-1634), an Elizabethan poet, started translating Homer from the 1590s and finished it in 1616.
② **Apollo**: Known as sungod, Apollo is also in charge of poetry.
③ **Cortez**: Hermando Cortez (1485-1547), a Spanish explorer who conquered Mexica. It's Vasco Balboa (1475-1517), another Spanish explorer, not Cortez, who discovered the Pacific in 1513.
④ **Darien**: the Isthmus of Darien in Panama, where Balboa discovered the Pacific.

Chapter Six　The Victorian Age

1. Introduction

1.1　Historical Background

The Victorian period in British literature roughly corresponds with the period of time when Queen Victoria was on the throne from 1837 to 1901. With great changes brought about by industrialization, it has generally been regarded as one of the most glorious periods in the history of the country. It was an age of imperial expansion, urbanization, and steam power, and Britain then became the most powerful country in the world. Rising from an island country to a great empire, it also saw the appearance of class conflict, Darwinism, religious crisis, bureaucratization and much more.

With industrial growth the middle class became more and more powerful. In 1832 the Reform Bill was passed in Parliament and the landed aristocrats gradually lost their political power. But the working class people, most of them peasants who had either flooded to industrial towns as a result of Enclosure or come to try their fortune, had to work in poor light and deafening noise for long hours in factories. Only a handful of them, through various means, became rich, while an overwhelming majority of workers who hoped to raise their social position and change their economic condition, worked hard, only to find that they were mistaken. Unemployment and low wages made life for most of them miserable and unbearable, which resulted in widespread protests. The nationwide Chartist Movement failed to bring about any substantial change either.

In the late 19th century, the unsettling of religious belief by new advances in science, particularly the theory of evolution and the historical study of the Bible, made the Victorian people experience a disillusionment of religion. In 1859 Charles Darwin published *The Origin of Species* and in 1870 *Descent of Man*, both hypothesizing that man had evolved from lower forms of life. Consequently the Christians had to face conflicting moral beliefs: While they were attracted by utilitarianism and the lifestyle of pleasure-seeking, they couldn't be free from the constricting influences of religion and the moral codes of Evangelists.

1.2　Literary Characteristics

In the first few decades of the Victorian period, romantic forms continued to dominate English literature in poetry and prose, but many writers shifted their attention to the growth of English democracy and the education of the masses. Many writers were drawn away from the immemorial subjects of literature into considerations of problems of faith and truth. The spiritual frustration of this age became a recurrent subject in many writers' works. The

Victorian literature speaks for an age of material comfort.

Since most of the writers during this period realistically showed the society as it was, their works came to be called realist writings. They depicted life around them, and familiar aspects of contemporary society and everyday scenes are represented in a straightforward or matter-of-fact manner. Literary realism focuses on commonness of the lives of the common people who are customarily ignored by the arts. Realists wrote about individual characters confronted by hardships and moral dilemmas; about the seamy side of human nature: cruelty, greed, hypocrisy, and stupidity. In their writings, life was presented as it was, not the picturesque, adventurous, heroic style characteristic of romantic writers. Realism thereby came to be seen and practiced as an art form which dominated the literary scene, until its extension into naturalism in the last few decades of the nineteenth century.

As Darwin's ideas became widely known, some people accepted the more negative implications of evolutionary theory and even used it to account for the behavior of characters in literary works: Characters were conceived as more or less complex combinations of inherited attributes and habits conditioned by social and economic forces. As the influential French theorist and novelist Emile Zola put the matter in his essay "The Experimental Novel":

In short, we must operate with characters, passions, human and social data as the chemist and the physicist work on inert bodies, as the physiologist works on living bodies. Determinism governs everything. It is scientific investigation; it is experimental reasoning that combats one by one the hypotheses of the idealists and will replace novels of pure imagination by novels of observation and experiment.

In naturalistic writings the reader can see the shattering of the optimistic idealism of the Enlightenment and its belief in the dignity of man, the faith in the democratic system, its hope for human growth and progress. The naturalist found in scientific discovery only a confirmation of man's helplessness in the face of overwhelming forces. In the eyes of naturalists, man is subject to the laws of nature, which may not only be indifferent but also hostile to man. As a result, they described lives objectively without emotion— "scientifically". They avoid a highly literary prose because they have little feeling for style and imagery.

First published in installments in periodicals, novels were the most widely read and the most challenging expression of progressive thought. A group of novelists such as Charles Dickens, William Makepeace Thackeray (1811-1863, known for his *Vanity Fair* published in 1848), and Thomas Hardy contributed a lot to the development of the English novel. They shared one thing in common: All were concerned about the fate of the ordinary people. With portrayal of urban life for all classes, the novels of Charles Dickens are full of humor and vivid characters. Most of Hardy's novels are set in Wessex and thus are labeled as local-color writing.

The Victorian age also witnessed great achievements in literature made by some women writers—Emily and Charlotte Bronte, George Eliot (Marian Evans), and Elizabeth Gaskell (1810-1865)—who struggled and finally succeeded in a male-dominated society.

The same spirit of social criticism inspired the plays of the Irish-born George Bernard Shaw, who awakened the drama, and the plays of Oscar Wilde (1854-1900), who showed the absurdity of life in his parodies and satire such as *The Importance of Being Earnest* (1895).

The major poets of the Victorian age were Alfred Tennyson and Robert Browning. The poetry of Robert Browning's wife, Elizabeth Barrette Browning, was also immensely popular.

Thomas Carlyle (1795-1881) and Mathew Arnold (1822-1888) were among the major prose writers of the period. Carlyle, the son of a Scottish peasant, wrote *Sartor Resartus* (1836), *The French Revolution* (1837), and *Past and Present* (1843) to show his conversion from Scottish Calvinism to German philosophy. Arnold, interested in literary and social criticism, wrote *Essays in Criticism* (1865, 1888), *Culture and Anarchy* (1869), *Literature and Dogma* (1873), and "Literature and Science" (1882).

2. Alfred Lord Tennyson (1809-1892)

Alfred, Lord Tennyson was born in Somersby, Lincolnshire. After spending four unhappy years in school he was tutored at home. Tennyson then studied at Trinity College, Cambridge, where he joined the literary club "The Apostles" and met Arthur Hallam, who became his closest friend. Tennyson began to write poetry at an early age in the style of Byron, and in 1830 he published *Poems, Chiefly Lyrical*, which included the popular "Mariana".

Alfred, Lord Tennyson

His next book, *Poems* (1833), received unfavorable reviews; Hallam died suddenly in the same year in Vienna, which was a heavy blow to Tennyson, who ceased to publish in the following ten years, although he began to write "In Memoriam", an elegy for his late friend—the work took seventeen years to write. "The Lady of Shalott", "The Lotus-Eaters", "Morte d'Arthur", and "Ulysses" appeared in 1842 in the two-volume *Poems*, which established his reputation as a writer.

Tennyson succeeded Wordsworth as poet laureate in 1850. After marrying Emily Sellwood, the couple settled in Farringford, and in 1869 moved to Aldworth, Surrey. The patriotic poem "The Charge of the Light Brigade", published in *Maud* (1855), is now considered to be one of Tennyson's best known works. *Enoch Arden* (1864) was based on a true story of a sailor thought drowned at sea who returned home after several years to find that his wife had remarried. *Idylls of the King* (1869) dealt with the Arthurian theme.

In the 1870s Tennyson wrote several plays, among them the poetic dramas *Queen Mary* (1875) and *Harold* (1876). In 1884 he was made a baron. Tennyson died at Aldworth and was buried in the Poet's Corner in Westminster Abbey.

A master in metrical verse, Tennyson worshipped heroes in his poetry. His influence can be found in the works of both Western and Eastern writers, the Chinese poet Wen Yiduo being among them.

3. Robert Browning (1812-1889) and Elizabeth Browning (1806-1861)

Robert Browning and Elizabeth Browning

Robert Browning was born in Camberwell, a suburb of London. Young Robert spent much of his time in his father's private library, the chief source of his education. In 1844, when Browning was 32 he became an admirer of Elizabeth Barrett, the author of "The Cry of the Children" (1843). He began corresponding with her by letter, her father not allowing his eleven children to receive visitors or to marry. This was the start of one of the world's most famous romances. Their courtship lasted until 1846 when they eloped to Italy.

Already a prominent woman of letters, Elizabeth wrote *Sonnets from the Portuguese* (1850) and a verse novel *Aurora Leigh* (1857). Robert, however, did not become recognized as a poet until after Elizabeth's death. His early poems and plays, including *Pauline*, *Paracelsus*, *Sordello*, and eight volumes of the *Bells and Pomegranates* series, were not successful, and he turned to the writing of a new genre in poetry, the "dramatic monologue". Four successive volumes—*Dramatic Lyrics* (1842), *Dramatic Romances and Lyrics* (1845), *Men and Women* (1855), and *Dramatis Personae* (1864)—appeared, and gradually his fame as a poet was established. His last important work, *The Ring and the Book* (1868-1869), is based on an Italian murder story. Browning died in 1889, and was buried in the Poets' Corner, Westminster Abbey, beside Tennyson.

Robert Browning is perhaps best-known for his dramatic monologue technique: He spoke in the voice of an imaginary or historical character. He had a fondness for people who lived during the Renaissance. Most of his monologues portray persons at dramatic moments in their lives.

4. Charles Dickens (1812-1870)

4.1 Life and Career

Charles Dickens

The second of eight children, Charles Dickens was born in Portsmouth. His father was a clerk in the Navy Pay Office, who was well paid but ended up in financial troubles. Finally the family moved to London, where Dickens began to work in a blacking warehouse for 6 shillings a week. Soon his family was sent to a debtor's prison in 1824. After the family was set free Charles was sent to school and became a law office clerk in 1827, then worked as a newspaper reporter, and this led to his writing literary sketches under the pseudonym Boz. *Sketches by Boz* and *The Pickwick Papers* were published in 1836. In the same year he married Catherine Hogarth, the daughter of a journalist.

Dickens' novels first appeared in serial installments, including *Oliver Twist* (1838), which depicts the London underworld and hard years of the foundling Oliver Twist, *Nicholas Nickelby* (1838-1839), a tale of young Nickleby's struggles to seek his fortune, and *The Old Curiosity Shop* (1840-1841).

In the 1840s Dickens spent much time traveling and campaigning against many of the social evils of his time. He published *Martin Chuzzlewit* (1843), *A Christmas Carol* (1843), the first of a series of Christmas books, and *Dombey and Son* (1846-1848). In the 1850s Dickens was founding editor of *Household Words* and its successor *All the Year Round* (1859-1870). Among his later works are *David Copperfield* (1849-1850), in which Dickens used his own personal experiences of work in a factory, *Bleak House* (1852-1853), *Hard Times* (1854), *A Tale of Two Cities* (1859) set in the years of the French Revolution, and *Great Expectations* (1860-1861).

Dickens died at Gadshill in 1870. The unfinished mystery novel *The Mystery of Edwin Drood* was published in the same year.

4.2　*David Copperfield* (synopsis)

David, a posthumous child, lives with his gentle, weak mother, his stepfather Mr Murdstone, and Jane, Murdstone's elder sister. Fond of reading fiction but poor at arithmetic and reciting texts, he finds himself constantly under the firm supervision of Murdstone and his fault-finding sister, both of whom consider him recalcitrant and send him to school, where David is mistreated by the headmaster Creakle but makes two friends, Steerforth and Traddles. After the death of his mother, David is taken out of school, and has to work in a blacking factory in London, where he makes the acquaintance of the lively but penniless Mr Micawber. Running away from the factory, he walks all the way to Dover to join the family of his aunt Betsey Trotwood, who sends him to a school in Canterbury, where he stays with the family of Mr Wickfield, Trotwood's lawyer who has a sweet daughter Agnes. Apprenticed to Mr Spenlow, David then enters Doctors' Commons to study law. Meanwhile he is seen together with Steerforth occasionally, whom he introduces to his old nurse Clara Peggotty and her family, which consists of Mr Peggotty (a Yarmouth fisherman), his nephew Ham, and Little Em'ly, Ham's cousin and fiancée. Induced by Steerforth, Little Em'ly runs away with him to mainland Europe, and Mr Peggotty has to trace them everywhere, only to find her cast off by Steerforth who, on his way back to England, encounters a shipwreck off Yarmouth and is drowned. Ham is also drowned while attempting to save him.

Copperfield, blind to Agnes's love for him, marries Dora, Mr Spenlow's daughter, who dies a few years later. Copperfield turns out to be a well-known writer. Uriah Heep, Mr Wickfield's clerk, tries to make Agnes marry him after he has secretly seized Wickfield's business. With the help of Traddles, a barrister now, Micawber, now Heep's clerk, discloses his boss' forgery, and Heep is sentenced to life imprisonment. Copperfield marries Agnes, and Micawber becomes a colonial magistrate in Australia, where Mr Peggotty and Em'ly have prospered after emigrating there.

5. The Brontë Sisters

5.1　Literary Career

The daughters of a curate, Charlotte, Emily, and Anne Brontë were born in 1816, 1818, and 1820 respectively in Thornton, Yorkshire, in the north of England. In 1820 their father moved the family, which composed of the parents and six children—five daughters and one son—to Haworth amid the Yorkshire moors, where the mother died the next year. The sisters were sent to Clergy Daughter's School where the two eldest sisters died because of the harsh conditions. Charlotte was left with her sisters Emily and Anne and brother Branwell to the care of their father, and their strict, religious aunt, Elisabeth Branwell. The children pursued their education at home. Both being sensitive and reserved, Emily and Anne were very close to each other. In 1831 Charlotte went to Miss Wooler's school at Roe Head, where she later worked as a teacher and where Emily attended in 1835. In 1838 Emily found a teaching job while

Charlotte tried to earn her living as a governess after quitting Roe Head. In 1842 Charlotte and Emily went to Brussels to learn French, German, and management. Their attempt in 1844 to open a school failed.

In 1845 Charlotte "discovered" the poems of Emily. In the next year, *Poems by Currer, Ellis and Acton Bell*, a collection of poems which she wrote with her sisters—Emily and Anne, was published, but only two copies were sold. By this time each had finished a novel: Charlotte's *The Professor* (1857) never found a publisher in her lifetime, but Emily's *Wuthering Heights* and Anne's *Agnes Grey* were accepted in 1847 and published the next year. Not discouraged, Charlotte finished *Jane Eyre*, which appeared in 1847, and became an immediate success. Meanwhile Emily wrote more poems which are profoundly metaphysical and original, and Anne finished a second novel—*The Tenant of Wildfell Hall* (1848) as well as some poems. In September 1848, Branwell died, probably due to his heavy drinking and drug abuse. At his funeral Emily caught a cold and died of tuberculosis three months later. In the next year Anne died of the same disease. Charlotte's grief can be found in *Shirley* (1849), followed by *Villette* (1853), which was based on her memories of Brussels. In 1854 Charlotte married her father's curate, Arthur Bell Nicholls. She died during her pregnancy on March 31, 1855.

5.2 Major Works

5.2.1 *Wuthering Heights* (synopsis)

In reminiscences and with stories told (to Lockwood, a new tenant at the Thrushcross Grange) by Nelly Dean, who has long been a servant at Thrushcross and Wuthering Heights, *Wuthering Heights* is a novel about two families—the Earnshaws and the Lintons—and an intruder—Heathcliff—and their stormy life between 1760 and 1801.

Mr Earnshaw, a gentleman-farmer, brings from a trip to Liverpool a little gypsy boy—a foundling—home to join his own family of his wife, his son Hindley, and his daughter Catherine at Wuthering Heights. He names the boy Heathcliff. All the other members of the household do not like Heathcliff, except for Catherine, who becomes fast friends with him. Some years later, Earnshaw dies. Hindley, after attending college, becomes the new master of Wuthering Heights, marries Frances, and uses his new power to reduce Heathcliff to the level of a servant. Meanwhile Heathcliff and Catherine continue their intimacy.

Emily Brontë

Locked out one day, Heathcliff and Catherine venture to the Grange, a house where the more civilized Lintons live with their children Edgar and Isabella. Catherine is caught by a bulldog. When the Lintons find out that the girl is Miss Earnshaw, they take good care of her and throw Heathcliff out. In the next few years, Catherine manages to maintain her relationship with Heathcliff while socializing with the elegant Linton children.

After Frances' death while giving birth to a son, Hareton, Hindley falls into wild despair and alcoholism. Edgar Linton falls in love with Catherine, who is attracted by what he represents, although she loves Heathcliff much more seriously. One night Heathcliff overhears a conversation between Catherine and Nelly to the effect that Heathcliff has been brought so low by Hindley that it will degrade her to marry him. Heathcliff disappears.

Three years later Catherine and Edgar become engaged. They live fairly harmoniously together for some time until Heathcliff returns one day. He has mysteriously acquired gentlemanly manners, education, and some money, and he gradually gains financial control of the Heights by paying Hindley's gambling debts. One day while visiting the Thrushcross Edgar orders Heathcliff thrown out of the Grange. Later Heathcliff elopes with Isabella.

Several months later, Heathcliff and Isabella return to Wuthering Heights, where he has a passionate reunion with Catherine, in which they forgive each other as much as possible for their mutual betrayals and Catherine dies that night after giving birth to a daughter, Catherine. Heathcliff is wildly grieved and he begs Catherine's ghost to haunt him. Isabella, who has been mistreated by her husband, escapes to London, where she gives birth to a son, Linton. Hindley dies a few months after the death of Catherine. During the following years, Hareton grows into an illiterate boy in the custody of Heathcliff. Linton, a peevish and effeminate boy, is taken back to Wuthering Heights after Isabella's death.

When younger Catherine is sixteen, Heathcliff kidnaps her and forces her to marry Linton, who is very ill and dying at the moment, so as to ensure himself of Edgar's land after his death. Catherine escapes in time to see Edgar before he dies. After Linton dies, Catherine becomes lonely enough to seek Hareton's company at Wuthering Heights. Heathcliff, still obsessed by his beloved Catherine, dies finally in a delirious state. The novel ends with younger Catherine and Hareton planning to marry and move to the Grange.

5.2.2 *Jane Eyre* (synopsis)

Charlotte Brontë

The story can be divided into five sections which correspond to the five periods of time spent in five different places in the heroine's life.

A. An orphan, Jane Eyre is passed into the care of Mrs Reed, the mistress of Gateshead Hall and wife of Jane's mother's brother who is now dead. Jane stays there for 10 years. She doesn't like the life there because she is occasionally bullied by her cousins. Once she is knocked to the floor. When she fights back, Mrs Reed punishes her by dragging her to the dark room in which Mr Reed died. There Jane loses consciousness.

B. Because of Jane's unbending spirit, she is sent to Lowood School, a charity institution for unwanted children. There, together with other pupils, she is subject to severe discipline. Also, the food there is unpalatable. Still, Jane works very hard, which makes her a favorite pupil of Miss Temple, the mistress of Lowood. During her schooling there, an epidemic of fever causes many deaths among the pupils, including her best friend Helen Burns. Subsequently an investigation is made, which brings some improvements. After her graduation, Jane becomes a teacher in Lowood.

C. When Miss Temple gets married, Jane leaves Lowood and finds a position as governess at Thornfield Park for Adele, an illegitimate daughter and ward of Jane's employer, Edward Fairfax Rochester. With the quiet country life and the natural beauty around the house, Jane enjoys herself greatly at Thornfield Park. One time when she is taking a walk outdoors, she meets, for the first time, Rochester, who is thrown by his horse to the ground. Thinking that he must have been hurt, she goes to his aid, not knowing he is her master. After some contact, Rochester finds the plain governess different from those empty-headed, money worshiping, beautiful upper class ladies he meets in Europe such as Celine Varens, the mother of Adele, and Blanche Ingram, an admirer of Rochester. Gradually they fall in love with each other, Jane by his passion, Rochester by her strong sense of dignity and equality, her sympathy and intelligence.

One day Bessie Leaven, the Gateshead Hall nurse, comes to inform Jane of the approaching death of Mrs Reed, who wishes to see her former ward. When Jane gets back to Gateshead Mrs Reed gives her a letter from John Eyre, Jane's uncle, who wrote three years ago from Madeira to Mrs Reed that he wanted to adopt his niece. On her deathbed Mrs Reed confesses that she has replied to John Eyre, telling him that Jane has died during the epidemic in Lowood.

After Jane returns to Thornfield, Rochester proposes marriage one night and she readily accepts it. Soon Jane writes a letter to her uncle in Madeira, informing him that she is to marry Rochester and explaining Mrs Reed's deception.

Strange things occasionally occur at Thornfield. One night Rochester's bed is set on fire; a visitor is wounded another night; late one night shortly before the wedding Jane is awakened by the movement of a woman who tries on the wedding veil before destroying it. When pressed for some explanation, Rochester tells Jane it's only her imagination. Jane finds that she is kept in the dark about something, which is confirmed at the wedding when a stranger declares an impediment to the marriage—Rochester has been married. Later Rochester leads the guests to a chamber at Thornfield where they find Bertha Mason, now a raving maniac, and Rochester admits that he was cheated by his family into a marriage with that woman fifteen years ago. Instead of staying with her beloved as his mistress, she leaves Thornfield as a dignified, virtuous and independent woman.

D. She gets to the moors of a north midland shire, where, penniless, she almost starves to death. Finally she is spotted by St John Rivers and his sisters, Mary and Diana, who bring her home and nurse her back to health. They later turn out to be Jane's cousins on her father's side. There Jane also inherits a large sum of money from John Eyre who has just died and Jane insists on sharing the legacy with her cousins. Later St John Rivers decides to go to India as a missionary and asks Jane to go with him as his wife. Although Jane is very grateful to him, she hesitates to accept his proposal because of lack of true love for him.

E. One night Jane dreams that Mr Rochester is calling her name. The next day she rushes to Thorfield, only to find its ruin. She learns from the neighbours that the mad woman had set it on fire and Rochester was injured and lost his eyesight while trying to get Bertha down from the roof. The wife has been killed in the fire. Jane finds Rochester a miserable and lonely man who lives now at Ferndean, a secluded country house. There she stays and later they get married. Two years later Rochester gains the sight of one eye and is happy to see his first child when it is handed to him.

6. George Eliot (1819-1880)

6.1 Life and Career

George Eliot

The daughter of a land agent, Marian Evans was born in Warwickshire. Educated at home and in several schools, she developed a strong evangelical piety. When her mother died in 1836, she left school and took charge of the family household. Meanwhile she managed to teach herself Italian, German, music, and medicine. In 1841 the family moved to Coventry, where she became acquainted with some religious free-thinkers. In 1846 she translated *The Life of Jesus* by D. F. Strauss. Through her own studies of theology, Eliot gradually rejected her dogmatic faith. After her father's death in 1849, she settled in London and became an assistant editor of *Westminster Review*, which later enjoyed success under Eliot's control. In London she became the centre of an intellectual circle, one of the members being George Henry Lewes, whose wife was mentally unbalanced. In 1854 Eliot went to Germany with Lewes. Their unconventional union caused some difficulties because Lewes was unable to obtain a divorce, which resulted in 25 years of alienation from her brother and some close friends. In the same year she published one of her translation works *Das Wesen des Christentums* (*The Essence of Christianity*) by Ludwig Feuerbach, a German philosopher and critic of the Bible.

Eliot's first collection of tales, *Scenes from Clerical Life*, appeared in installments in magazines in 1858 under the pseudonym George Eliot. It was followed by her first novel, *Adam Bede* (1859), a tragic love story in which the model for the title character was Eliot's father. The book was a brilliant success. Her other major early works include *The Mill on the Floss* (1860), a story of destructive family relations, and *Silas Marner* (1861), the story of a linen-weaver.

In the early 1860s Eliot spent some time in Italy collecting material for her historical romance *Romola*. It was published serially first in the *Cornhill Magazine* and in book form in 1863. *Felix Holt the Radical*, a political novel, appeared in 1866, and two years later *The Spanish Gypsy*, which was a dramatic poem. *Middlemarch* (1871-1872), her greatest novel, probably inspired by her life at Coventry, was published in installments, and, *Daniel Deronda*, her last great work, in the same way in 1876. By that time Eliot was widely recognized as the greatest living English novelist.

In 1878 Lewes died and Eliot seemed to have never recovered from the grief. The next year saw the appearance of *The Impressions of Theophrastus Such*, a volume of essays. Eliot married J. W. Cross, an admirer, in May 1880, which brought a reunion with her brother. Eliot died seven months later.

6.2 *Middlemarch* (synopsis)

The scene is laid in the provincial town of Middlemarch around 1830. Dorothea Brooke is an ardent, intelligent and idealistic young woman of the middle class. Tired of the selfishness and superficial conventions of her own class, she is determined to devote herself to "something greater; even if you don't know what it is". When Edward Casaubon, an elderly clergyman who is devoting his life to constructing a meaningless concordance of religious myths which, to Dorothea's uninformed vision, is necessarily a work of profound scholarship and social significance, proposes to her, she is therefore overwhelmed with joy. They are engaged and get married despite the doubts and advice of her sister Celia, her neighbour and suitor Sir James Chettam (who later marries Celia), and Mrs Cadwallader, the rector's outspoken wife. Shortly after marriage, Dorothea finds herself disillusioned: She realizes during their honeymoon in Rome that Casaubon's plans to write a great work are doomed. She is sustained by the friendship of Casaubon's cousin, Will Ladislaw, a lively, light-hearted and good-natured young man. Casaubon hates Ladislaw and when he finds that Dorothea has affection for Ladislaw, he, now terminally ill, has a codicil added to his will by which Dorothea will be disinherited if she marries Ladislaw. Soon the old man dies.

Tertius Lydgate is an ambitious and idealistic doctor who has come from London to the small town in the hope of doing something good for the townspeople and something great for the world. He is interested in medical reform and scientific studies. But he gets trapped into a marriage with a beautiful woman, Rosamond Vincy, daughter of the mayor of Middlemarch. The marriage is ruined by Rosamond's selfishness and extravagance. Soon Lydgate finds himself heavily in debt, and has to borrow some money from the banker—Mr Bulstrode, the mayor's brother-in-law and a religious hypocrite. What's more, Lydgate gets entangled in a scandal concerning the death of Raffles, who has most probably been killed by Bulstrode because he has been involved with the banker's shady past. Only Dorothea understands him, but she is shocked to find Ladislaw and Rosamond together. Later Rosamond explains that Ladislaw has remained faithful to Dorothea, though with no prospect of any good result. At last Dorothea and Ladislaw confess their love to each other and get married. Lydgate has to give up his reform and research, and subdues himself to being just a pragmatic physician and, his ambitions frustrated, he dies at 50. Ladislaw becomes an ardent public man and a Member of Parliament while his wife Dorothea turns out to live a conventional life of a woman, content in giving Ladsilaw her "wifely" help.

Crisscrossing these two major threads there is also the love story of Fred Vincy, Rosamond's brother, and his childhood sweetheart Mary Garth, a practical, shrewd, poor and plain young woman who will not pledge herself to Fred unless he abandons his father's plan for him to enter the church and proves himself stable and self-sufficient; and the story of the old miser Mr Featherstone, who, on his deathbed, fights his last battle against his greedy relatives.

7. Thomas Hardy (1840-1928)

7.1 Life and Career

Thomas Hardy

Thomas Hardy was born in Dorset, in what is known as Wessex in 1840. His father was a stonemason and building contractor. After his schooling in Dorchester Hardy was apprenticed to an architect. At the age of 22 Hardy went to London and worked as an assistant in an architectural firm. Meanwhile he managed to find time for extensive reading and became interested in fiction and poetry. He also tried writing poems. In 1867 he returned home and continued architectural work. Unable to find a publisher for his poems, Hardy began to write novels. His first published novel, *Desperate Remedies*, appeared in 1871. It was followed by *Under the Greenwood Tree* (1872), and *A Pair of Blue Eyes* (1873). The success of his next novel, *Far from the Madding Crowd* (1874), enabled him to give up architecture for writing and marry Emma Gifford. In the following twenty-three years Hardy wrote altogether sixteen local-color novels until 1896 when he, disgusted with the criticism against his last two books—*Tess of the D'Urbervilles* (1891) and *Jude the Obscure* (1895), returned to the writing of poetry, which he had always regarded as superior to fiction. He wrote 918 poems in all, the most famous being *The Dynasts* (1904-1908), a long epic-drama about the Napoleonic Wars.

Emma Hardy died in 1912 and in 1914 Hardy married his secretary, Florence Dugdale, a woman in her 30's. Hardy died in Dorchester, Dorset, on January 11, 1928, and was buried with impressive ceremonies in the Poets' Corner in Westminster Abbey.

In addition to those mentioned above, Hardy's major writings include *The Return of the Native* (1878), *The Trumpet-Major* (1880), *The Mayor of Casterbridge* (1886), *The Woodlanders* (1887), *Wessex Tales* (1888, a collection of short stories), and *Wessex Poems* (1898).

7.2 *Tess of the D'Urbervilles* (synopsis)

Jack Durbeyfield is a poor villager of Blackmoor Vale who has never done more work than is necessary to keep his family alive. When he is told that he is descended from the famous D'Urberville family, he, together with his wife, thinks that they should lead a better life with less effort. Thus they persuade their eldest daughter, Tess, to go to a prosperous family by that name to claim kindred. Being a dutiful girl, Tess leaves her family for the D'Urbervilles, who have recently acquired wealth and bought their way into the gentry class, only to find a blind mother and a dapper son, Alec, who, after making Tess unhappy with his improper remarks to her, tricks the innocent girl into working as a poultry maid and tries to possess her. Aware of this Tess decides to look for work elsewhere, but Alec at last manages to get her alone and have her chastity. She returns home and, without Alec's knowledge, gives birth to a baby in disgrace. Soon the baby dies in infancy.

To escape the infamy Tess goes to work in a dairy farm where she meets Angel Clare, son of a clergyman, who has rejected the ministry and is working on different farms to get some experience in the hope of owning a farm some day. He falls in love with Tess, despite their differences in family background. Tess, however, refuses his proposal because of her shameful past. But her parents urge her to marry someone so that the husband can help the family financially. Tess finally agrees to marry Angel after his repeated proposals. Before the wedding, she writes Angel a note telling everything about her past, but Angel fails to see the note. On their wedding night, after Angel's confession of his past relation with another woman, Tess tells him of her own story. But while she forgives him readily, Angel is too much a hypocrite and snob and thinks too much of his reputation and honour to forgive her. He sends her home and leaves for Brazil. When her mother learns the news of their separation, she, instead of comforting Tess, blames her for losing her husband by confessing something he doesn't need to know. Angel has left Tess some money and some jewels which have been given to him by his godmother. The jewels Tess puts in a bank; the money she spends on her parents. It is soon gone.

Poverty forces her to leave her parents again who still think themselves too high-born to work for a living, and this time she works at the notorious Flintcomb-Ash farm where she meets Alec again, now a practicing preacher. The sight of Tess causes a lapse in his new religious fervour and he begins to pursue her once more. Frightened, Tess writes a letter to Angel, begging him to forgive her and to return to her because she is in danger. But unfortunately it takes a long time for the letter to reach Angel. When she doesn't receive any reply from Angel she becomes desperate. Then comes the news of her father's death and the expulsion of her family from their cottage because her father is a life-holder and his death automatically ends their tenantry on the land. Finally Tess goes to Alec, who is now very kind to her and generous to her family. Before long, Angel, ashamed of his unfair treatment of his wife, returns from abroad to tell Tess that he has forgiven her, but only to find her and Alec together. After accusing Tess of being unfaithful he leaves in anger. Seeing that Alec's relation with her has once again prevented her from her union with Angel, whom she really loves, she stabs Alec while he is asleep. After spending a few happy days with Angel, who has finally forgiven her, she is spotted, arrested, tried, convicted and hanged.

8. George Bernard Shaw (1856-1950)

8.1　Life and Career

George Bernard Shaw

Born in Dublin, George Bernard Shaw went to various schools, including the Dublin English Scientific and Commercial Day School. At the age of 15 he started to work as a junior clerk. In 1876 he went to London, and was away from Ireland for nearly thirty years. In 1884 Shaw joined the Fabian Society, a middle-class socialist group and served on its executive committee from 1885 to 1911.

Shaw's early plays, including *Widowers' Houses* (1892), *Arms and the Man* (1894), and *The Devil's Disciple* (1897), were not well received. In 1895 Shaw became a drama critic for the *Saturday Review*. His articles were later collected into *Our Theatres in the Nineties* (1932). Shaw also wrote music and art criticism.

In 1898 Shaw married the wealthy Charlotte Payne-Townshend. *Caesar and Cleopatra* appeared three years later. They settled in 1906 in the Hertfordshire village of Ayot St. Lawrence. Shaw remained with Charlotte until her death, although he carried on correspondences over the years with Mrs. Patrick Campbell, a widow and actress, and other women.

His "unpleasant plays", ideological attacks on the evils of capitalism and explorations of moral and social problems, were followed with more entertaining but equally principled productions like *Candida* (1897) and *John Bull's Other Island* (1904). *Major Barbara* (1905) depicts an officer of the Salvation Army, who learns from her father, a manufacturer of armaments, that money and power can be better weapons against evil than love. *Pygmalion* (1913) was originally written for Mrs. Patrick Campbell, and became later the basis for two films and a musical. Shaw's popularity declined after his essay "Common Sense about the War" (1914), which was considered unpatriotic. With *Saint Joan* (1924) he was again accepted by the post-war public and recognized as a literary critic.

In 1925 George Bernard Shaw was awarded the Nobel Prize for Literature. He accepted the honor but refused the money. In many of his plays, with the use of the latest economic and sociological theories, Bernard Shaw exposed the sickness of individuals and societies of the modern world, showing his great satirical skill. Shaw wrote over 50 plays and was a leading figure in the revival of drama in late Victorian period and the early 20th century.

8.2　*Mrs. Warren's Profession* (synopsis)

Mrs. Warren's Profession, a play in four acts, was written in 1893 and published in 1898 but not performed until 1902 because of government censorship.

Vivie Warren, a young woman who has obtained "Crofts scholarship" and made "magnificent achievements" at Cambridge, discovers that her mother has attained her present status and affluence by fostering prostitution and that she now has financial interests in several brothels throughout Europe. For years, Sir George Crofts, an aristocratic friend of the family, has been her partner. Vivie also discovers that the clergyman father of Frank, her suitor, was once a client of her mother's. Worst of all, Vivie feels greatly disappointed when her mother even fails to tell her who her father is.

In a conversation with her daughter, Mrs Warren asserts that life in a brothel is preferable to a life of poverty as a factory worker. Although she acknowledges her mother's courage in overcoming her past, Vivie, disgusted with Mrs Warren's profession, leaves her mother, and, rejecting Frank, starts a career of an independent professional woman.

9. Selected Writings

9.1 "Ulysses" ① by Tennyson

<pre>
            It little profits that an idle king,
       By this still hearth, among these barren crags②,
          Matched with and aged wife, I mete and dole
                 Unequal laws③ unto a savage race,
5   That hoard, and sleep, and feed, and know not me.

              I cannot rest from travel: I will drink
            Life to the lees④: all times I have enjoyed
           Greatly, have suffered greatly, both with those
            That loved me, and alone; on shore, and when
10   Through scudding drifts the rainy Hyades⑤
               Vexed the dim sea: I am become a name;
                For always roaming with a hungry heart
              Much have I seen and known; cities of men
              And manners, climates, councils, governments,
15   Myself not least, but honoured of them all⑥;
</pre>

---

① **Ulysses**: See the note to "Ulysses" in "Of Marriage and Single Life" by Francis Bacon. Dante told how, after he returns to Ithaca at the end of the war and to the throne of his island state, Ulysses becomes restless and calls his followers together to go on another voyage of exploration (Inferno XX VI). This poem is a dramatic monologue supposed to be made by Ulysses before they set out.

② **this still hearth**: the quiet family life; **these barren crags**: the island of Ithaca.

③ **unequal laws**: rewards and punishments, which are thought to be measured out "unequally".

④ **drink/Life to the lees**: keep traveling and exploring till the end of his life.

⑤ **Hyades**: a group of stars in the constellation of Taurus, whose rising is often accompanied by rain.

⑥ **honoured of them all**: (I am) honoured by all of them.

     And drunk delight of battle with my peers,
     Far on the ringing plains of windy Troy①.
     I am a part of all that I have met;
     Yet all experience is an arch wherethrough
20   Gleams that untravelled world, whose margin fades
     For ever and for ever when I move.
     How dull it is to pause, to make an end,
     To rust unburnished, not to shine in use!
     As though to breathe were life. Life piled on life
25   Were all too little, and of one to me
     Little remains: but every hour is saved
     From that eternal silence, something more,
     A bringer of new things; and vile it were
     For some three suns② to store and hoard myself,
30   And this grey spirit yearning in desire
     To follow knowledge like a sinking star,
     Beyond the utmost bound of human thought.

     This is my son, mine own Telemachus,
     To whom I leave the sceptre and the isle—
35   Well-loved of me, discerning to fulfil
     This labour, by slow prudence to make mild
     A rugged people, and through soft degrees
     Subdue them to the useful and the good.
     Most blameless is he, centred in the sphere
40   Of common duties, decent not to fail
     In offices of tenderness, and pay
     Meet adoration to my household gods③,
     When I am gone. He works his work, I mine.

     There lies the port; the vessel puffs her sail:
45   There gloom the dark broad seas. My mariners,
    Souls that have toiled, and wrought, and thought with me—
     That ever with a frolic welcome took
     The thunder and the sunshine, and opposed
     Free hearts, free foreheads—you and I are old;
50   Old age hath yet his honour and his toil;

---

 ① **Troy**: the city (site of the Trojan War) which took Ulysses and other Greek princes ten years to capture.
 ② **three suns**: three years.
 ③ **household gods**: gods worshipped at home to protect the family.

                    Death closes all: but something ere the end,

                    Some work of noble note, may yet be done,
                    Not unbecoming① men that strove with Gods.
                    The lights begin to twinkle from the rocks:
55   The long day wanes: the slow moon climbs: the deep
                    Moans round with many voices. Come, my friends,
                    'Tis not too late to seek a newer world.
                    Push off, and sitting well in order smite
                    The sounding furrows; for my purpose holds
60   To sail beyond the sunset, and the baths
                    Of all the western stars②, until I die.
                    It may be that the gulfs will wash us down:
                    It may be we shall touch the Happy Isles③,
                    And see the great Achilles④, whom we knew.
65   Though much is taken, much abides; and though
                    We are not now that strength which in old days
                    Moved earth and heaven; that which we are, we are;
                    One equal temper of heroic hearts,
                    Made weak by time and fate, but strong in will
70   To strive, to seek, to find, and not to yield.

Questions

1. What can we learn from this poem about the author's attitude towards heroes?
2. What is the verse form of this piece of writing?
3. Ulysses is said to represent the Victorian age. What is your understanding of this remark?

9.2 "Break, Break, Break" by Tennyson

                    Break, break, break,
                    On thy cold gray stones, O Sea!
                    And I would that my tongue could utter
                    The thoughts that arise in me.

                    O, well for⑤ the fisherman's boy,
                    That he shouts with his sister at play!

---

① **not unbecoming**: not unfit.
② **the baths/Of all the western stars**: the outer ocean or river which, according to Greek cosmology, surrounded the flat earth in a circle and into which the stars descended (like into "baths").
③ **the Happy Isles**: Elysium, or the Island of the Blessed. Heroes like Achilles were supposed to live there after death.
④ **Achilles**: a hero who died in the Trojan War and became immortal after death.
⑤ **O, well for**: It would be well for ...

O, well for the sailor lad,
That he sings in his boat on the bay!

And the stately ships go on
To their haven under the hill;
But O for① the touch of a vanish'd hand②,
And the sound of a voice that is still!

Break, break, break,
At the foot of thy crags, O Sea!
But the tender grace of a day that is dead
Will never come back to me.

Questions

1. What's the rhyme scheme of the poem?
2. In the poem we can find the following sentences "the fisherman's boy ... shouts with his sister at play", "the sailor lad sings in his boat", "the stately ships go on to their haven". What is the tone of these pictures? And what's the mood of the poet when he sees all these? Is there a sharp contrast between them?

9.3 "My Last Duchess"③ by Robert Browning

Ferrara

That's my last duchess painted on the wall,
Looking as if she were alive. I call
That piece a wonder, now; Fra Pandolf's④ hands
Worked busily a day, and there she stands.
5   Will't please you sit and look at her? I said
"Fra Pandolf" by design, for never read
Strangers like you that pictured countenance,
That depth and passion of its earnest glance,
But to myself they turned (since none puts by
10   The curtain drawn for you, but I)
And seemed as they would ask me, if they durst,
How such a glance came there; so not the first

---

 ① **O for**: How I wish for ...
 ② **a vanish'd hand**: the poet's late friend Hallam's hand, and in the next line **a voice** meaning Hallam's voice.
 ③ The poem takes its sources from the life of Alfonso II, Duke of Ferrara (a city near Venice) of the 16th century Italy, whose young wife died after three years of marriage. Not long after her death, the duke managed to arrange a marriage with the niece of the Count of Tyrol. This dramatic monologue is the duke's speech addressed to the agent who comes to negotiate the marriage.
 ④ **Frà Pandolf**: an imaginary painter.

  Are you to turn and ask thus. Sir, 't was not
Her husband's presence only, called① that spot
15   Of joy into the Duchess' cheek: perhaps
Fra Pandolf chanced to say "Her mantle laps
Over my lady's wrist too much", or "Paint
    Must never hope to reproduce the faint
Half-flush that dies along her throat": such stuff
20   Was courtesy, she thought, and cause enough
For calling up that spot of joy. She had
A heart—how shall I say? —too soon made glad,
    Too easily impressed: she liked whate'er
She looked on, and her looks went everywhere.
25   Sir, 'twas all one②. My favour③ at her breast,
The dropping of the daylight in the West,
The bough of cherries some officious fool
Broke in the orchard for her, the white mule
She rode with round the terrace—all and each
30   Would draw from her alike the approving speech,
Or blush, at least. She thanked men—good! but thanked
Somehow—I know not how—as if she ranked
My gift of a nine-hundred-years-old name④
With anybody's gift. Who'd stoop to blame
35   This sort of trifling? Even had you skill
In speech—(which I have not)—to make your will
Quite clear to such an one, and say, "Just this
Or that in you disgusts me; here you miss,
Or there exceed the mark" —and if she let
40   Herself be lessoned so, nor plainly set
Her wits to yours, forsooth, and made excuse
—E'en then would be some stooping; and I choose
Never to stoop. Oh sir, she smiled, no doubt,
Whene'er I passed her; but who passed without
45   Much the same smile? This grew; I gave commands;
Then all smiles stopped together. There she stands
As if alive. Will 't please you rise? We'll meet

---

 ① **called**: caused.
 ② **'twas all one**: It was all the same.
 ③ **favour**: gift.
 ④ **a nine-hundred-years-old name**: The title of the Duchess of Ferrara I gave her through marriage has a family history of over 900 years.

                    The company below, then. I repeat,
                The Count your master's known munificence
50   Is ample warrant that no just pretence
                Of mine for dowry will be disallowed;
                Though his fair daughter's self, as I avowed
                At starting is my object. Nay, we'll go
                Together down, sir. Notice Neptune①, though,
55   Taming a sea-horse, thought a rarity,
                Which Claus of Innsbruck② cast in bronze for me.

Questions

1. What is your understanding of "my last (duchess)"?
2. What can we learn from this poem about the life of the upper class in Italy at that time?
3. Why does the duke hide the portrait behind the curtain?
4. Comment on the use of favourable and/or unfavorable words used in the poem.
5. Why does he show the servant the statue of Neptune when they are going downstairs?

9.4 "Home Thoughts, from the Sea" by Robert Browning

        Nobly, nobly Cape Saint Vincent③ to the North-west died away;
        Sunset ran, one glorious blood-red, reeking into Cadiz Bay④;
        Bluish 'mid the burning water, full in face Trafalgar⑤ lay;
    In the dimmest North-east distance dawned Gibraltar⑥ grand and grey;
    "Here and here did England help me: how can I help England?"—say,
        Whoso turns as I, this evening, turn to God to praise and pray,
        While Jove's planet rises yonder, silent over Africa.

Questions

1. What's the rhyme scheme of the poem? What does it imply?
2. What's the mood of the poet shown in the poem and how is it reflected?
3. Why does the poet turn to God to praise and pray?

---

① **Neptune**: the Roman god of the sea, whose chariot is often shown pulled by sea-horses.
② **Claus of Innsbruck**: an imaginary sculptor; Innsbruck, renowned for its sculpture that Browning visited in 1838, is the capital of the Count of Tyrol.
③ **Cape Saint Vincent**: promontory on the coast of the Atlantic Ocean in southern Portugal.
④ **Cadiz Bay**: located in the east of Cape Saint Vincent.
⑤ **Trafalgar**: a cape in the west of Gibraltar. British Admiral Horatio Nelson defeated Napoleon's naval force here in 1805.
⑥ **Gibraltar**: a rocking peninsula at the tip of southern Spain and strategically important area between Spain and Morocco.

9.5 "How Do I Love Thee? Let me Count the Ways.[①]" by Elizabeth Browning

How do I love thee? Let me count the ways.
I love thee to the depth and breadth and height
My soul can reach, when feeling out of sight
For the ends of Being and ideal Grace.
I love thee to the level of everyday's
Most quiet need, by sun and candlelight.
I love thee freely, as men strive for Right;
I love thee purely, as they turn from Praise.
I love thee with the passion put to use
In my old griefs, and with my childhood's faith.
I love thee with a love I seemed to lose
With my lost saints—I love thee with the breath,
Smiles, tears, of all my life! —and, if God choose,
I shall but love thee better after death.

Questions

1. To whom is the poem addressed? What kind of love does the author have for the addressee?
2. What can we learn about the author's ideas of men?

9.6 "Biographical Notice of Ellis and Acton Bell" by Charlotte Bronte

It has been thought that all the works published under the names of Currer, Ellis, and Acton Bell were, in reality, the production of one person. This mistake I endeavoured to rectify by a few words of disclaimer prefixed to the third edition of *Jane Eyre*. These, too, it appears, failed to gain general credence, and now, on the occasion of a reprint of *Wuthering Heights*, I am advised distinctly to state how the case really stands.

Indeed, I feel myself that it is time the obscurity attending those two names—Ellis and Acton—was done away. The little mystery, which formerly yielded some harmless pleasure, has lost its interest; circumstances are changed. It becomes, then, my duty to explain briefly the origin and authorship of the books written by Currer, Ellis, and Acton Bell.

About five years ago, my two sisters and myself, after a somewhat prolonged period of separation, found ourselves reunited, and at home. Resident in a remote district[②], where education had made little progress, and where, consequently, there was no inducement to seek social intercourse beyond our own domestic circle, we were wholly dependent on ourselves and each other, on books and study, for the enjoyments and occupations of life. The highest stimulus, as well as the liveliest pleasure we had known from childhood upwards, lay in attempts at literary composition; formerly we used to show each other what we wrote, but of

---

① This is the 43rd sonnet in *Sonnets from the Portuguese*.
② **Resident in a remote district**: Haworth, Yorkshire.

late years this habit of communication and consultation had been discontinued; hence it ensued, that we were mutually ignorant of the progress we might respectively have made.

One day, in the autumn of 1845, I accidentally lighted on a MS. volume of verse in my sister Emily's handwriting. Of course, I was not surprised, knowing that she could and did write verse: I looked it over, and something more than surprise seized me—a deep conviction that these were not common effusions, nor at all like the poetry women generally write. I thought them condensed and terse, vigorous and genuine. To my ear they also had a peculiar music—wild, melancholy, and elevating.

My sister Emily was not a person of demonstrative character, nor one on the recesses of whose mind and feelings even those nearest and dearest to her could, with impunity, intrude unlicensed; it took hours to reconcile her to the discovery I had made, and days to persuade her that such poems merited publication. I knew, however, that a mind like hers could not be without some latent spark of honourable ambition, and refused to be discouraged in my attempts to fan that spark to flame.

Meantime, my younger sister quietly produced some of her own compositions, intimating that, since Emily's had given me pleasure, I might like to look at hers. I could not but be a partial judge, yet I thought that these verses, too, had a sweet, sincere pathos of their own.

We had very early cherished the dream of one day becoming authors. This dream, never relinquished even when distance divided and absorbing tasks occupied us, now suddenly acquired strength and consistency: it took the character of a resolve. We agreed to arrange a small selection of our poems, and, if possible, get them printed. Averse to personal publicity, we veiled our own names under those of Currer, Ellis, and Acton Bell; the ambiguous choice being dictated by a sort of conscientious scruple at assuming Christian names positively masculine, while we did not like to declare ourselves women, because—without at that time suspecting that our mode of writing and thinking was not what is called "feminine"—we had a vague impression that authoresses are liable to be looked on with prejudice; we had noticed how critics sometimes use for their chastisement the weapon of personality, and for their reward, a flattery, which is not true praise.

The bringing out of our little book was hard work. As was to be expected, neither we nor our poems were at all wanted; but for this we had been prepared at the outset; though inexperienced ourselves, we had read the experience of others. The great puzzle lay in the difficulty of getting answers of any kind from the publishers to whom we applied. Being greatly harassed by this obstacle, I ventured to apply to the Messrs. Chambers, of Edinburgh, for a word of advice; they may have forgotten the circumstance, but I have not, for from them I received a brief and business-like, but civil and sensible reply, on which we acted, and at last made a way[①].

The book was printed: it is scarcely known, and all of it that merits to be known are the poems of Ellis Bell. The fixed conviction I held, and hold, of the worth of these poems has not indeed received the confirmation of much favourable criticism; but I must retain it

---

① **made a way**: made some progress.

notwithstanding.

Ill-success failed to crush us; the mere effort to succeed had given a wonderful zest to existence; it must be pursued. We each set to work on a prose tale: Ellis Bell produced "Wuthering Heights", Acton Bell "Agnes Grey", and Currer Bell also wrote a narrative in one volume①. These MSS. were perseveringly obtruded upon various publishers for the space of a year and a half; usually, their fate was an ignominious and abrupt dismissal.

At last *Wuthering Heights* and *Agnes Grey* were accepted on terms somewhat impoverishing to the two authors; Currer Bell's book found acceptance nowhere, nor any acknowledgment of merit, so that something like the chill of despair began to invade her heart. As a forlorn hope, she tried one publishing house more—Messrs. Smith, Elder and Co. Ere long, in a much shorter space than that on which experience had taught her to calculate—there came a letter, which she opened in the dreary expectation of finding two hard, hopeless lines, intimating that Messrs. Smith, Elder and Co. "were not disposed to publish the MS.", and, instead, she took out of the envelope a letter of two pages. She read it trembling. It declined, indeed, to publish that tale, for business reasons, but it discussed its merits and demerits so courteously, so considerately, in a spirit so rational, with a discrimination so enlightened, that this very refusal cheered the author better than a vulgarly expressed acceptance would have done. It was added, that a work in three volumes would meet with careful attention.

I was just then completing "Jane Eyre", at which I had been working while the one-volume tale was plodding its weary round in London: in three weeks I sent it off; friendly and skilful hands took it in. This was in the commencement of September, 1847; it came out before the close of October following, while "Wuthering Heights" and "Agnes Grey", my sisters' works, which had already been in the press for months, still lingered under a different management②.

They appeared at last. Critics failed to do them justice. The immature but very real powers revealed in "Wuthering Heights" were scarcely recognised; its import and nature were misunderstood; the identity of its author was misrepresented; it was said that this was an earlier and ruder attempt of the same pen which had produced *Jane Eyre*. Unjust and grievous error! We laughed at it at first, but I deeply lament it now. Hence, I fear, arose a prejudice against the book. That writer who could attempt to palm off an inferior and immature production under cover of one successful effort, must indeed be unduly eager after the secondary and sordid result of authorship, and pitiably indifferent to its true and honourable meed. If reviewers and the public truly believed this, no wonder that they looked darkly on the cheat.

Yet I must not be understood to make these things subject for reproach or complaint; I dare not do so; respect for my sister's memory forbids me. By her any such querulous manifestation would have been regarded as an unworthy and offensive weakness.

It is my duty, as well as my pleasure, to acknowledge one exception to the general rule of

---

① **a narrative in one volume**: *The Professor* by the author of this passage.
② **a different management**: another publishing house.

criticism. One writer[①], endowed with the keen vision and fine sympathies of genius, has discerned the real nature of "Wuthering Heights", and has, with equal accuracy, noted its beauties and touched on its faults. Too often do reviewers remind us of the mob of Astrologers, Chaldeans, and Soothsayers gathered before the "writing on the wall", and unable to read the characters or make known the interpretation. We have a right to rejoice when a true seer comes at last, some man in whom is an excellent spirit, to whom have been given light, wisdom, and understanding; who can accurately read the "Mene, Mene, Tekel, Upharsin" [②] of an original mind (however unripe, however inefficiently cultured and partially expanded that mind may be); and who can say with confidence, "This is the interpretation thereof."

Yet even the writer to whom I allude shares the mistake about the authorship, and does me the injustice to suppose that there was equivoque in my former rejection of this honour (as an honour I regard it). May I assure him that I would scorn in this and in every other case to deal in equivoque; I believe language to have been given us to make our meaning clear, and not to wrap it in dishonest doubt.

"The Tenant of Wildfell Hall", by Acton Bell, had likewise an unfavourable reception. At this I cannot wonder. The choice of subject was an entire mistake. Nothing less congruous with the writer's nature could be conceived. The motives which dictated this choice were pure, but, I think, slightly morbid. She had, in the course of her life, been called on to contemplate, near at hand, and for a long time, the terrible effects of talents misused and faculties abused[③]: hers was naturally a sensitive, reserved, and dejected nature; what she saw sank very deeply into her mind; it did her harm. She brooded over it till she believed it to be a duty to reproduce every detail (of course with fictitious characters, incidents, and situations), as a warning to others. She hated her work, but would pursue it. When reasoned with on the subject, she regarded such reasonings as a temptation to self-indulgence. She must be honest; she must not varnish, soften, nor conceal. This well-meant resolution brought on her misconstruction, and some abuse, which she bore, as it was her custom to bear whatever was unpleasant, with mild, steady patience. She was a very sincere and practical Christian, but the tinge of religious melancholy communicated a sad shape to her brief, blameless life.

Neither Ellis nor Acton allowed herself for one moment to sink under want of encouragement; energy nerved the one, and endurance upheld the other. They were both prepared to try again; I would fain think that hope and the sense of power were yet strong within them. But a great change approached; affliction came in that shape which to anticipate is dread; to look back on, grief. In the very heat and burden of the day, the labourers failed over their work.

---

① **One writer**: See the *Palladium* for September 1850 (Palladium, i. e. the Greek goddess Athena, is the name of a periodical at that time).

② **"Mene, Mene, Tekel, Upharism"**: the "writing on the wall" which means a puzzle. It is taken from the Old Testament.

③ **talents misused and faculties abused**: a reference to Branwell, the only brother of the Bronte sisters. A talented youth, he participated in their literary creation, but later got addicted to both drugs and alcohol which probably caused his death.

My sister Emily first declined. The details of her illness are deep-branded in my memory, but to dwell on them, either in thought or narrative, is not in my power. Never in all her life had she lingered over any task that lay before her, and she did not linger now. She sank rapidly. She made haste to leave us. Yet, while physically she perished, mentally she grew stronger than we had yet known her. Day by day, when I saw with what a front she met suffering, I looked on her with an anguish of wonder and love. I have seen nothing like it; but, indeed, I have never seen her parallel in anything. Stronger than a man, simpler than a child, her nature stood alone. The awful point was, that while full of ruth for others, on herself she had no pity; the spirit was inexorable to the flesh; from the trembling hand, the unnerved limbs, the faded eyes, the same service was exacted as they had rendered in health. To stand by and witness this, and not dare to remonstrate, was a pain no words can render.

Two cruel months of hope and fear passed painfully by, and the day came at last when the terrors and pains of death were to be undergone by this treasure①, which had grown dearer and dearer to our hearts as it wasted before our eyes. Towards the decline of that day, we had nothing of Emily but her mortal remains as consumption left them. She died December 19, 1848.

We thought this enough: but we were utterly and presumptuously wrong. She was not buried ere Anne fell ill. She had not been committed to the grave a fortnight, before we received distinct intimation that it was necessary to prepare our minds to see the younger sister go after the elder. Accordingly, she followed in the same path with slower step, and with a patience that equalled the other's fortitude. I have said that she was religious, and it was by leaning on those Christian doctrines in which she firmly believed, that she found support through her most painful journey. I witnessed their efficacy in her latest hour and greatest trial, and must bear my testimony to the calm triumph with which they brought her through. She died May 28, 1849.

What more shall I say about them? I cannot and need not say much more. In externals, they were two unobtrusive women; a perfectly secluded life gave them retiring manners and habits. In Emily's nature the extremes of vigour and simplicity seemed to meet. Under an unsophisticated culture, inartificial tastes, and an unpretending outside, lay a secret power and fire that might have informed the brain and kindled the veins of a hero; but she had no worldly wisdom; her powers were unadapted to the practical business of life; she would fail to defend her most manifest rights, to consult her most legitimate advantage. An interpreter ought always to have stood between her and the world. Her will was not very flexible, and it generally opposed her interest. Her temper was magnanimous, but warm and sudden; her spirit altogether unbending.

Anne's character was milder and more subdued; she wanted the power, the fire, the originality of her sister, but was well endowed with quiet virtues of her own. Long-suffering, self-denying, reflective, and intelligent, a constitutional reserve and taciturnity placed and kept her in the shade, and covered her mind, and especially her feelings, with a sort of nun-like

---

① **this treasure**: Emily.

veil, which was rarely lifted. Neither Emily nor Anne was learned; they had no thought of filling their pitchers at the well-spring of other minds; they always wrote from the impulse of nature, the dictates of intuition, and from such stores of observation as their limited experience had enabled them to amass. I may sum up all by saying, that for strangers they were nothing, for superficial observers less than nothing; but for those who had known them all their lives in the intimacy of close relationship, they were genuinely good and truly great.

This notice has been written because I felt it a sacred duty to wipe the dust off their gravestones, and leave their dear names free from soil.

Questions

1. For what purpose did the author write this notice?
2. Why did the Bronte sisters choose the names Currer, Ellis and Acton Bell?
3. What difficulty did they meet with in bringing out their works at first?
4. Does this passage shed any light on *Wuthering Heights* and *The Tenant of Wildfell Hall*?

Vocabulary

notice 评介，短评
endeavour 努力，力图
rectify 纠正
disclaimer 否认
prefix 把……放在前
credence 接受，信任
distinct 清楚的，显著的
obscurity 模糊
attend 伴随
yield 产生，导致
authorship 原创者
prolong 延长，拉长
resident 居住的，常驻的
inducement 诱因，动机
intercourse 交往
stimulus 刺激，鼓舞
upwards 向上地，上升地
literary 文学的
composition 创作
discontinue 停止
ensue 接着而来，结果是
mutually 互助地
respectively 各自
light on 发现
conviction 相信
effusion 诗文
condense 精简，缩短，精炼
terse 简洁的，扼要的

vigorous 强有力的
genuine 真诚，坦率
peculiar 特殊的，奇怪的
melancholy 悲伤的，忧郁的
elevate 举起，提高，提拔
demonstrative 外露的
recess 内心深处
impunity 免罚，不受伤害
intrude 闯入
unlicensed 未经允许的
reconcile 和解，调停，使顺从
merit 应该得到，值得
latent 潜在的
spark 火星，火花
produce 拿出
flame 火焰
intimate 表示，暗示
partial 公正的
pathos 哀婉情调
cherish 抱有（希望）
relinquish 放弃
absorbing 吸引人的
consistency 坚实，坚定
resolve 决心，决定
averse 不情愿的
publicity 公开，抛头露面
veil 遮掩
ambiguous 模糊的

dictate 决定，指令，命令
conscientious 谨慎的，诚心诚意的
scruple （由于道德上的原因）迟疑不安，踌躇，顾虑
assume 采用
positive 确定，明确
masculine 男性的，阳性的
suspect 觉得，怀疑
feminine 女性的
liable 易于……
prejudice 偏见
chastisement 惩罚，鞭打
flattery 奉承，谄媚，恭维
harass 侵袭，使苦恼
obstacle 障碍
venture 冒险，敢于……
civil 有礼貌的
retain 保持，保留，记住
notwithstanding 虽然，尽管
crush 压垮
zest 兴趣
perseveringly 坚持不懈地，倔强地
obtrude 闯入，莽撞
ignominious 可耻的，没面子的
dismissal 打发，拒绝
impoverish 使成赤贫，耗尽力气

forlorn 孤零的，不幸的
calculate on 指望
dreary 无精打采的
expectation 心情，期待
decline 拒绝，终止
demerit 缺点
courteously 有礼貌
rational 理性的
vulgar 粗俗的，一般的
plod 缓步走
commencement 开始
import 意义，含义
grievous 悲伤的，痛心的
lament 悲伤，悲痛
palm off 把……强加于
unduly 过度，不正当地
sordid 污秽的，不洁的
meed 报答，报应，报酬，奖赏
subject 原因，理由
reproach 责备
querulous 不满的，爱发牢骚的
offensive 攻击的，令人不悦的
discern 识别，看出，辨出
mob 暴民
astrologer 占星学家
soothsayer 占卜者，预言家
rejoice 感到高兴
seer 先知
equivoque 暧昧之词

congruous 适当的，一致的，和谐的
conceive 构想出
morbid 病态的，不正常的
deject 使沮丧
brood 沉思，筹划
fictitious 虚构的
varnish 掩饰
reason 劝说
self-indulgence 自我放纵
misconstruction 误解，曲解
abuse 攻击
tinge 色调
melancholy 悲伤，忧郁
fain 乐意，欣然，宁愿
affliction 苦恼，困苦，灾难
anticipate 预期，预料
deep-branded 深深烙上的
grief 悲伤，极度苦恼
front 态度，气概
anguish 痛苦，烦恼
parallel 同等的人
ruth 怜悯，悲哀
inexorable 无情，残酷的
limb 四肢，手足
witness 目击
remonstrate 抗议，忠告
render 给予，致使，表达

terror 恐怖，惊骇
undergo 经历
consumption 肺病
presumptuous 胆大妄为的
intimation 通知
fortitude 坚韧，刚毅
doctrine 教义，教条
efficacy 效果
testimony 证明
triumph 成功，胜利
externals 外表
unobtrusive 不显眼的，谦虚的
secluded 与世隔绝的，隐居的
retiring 腼腆的
manifest 明显的
consult 考虑
legitimate 正当的
interpreter 解说者
flexible 易改变的，易弯曲的
magnanimous 宽宏大量的
unbending 不屈服的
subdued 温顺的
originality 原创性
constitutional 生来的，体质的
taciturnity 沉默寡言
intimacy 亲密，亲近，友好
sacred 神圣的
gravestone 墓碑

Chapter Seven   The Twentieth Century

1. Introduction

1.1 Historical Background

The Victorian Age, which saw rapid industrialization and large scale colonial expansion, came to an end with the death of Queen Victoria in 1901. With one quarter of the world's population and area, the British Empire, where "the sun never set", had become the most powerful country in the world. With the great wealth grabbed from every corner of the earth, London became the financial center of the globe. In the early years of the 20th century, however, America, France and Germany became more and more powerful and joined in the competition for the world market. Among them the newly united German state emerged as the biggest threat to Britain which had the largest number of colonies. As a result and as part of the competition, the First World War broke out in 1914 and many countries became involved in it. With around one million young men killed, Britain suffered heavy losses during the war, and the nation's wealth was drained.

After World War I, Britain began to face new problems: unemployment (even for war veterans), the sharp contrast between the working class and the middle class, and widespread strikes. Social unrest led to four general elections within a five-year period in the 1920s, including one which in 1924 brought the Labour Party to power for the first time. The situation in Britain hardly improved when the New York Stock Market crashed in 1929 and by 1931 Britain was already in the Great Depression. Improvements were made in the middle 1930s. In 1936 Edward VIII (1894-1972) became the monarch after his father George V (1865-1936). When he planned to marry Mrs Wallis Simpson, an American who had been divorced, there appeared a constitutional crisis, and the King abdicated. Edward's brother was put on the throne as George VI (1895-1952). Edward married Mrs Simpson in 1937 and was made Duke of Windsor.

The problems at home exhausted the British who somewhat neglected their involvement in European affairs, which gave rise to Nazism in Germany. Furthermore, Prime Minister Nevile Chamberlain's policy of appeasement made Adolf Hitler become more and more aggressive, which led to the outbreak of the Second World War in 1939. Winston Churchill took over as Prime Minister in 1940 and, after London survived the Blitz, he led the country and won the War in 1945. After World War II, however, the British Empire began to collapse: Most of her former colonies gained independence one after another, first India, followed by Burma, Newfoundland and so on. The Cold War began. The United States and the former Soviet Union became more powerful. It took nearly twenty years for most British people to accept the fact that Britain no longer stood at the center of the world political arena. Social Security was established in post-war Britain. Elizabeth II was crowned in 1952. The 1950s saw a small economic boom in Britain: Unemployment rate was low; more and more people were buying cars and going on holidays. By the 1960s the U. K. was one of the world's leading industrial as well as nuclear powers. In 1973 Britain became a full member of the European Economic Community (now EU). In 1979 the Conservative Party again came to power under Margaret Thatcher, the first woman Prime Minister in Britain. Through privatization, the economy grew rapidly, and she was twice re-elected.

The Victorian Age marked a return to rational philosophy after the great Romantic Movement. Traditional ideas were accepted and conventional values shaped people's thinking and behavior. The late Victorian period also saw the rise of determinism. People thought that their life and future were controlled either by the environment, hereditary traits or by one's own character. Pessimism became widespread as European philosophy was introduced into Britain. Arthur Schopenhauer (1788-1860) started a rebellion against rationalism, the then dominant philosophy in Europe, by stressing the importance of will and intuition in his *The World as Will and Representation* (1819). Friedrich Nietzsche (1844-1900) further sharpened the criticism of rationalism by advocating the doctrines of power and superman and rejecting Christian morality completely.

1.2 Modernism

With the world entering a new century and with the advancement of scientific research, new ideas appeared. Sigmund Freud (1856-1939), the world famous doctor of Vienna, changed the way we look at mental problems. His theory of psychoanalysis has greatly altered our conception of human nature. Karl Marx (1815-1883), a German thinker, who thought that the pursuit of profits was responsible for various social problems, showed us another aspect of human nature. Einstein's (1879-1955) special theory of relativity changed the way people look at space and time. Henri Bergson (1859-1941), a French philosopher who believed in the primacy of creative inner experience, established his irrational philosophy, with emphasis on creation and intuition. His conceptions of life impulse and psychic time greatly influenced the intellectuals in the Western world. The two world wars in the first half of the 20th century, with their massive killing of civilians, confirmed or served as the basis of some of the theories. People realized that human beings were not rational at all. They were controlled by will and passions. Apart from the influence of Nietzsche's ideas, the wars made people believe that the universe had not been, as it was stated in the Old Testament, created by Jehovah; instead, God was created by human beings. More and more people lost their religious beliefs, and many were seized by despair.

Amid all the above-mentioned ideas and disillusionment Modernism was born. As an artistic movement, it covered all the major art forms, such as painting, sculpture, music, and dance. As far as literature is concerned, it appeared with the French symbolism which flourished in the late 19th century. "Modernism" is the name of a major artistic movement that attempted to develop a response to the sense of social breakdown occurring in the aftermath of

World War I. Various trends of Modernism all made their appearances: expressionism, surrealism, futurism, Dadaism, imagism and streams of consciousness. Modernists developed new ways of looking at man's position and function in the universe. In the 1930s the modernist movement somewhat declined, but after the Second World War varieties of Modernism, or Post-modernism, such as existentialist literature, theatre of absurd, new novels and black humor, rose again. This, in part, had something to do with Jean-Paul Sartre (1905-1980), a philosopher, novelist and the principal exponent of Existentialism in France. Sartre emphasized the unique and particular in human experience: Everyone has his own ideas, and the human society is filled with conflict. An individual can not follow his own free will, but frequently encounters restrictions and barriers, which makes him lose his identity and ego. Without any real existence, the individual is lonely in a world that is absurd.

In Britain Modernism is usually associated with writers like T. S. Eliot, James Joyce, Virginia Woolf, among others.

1.3 Literary Characteristics

Although Modernists differ greatly in writing style, subject matter, and so on, they share the following:

Firstly, modernist writing evolves from the irrational philosophy and the idea of psychoanalysis. Modernists tried to show the inner feelings of their characters, with emphasis shifted from the actual world to the human mind, from the outside to the inside, from the objective to the subjective.

Secondly, with no respect for fixed rules, modernists cast away almost all the traditional elements in literature, like story, plot, character, chronological narration, etc. Modernism is marked by a persistent experimentalism. A typical modernist work begins arbitrarily, advances without explanation, and ends without resolution. There are shifts in perspective, voice, and tone. To a great extent, fragments make up modernist writing. Fragments can be drawn from diverse areas of experience, including areas previously deemed inappropriate for literature, such as the life of the street or of the mind. Segments are juxtaposed without cushioning or integrating transitions. Its rhetoric is understated, and ironic.

Thirdly, with many dreamlike scenes and seeming illogicality, a modernist work, in one sense, is the writer's futile attempts to find order in a disorderly world. A piece of modernist writing suggests rather than asserts, making more use of symbols and images than statements. While symbolism draws on objects or actions that represent things beyond themselves, imagism has dependence on the poetic image because it is the essential vehicle of aesthetic communication.

Finally, in modernist work the reader can frequently find numerous allusions to classical mythology, religion, especially Christianity, history and ancient literature. It is a big challenge for readers of modern writing.

Disappointment, despair, and disillusionment became the themes of modernist writings. Modernists tried to show the distorted, alienated and ill relationships between man and nature, man and society, man and man, and man and himself.

In addition to those of the modernists, some other voices were heard in 20th century Britain. The early 20th century saw the appearance of some realists, notably, Arnold Bennett (1867-1931), best known for *The Old Wives' Tale* (1908). Katherine Mansfield (1888-1923), who used interior monologues and who wrote in an impressionistic style, is known for her short stories like "The Daughters of the Late Colonel" (1922). George Orwell (pseudonym of Eric Arthur Blair, 1903-1950) wrote *Animal Farm* (1945) and *Nineteen Eighty-Four* (1949) to show that limitations on individual freedom would probably be imposed by the modern state in the post-WW II era. A dystopian novel, *Nineteen Eighty-Four* is written in the tradition of Aldous Huxley's *Brave New World* (1932). As George Woodcock put it, "In it he (George Orwell) portrays the kind of society he believed could evolve if man allowed politicians to establish and perpetuate totalitarian rule by a systematic distortion of the truth and a continuous rewriting of history."

2. Joseph Conrad (1857-1924)

2.1 Life and Career

Joseph Conrad was born of Polish parents in the Russian-dominated Ukraine in 1857. Because of his father's nationalist activities, the family was exiled to northern Russia, where his mother died when he was seven. After their return to Poland his father also died, and Joseph was passed into the care of his maternal uncle, Thaddeus Bobrowski. At the age of seventeen he went to Marseilles, embarked on a French vessel and began his 20-year career as a sailor. In 1878 Joseph joined the British merchant service and, after years of hard work, he rose to the rank of captain. Also, he gradually picked up the English language. In 1886 he became a British subject. Four years later Conrad took a steamboat up the Congo River in Africa, colonies of European countries at that time. This experience provided him the material for *Heart of Darkness* (1902), his masterwork.

Joseph Conrad

In 1894 Conrad settled in England and began to write in reminiscences about his great voyages. His first novel, *Almayer's Folly* appeared in 1895, the year he married Jessie George. In 1897 he published *The Nigger of the "Narcissus"*, a novel which shows his mastery of both literary technique and the English language. In 1900 he published *Lord Jim*, followed by *Youth and Two Other Stories* (1902), *Typhoon and Other Stories* (1903) and *Nostromo* (1904), an imaginative novel which explores one of Conrad's chief preoccupations— man's vulnerability and corruptibility. In 1907 he published *The Secret Agent* and in 1911 *Under Western Eyes*, two political novels. Conrad's novels and short stories were not well received by critics or readers of his day, and he was constantly plagued with money problems.

Chance (1913) is the first novel that brought him popularity and financial success. By the time of his death in 1924 Conrad was well established as one of the leading Modernists.

Conrad's other major works include: *The Mirror of the Sea* (1906), *Victory* (1915), *The Shadow Line* (1917), *The Arrow of Gold* (1919), *The Rescue* (1920), and *The Rover* (1923).

2.2 *Heart of Darkness* (synopsis)

On board a boat anchored peacefully in the Thames the narrator, Marlow, tells the story of his journey on another river.

Travelling in Africa to join a cargo boat, Marlow grows disgusted by what he sees of the greed of the ivory traders and their brutal exploitation of the natives. At a company station he hears of the remarkable Mr Kurtz who is stationed in the very heart of the ivory country and is the company's most successful agent. Leaving the river, Marlow makes a long and arduous crosscountry trek to join the steamboat which he will command on an ivory collecting journey into the interior, but at the Central Station he finds that his boat has been mysteriously wrecked. He learns that Kurtz has dismissed his assistant and is seriously ill. The other agents, jealous of Kurtz's success and possible promotion, hope that he will not recover and it becomes clear that Marlow's arrival at the Inner Station is being deliberately delayed. With repairs finally completed Marlow sets off on the two-month journey towards Kurtz. The river passage through the heavy motionless forest fills Marlow with a growing sense of dread. The journey is "like travelling back to the earliest beginnings of the world". Ominous drumming is heard and dark forms are glimpsed among the trees. Nearing its destination the boat is attacked by tribesmen and a helmsman is killed. At the Inner Station Marlow is met by a naive young Russian sailor who tells Marlow of Kurtz's brilliance and the semi-divine power he exercises over the natives. A row of severed heads on stakes round the hut give an intimation of the barbaric rites by which Kurtz has achieved his ascendancy. Ritual dancing has been followed with human sacrifice and, without the restraints imposed by his society, Kurtz, an educated and civilized man, has used his knowledge and his gun to reign over this dark kingdom. While Marlow attempts to get Kurtz back down the river Kurtz tries to justify his actions and his motives: he has seen into the very heart of things. But dying, his last words are: "The horror! The horror!" Marlow is left with two packages to deliver, Kurtz's report for the Society for Suppression of Savage Customs, and some letters for his girlfriend. Faced with the girl's grief Marlow tells her simply that Kurtz died with her name on his lips.

3. William Butler Yeats (1865-1939)

The eldest son of an Irish painter, William Butler Yeats spent his childhood in Dublin, in London, and occasionally in his mother's home country Sligo, which is located in the west of Ireland. After attending high school, Yeats entered the School of Art in Dublin, but in 1886 he switched to writing. *The Wanderings of Oisin*, a narrative poem based on the legend of Oisin (a hero in Celtic mythology), came out in 1889, the year when he met and fell in love with

Maud Gonne, an actress and Irish nationalist. His unrequited love for Maud informs such plays as *The Land of Heart's Desire* (1894) and *Deirdre* (1907). *The Countess Cathleen*, a verse play about Countess Kathleen O'Shea who sells her soul to the demons to get food for starving peasants, was published in 1892. In the next year Yeats edited *The Poems of William Blake*, and a dozen years later *The Poems of Spenser*. In 1896 Yeats met Lady Gregory, a writer who helped him to organize the Irish dramatic movement in 1899 and to found the Irish National Theatre at the Abbey Theatre in Dublin in 1904. He haunted her country house, Coole Park, and was deeply impressed by the winding stair inside a Norman tower on her land. *Cathleen Ni Houlihan* was acted with great success in 1902.

William Butler Yeats

Though a nationalist himself, Yeats grew tired of the conflict between Catholicism and Protestantism in Ireland, and "Easter, 1916", a poem written after the Irish rebellion against British rule caused by the delay of implementation of the Home Rule Act (1914), shows his ambivalence. In 1922 the Irish Free State (later the Republic of Ireland) came into being, and Yeats was appointed a senator, and he held the position until 1928. In 1923 Yeats was awarded the Nobel Prize for literature. He died in France and his body was carried back to Ireland and buried at Sligo in 1948.

Yeats' *The Wild Swans at Coole* (1919) and *Michael Robartes and the Dancer* (1921), two collections of poems, are highly acclaimed, and, together with *The Tower* (1928), *The Winding Stair and Other Poems* (1933), and *Last Poems and Plays* (1940), made him one of the most outstanding symbolist poets: The moon, water, winding stairs, spinning tops, etc., are used as symbols in his poetry. In *A Vision* (1925), he developed, based on the automatic writing of his wife Georgie Hyde Lees, the symbolic system. Remembered today mainly as a lyricist, Yeats wrote about the paradoxes of time and eternity, art and life, change and order, cyclical patterns of life. Yeats was interested in esoteric studies, and his writings deal with Irish folklore, which made him one of the central figures in the revival of Irish literature; they also show his fascination with mysticism, which reflects the influence of Blake. Yeats' influence can be found in the writings of W. H. Auden, Seamus Heaney (1939-), and many others.

4. E. M. Forster (1879-1970)

4.1 Life and Career

Edward Morgan Forster was born in London in 1879. His father died in the next year. Generally speaking, Edward enjoyed a happy childhood. But while he was attending Tonbrigde School he was deeply unhappy and developed a lasting dislike of public school values. In 1897

E. M. Forster

he attended King's College, Cambridge and was attracted by the free intellectual discussions of the Apostle to which he was later elected. He was especially interested in the Cambridge philosopher, G. E. Moore's idea of true friendship in a stuffy and hypocritical world. In 1901 he traveled with his mother in Italy and Greece, which provided the material for his early novels that satirize the attitude of English tourists abroad.

Back in England Forster began to write for the new *Independent Review* which published his first short story in 1904. His first novel, *Where Angels Fear to Tread*, appeared the next year.

In the following year he became tutor to an Indian Muslim patriot, Syed Masood and developed an intense affection for him. *The Longest Journey*, a partially autobiographical novel, appeared in 1907, followed by *A Room with a View* (1908). The next novel, *Howard's End* (1910), made Forster an important writer. *The Celestial Omnibus*, a collection of short stories, appeared in 1911. In 1912-1913 he visited India, a British colony at that time, meeting Masood and traveling with him. It led to the writing of his masterpiece *A Passage to India*, which was completed after his second trip to India in 1921-1922 and published in 1924. It was well received by both critics and readers.

After 1924, Forster's writings became varied. In 1927 he gave some lectures at Cambridge, which were later collected in *Aspects of the Novel* (1927). *The Eternal Moment* (1928) is a volume of pre-1914 short stories. *Goldsworthy Lowes Dickinson* (1934) and *Marianne Thornton* (1956) are two biographies. *The Hill of Devi* (1953) is some reminiscences of India. His major writings after 1924 are two large collections of essays, reviews and broadcasts over the BBC: *Abinger Harvest* (1936) and *Two Cheers for Democracy* (1951).

Being a member of the Bloomsbury Group, Forster maintained a good relationship with some famous English intellectuals of his time. He spent his last years in King's College. *Maurice*, which circulated privately after it was first written in the 1920s, is a novel with a homosexual theme. It was published posthumously in 1971, and was followed by *The Life to Come* (1972), a collection of short stories, many with similar themes.

4.2 *A Passage to India* (synopsis)

The novel is divided into three parts: I, Mosque, II, Cave, and III, Temple. Mrs Moore, an elderly British lady, has come to India to visit her son, Ronny Heaslop, the magistrate of Chandrapore, an Indian city. Miss Adela Quested, Ronny's fiancée, has come with her to get married to Ronny. Both women have strong liberal ideas and are eager to meet people of a different culture and to know the "real" India. During a chance meeting at the mosque Mrs Moore meets Aziz, a young Muslim Indian doctor who once studied in Britain, and they have a friendly conversation. Later at a tea party given by Mr Cyril Fielding, an educated Englishman who works in India as the principal of the Government College, Aziz invites the two ladies and Fielding to visit the local Marabar Caves, a prehistorical site some 20 miles from the city. Unfortunately, Fielding misses the train on the scheduled day of visit, and Aziz accompanies the two ladies to visit the caves. Because of the heat and the stuffy, echoing caves Mrs Moore is soon exhausted and stays behind, leaving Adela and Aziz with a guide to continue the visit. Adela and Aziz carry on a conversation of questions and answers and one of her questions offends him. Without showing any anger he gets into one of the many caves and Adela, unaware that she has said the wrong thing, gets into another cave. When Aziz gets out one moment later, she is seen rushing down hill alone. Later Adela accuses Aziz of having insulted her and he is arrested. Soon antagonism arises between the two peoples in Chandrapore and the English try to prove Aziz guilty and punish him to warn other Indians whom they consider are dirty-minded when they are together with white ladies. Fielding is the only Englishman who thinks Aziz innocent. During the trial, Adela recovers from her hysteria and declares in court: "I have made a mistake ... Dr Aziz never followed me into the cave." Aziz is set free. While the Indians are celebrating their "victory", Adela is deserted by all her fellow British men in that city except Fielding who later helps her get back to England. In the third part of the story Aziz, who has turned furiously away from the British, has moved to a post in a native state, and is bringing up his family in peace, writing poetry and so on. His friend Fielding returns to India two years later and when he comes to visit Aziz, the latter prophesies that only when the British are driven out can he and Fielding really be friends.

5. James Joyce (1882-1941)

5.1 Life and Career

Born in Dublin, James Joyce was educated at Jesuit schools, and then at University College, Dublin. Interested in literature, in his teens he began to read Ibsen, Dante, Yeats, and some other writers. After graduation in 1902 Joyce went to Paris, where he discovered the use of "interior monologue." Tired of what he saw as the narrowness and bigotry of Irish Catholicism, Joyce lived from 1904 in voluntary exile from Ireland, although Irish life continued to provide the raw material for his writing. With Nora Barnacle, a chambermaid from Galway (they formally married in 1931), he stayed in Paris, Trieste, Rome, and Zurich (during the First World War), with only occasional brief visits to Ireland. Joyce worked as a journalist and teacher temporarily. Those years were nomadic, poverty-stricken, yet productive. They settled in Paris in 1920 and stayed until December 1940, when

James Joyce

WW II drove them to Switzerland, where he died several weeks later.

His first book, the poetry collection *Chamber Music*, appeared in 1907. The short story collection *Dubliners* was published in 1914, and acclaimed by Ezra Pound, whose support helped Joyce establish a literary career. In 1916 appeared *Portrait of the Artist as a Young Man*, an autobiographical novel. By this time Pound and W. B. Yeats had obtained for Joyce some financial support, but he continued to be in need of money for most of his life. In 1917 Joyce suffered from a severe attack of glaucoma, and had many operations in later years. His only play, *Exiles*, was published in 1918. Joyce's masterpiece—*Ulysses* (1922) was banned on publication. Another major work, *Finnegans Wake* (1939), was the last and most innovative work of the author. These two books revolutionized the form and structure of the novel and changed the course of interior monologue.

Disgusted with the commonplaceness and vulgarity of modern life, James Joyce created a world of depravation, nihility, and debauchery to show his longing for the heroic age of the ancient world in addition to the loneliness of modern men. His characters are shown to live a dreamlike existence which is thought to be typical of the world around the author. During his career Joyce suffered from rejections from publishers, suppression by censors, attacks by critics, and misunderstanding by readers. Noted for his experimental use of language and the use of the stream-of-consciousness technique in such works as *Ulysses* and *Finnegans Wake*, James Joyce has attracted worldwide attention of scholars, critics and readers.

5.2 *Ulysses* (synopsis)

Ulysses parallels the major events in Odysseus' journey home (see Chapter One) and gives an account of several ordinary men's trivial lives and thoughts in Dublin, Ireland, on June 16, 1904, a day chosen, most probably, at random. The main characters are Leopold Bloom, a Jewish advertising canvasser, his wife Molly, an opera singer, and Stephen Dedalus, the hero in *Portrait of the Artist as a Young Man*.

The whole book is divided into eighteen episodes in correspondence with the eighteen hours of the day. The first three episodes are mainly concerned with Stephen Dedalus, who gets up at eight o'clock, teaches a history class at a boy's school, gets his pay, and walks along the strand to town with random thoughts in mind. During the course of the day, Stephen also wanders aimlessly in the town, pondering over his theory on Shakespeare's *Hamlet* at the National Library, drinking at the students' common room of the hospital, visiting a brothel in the "Nighttown" where he gets drunk and is rescued by Bloom. The next fourteen episodes are largely about Leopold Bloom, who prepares breakfast for him and his wife, takes a Turkish bath, calls in the National Library, attends the funeral of a friend, and transacts business at the newspaper office where he sells advertising. After lunch, Bloom wanders about in the city, meeting people in streets, at pubs, in shops, worrying about his unfaithful wife, his money, his daughter, his digestion, ruminating over his past, the death of his father and baby son, but also lending an ear to what is going on around him. Then he roams along a beach at twilight, sitting at a place to watch a girl and daydream. In the evening, he visits a lying-in hospital to inquire about the birth of a friend's baby. Then he comes across Stephen and takes him home for a meal. Stephen leaves in the early hours of the next morning and Bloom goes to bed. While Bloom is wandering in town, his wife Molly meets Blazes Boylan, her concert manager, and has an affair at home. The last episode is the famous monologue by Molly, who is musing in a half-awake state over her personal experiences in the past and at the present.

6. Virginia Woolf (1882-1941)

6.1 Life and Career

Virginia Woolf was born into an intellectual family at Hyde Park Gate, London, in 1882. A sensitive girl who often suffered from nervous stress, she grew up in a talented family. Her father, Laslie Stephen, was a historian, philosopher, and literary critic. She got her education from her tutors, her extensive reading in her father's library and from the frequent contact with her father's eminent, scholarly friends. After her father's death in 1904, Virginia moved with her sisters and brothers to the Bloomsbury district of London. Their home soon became the gathering place of a group of free-minded intellectuals known as the Bloomsbury Group, who would meet to discuss various issues of the day. In 1905 Virginia began to write for the *Times Literary Supplement*. In 1912, she married Leonard

Virginia Woolf

Woolf, a member of Bloomsbury and writer of political and historical books. By that time she was already working on her first novel *The Voyage Out* (1915). In 1917, Woolf and her husband set up the Hogarth Press, which later published the earlier works of T. S. Eliot, E. M. Forster, Katherine Mansfield (1888-1923) and a few other writers who later became well-known. Her second novel, *Night and Day*, was published in 1919. Not satisfied with her first two novels which were cast in the traditional and realistic form, Woolf began to experiment with new techniques in novel writing. Her next novel, *Jacob's Room* (1922), marked a new development in the art of fiction. In this book, she tried exploring her characters' inner lives by presenting their interior monologue instead of describing mainly their external action. Woolf's subsequent major works, *Mrs. Dalloway* (1925), *To the Lighthouse* (1927), and *The Waves* (1931) made her one of the principal exponents of modernism. In these novels, she handled the "stream of consciousness" with a carefully modulated poetic flow and brought into prose fiction something of the rhythms and the imagery of lyric poetry.

Tormented with mental illness and ill health, Woolf carried on her literary creation. In addition to her novels and short stories, she wrote a large number of essays, expressing her literary and feministic ideas. *A Room of One's Own* (1929) is a classic of the feminist movement. *Three Guineas*, which contains discussions of women's problems, was published in 1938.

Shortly after she finished *Between the Acts* (1941), her last novel, Woolf drowned herself in a river near her country house in Sussex.

Woolf's other major writings include: *Orlando* (1928), a fantastic biography; two series of *The Common Reader* (1925 and 1932), which contain her critical essays, *The Years* (1937), a conventional novel, and *A Haunted House* (1943), a volume of short stories.

6.2 *To the Lighthouse* (synopsis)

The story is based on the author's family holidays at St Ives, Cornwall. With minimal action, the novel focuses on the thoughts, moods, and mental impressions of the characters.

The novel is made up of three sections: Ⅰ. The Window, Ⅱ. Time Passes, and Ⅲ. The Lighthouse. In the first section which is set on one evening before WW Ⅰ, the Ramsays, spending the summer with their visiting guests, are discussing a trip to a lighthouse not very far from their summerhouse. James, the youngest son, wants to go to the lighthouse. Mrs. Ramsay, the managing, gracious, and imaginative mother, does not object to the idea; however, Mr. Ramsay, the self-centered, self-pitying father, tries to thwart his son by saying that they will have terrible weather conditions the next day. James is bearing some hatred for his father, but as night falls the weather turns from bad to worth.

The second section is a brief account of what has occurred in the next decade: Mrs. Ramsay has passed away; Andrew, one of the sons, is killed in the war, and Prue, one of the daughters, has also died while giving birth to a baby. The family summerhouse is deserted. But after the war it is occupied again by the living members of the Ramsay family who, at the end of this section, are expecting the arrival of Lily Briscoe, a painter, and Mr. Carmichael, an elderly poet.

In the third section, Mr. Ramsay, now lonely, grants his children's wish by making a trip to the lighthouse together with two of his children, Camilla and James. Meanwhile Lily Briscoe manages to finish the picture which she began on the first visit.

7. D. H. Lawrence (1885-1930)

7.1 Life and Career

David Herbert Lawrence was born in a mining village of Eastwood, Nottinghamshire. His father was a coal-miner with little education. His mother, once a school teacher, tried to raise the cultural level of her sons in order to keep them out of the mines. His ill-suited parents quarreled frequently and David was usually on his mother's side. At 13, he won a scholarship to Nottingham High School, but at 15 was forced to give up his education. After working first as a clerk and then as a teacher for a few years he went to Nottingham University College to study for a teacher's certificate, and in 1908 became a regular teacher at Croydon, which is located in the southern suburb of London. While teaching, Lawrence began writing poems and short stories. He published some poems in the *English Review* in 1909. He also began writing novels around this time and *The White Peacock*, his first novel, was published in 1911, followed by *The Trespasser* (1912). After the death of his mother he became seriously ill and gave up teaching.

In 1912, while visiting his former French teacher, Prof. Weekley, at Nottingham University College, Laurence met Frieda, the professor's wife and mother of three children. They fell in love and ran away to Germany. Living abroad, Lawrence finished an autobiographical novel, *Sons and Lovers* (1913), his masterpiece. After Frieda had been divorced, they got married in 1914.

The war brought them back to Britain, where Frieda's German origins and his anti-war attitude gave them much trouble. His next novel, *The Rainbow*, appeared in 1915, but was declared obscene and banned. He finished *Women in*

D. H. Lawrence

Love (1921) in 1916 but was unable to find a publisher at that time. When the war was over, the Lawrences began to travel endlessly, first to Italy, then to Ceylon, Australia, New Zealand, the South Seas, America, Mexico and back to England, Italy. Lawrence died of tuberculosis in France on March 2, 1930.

Living an unsettled life, Lawrence went on writing. *Aaron's Rod*, a novel which shows the influence of Nietzsche, came out in 1922. *Kangaroo*, written while he was in Australia, appeared in the next year. *The Plumed Serpent*, set in Mexico, was published in 1926. *Lady Chatterley's Lover*, his last novel which caused more furore than any other of his works, was printed, first privately, in Florence by one of his good friends and finally published in unexpurgated editions in the United States and England 30 years later.

Besides his novels, short stories and poems, Lawrence wrote a large number of works of nonfiction: *Twilight in Italy* (1916), *Sea and Sardinia* (1921), *Mornings in Mexico* (1927), *Etruscan Places* (1932), *Movements in European History* (1921), *Psychoanalysis and the Unconscious* (1921), *Fantasia of the Unconscious* (1922), and *Studies in Classic American Literature* (1923).

7.2 *Sons and Lovers* (synopsis)

The story opens with the union of Walter Morel, a coalminer with little education, and Gertrude, a schoolteacher once who is fascinated by Walter and marries beneath her. After marriage, the initial stage of happiness is followed by the class difference which starts to estrange them. Walter works in the dark moist pits all day long. She tries to change him but fails. Walter also proves to be an irresponsible breadwinner, and quarrels arise between husband and wife who always complains. A coalminer is confronted by the danger of collapse every moment. Only alcohol can make them forget the worry and exhaustion. Walter often visits pubs, and getting drunk frequently, returns home bad-tempered. This leads to more quarrelling and sometimes even fighting. They become quieter after having children. Now seeking missing love from her sons, Gertrude gives all her love to the children, especially the eldest son—William, although the husband complains a lot. She is determined to keep her sons out of those mines, and her children love her. Gradually, the father seems to be excluded from family life.

Later, William goes to London to work as a clerk, where he develops pneumonia and dies soon afterwards. The mother can not bring herself out of the sorrow. Not until Paul, the second son, also gets sick does she realize that her duty lies with the living rather than with the dead. Now she shifts all her attention on Paul, who is more sensitive than his brothers and sister and is closer to his mother. Paul likes painting. At 16 he meets the 15-year old Miriam. Although Mrs Morel doesn't care for Miriam, Paul is attracted by her inner charm. When he is over twenty, Paul realizes that Miriam loves him deeply and that he loves her, too. But for some reason he can't bring himself to touch her. Mrs Morel has urged Paul to give up Miriam, but he can't make up his mind because he feels he belongs to her in some way.

Then through Miriam, Paul gets to know Clara and is attracted by the beautiful woman who becomes his mistress. But Clara refuses to leave her husband to join Paul. And Paul is not sure whether he really wants to marry Clara. Her husband, Baxter, has once threatened Paul when he learns about their relationship, but Paul continues to meet Clara. Meanwhile, Paul devotes much of his time and attention to his mother to make her happy. Annie, his younger sister, has got married and gone to live with her husband, and Arthur, his younger brother, has also got married. Paul is the only child in the family who remains single.

Paul has got a job as a clerk with Mr Jordon, a manufacturer of surgical appliances. Later he is made an overseer and he can make enough money to give his mother the things her husband has failed to provide. Meanwhile, he manages to find some time to paint and has won four prizes for his paintings. He wants to go abroad to become an artist but he can't bear to leave his mother behind. One day, it is found that Mrs Morel has cancer and only morphine can lessen her pain. Paul is tortured by his mother's approaching death. In order to relieve her suffering, Paul gives her an overdose of morphine one night and Mrs Morel dies the next day.

For some time Paul seems unable to find any purpose in life after the death of his mother. He can't turn to Clara now because he himself has brought about a reconciliation between her and her husband. Then he goes to Miriam, but after some time he realizes more than ever that Miriam is not the one he really wants to marry. Now there is no one to turn to for love or help. He can't make any decision as to what to do next. The novel ends with Paul's decision, which is made after a long time of aimlessness, to start a new life.

8. T. S. Eliot (1888-1965)

The son of a prosperous businessman and an amateur poetess, Thomas Stearns Eliot was born in St. Louis, Missouri, USA. He first attended Smith Academy in St Louis, and then in 1906 Harvard, where, as an undergraduate and then graduate, he studied philosophy and logic. He was interested in Elizabethan and Jacobean literature, the Italian Renaissance and Indian mystical philosophy of Buddhism. He was also attracted by the French symbolist poetry. In 1910 he went to study at the Sorbonne in Paris and then went to Oxford, England, where he began to work on his doctorate thesis, a study of the Oxford philosopher, F. H.

Bradley (1846-1924). He didn't get a doctor's degree because of the outbreak of World War I. In 1915 he married Vivienne Haigh-Wood, an English writer, and settled down in London, working first as a teacher and then as a bank clerk. Meanwhile he gave lectures, wrote book-reviews and did editorial work: first the assistant editor of *The Egoist* and then the editor of *The Criterion*, which he founded in 1922. His first important poem "The Love Song of J. Alfred Prufrock" (1915), appeared in Chicago's *Poetry* magazine. Two years later, his first book, *Prufrock and Other Observations*, appeared. It was followed by *Poems* (1919), printed by L. and V. Woolf at the Hogarth Press. In 1922, "The Waste Land" appeared in *The Criterion*. In 1927, Eliot was confirmed in the Anglican Church and took British citizenship. Three years later, "Ash Wednesday" was published.

T. S. Eliot

Eliot also wrote some plays, and in 1935, he published *Murder in the Cathedral*, which is written for the Canterbury Festival of that year. The next year saw the publication of *Collected Poems*. Another play, *The Family Reunion*, although not generally considered successful as drama, appeared in 1939. *The Cocktail Party* (1949), *The Confidential Clerk* (1953), and *The Elder Statesman* (1958) created interest as experimental theater.

Eliot's later masterpiece, *Four Quartets*, was published in 1943. Five years later, Eliot was awarded the Nobel Prize for literature, one year after the death of his wife. In 1957, he married his assistant. By the time of his death in 1965, he had become a social and cultural institution.

In the preface of the critical volume *For Lancelot Andrewes* (1928), Eliot described himself as "a royalist in politics, a classicist in literature, and an Anglo-Catholic in religion". He was a scholar in many fields and he tried to include much knowledge in his works, just as James Joyce did. Eliot was regarded by many people as the greatest poet in the west in the 20th century and "The Waste Land" is highly acclaimed because it is filled with literary, religious and historical allusions, images of contemporary life, myth, and legend.

9. Samuel Beckett (1906-1989)

Samuel Beckett was born into a Protestant family near Dublin, and attended Trinity College, Dublin, specializing in French and Italian. In 1928 he went to Paris and taught English at the Ecole Normale Superieure; there he met James Joyce, with whom he formed a lifelong friendship. He published an essay on Joyce's *Finnegans Wake* the next year and a study of Proust in 1931. After returning to Ireland he taught French at Trinity College until 1932, and then he went again to Europe and settled permanently in Paris in 1937. *Murphy*, a full-length novel, came out the next year. During WW II he tried to help the French people fighting against Fascists. After the War, he produced the major prose narrative trilogy—*Molloy* (1951), *Malone Meurt* (1951, Malone Dies), and *L'innommable* (1953, The

Samuel Beckett

Unnameable), which were written first in French. *Watt*, another novel, came out in 1953.

Waiting for Godot, first written in French and published in English in 1954, brought Beckett international fame and made him known as a playwright associated with the theater of the absurd. More plays of the same kind appeared in later years: *Endgame* (1958), *Krapp's Last Tape* (1959), *Happy Days* (1961), *Come and Go* (1967), and *Not I* (1973). Beckett was awarded the Nobel Prize for Literature in 1969.

Influenced by Joyce, Beckett used interior monologue as a major device to convey his sense of isolation and anxiety in the post-war era. In his writings for the theater Beckett also showed influence of burlesque, vaudeville, the music hall, commedia dell'arte, and the silent-film style of such figures as Keaton and Chaplin. Beckett's plays are concerned with the state of human existence, and his characters are struggling with meaninglessness in life. For this reason he is recently regarded a postmodernist.

10. Wystan Hugh Auden (1907-1973)

Wystan Hugh Auden, the son of a doctor, was born in Yorkshire. Educated first at Gresham's School and then at Christ Church, Oxford, he became interested in Anglo-Saxon and Middle English poetry. After Oxford, he became a schoolteacher, and regularly visited Germany, staying with his friend Isherwood (1904-1986), a novelist. His first volume, *Poems* (1930), was accepted for publication by T. S. Eliot and turned out a great success, and it was followed by *The Orators* (1932). Auden also began to write plays in the early 1930s. *The Dance of Death* was produced in 1933, and it was followed by *The Dog beneath the Skin* (1935), which was collaborated with Isherwood.

Wystan Hugh Auden

In 1935 Auden married Erika Mann to help her escape Nazi Germany. While in Spain during the Civil War, he grew tired of the devastation of many of the Roman Catholic churches by the Republicans, whom he supported previously. He published another volume of poems, *Look Stranger !*, the next year, and produced another play *The Ascent of F6*, also in collaboration with Isherwood, followed by *On the Frontier* (1938), another play. *Journey to a War* (1939) records a journey to China. In 1939 he immigrated to the US, where *Another Time* (1940), containing some of his most important poems, appeared. He made a lifelong friend with Chester Kallman, an American writer, and this is reflected in *About the House* (1965). Religiously Auden became a member of the Church of England, and after 1941 his poetry became increasingly Christian in tone, which might have something to do with the death of his devout Anglo-Catholic mother. *The Sea and the Mirror*, a series of dramatic monologues, appeared in 1944. Two years later Auden became a citizen of the United States. *The Age of Anxiety: A Baroque Eclogue*, a long dramatic poem, was published in 1948.

Regarded as a master of verse form, Auden became professor of poetry at Oxford in 1956. His major later collections of poems include: *Nones* (1951), *The Shield of Achilles* (1955), and *Homage to Clio* (1960). Auden died in Vienna in 1973.

11. William Golding (1911-1993)

11.1 Life and Career

Born in Cornwall, England, William Golding was educated at the Marlborough Grammar school, where his father worked as the schoolmaster. In 1930 he was admitted by Brasenose College, Oxford, where he read Natural Sciences for two years before transferring to English Literature. A book of his poems was published, with the help of his Oxford friend Adam Bittleston, by Macmillan & Co. in 1934. Golding became a schoolmaster teaching Philosophy and English in 1939, then just English from 1945 to 1962 at Bishop Wordsworth's School in Wiltshire. Golding married Ann Brookfield, an analytic chemist, in 1939.

William Golding

During the Second World War, he served as a naval officer, taking part in a number of combat operations. After the war, Golding devoted himself to teaching and writing. *Lord of the Flies*, completely out of key with contemporary realism and provincialism, was turned down by twenty-one publishers before it finally appeared in 1954. In 1961 Golding resigned from teaching and devoted himself entirely to writing. Altogether he wrote 12 novels besides *Lord of the Flies*. His other works include *The Inheritors* (1955), *Pincher Martin* (1956), *Free Fall* (1959), *The Spire* (1964), *The Pyramid* (1967), *The Scorpion God* (three short novels, 1971), *Darkness Visible* (1979), *Rites of Passage* (1980), *The Paper Men* (1984), *Close Quarters* (1987), and *Fire Down Below* (1989). He left his last novel, *The Double Tongue*, in draft at his death in 1993 and it was published in 1995.

William Golding won the Booker Prize in 1980, and three years later he was awarded the Nobel Prize for Literature. In 1988 Golding was appointed as a Knight Bachelor. Golding's novels, as the Swedish Academy said, "illuminate the human condition in the world of today" "with the perspicuity of realistic narrative art and the diversity and universality of myth". His fame has been in part due to his inventiveness in realistic fantasy, his richness in biblical symbolism, and his disposition to use the novel form as a fable.

11.2 *Lord of the Flies* (synopsis)

A fictional story set during a period of nuclear war, *Lord of the Flies* is about a group of British boys who experience a plane crash. The only survivors of the crash are several boys under the age of 13. Strangers to each other at first, they band together and a hierarchy of leadership forms as they come to know each other after some time. Two leaders emerge among the boys, Ralph and Jack. In such activities as hunting for food, building shelters, and keeping a fire for a rescue signal, the children soon abandon all the civilized conducts that have been taught them and start killing each other. As time goes on, the two separate the group into two groups, and the two leaders head in separate ways to try and survive the island. Ralph, the protagonist, symbolizes order and civilization; Jack, the antagonist, the savagery and the desire for power. One group seems to live by a more civilized code in which they work together to survive while the other group seems to live like savages. Eventually the boys are rescued, but not all survive the struggle of island life.

The novel helps to show that deep down we are all savages in a sense. It all depends on whether one can control the savage in themselves.

12. Doris Lessing (1919-2013)

12.1 Life and career

Doris Lessing

Now a British novelist, poet, playwright, librettist, biographer and short story writer, Doris Lessing was born in Iran of British parents, known as Persia then. Before settling in England, Lessing lived on a farm in southern Rhodesia (now Zimbabwe) from 1924 to 1949. In 1950 she published *The Grass Is Singing*, her first novel. With colonial settings, it shows the racist contempt of the English for the Africans. Her five-volume sequence of novels (*Martha Quest*, *A Proper Marriage*, *A Ripple from the Storm*, *Landlocked*, and *The Four-Gated City*) with the general title *Children of Violence* (1952-1969) again explores the relationship between blacks and whites in southern Africa. Her novel, *The Golden Notebook* (1962), combines psychological introspection, political analysis, social documentary, and feminism. In *Briefing for a Descent into Hell* (1971) and *The Memoirs of a Survivor* (1974), she explores myth and fantasy. *Canopus in Argus Archives* (1979-1983), a series of novels based on the Bible, the Apocrypha, and the Koran, breaks away from traditional realism. *The Good Terrorist* (1985) is also written in the style of documentary realism, but *The Fifth Child* (1988) combines elements of realism and fantasy. She published in the following decades two volumes of autobiography, *Under My Skin* (1994) and *Waiting in the Shade: 1949-1962* (1997), four short novels that comprise *The Grandmothers* (2004), several other novels, and a series of short stories.

In 2007 Doris Lessing was awarded the Nobel Prize for literature. In her writings, Lessing has consistently explored and tested the boundaries of realist technique without resort to formal experimentalism.

12.2 *The Golden Notebook* (synopsis)

The story opens in London in 1957 with a section entitled "Free Women", in which two friends are having a conversation. The central character of *The Golden Notebook* is Anna Wulf, a novelist who has not published for many years. She lives on the proceeds of her first book, *Frontiers of War*, a story about the racial situation in central Africa during World War Ⅱ. Throughout the period covered by *The Golden Notebook*, Anna's writing efforts are concentrated on four separate notebooks which she keeps hidden in her room. Only Tommy, the son of her friend Molly, ever reads them which read: "I keep four notebooks, a black notebook, which is to do with Anna Wulf the writer; a red notebook, concerned with politics; a yellow notebook, in which I make stories out of my experience; and a blue notebook which tries to be a diary." The four notebooks, making up the greater portion of the novel, are all written in the first person, and they cover the years from 1950 to 1957. In addition, the novel has a fifth notebook, "The Golden Notebook," also written by Anna in 1957 and relating only the events taking place that year. *The Golden Notebook* is regarded as one of the key texts of the Women's movement of the 1960s.

13. Sir V. S. Naipaul (1932-   )

13.1 Life and Career

Sir V. S. Naipaul

Vidiadhar Surajprasad Naipaul was born to a family of Indian descent in Trinidad and educated at Queen's Royal College, Port of Spain, and at University College, Oxford. After settling in England in 1950, he became editor of the *Caribbean Voices* program for the BBC (1954-1956) and fiction reviewer for the *New Statesman* (1957-1961). Naipaul's first three books, *The Mystic Masseur* (1957), *The Suffrage of Elvira* (1958), and *Miguel Street* (short stories, 1959), are comedies of manners. Naipaul married Patricia Ann Hale in 1955. She served as first reader, editor, and critic of his writings until her death in 1996. *A House for Mr. Biswas* (1961), Naipaul's first major novel which is partly based on his father's experience, traces the disintegration of a traditional way of life in Trinidad. He won the Booker Prize in 1971 for *In a Free State* (1971), and received the Nobel Prize for Literature in 2001. He continues to live and write in England. Other novels by Naipaul include *Mr Stone and the Knights Companion* (1963), *The Mimic Men* (1967), *Guerrillas* (1875), *A Bend in the River* (1979), *The Enigma of Arrival* (1987), and *Half a Life* (2001), all exploring the desperate and destructive conditions facing individuals as they struggle with cultures in complicated states of transition and development. Naipaul has also produced essays, which are collected into *Among the Believers: An Islamic Journey* (1981), *A Turn in the South* (1989) and *Beyond Belief: Islamic Excursions among the Converted Peoples* (1998). He was knighted in 1989. V. S. Naipaul is generally considered the leading novelist of the English-speaking Caribbean.

Central themes in Naipaul's works are damaging effects of colonialism upon the people of the Third World. He has been compared to Joseph Conrad because of similar pessimistic portrayal of human nature and the themes of exile and alienation.

13.2　*A House for Mr. Biswas* (synopsis)

Divided into two parts, the novel opens with a prologue and it ends with an Epilogue. It takes the form of fictive biography, beginning with the inauspicious birth of Mr. Biswas in an obscure village, and ending with his death in the city forty-six years later. Biswas begins his career as a sign-writer, is apprenticed to a Hindu priest, runs a grocery store, and finally becomes a journalist. Trapped into marriage, he is almost absorbed by his wife's Indian family, the Tulsis. He continues to seek independence, which is symbolized by the house which he acquires shortly before his death. Inevitably, the novel has been seen as providing a picture of Indian life in the West Indies, with Hanuman House, the Tulsi family residence at Arwacas, becoming representative.

14. Selected Writings

14.1　"Down by the Salley Gardens" [①] by Yeats

Down by the salley gardens
My love and I did meet;
She passed the salley gardens

[①] "This is an attempt to reconstruct an old song from three lines imperfectly remembered by an old peasant woman in the village of Ballysodare, Sligo, who often sings them to herself." (Yeats) **"salley"**: a variant of sallow.

With little snow-white feet.
She bid me take love easy,
As the leaves grow on the tree;
But I, being young and foolish,
With her would not agree.
In a field by the river
My love and I did stand,
And on my leaning shoulder
She laid her snow-white hand.
She bid me take life easy,
As the grass grows on the weirs;
But I was young and foolish,
And now am full of tears

Questions

1. What attitude does the poetic personae take at first towards life and love? What change has he undergone in life's journey?
2. What is the theme of this poem?

14.2 "Leda and the Swan" [①] by Yeats

A sudden blow: the great wings beating still
Above the staggering girl, her thighs caressed
By his dark webs, her nape caught in his bill,
He holds her helpless breast upon his breast.

How can those terrified vague fingers push
The feathered glory from her loosening thighs?
How can anybody, laid in that white rush,
But feel the strange heart beating where it lies?

A shudder in the loins, engenders there
The broken wall, the burning roof and tower
And Agamemnon[②] dead.
Being so caught up,

---

① **Leda and the Swan**: Leda in Greek mythology is the wife of Tyndareus, king of Sparta. Her beauty fascinates Zeus, who, disguised as a swan (so that his wife Hera would not find out about his adultery), goes to her, seizes her by the nape of her neck, and rapes her. Consequently the famous beauty Helen is born, out of an egg.

② **Agamemnon**: king of Mycenae and husband of Clytemnestra, younger sister of Helen. Being the brother of Menelaus (king of Sparta after Tyndareus), he serves as the leader of the Greeks in the Trojan War. After the sack of Troy, Agamemnon acquires Cassandra, the daughter of King Priam of Troy, as his concubine, and takes her home with him to Greece. He finds Clytemnestra has a lover (Aegisthus), and the later two together murder Agamemnon and Cassandra shortly after their arrival.

So mastered by the brute blood of the air,
Did she put on his knowledge with his power
Before the indifferent beak could let her drop?

Questions

1. In what way is the tale of "Leda and the swan" related to the death of Agamemnon?
2. What did the author have in mind when he described the rape and violence in the poem?
3. Which line in the poem describes the scene portrayed in "The Palace of Deiphobus ascends/ In smoky flame, and catches on his friends/Ucalegon burns next: seas are bright/With splendeur, not their own, and shine with Trojan light"?

14.3 "Sailing to Byzantium①" by Yeats

That is no country for old men. The young
In one another's arms, birds in the trees
—Those dying generations—at their song,
The salmon falls, the mackerel-crowded seas,
Fish, flesh, or fowl, commend all summer long
Whatever is begotten, born, and dies.
Caught in that sensual music all neglect
Monuments of unageing intellect.

An aged man is but a paltry thing,
A tattered coat upon a stick, unless
Soul clap its hands and sing, and louder sing
For every tatter in its mortal dress,
Nor is there singing school but studying
Monuments of its own magnificence;
And therefore I have sailed the seas and come
To the holy city of Byzantium.

O sages standing in God's holy fire
As in the gold mosaic of a wall,
Come from the holy fire, perne in a gyre,
And be the singing masters of my soul.
Consume my heart away; sick with desire
And fastened to a dying animal
It knows not what it is; and gather me
Into the artifice of eternity.

---

① **Byzantium**: now Istanbul, Turkey, christened Constantinople after Constantine the Great (280? A. D.-337 A. D.) made it the capital of the Byzantine Empire (Eastern Roman Empire) in 330 A. D.

Once out of nature I shall never take
My bodily form from any natural thing,
But such a form as Grecian goldsmiths make
Of hammered gold and gold enameling
To keep a drowsy Emperor awake①;
Or set upon a golden bough to sing
To lords and ladies of Byzantium
Of what is past, or passing, or to come.

Questions

1. Why have "I" come to Byzantium?
2. What, according to the poem, is transitory? And what is permanent?
3. Modernists try to create order in a chaotic world. Is this poem a modernist one? Why or why not?

14.4 "The Second Coming" by Yeats

Turning and turning in the widening gyre②
The falcon cannot hear the falconer;
Things fall apart; the centre cannot hold;
Mere anarchy is loosed upon the world,
The blood-dimmed tide is loosed, and everywhere
The ceremony of innocence is drowned;
The best lack all conviction, while the worst
Are full of passionate intensity.

Surely some revelation is at hand;
Surely the Second Coming is at hand.
The Second Coming! Hardly are those words out
When a vast image out of *Spiritus Mundi*③
Troubles my sight: somewhere in sands of the desert
A shape with lion body and the head of a man,
A gaze blank and pitiless as the sun,
Is moving its slow thighs, while all about it
Reel shadows of the indignant desert birds.

---

① **Grecian goldsmiths ... a drowsy Emperor awake**: "I have read somewhere ... that in the Emperor's palace at Byzantium was a tree made of gold and silver and artificial birds that sang". (Yeats)

② **gyre**: "The end of an age, which always receives the revelation of the character of the next age, is represented by the coming of one gyre (a spiraling motion in the shape of a cone) to its place of greatest expansion and of the other to that of its greatest contraction". (Yeats)

③ *Spiritus Mundi*: the spirit of the universe. (Latin)

The darkness drops again; but now I know
That twenty centuries of stony sleep
Were vexed to nightmare by a rocking cradle,
And what rough beast, its hour come round at last,
Slouches towards Bethlehem① to be born?

Questions

1. What is described in the last four lines of the first stanza?
2. What does the title mean? What do you know about the first coming?
3. What can we learn about the author's view of social development from this poem?

14.5 "My Wood" by Forster

A few years ago I wrote a book which dealt in part with the difficulties of the English in India②. Feeling that they would have had no difficulties in India themselves, the Americans read the book freely. The more they read it the better it made them feel, and a cheque to the author was the result. I bought a wood with the cheque. It is not a large wood—it contains scarcely any trees, and it is intersected, blast it, by a public foot-path. Still, it is the first property that I have owned, so it is right that other people should participate in my shame, and should ask themselves, in accents that will vary in horror, this very important question: What is the effect of property upon the character? Don't let's touch economics; the effect of private ownership upon the community as a whole is another question—a more important question, perhaps, but another one. Let's keep to psychology. If you own things, what's their effect on you? What's the effect on me of my wood?

In the first place, it makes me feel heavy. Property does have this effect. Property produces men of weight, and it was a man of weight who failed to get into the Kingdom of Heaven. He was not wicked, that unfortunate millionaire in the parable, he was only stout; he stuck out in front, not to mention behind, and as he wedged himself this way and that in the crystalline entrance and bruised his well-fed flanks, he saw beneath him a comparatively slim camel passing through the eye of a needle and being woven into the robe of God③. The Gospels all through couple stoutness and slowness. They point out what is perfectly obvious, yet seldom realized: that if you have a lot of things you cannot move about a lot, that furniture requires dusting, dusters require servants, servants require insurance stamps, and the whole tangle of them makes you think twice before you accept an invitation to dinner or go for a bathe

---

① **Bethlehem**: Located five and half miles from Jerusalem, it is the birthplace of Jesus Christ.
② **a book**: *A Passage to India* (1924); **the difficulties of the English in India**: India was a colony of Britain when the book was written, and there was strife between the British and the Indians.
③ "It is easier for a camel to pass through the eye of a needle than for a rich man to enter the kingdom of God." (Matthew 19: 24)

in the Jordan①. Sometimes the Gospels proceed further and say with Tolstoy② that property is sinful; they approach the difficult ground of asceticism here, where I cannot follow them. But as to the immediate effects of property on people, they just show straightforward logic. It produces men of weight. Men of weight cannot, by definition, move like the lightning from the East unto the West, and the ascent of a fourteen-stone③ bishop into a pulpit is thus the exact antithesis of the coming of the Son of Man. My wood makes me feel heavy.

In the second place, it makes me feel it ought to be larger. The other day I heard a twig snap in it. I was annoyed at first, for I thought that someone was blackberrying, and depreciating the value of the undergrowth. On coming nearer, I saw it was not a man who had trodden on the twig and snapped it, but a bird, and I felt pleased. My bird. The bird was not equally pleased. Ignoring the relation between us, it took flight as soon as it saw the shape of my face, and flew straight over the boundary hedge into a field, the property of Mrs. Henessy, where it sat down with a loud squawk. It had become Mrs. Henessy's bird. Something seemed grossly amiss here, something that would not have occurred had the wood been larger. I could not afford to buy Mrs. Henessy out, I dared not murder her, and limitations of this sort beset me on every side. Ahab④ did not want that vineyard—he only needed it to round off his property, preparatory to plotting a new curve—and all the land around my wood has become necessary to me in order to round off the wood. A boundary protects. But—poor little thing—the boundary ought in its turn to be protected. Noises on the edge of it. Children throw stones. A little more, and then a little more, until we reach the sea. Happy Canute⑤! Happier Alexander⑥! And after all, why should even the world be the limit of possession? A rocket containing a Union Jack, will, it is hoped, be shortly fired at the moon. Mars. Sirius. Beyond which... But these immensities ended by saddening me. I could not suppose that my wood was the destined nucleus of universal dominion—it is so very small and contains no mineral wealth beyond the blackberries. Nor was I comforted when Mrs. Henessy's bird took alarm for the second time and flew clean away from us all, under the belief that it belonged to itself.

In the third place, property makes its owner feel that he ought to do something to it. Yet he isn't sure what. A restlessness comes over him a vague sense that he has a personality to express—the same sense which, without any vagueness, leads the artist to an act of creation. Sometimes I think I will cut down such trees as remain in the wood, at other times I want to fill

---

① **the Jordan**: The Jordan is the river in which John the Baptist christened repentant sinners.

② **Tolstoy**: a Russian prose writer (1828-1910), author of *War and Peace* (1863-1869) and *Anna Karenina* (1873-1877). This is a reference to a short story by Tolstoy entitled "How Much Land Does a Man Need?"

③ **stone**: a British unit of weight which is equal to 14 pounds.

④ **Ahab**: ninth century B.C. pagan king of Israel and husband of Jezebell who, according to the Old testament, was overthrown by Jehu.

⑤ **Canute**: Canute (Cnut) (995-1035), King of England (1016-1035), Denmark (1018-1035), and Norway (1028-1035). He invaded Scotland in about 1027, and conquered Norway in 1028. His reign, at first brutal, was later marked by wisdom and temperance, but his empire broke up after his death. He is the subject of many legends.

⑥ **Alexander**: Known as Alexander the Great (356-323 B.C.), he became King of Macedon in 336 and conquered Asia Minor, Syria, Egypt, Babylonia, India, and Persia in only a dozen years.

up the gaps between them with new trees. Both impulses are pretentious and empty. They are not honest movements towards moneymaking or beauty. They spring from a foolish desire to express myself and from an inability to enjoy what I have got. Creation, property, enjoyment form a sinister trinity in the human mind. Creation and enjoyment are both very, very good, yet they are often unattainable without a material basis, and at such moments property pushes itself in as a substitute, saying, "Accept me instead—I'm good enough for all three." It is not enough. It is, as Shakespeare said of lust, "The expense of spirit in a waste of shame" ①: it is "Before, a joy proposed; behind, a dream." Yet we don't know how to shun it. It is forced on us by our economic system as the alternative to starvation. It is also forced on us by an internal defect in the soul, by the feeling that in property may lie the germs of self-development and of exquisite or heroic deeds. Our life on earth is, and ought to be material and carnal. But we have not yet learned to manage our materialism and carnality properly; they are still entangled with the desire for ownership, where (in the words of Dante②) "Possession is one with loss."

And this brings us to our fourth and final point: the blackberries. Blackberries are not plentiful in this meagre grove, but they are easily seen from the public footpath which traverses it, and all too easily gathered. Foxgloves, too—people will pull up the foxgloves, and ladies of an educational tendency even grub for toadstools to show them on the Monday in class. Other ladies, less educated, roll down the bracken in the arms of their gentlemen friends. There is paper, there are tins. Pray, does my wood belong to me or doesn't it? And, if it does, should I not own it best by allowing no one else to walk there? There is a wood near Lyme Regis③, also cursed by a public footpath, where the owner has not hesitated on this point. He has built high stone walls each side of the path, and has spanned it by bridges, so that the public circulate like termites while he gorges on the blackberries unseen. He really does own his wood, this able chap. Dives in Hell did pretty well, but the gulf dividing him from Lazarus could be traversed by vision, and nothing traverses it here. And perhaps I shall come to this in time. I shall wall in and fence out until I really taste the sweets of property. Enormously stout, endlessly avaricious, pseudocreative, intensely selfish, I shall weave upon my forehead the quadruple crown of possession until those nasty Bolshies④ come and take it off again and thrust me aside into the outer darkness.

Questions

1. What can we learn about the author's attitudes toward wealth and property? Do properties mean impediments to salvation to him?
2. Why does the author cite the sonnet by Shakespeare—"The Expense of Spirit in a Waste of Shame"?

---

① **Th' expense of spirit in a waste of shame**: the first line of a sonnet (129) by William Shakespeare.
② **Dante**: Dante Alighieri (1265-1321), Italian poet and author of *The Divine Comedy*.
③ **Lyme Regis**: a resort city in the county of Dorset on the southwest coast of England.
④ **Bolshies**: members of the left-wing majority group of the Russian Social Democratic Workers' Party that adopted Lenin's theses on party organization in 1903, or members of the Russian Social Democratic Workers' Party that seized power in that country in November 1917, or members of a Marxist-Leninist party or supporters of it.

3. What can we learn about the author's reaction to the revolution in Russia in 1917?

Vocabulary

intersect 横切，横断
blast 毁灭
blast it 该死
weight 负担，重累
parable 寓言，比喻
stout 胖的
wedge 楔入，把……挤进
crystalline 水晶的
bruise 打伤，撞伤
flank 肋（腹）
Gospel 福音书
couple 连接，结合
dusting 打扫
duster 抹布
tangle 混乱状态
asceticism 禁欲主义，苦行
straightforward 坦率，简单
ascent 上升，攀登
bishop 主教
pulpit （教堂的）讲道坛
antithesis 对立面，相反
twig 树枝
snap 突然折断

blackberry 黑莓
depreciate 贬低
undergrowth 矮树丛
tread 踩，踢
hedge 树篱，篱笆
squawk 叫声
amiss 有毛病的，出差错的
beset 困扰
vineyard 葡萄园
Union jack 英国国旗
Sirius 天狼星
immensity 广大，巨大，浩瀚
destined 注定的，预定的
nuclear 核子，原子
dominion 主权，统治权
restlessness 不平静
pretentious 狂妄，自负
sinister 险恶的，不吉祥的
trinity 三位一体，三个一组的（事物）
unattainable 不可到达的
substitute 代用品，替代品

shun 避免，躲开
germ 萌芽
exquisite 优美的，高雅的
carnal 肉体的，肉欲的
entangle 使缠上，纠缠
meagre 瘦的，贫弱的
grove 小树林
traverse 横越
foxglove 洋地黄
tendency 癖好
toadstool 伞菌，毒菌
roll down 把……碾平
bracken 欧洲蕨
tin 罐头
span 横越
termite 白蚁
gorge 狼吞虎咽
Dives 富豪（源出《圣经》）
Lazarus [圣经] 拉撒路
enormously 非常地，巨大地
avaricious 贪财的，贪婪的
quadruple 四倍

14.6 "Araby①" by Joyce

North Richmond Street②, being blind, was a quiet street except at the hour when the Christian Brothers' School set the boys free. An uninhabited house of two storeys stood at the blind end, detached from its neighbours in a square ground. The other houses of the street, conscious of decent lives within them, gazed at one another with brown imperturbable faces.

The former tenant of our house, a priest, had died in the back drawing-room. Air, musty from having been long enclosed, hung in all the rooms, and the waste room behind the kitchen was littered with old useless papers. Among these I found a few paper-covered books, the pages of which were curled and damp: *The Abbot*, by Walter Scott, *The Devout Communnicant*

---

① **Araby**: a term used to express the romantic view of the east that had been popular since Napoleon's triumph over Egypt.

② **North Richmond Street**: In 1894 the Joyces moved to 17 North Richmond Street, Dublin, and earlier Joyce had briefly attended the Christian Brothers' School a few doors away.

and *The Memoirs of Vidocq*①. I liked the last best because its leaves were yellow. The wild garden behind the house contained a central apple-tree and a few straggling bushes under one of which I found the late tenant's rusty bicycle-pump. He had been a very charitable priest; in his will he had left all his money to institutions and the furniture of his house to his sister.

When the short days of winter came dusk fell before we had well eaten our dinners. When we met in the street the houses had grown sombre. The space of sky above us was the colour of ever-changing violet and towards it the lamps of the street lifted their feeble lanterns. The cold air stung us and we played till our bodies glowed. Our shouts echoed in the silent street. The career of our play brought us through the dark muddy lanes behind the houses where we ran the gauntlet of the rough tribes from the cottages, to the back doors of the dark dripping gardens where odours arose from the ashpits, to the dark odorous stables where a coachman smoothed and combed the horse or shook music from the buckled harness. When we returned to the street light from the kitchen windows had filled the areas. If my uncle was seen turning the corner we hid in the shadow until we had seen him safely housed. Or if Mangan②'s sister came out on the doorstep to call her brother in to his tea we watched her from our shadow peer up and down the street. We waited to see whether she would remain or go in and, if she remained, we left our shadow and walked up to Mangan's steps resignedly. She was waiting for us, her figure defined by the light from the half-opened door. Her brother always teased her before he obeyed and I stood by the railings looking at her. Her dress swung as she moved her body and the soft rope of her hair tossed from side to side.

Every morning I lay on the floor in the front parlour watching her door. The blind was pulled down to within an inch of the sash so that I could not be seen. When she came out on the doorstep my heart leaped. I ran to the hall, seized my books and followed her. I kept her brown figure always in my eye and, when we came near the point at which our ways diverged, I quickened my pace and passed her. This happened morning after morning. I had never spoken to her, except for a few casual words, and yet her name was like a summons to all my foolish blood.

Her image accompanied me even in places the most hostile to romance. On Saturday evenings when my aunt went marketing I had to go to carry some of the parcels. We walked through the flaring streets, jostled by drunken men and bargaining women, amid the curses of labourers, the shrill litanies of shop-boys who stood on guard by the barrels of pigs' cheeks, the nasal chanting of street-singers, who sang a come-all-you about O'Donovan Rossa③, or a ballad about the troubles in our native land. These noises converged in a single sensation of life for me: I imagined that I bore my chalice safely through a throng of foes. Her name sprang to

---

① **The Abbot, by Walter Scott, The Devout Communicant, and The Memoirs of Vidocq**: *The Abbot* is a historical novel concerned with that period of the life of Mary Queen of Scots which she spent in imprisonment, her escape, the rally of her supporters and their defeat at a battle, and her withdrawal across the border to England. *The Devout Communicant* is a Catholic religious manual. *The Memoirs of Vidocq* is a book about Francois Eugene Vidocq (1775-1857), a French detective.

② **Mangan**: James Clarence Mangan (1803-1849), an Irish romantic poet who was fond of writing about "Araby".

③ **come-all-you about O'Donovan Rossa**: street ballad, so called from its opening words. This one is about the 19th century Irish nationalist Jeremiah Donovan, popularly known as O'Donovan Rossa.

my lips at moments in strange prayers and praises which I myself did not understand. My eyes were often full of tears (I could not tell why) and at times a flood from my heart seemed to pour itself out into my bosom. I thought little of the future. I did not know whether I would ever speak to her or not or, if I spoke to her, how I could tell her of my confused adoration. But my body was like a harp and her words and gestures were like fingers running upon the wires.

One evening I went into the back drawing-room in which the priest had died. It was a dark rainy evening and there was no sound in the house. Through one of the broken panes I heard the rain impinge upon the earth, the fine incessant needles of water playing in the sodden beds. Some distant lamp or lighted window gleamed below me. I was thankful that I could see so little. All my senses seemed to desire to veil themselves and, feeling that I was about to slip from them, I pressed the palms of my hands together until they trembled, murmuring: "O love! O love!" many times.

At last she spoke to me. When she addressed the first words to me I was so confused that I did not know what to answer. She asked me was I going to Araby. I forgot whether I answered yes or no. It would be a splendid bazaar, she said she would love to go.

"And why can't you?" I asked.

While she spoke she turned a silver bracelet round and round her wrist. She could not go, she said, because there would be a retreat that week in her convent. Her brother and two other boys were fighting for their caps and I was alone at the railings. She held one of the spikes, bowing her head towards me. The light from the lamp opposite our door caught the white curve of her neck, lit up her hair that rested there and, falling, lit up the hand upon the railing. It fell over one side of her dress and caught the white border of a petticoat, just visible as she stood at ease.

"It's well for you," she said.

"If I go," I said, "I will bring you something."

What innumerable follies laid waste my waking and sleeping thoughts after that evening! I wished to annihilate the tedious intervening days. I chafed against the work of school. At night in my bedroom and by day in the classroom her image came between me and the page I strove to read. The syllables of the word Araby were called to me through the silence in which my soul luxuriated and cast an Eastern enchantment over me. I asked for leave to go to the bazaar on Saturday night. My aunt was surprised and hoped it was not some Freemason affair①. I answered few questions in class. I watched my master's face pass from amiability to sternness; he hoped I was not beginning to idle. I could not call my wandering thoughts together. I had hardly any patience with the serious work of life which, now that it stood between me and my desire, seemed to me child's play, ugly monotonous child's play.

On Saturday morning I reminded my uncle that I wished to go to the bazaar in the evening. He was fussing at the hallstand, looking for the hat-brush, and answered me curtly:

---

① **Freemason affair**: international secret service society, also called the Free and Accepted Masons, reputedly anti-Catholic. His aunt shares her church's distrust of the Freemasons.

"Yes, boy, I know."

As he was in the hall I could not go into the front parlour and lie at the window. I left the house in bad humour and walked slowly towards the school. The air was pitilessly raw and already my heart misgave me.

When I came home to dinner my uncle had not yet been home. Still it was early. I sat staring at the clock for some time and, when its ticking began to irritate me, I left the room. I mounted the staircase and gained the upper part of the house. The high cold empty gloomy rooms liberated me and I went from room to room singing. From the front window I saw my companions playing below in the street. Their cries reached me weakened and indistinct and, leaning my forehead against the cool glass, I looked over at the dark house where she lived. I may have stood there for an hour, seeing nothing but the brown-clad figure cast by my imagination, touched discreetly by the lamplight at the curved neck, at the hand upon the railings and at the border below the dress.

When I came downstairs again I found Mrs. Mercer sitting at the fire. She was an old garrulous woman, a pawnbroker's widow, who collected used stamps for some pious purpose. I had to endure the gossip of the tea-table. The meal was prolonged beyond an hour and still my uncle did not come. Mrs. Mercer stood up to go: she was sorry she couldn't wait any longer, but it was after eight o'clock and she did not like to be out late as the night air was bad for her. When she had gone I began to walk up and down the room, clenching my fists. My aunt said:

"I'm afraid you may put off your bazaar for this night of Our Lord."

At nine o'clock I heard my uncle's latchkey in the halldoor. I heard him talking to himself and heard the hallstand rocking when it had received the weight of his overcoat. I could interpret these signs. When he was midway through his dinner I asked him to give me the money to go to the bazaar. He had forgotten.

"The people are in bed and after their first sleep now," he said.

I did not smile. My aunt said to him energetically:

"Can't you give him the money and let him go? You've kept him late enough as it is."

My uncle said he was very sorry he had forgotten. He said he believed in the old saying: "All work and no play makes Jack a dull boy." He asked me where I was going and, when I told him a second time he asked me did I know The Arab's Farewell to his Steed①. When I left the kitchen he was about to recite the opening lines of the piece to my aunt.

I held a florin tightly in my hand as I strode down Buckingham Street towards the station. The sight of the streets thronged with buyers and glaring with gas recalled to me the purpose of my journey. I took my seat in a third-class carriage of a deserted train. After an intolerable delay the train moved out of the station slowly. It crept onward among ruinous house and over the twinkling river. At Westland Row Station a crowd of people pressed to the carriage doors;

---

① **The Arab's Farewell to his Steed**: name of a poem by Caroline Norton about an Arab boy who sells for gold coins the thing that he loves the most in the world, his horse. But as the horse is being led away the boy changes his mind and reclaims it by returning the money to the buyer.

but the porters moved them back, saying that it was a special train for the bazaar. I remained alone in the bare carriage. In a few minutes the train drew up beside an improvised wooden platform. I passed out on to the road and saw by the lighted dial of a clock that it was ten minutes to ten. In front of me was a large building which displayed the magical name.

I could not find any sixpenny entrance and, fearing that the bazaar would be closed, I passed in quickly through a turnstile, handing a shilling to a weary-looking man. I found myself in a big hall girdled at half its height by a gallery. Nearly all the stalls were closed and the greater part of the hall was in darkness. I recognised a silence like that which pervades a church after a service. I walked into the centre of the bazaar timidly. A few people were gathered about the stalls which were still open. Before a curtain, over which the words Cafe Chantant① were written in coloured lamps, two men were counting money on a salver. I listened to the fall of the coins.

Remembering with difficulty why I had come I went over to one of the stalls and examined porcelain vases and flowered tea-sets. At the door of the stall a young lady was talking and laughing with two young gentlemen. I remarked their English accents and listened vaguely to their conversation.

"O, I never said such a thing!"

"O, but you did!"

"O, but I didn't!"

"Didn't she say that?"

"Yes. I heard her."

"O, there's a ... fib!"

Observing me the young lady came over and asked me did I wish to buy anything. The tone of her voice was not encouraging; she seemed to have spoken to me out of a sense of duty. I looked humbly at the great jars that stood like eastern guards at either side of the dark entrance to the stall and murmured:

"No, thank you."

The young lady changed the position of one of the vases and went back to the two young men. They began to talk of the same subject. Once or twice the young lady glanced at me over her shoulder.

I lingered before her stall, though I knew my stay was useless, to make my interest in her wares seem the more real. Then I turned away slowly and walked down the middle of the bazaar. I allowed the two pennies to fall against the sixpence in my pocket. I heard a voice call from one end of the gallery that the light was out. The upper part of the hall was now completely dark.

Gazing up into the darkness I saw myself as a creature driven and derided by vanity; and my eyes burned with anguish and anger.

---

① **Café Chantant**: a coffee house where musical entertainment is provided.

Questions

1. What's the tone of the story? How does the author achieve it?
2. What kind of feeling does the boy have for Mangan's sister? Have you experienced puppy love?
3. What do you think the bazaar represents?
4. How do you understand the title of the story?

Vocabulary

blind a. 一端不通的
n. 窗帘
uninhabited 空着的
detached 隔开的
decent 得体的，体面的
imperturbable 沉着的
tenant 居住者
drawing-room 客厅
musty 发霉的
litter 乱扔
curl 卷曲
damp 潮湿的
straggle 零落分布，蔓延
rusty 生锈的
bicycle pump 打气筒
charitable 大慈大悲的
institution 公共团体
sombre 昏暗的，阴森的
violet 紫罗兰属植物
feeble 微弱的
sting 刺
glow 发红；发热
gauntlet 夹笞刑（run the ~ 受夹道鞭打）
ashpit 火炉的灰坑
buckled 有带扣的

harness 马具，行头
resignedly 顺从地
railing 扶手，栏杆
tease 取笑
sash 框格，窗扉
diverge （路）分岔
summons 召唤，号召
flaring 闪耀的，闪烁的
jostle 推，挤
litany 连祷，应答祈祷
barrel 动物躯体
converge 聚合，收敛
chalice 圣餐杯，高脚杯
throng 一大群，太多
adoration 崇敬，爱慕
harp 竖琴
impinge 侵入
incessant 不停的
sodden 浸湿的
bazaar （东方）市场，集市
retreat 避静，静修
convent 修女团，女修道院
petticoat 衬裙，裙子
lay waste 损毁，蹂躏
annihilate 灭绝，废止
chafe 焦躁，摩擦

luxuriate 沉溺于……中
hallstand 帽架
curt 简略的
raw 湿冷的
misgive 使起疑，使担忧
staircase 楼梯，阶梯
discreet 谨慎的
garrulous 饶舌的，多嘴的
pawnbroker 典当商
pious 虔诚的
clench 握紧
latchkey 闩锁钥匙，弹簧锁钥匙
florin 银币
improvise 临时而作
dial 指针盘，标度盘
turnstile 旋转式的门
girdle 环绕，包围，缚
gallery 看台，货摊
pervade 蔓延，充满
salver 盘子
porcelain 陶瓷
remark 注意到，察觉
fib 小谎，无关紧要的谎话
linger 逗留，徘徊
deride 嘲弄，嘲笑
anguish 极度痛苦

14.7 "Dorothy Wordsworth[①]" by Woolf

Two highly incongruous travellers, Mary Wollstonecraft[②] and Dorothy Wordsworth, followed close upon each other's footsteps. Mary was in Altona[③] on the Elbe in 1795 with her baby; three years later Dorothy came there with her brother and Coleridge. Both kept a record of their travels; both saw the same places, but the eyes with which they saw them were very different. Whatever Mary saw served to start her mind upon some theory, upon the effect of government, upon the state of the people, upon the mystery of her own soul. The beat of the oars on the waves made her ask, "Life, what are you? Where goes this breath? This I so much alive? In what element will it mix, giving and receiving fresh energy?" And sometimes she forgot to look at the sunset and looked instead at the Baron Wolzogen. Dorothy, on the other hand, noted what was before her accurately, literally, and with prosaic precision. "The walk very pleasing between Hamburgh and Altona. A large piece of ground planted with trees, and intersected by gravel walks... The ground on the opposite side of the Elbe appears marshy." Dorothy never railed against "the cloven hoof of despotism[④]". Dorothy never asked "men's questions" about exports and imports; Dorothy never confused her own soul with the sky. This "I so much alive" was ruthlessly subordinated to the trees and the grass. For if she let "I" and its rights and its wrongs and its passions and its suffering get between her and the object, she would be calling the moon "the Queen of the Night"; she would be talking of dawn's "orient beams"; she would be soaring into reveries and rhapsodies and forgetting to find the exact phrase for the ripple of moonlight upon the lake. It was like "herrings in the water"—she could not have said that if she had been thinking about herself. So while Mary dashed her head against wall after wall, and cried out, "Surely something resides in this heart that is not perishable—and life is more than a dream", Dorothy went on methodically at Alfoxden[⑤] noting the approach of spring. "The sloe in blossom, the hawthorn green, the larches in the park changed from black to green, in two or three days." And next day, 14th April 1798, "the evening very stormy, so we stayed indoors. *Mary Wollstonecraft's Life*, &c., came." And the day after they walked in the squire's grounds and noticed that "Nature was very successfully striving to make beautiful what art had deformed—ruins, hermitages, &c., &c." There is no reference to Mary Wollstonecraft; it seems as if her life and all its storms had been swept away in one of those compendious *et ceteras*, and yet the next sentence reads like an

---

① **Dorothy Wordsworth** (1771-1855): sister of William Wordsworth. Following their father's death she was separated from her brothers from 1782 to 1795. Then she lived with Wordsworth, through his marriage until his death. She made many detailed notes of the poetic composition of William Wordsworth.

② **Mary Wollstonecraft** (1759-1797): a feminist and author of *A Vindication of the Rights of Women*. In 1797 she married William Godwin and later gave birth to Mary, who in 1814 eloped with Shelley and later became his wife. (See the life of Percy Bysshe Shelley)

③ **Altona**: a town in Northern Germany, near Hamburg.

④ **the cloven hoof of despotism**: In Christian countries people used to believe that devils had cloven hoof.

⑤ **Alfoxden**: a place where William Wordsworth and Dorothy lived (1797-1798) and where Dorothy began her first journal.

unconscious comment. "Happily we cannot shape the huge hills, or carve out the valleys according to our fancy." No, we cannot reform, we must not rebel; we can only accept and try to understand the message of Nature. And so the notes go on.

 Spring passed; summer came; summer turned to autumn; it was winter, and then again the sloes were in blossom and the hawthorns green and spring had come. But it was spring in the North now, and Dorothy was living alone with her brother in a small cottage at Grasmere in the midst of the hills. Now after the hardships and separations of youth they were together under their own roof; now they could address themselves undisturbed to the absorbing occupation of living in the heart of Nature and trying, day by day, to read her meaning. They had money enough at last to let them live together without the need of earning a penny. No family duties or professional tasks distracted them. Dorothy could ramble all day on the hills and sit up talking to Coleridge all night without being scolded by her aunt for unwomanly behaviour. The hours were theirs from sunrise to sunset, and could be altered to suit the season. If it was fine, there was no need to come in; if it was wet, there was no need to get up. One could go to bed at any hour. One could let the dinner cool if the cuckoo were shouting on the hill and William had not found the exact epithet he wanted. Sunday was a day like any other. Custom, convention, everything was subordinated to the absorbing, exacting, exhausting task of living in the heart of Nature and writing poetry. For exhausting it was. William would make his head ache in the effort to find the right word. He would go on hammering at a poem until Dorothy was afraid to suggest an alteration. A chance phrase of hers would run in his head and make it impossible for him to get back into the proper mood. He would come down to breakfast and sit "with his shirt neck unbuttoned, and his waistcoat open", writing a poem on a Butterfly which some story of hers had suggested, and he would eat nothing, and then he would begin altering the poem and again would be exhausted.

 It is strange how vividly all this is brought before us, considering that the diary is made up of brief notes such as any quiet woman might make of her garden's changes and her brother's moods and the progress of the seasons. It was warm and mild, she notes, after a day of rain. She met a cow in a field. "The cow looked at me, and I looked at the cow, and whenever I stirred the cow gave over eating." She met an old man who walked with two sticks—for days on end she met nothing more out of the way than a cow eating and an old man walking. And her motives for writing are common enough—"because I will not quarrel with myself, and because I shall give William pleasure by it when he comes home again". It is only gradually that the difference between this rough notebook and others discloses itself; only by degrees that the brief notes unfurl in the mind and open a whole landscape before us, that the plain statement proves to be aimed so directly at the object that if we look exactly along the line that it points we shall see precisely what she saw. "The moonlight lay upon the hills like snow." "The air was become still, the lake of a bright slate colour, the hills darkening. The bays shot into the low fading shores. Sheep resting. All things quiet." "There was no one waterfall above another—it was the sound of waters in the air—the voice of the air." Even in such brief notes one feels the suggestive power which is the gift of the poet rather than of the naturalist, the power which, taking only the simplest facts, so orders them that the whole scene comes before us, heightened and composed, the lake in its quiet, the hills in their splendour. Yet she was no descriptive writer in the usual sense. Her first concern was to be truthful—grace and symmetry must be made subordinate to truth. But then truth is sought because to falsify the look of the stir of the breeze on the lake is to tamper with the spirit which inspires appearances. It is that spirit which goads her and urges her and keeps her faculties for ever on the stretch. A sight or a sound would not let her be till she had traced her perception along its course and fixed it in words, though they might be bald, or in an image, though it might be angular. Nature was a stern taskmistress. The exact prosaic detail must be rendered as well as the vast and visionary outline. Even when the distant hills trembled before her in the glory of a dream she must note with literal accuracy "the glittering silver line on the ridge of the backs of the sheep", or remark how "the crows at a little distance from us became white as silver as they flew in the sunshine, and when they went still further, they looked like shapes of water passing over the green fields". Always trained and in use, her powers of observation became in time so expert and so acute that a day's walk stored her mind's eye with a vast assembly of curious objects to be sorted at leisure. How strange the sheep looked mixed with the soldiers at Dumbarton Castle! For some reason the sheep looked their real size, but the soldiers looked like puppets. And then the movements of the sheep were so natural and fearless, and the motion of the dwarf soldiers was so restless and apparently without meaning. It was extremely queer. Or lying in bed she would look up at the ceiling and think how the varnished beams were "as glossy as black rocks on a sunny day cased in ice". Yes, they crossed each other in almost as intricate and fantastic a manner as I have seen the underboughs of a large beech-tree withered by the depth of the shade above... It was like what I should suppose an underground cave or temple to be, with a dripping or moist roof, and the moonlight entering in upon it by some means or other, and yet the colours were more like melted gems. I lay looking up till the light of the fire faded away... I did not sleep much.

Indeed, she scarcely seemed to shut her eyes. They looked and they looked, urged on not only by an indefatigable curiosity but also by reverence, as if some secret of the utmost importance lay hidden beneath the surface. Her pen sometimes stammers with the intensity of the emotion that she controlled, as De Quincey said that her tongue stammered with the conflict between her ardour and her shyness when she spoke. But controlled she was. Emotional and impulsive by nature, her eyes "wild and starting", tormented by feelings which almost mastered her, still she must control, still she must repress, or she would fail in her task—she would cease to see. But if one subdued oneself, and resigned one's private agitations, then, as if in reward, Nature would bestow an exquisite satisfaction. "Rydale① was very beautiful, with spear-shaped streaks of polished steel... It calls home the heart to quietness. I had been very melancholy", she wrote. For did not Coleridge come walking over the hills and tap at the cottage door late at night—did she not carry a letter from Coleridge hidden safe in her bosom?

Thus giving to Nature, thus receiving from Nature, it seemed, as the arduous and ascetic

---

① **Rydale**: name of a place near Grasmere. (See "Life and career" of William Wordsworth)

days went by, that Nature and Dorothy had grown together in perfect sympathy—a sympathy not cold or vegetable or inhuman because at the core of it burnt that other love for "my beloved", her brother, who was indeed its heart and inspiration. William and Nature and Dorothy herself, were they not one being? Did they not compose a trinity, self-contained and self-sufficient and independent whether indoors or out? They sit indoors. It was about ten o'clock and a quiet night. The fire flickers and the watch ticks. I hear nothing but the breathing of my Beloved as he now and then pushes his book forward, and turns over a leaf.

And now it is an April day, and they take the old cloak and lie in John's grove out of doors together.

William heard me breathing, and rustling now and then, but we both lay still and unseen by one another. He thought that it would be sweet thus to lie in the grave, to hear the peaceful sounds of the earth, and just to know that our dear friends were near. The lake was still; there was a boat out.

It was a strange love, profound, almost dumb, as if brother and sister had grown together and shared not the speech but the mood, so that they hardly knew which felt, which spoke, which saw the daffodils or the sleeping city; only Dorothy stored the mood in prose, and later William came and bathed in it and made it into poetry. But one could not act without the other. They must feel, they must think, they must be together. So now, when they had lain out on the hill-side they would rise and go home and make tea, and Dorothy would write to Coleridge, and they would sow the scarlet beans together, and William would work at his "Leech Gatherer", and Dorothy would copy the lines for him. Rapt but controlled, free yet strictly ordered, the homely narrative moves naturally from ecstasy on the hills to baking bread and ironing linen and fetching William his supper in the cottage.

The cottage, though its garden ran up into the fells, was on the highroad. Through her parlour window Dorothy looked out and saw whoever might be passing—a tall beggar woman perhaps with her baby on her back; an old soldier; a coroneted landau with touring ladies peering inquisitively inside. The rich and the great she would let pass—they interested her no more than cathedrals or picture galleries or great cities; but she could never see a beggar at the door without asking him in and questioning him closely. Where had he been? What had he seen? How many children had he? She searched into the lives of the poor as if they held in them the same secret as the hills. A tramp eating cold bacon over the kitchen fire might have been a starry night, so closely she watched him; so clearly she noted how his old coat was patched "with three bell-shaped patches of darker blue behind, where the buttons had been", how his beard of a fortnight's growth was like "grey plush". And then as they rambled on with their tales of seafaring and the press-gang and the Marquis of Granby①, she never failed to capture the one phrase that sounds on in the mind after the story is forgotten, "What, you are stepping westward?" "To be sure there is great promise for virgins in Heaven." "She could trip lightly by the graves of those who died when they were young." The poor had their poetry as the hills had theirs. But it was out of doors, on the road or on the moor, not in the cottage parlour,

---

① **the Marquis of Granby**: an 18th century British general.

that her imagination had freest play. Her happiest moments were passed tramping beside a jibbing horse on a wet Scottish road without certainty of bed or supper. All she knew was that there was some sight ahead, some grove of trees to be noted, some waterfall to be inquired into. On they tramped hour after hour in silence for the most part, though Coleridge, who was of the party, would suddenly begin to debate aloud the true meaning of the words majestic, sublime, and grand. They had to trudge on foot because the horse had thrown the cart over a bank and the harness was only mended with string and pocket-handkerchiefs. They were hungry, too, because Wordsworth had dropped the chicken and the bread into the lake, and they had nothing else for dinner. They were uncertain of the way, and did not know where they would find lodging: all they knew was that there was a waterfall ahead. At last Coleridge could stand it no longer. He had rheumatism in the joints; the Irish jaunting car provided no shelter from the weather; his companions were silent and absorbed. He left them. But William and Dorothy tramped on. They looked like tramps themselves. Dorothy's cheeks were brown as a gipsy's, her clothes were shabby, her gait was rapid and ungainly. But still she was indefatigable; her eye never failed her; she noticed everything. At last they reached the waterfall. And then all Dorothy's powers fell upon it. She searched out its character, she noted its resemblances, she defined its differences, with all the ardour of a discoverer, with all the exactness of a naturalist, with all the rapture of a lover. She possessed it at last—she had laid it up in her mind for ever. It had become one of those "inner visions" which she could call to mind at any time in their distinctness and in their particularity. It would come back to her long years afterwards when she was old and her mind had failed her; it would come back stilled and heightened and mixed with all the happiest memories of her past—with the thought of Racedown① and Alfoxden and Coleridge reading "Christabel②", and her beloved, her brother William. It would bring with it what no human being could give, what no human relation could offer—consolation and quiet. If, then, the passionate cry of Mary Wollstonecraft had reached her ears—"Surely something resides in this heart that is not perishable—and life is more than a dream"—she would have had no doubt whatever as to her answer. She would have said quite simply, "We looked about us, and felt that we were happy".

Questions

1. What do you know about Mary Wollstonecraft? What difference, according to the passage, exists between her and Dorothy Wordsworth?
2. Woolf herself is a feminist. Do you think she wants to express in this essay the idea that a woman should do what she likes, without regard to social convention?
3. What connection can we find in this piece of writing between the poetic creation of William Wordsworth and Dorothy's various help? Do you think Dorothy's journal sheds much light on the poetry of her brother according to this passage?
4. What can we learn about William and Dorothy Wordsworth from the description of their trip

---

① **Racedown**: name of a place in Dorsetshire. (See "Life and career" of William Wordsworth)
② **Christabel**: name of a poem by Coleridge.

to the waterfall?
5. Dorothy is a keen observer. Can you find in the passage any detail that shows she also possesses powerful imagination?

Vocabulary

incongruous 大不相同的
oar 船桨
literally 逐字，照字义
prosaic 如实的，无诗意的
precision 准确
intersect 横切，横断
gravel 沙砾
marshy 多沼泽的
rail 责骂
cloven 分趾的，偶蹄的
hoof 蹄
despotism 专制，暴政
ruthlessly 残酷地，无条件地
subordinate 从属
passion 热情
orient （太阳）上升的
beam 光线，光芒
soar 翱翔
revery 梦幻，空想
rhapsody 狂想，狂想曲
ripple 微波
herring 鲱鱼
reside 居住
perishable 易死的
methodically 有条不紊地
sloe 野李树
blossom 花，开花
hawthorn 山楂
larch 落叶松
squire 乡绅
ground 房子周围的场地，庭园
strive 努力，力求
art 人工，人力
deform 使变形，使丑陋
hermitage 隐士住处
compendious 简略的
et ceteras 等等
carve 雕刻
fancy 设想，幻想
address oneself to 致力于

occupation 天命
distract 分散……的注意力
ramble 闲逛
scold 骂
unwomanly 不守妇道的
alter 改变
cuckoo 杜鹃，布谷鸟
epithet 形容词
custom 习俗，习惯
convention 传统
exhaust 使……筋疲力尽
hammer at 埋头于，致力于
alteration 修改
waistcoat 背心
butterfly 蝴蝶
vivid 惟妙惟肖的
stir 走动，移动
out of the way 不寻常的
motive 目的
disclose 显露
unfurl 展开，打开
landscape 景色
slate 暗蓝灰色，石板色
fade 消失
shore 滨，岸
suggest 暗示
heighten 提高，使显著
compose 创作，做成
symmetry 对称
falsify 歪曲
tamper 损害，削弱
inspire 激励，引起
goad 刺激，驱使
faculty 才能
stretch 伸展
perception 观察，了解，知觉
bald 光秃秃的，无装饰的
image 意象，形象
angular 生硬的，笨拙的

stern 严厉的
taskmistress 女监工
prosaic 平淡无奇的
render 描绘，表达
visionary 幻觉的
outline 外形，轮廓
tremble 颤抖
glory 光荣，荣誉，壮丽
accuracy 准确
glitter 闪烁，闪闪发光
ridge 脊
crow 乌鸦
acute 敏锐
assembly 集合
sort 分类
leisure 闲暇
puppet 木偶
dwarf 矮子
restless 不安的
apparent 明显的
queer 奇怪的
varnish 给……涂清漆
beam 梁柱
glossy 有光泽的
case 放在……里面
intricate 错综复杂的
fantastic 奇异，幻想的
under-bough （在下面的）树枝
beech-tree 山毛榉
wither 枯萎
dripping 滴水的
moist 潮湿的
melted 色彩淡晕的
gem 宝石
scarcely 几乎没有
indefatigable 不知疲倦的
curiosity 好奇心
reverence 尊敬
utmost 极高的，最高程度的
stammer 口吃

intensity 热烈	tick (钟表) 滴答	ramble 漫谈,聊天
ardour 热情,激情	cloak 斗篷	seafaring 航海
impulsive 冲动的	grove 丛林	pressgang 拉兵,强征……入伍
torment 折磨	rustle 发出沙沙声	virgin 童男子
master 控制	profound 深刻的	trip 轻快地走
repress 克制	daffodil 水仙花	moor 荒地
cease 停止	prose 散文	play 才智等的运用,作用
subdue 征服,压抑	scarlet 红色的	jib 裹足不前
resign 舍弃	bean 菜豆	debate 辩论
agitation 兴奋	leech 水蛭	majestic 庄严的
bestow 给予	rapt 狂喜的	sublime 崇高
exquisite 绝妙的	ecstasy 狂喜	grand 雄伟
spear 幼芽	iron 熨	trudge 跋涉,蹒跚地走
streak 线条	linen 亚麻布做的衣服	harness 马具
polish 擦亮	fell 荒野,沼泽	string 绳子
melancholy 忧郁的	highroad 大路	lodging 寄宿
tap 敲	parlour 起居室	rheumatism 风湿症
bosom 内心,胸怀	coronet 小冠冕	joint 关节
arduous 辛勤的	landau 四轮马车	jaunt 作短途旅行
ascetic 苦修的	peer 透过……看	gipsy 吉普赛人
sympathy 同情,共鸣	inquisitively 好奇	gait 步伐
vegetable 呆板的	cathedral 大教堂	ungainly 笨拙的,难看的
inhuman 无人情味的	gallery 画廊,艺术馆	resemblance 外观,风貌
core 核心	tramp 流浪者	rapture 兴高采烈
inspiration 鼓舞	bacon 咸肉	distinctness 明显特征
compose 组成	starry 星光灿烂的	particularity 独特之处
trinity 三位一体	patch 补丁	consolation 抚慰
self-contained 自给自足的	beard 胡子	passionate 充满激情的
self-sufficient 自给自足的	fortnight 两星期	reside 居住
flicker 摇曳	plush 毛绒布,长毛绒	

14.8 "The Mark on the Wall" by Woolf

Perhaps it was the middle of January in the present that I first looked up and saw the mark on the wall. In order to fix a date it is necessary to remember what one saw. So now I think of the fire; the steady film of yellow light upon the page of my book; the three chrysanthemums in the round glass bowl on the mantelpiece. Yes, it must have been the winter time, and we had just finished our tea, for I remember that I was smoking a cigarette when I looked up and saw the mark on the wall for the first time. I looked up through the smoke of my cigarette and my eye lodged for a moment upon the burning coals, and that old fancy of the crimson flag flapping from the castle tower came into my mind, and I thought of the cavalcade of red knights riding up the side of the black rock. Rather to my relief the sight of the mark interrupted the fancy, for it is an old fancy, an automatic fancy, made as a child perhaps. The mark was a small round mark, black upon the white wall, about six or seven inches above the mantelpiece.

How readily our thoughts swarm upon a new object, lifting it a little way, as ants carry a blade of straw so feverishly, and then leave it... If that mark was made by a nail, it can't have been for a picture, it must have been for a miniature—the miniature of a lady with white powdered curls, powder-dusted cheeks, and lips like red carnations. A fraud of course, for the people who had this house before us would have chosen pictures in that way—an old picture for an old room. That is the sort of people they were—very interesting people, and I think of them so often, in such queer places, because one will never see them again, never know what happened next. They wanted to leave this house because they wanted to change their style of furniture, so he said, and he was in process of saying that in his opinion art should have ideas behind it when we were torn asunder, as one is torn from the old lady about to pour out tea and the young man about to hit the tennis ball in the back garden of the suburban villa as one rushes past in the train.

But as for that mark, I'm not sure about it; I don't believe it was made by a nail after all; it's too big, too round, for that. I might get up, but if I got up and looked at it, ten to one I shouldn't be able to say for certain; because once a thing's done, no one ever knows how it happened. Oh! Dear me, the mystery of life; The inaccuracy of thought! The ignorance of humanity! To show how very little control of our possessions we have—what an accidental affair this living is after all our civilization—let me just count over a few of the things lost in one lifetime, beginning, for that seems always the most mysterious of losses—what cat would gnaw, what rat would nibble—three pale blue canisters of book-binding tools? Then there were the bird cages, the iron hoops, the steel skates, the Queen Anne coal-scuttle, the bagatelle board, the hand organ—all gone, and jewels, too. Opals and emeralds, they lie about the roots of turnips. What a scraping paring affair it is to be sure! The wonder is that I've any clothes on my back, that I sit surrounded by solid furniture at this moment. Why, if one wants to compare life to anything, one must liken it to being blown through the Tube① at fifty miles an hour—landing at the other end without a single hairpin in one's hair! Shot out at the feet of God entirely naked! Tumbling head over heels in the asphodel meadows② like brown paper parcels pitched down a shoot in the post office! With one's hair flying back like the tail of a race-horse. Yes, that seems to express the rapidity of life, the perpetual waste and repair; all so casual, all so haphazard...

But after life. The slow pulling down of thick green stalks so that the cup of the flower, as it turns over, deluges one with purple and red light. Why, after all, should one not be born there as one is born here, helpless, speechless, unable to focus one's eyesight, groping at the roots of the grass, at the toes of the Giants? As for saying which are trees, and which are men and women, or whether there are such things, that one won't be in a condition to do for fifty years or so. There will be nothing but spaces of light and dark, intersected by thick stalks, and rather higher up perhaps, rose-shaped blots of an indistinct colour—dim pinks and blues—which will, as time goes on, become more definite, become—I don't know what...

And yet that mark on the wall is not a hole at all. It may even be caused by some round

---

① **Tube**: the metro in London.
② **asphodel meadows**: heaven (In ancient mythology asphodel flowers grew in the Elysian fields).

black substance, such as a small rose leaf, left over from the summer, and I, not being a very vigilant housekeeper—look at the dust on the mantelpiece, for example, the dust which, so they say, buried Troy three times over, only fragments of pots utterly refusing annihilation, as one can believe.

The tree outside the window taps very gently on the pane... I want to think quietly, calmly, spaciously, never to be interrupted, never to have to rise from my chair, to slip easily from one thing to another, without any sense of hostility, or obstacle. I want to sink deeper and deeper, away from the surface, with its hard separate facts. To steady myself, let me catch hold of the first idea that passes... Shakespeare... Well, he will do as well as another. A man who sat himself solidly in an arm-chair, and looked into the fire, so—A shower of ideas fell perpetually from some very high Heaven down through his mind. He leant his forehead on his hand, and people, looking in through the open door,—for this scene is supposed to take place on a summer's evening—But how dull this is, this historical fiction! It doesn't interest me at all. I wish I could hit upon a pleasant track of thought, a track indirectly reflecting credit upon myself, for those are the pleasantest thoughts, and very frequent even in the minds of modest mouse-coloured people, who believe genuinely that they dislike to hear their own praises. They are not thoughts directly praising oneself; that is the beauty of them; they are thoughts like this:

"And then I came into the room. They were discussing botany. I said how I'd seen a flower growing on a dust heap on the site of an old house in Kingsway①. The seed, I said, must have been sown in the reign of Charles the First②. What flowers grew in the reign of Charles the First?" I asked—(but, I don't remember the answer). Tall flowers with purple tassels to them perhaps. And so it goes on. All the time I'm dressing up the figure of myself in my own mind, lovingly, stealthily, not openly adoring it, for if I did that, I should catch myself out, and stretch my hand at once for a book in self-protection. Indeed, it is curious how instinctively one protects the image of oneself from idolatry or any other handling that could make it ridiculous, or too unlike the original to be believed in any longer. Or is it not so very curious after all? It is a matter of great importance. Suppose the looking glass smashes, the image disappears, and the romantic figure with the green of forest depths all about it is there no longer, but only that shell of a person which is seen by other people—what an airless, shallow, bald, prominent world it becomes! A world not to be lived in. As we face each other in omnibuses and underground railways we are looking into the mirror that accounts for the vagueness, the gleam of glassiness, in our eyes. And the novelists in future will realize more and more the importance of these reflections, for of course there is not one reflection but an almost infinite number; those are the depths they will explore, those the phantoms they will pursue, leaving the description of reality more and more out of their stories, taking a knowledge of it for granted, as the Greeks did and Shakespeare perhaps—but these

---

① **Kingsway**: name of a street in London.
② **Charles the First**: Charles I (1600-1649), King of Great Britain from 1625, whose conflict with the Parliament led to the outbreak of English Civil War (1642-1652). He was beheaded in 1649.

generalizations are very worthless. The military sound of the word is enough. It recalls leading articles, cabinet ministers—a whole class of things indeed which as a child one thought the thing itself, the standard thing, the real thing, from which one could not depart save at the risk of nameless damnation. Generalizations bring back somehow Sunday in London, Sunday afternoon walks, Sunday luncheons, and also ways of speaking of the dead, clothes, and habits—like the habit of sitting all together in one room until a certain hour, although nobody liked it. There was a rule for everything. The rule for tablecloths at that particular period was that they should be made of tapestry with little yellow compartments marked upon them, such as you may see in photographs of the carpets in the corridors of the royal palaces. Tablecloths of a different kind were not real tablecloths. How shocking, and yet how wonderful it was to discover that these real things, Sunday luncheons, Sunday walks, country houses, and tablecloths were not entirely real, were indeed half phantoms, and the damnation which visited the disbeliever in them was only a sense of illegitimate freedom. What now takes the place of those things I wonder, those real standard things? Men perhaps, should you be a woman; the masculine point of view which governs our lives, which sets the standard, which establishes Whitaker's Table of Precedency①, which has become, I suppose, since the war half a phantom to many men and women, which soon—one may hope, will be laughed into the dustbin where the phantoms go, the mahogany sideboards and the Landseer② prints, Gods and Devils, Hell and so forth, leaving us all with an intoxicating sense of illegitimate freedom—if freedom exists...

    In certain lights that mark on the wall seems actually to project from the wall. Nor is it entirely circular. I cannot be sure, but it seems to cast a perceptible shadow, suggesting that if I ran my finger down that strip of the wall it would, at a certain point, mount and descend a small tumulus, a smooth tumulus like those barrows on the South Downs③ which are, they say, either tombs or camps. Of the two I should prefer them to be tombs, desiring melancholy like most English people, and finding it natural at the end of a walk to think of the bones stretched beneath the turf... There must be some book about it. Some antiquary must have dug up those bones and given them a name.... What sort of a man is an antiquary, I wonder? Retired Colonels for the most part, I daresay, leading parties of aged labourers to the top here, examining clods of earth and stone, and getting into correspondence with the neighbouring clergy, which, being opened at breakfast time, gives them a feeling of importance, and the comparison of arrow-heads necessitates cross-country journeys to the county towns, an agreeable necessity both to them and to their elderly wives, who wish to make plum jam or to clean out the study, and have every reason for keeping that great question of the camp or the tomb in perpetual suspension, while the Colonel himself feels agreeably philosophic in

---

    ① **Whitaker's Table of Precedency**: Whitaker's Almanack, an annual compendium of information, prints a "Table of Precedency" which shows the order in which the various ranks in public life and society proceed on formal occasions.

    ② **Landseer**: Edwin Henry Landseer, 19th century animal painter, reproductions of whose "Stag at Bay", "Monarch of the Glen", and similar paintings were often found in Victorian homes.

    ③ **the South Downs**: also known as the Downs, a range of low hills in southeastern England.

accumulating evidence on both sides of the question. It is true that he does finally incline to believe in the camp; and, being opposed, indites a pamphlet which he is about to read at the quarterly meeting of the local society when a stroke lays him low, and his last conscious thoughts are not of wife or child, but of the camp and that arrowhead there, which is now in the case at the local museum, together with the foot of a Chinese murderess, a handful of Elizabethan nails, a great many Tudor clay pipes, a piece of Roman pottery, and the wine-glass that Nelson drank out of—proving I really don't know what.

No, no, nothing is proved, nothing is known. And if I were to get up at this very moment and ascertain that the mark on the wall is really—what shall we say?—the head of a gigantic old nail, driven in two hundred years ago, which has now, owing to the patient attrition of many generations of housemaids, revealed its head above the coat of paint, and is taking its first view of modern life in the sight of a white-walled fire-lit room, what should I gain?— Knowledge? Matter for further speculation? I can think sitting still as well as standing up. And what is knowledge? What are our learned men save the descendants of witches and hermits who crouched in caves and in woods brewing herbs, interrogating shrew-mice and writing down the language of the stars? And the less we honour them as our superstitions dwindle and our respect for beauty and health of mind increases... Yes, one could imagine a very pleasant world. A quiet, spacious world, with the flowers so red and blue in the open fields. A world without professors or specialists or house-keepers with the profiles of policemen, a world which one could slice with one's thought as a fish slices the water with his fin, grazing the stems of the water-lilies, hanging suspended over nests of white sea eggs... How peaceful it is drown here, rooted in the centre of the world and gazing up through the grey waters, with their sudden gleams of light, and their reflections—if it were not for Whitaker's Almanack—if it were not for the Table of Precedency!

I must jump up and see for myself what that mark on the wall really is—a nail, a rose-leaf, a crack in the wood?

Here is nature once more at her old game of self-preservation. This train of thought, she perceives, is threatening mere waste of energy, even some collision with reality, for who will ever be able to lift a finger against Whitaker's Table of Precedency? The Archbishop of Canterbury is followed by the Lord High Chancellor; the Lord High Chancellor is followed by the Archbishop of York. Everybody follows somebody, such is the philosophy of Whitaker; and the great thing is to know who follows whom. Whitaker knows, and let that, so Nature counsels, comfort you, instead of enraging you; and if you can't be comforted, if you must shatter this hour of peace, think of the mark on the wall.

I understand Nature's game—her prompting to take action as a way of ending any thought that threatens to excite or to pain. Hence, I suppose, comes our slight contempt for men of action—men, we assume, who don't think. Still, there's no harm in putting a full stop to one's disagreeable thoughts by looking at a mark on the wall.

Indeed, now that I have fixed my eyes upon it, I feel that I have grasped a plank in the sea; I feel a satisfying sense of reality which at once turns the two Archbishops and the Lord High Chancellor to the shadows of shades. Here is something definite, something real. Thus, waking from a midnight dream of horror, one hastily turns on the light and lies quiescent, worshipping the chest of drawers, worshipping solidity, worshipping reality, worshipping the impersonal world which is a proof of some existence other than ours. That is what one wants to be sure of... Wood is a pleasant thing to think about. It comes from a tree; and trees grow, and we don't know how they grow. For years and years they grow, without paying any attention to us, in meadows, in forests, and by the side of rivers—all things one likes to think about. The cows swish their tails beneath them on hot afternoons; they paint rivers so green that when a moorhen dives one expects to see its feathers all green when it comes up again. I like to think of the fish balanced against the stream like flags blown out; and of water-beetles slowly raiding domes of mud upon the bed of the river. I like to think of the tree itself:—first the close dry sensation of being wood; then the grinding of the storm; then the slow, delicious ooze of sap. I like to think of it, too, on winter's nights standing in the empty field with all leaves close-furled, nothing tender exposed to the iron bullets of the moon, a naked mast upon an earth that goes tumbling, tumbling, all night long. The song of birds must sound very loud and strange in June; and how cold the feet of insects must feel upon it, as they make laborious progresses up the creases of the bark, or sun themselves upon the thin green awning of the leaves, and look straight in front of them with diamond-cut red eyes... One by one the fibres snap beneath the immense cold pressure of the earth, then the last storm comes and, falling, the highest branches drive deep into the ground again. Even so, life isn't done with; there are a million patient, watchful lives still for a tree, all over the world, in bedrooms, in ships, on the pavement, living rooms, where men and women sit after tea, smoking cigarettes. It is full of peaceful thoughts, happy thoughts, this tree. I should like to take each one separately—but something is getting in the way... Where was I? What has it all been about? A tree? A river? The Downs①? Whitaker's Almanack? The fields of asphodel? I can't remember a thing. Everything's moving, falling, slipping, vanishing... There is a vast upheaval of matter. Someone is standing over me and saying—

"I'm going out to buy a newspaper."

"Yes?"

"Though it's no good buying newspapers... Nothing ever happens. Curse this war; God damn this war! ... All the same, I don't see why we should have a snail on our wall."

Ah, the mark on the wall! It was a snail.

Questions

1. Do you think this piece of writing an essay or a short story? Explain. In what way or ways is it different from traditional or conventional ones?
2. What are the characteristics of the technique of stream of consciousness?
3. What does the author say about modern life and modern man in this passage?
4. In paragraph 7 the author mentions novel-writing "in future". Has her prediction become a reality?

---

① **the Downs**: part of the sea off the east coast of Kent.

5. What feminist ideas can we find in the passage?

Vocabulary

film 薄层，薄膜
chrysanthemum 菊（花）
mantelpiece 壁炉台
lodge 固定，停留
crimson 深红色
flap 飘动，拍动
cavalcade 骑兵队
knight 骑士，武士
relief 调剂，解除，减轻
interrupt 打扰，打断
swarm 云集，涌往
feverish 狂热的，兴奋的
miniature 小画像
carnation 康乃馨
fraud 骗子，假货
queer 奇怪的
asunder 离散，分开
inaccuracy 不准确
ignorance 无知
humanity 人类
accidental 偶然的
gnaw 啃
nibble 啃，一点一点地咬
canister 罐
book-blinding 装订
hoop 圈，箍
skate 冰鞋
scuttle 桶
bagatelle 弹子游戏
opal 乳色玻璃，蛋白石
emerald 祖母绿，纯绿柱石
turnip 萝卜
scraping 刮擦的，吝啬的
pare 削减，修掉（角、边等）
liken 把……比作
hairpin 发夹
tumble （使）摔倒，（使）滚翻，弄乱
asphodel （植）日光兰
meadow 草地
parcel 包裹
pitch 投，掷

shoot 急速动作，奔流，射击
perpetual 永久的
casual 随便的
haphazard 没有计划的，任意的
stalk （草本植物）主茎，花梗
deluge 淹浸，使泛滥
grope （暗中）摸索，探索
intersect 横断
blot 污渍，墨水渍
indistinct 不清晰的，模糊的
vigilant 警醒的
fragment 碎片
utterly 完全，彻底
annihilation 歼灭
tap 敲
spacious 宽广的
hostility 敌对
obstacle 障碍
steady 使稳固
fiction （虚构的）小说
track 思路，轨道
credit 信任，相信
modest 谦虚的
mouse-colored 鼠色的，灰褐色的
botany 植物学
tassel 缨，穗，绶，流苏
dress up 给……穿上盛装，乔装打扮
stealthy 隐秘的，暗中的
adore 喜爱，敬慕
catch out 发觉某人的错误
instinctive 本能的
idolatry 偶像崇拜，盲目崇拜
ridiculous 滑稽的，可笑的
smash 碎裂
shallow 浅薄的，浅的
bald 光秃秃的，无树的
prominent 显要的，突出的
omnibus 公共汽车，公共马车
account for 解释，说明
vague 模糊的
gleam 微光，闪光，微量

glassy （眼睛）没有神采的，呆滞的
novelist 小说家
reflection 想法，丢脸，责难
phantom 幽灵，幻象，影子，（抽象品性等的）化身
generalization 总结，一般化
military 军事的，军人的，军队的
damnation 毁掉，罚入地狱
luncheon 午餐，午宴
tapestry 织锦，花毯，挂毯
compartment 分隔空间
corridor 走廊
illegitimate 非法的，不合理的
mahogany 桃花心木，红木
sideboard 餐具柜，络腮胡须
intoxicating 令人陶醉的
project 凸出，伸出，突出
circular 圆形的
cast 投（射），投（影）
perceptible 可察觉的
strip 条，带
mount 上升
descend 下降
tumulus 冢，古坟
barrow 冢，古坟
stretch 伸长
turf 草皮，草根土
antiquary 文物工作者
clod 土块
correspondence 联系
necessitate 使必须
plum 洋李，李，梅
suspension 暂停，中止
accumulate 积累
incline 趋向于
indite 作（诗、文），写
pamphlet 传单，小册子
stroke 中风
murderess 女凶手
ascertain 查明，弄清
gigantic 巨大的

attrition 磨损
reveal 显露
speculation 玄思，构思，沉思
descendant 后代
witch 女巫
hermit 隐士
crouch 蹲伏
brew 调制，熬（草药）
herb 草（药）
interrogate 询问
shrew 鼩鼱（一种似鼠的小动物）
superstition 迷信
dwindle 减少，衰落
profile 简介，侧面（像）
slice 把……分成部分，切
fin 鳍
graze 吃（草）
waterlily 睡莲
suspend 悬（挂）

crack 裂缝
self-preservation 自我保存
collision 冲突，碰撞
enrage 激怒
shatter 打碎，摔碎
prompt 敦促，激励
contempt 轻视
fullstop 休止，句号
disagreeable 不合意的，不爽快的
plank 木版
quiescent 静止的，沉默的
worship 崇拜，敬慕
solidity 坚固，稳健，可靠
impersonal 不受个人感情影响的，非个人的
proof 证明
meadow 草地
swish 嗖嗖作声

moorhen 母红松鸡
raid 攻入，突击
water-beetle 水甲
dome 圆顶，圆顶形
grind 推，摇
ooze 渗出，分泌
sap 树液
bullet 像子弹的东西
mast 柱，杆
laborious 吃力的，费劲
crease 折缝，折痕，皱痕
bark 树皮
awning 遮篷
diamond 金刚石，钻石
fibre 纤维，须根
snap 突然折断，拉断
upheaval 剧变
snail 蜗牛

14.9 "Tickets, Please" by Lawrence

There is in the Midlands a single-line tramway system which boldly leaves the county town and plunges off into the black, industrial countryside, up hill and down dale, through the long ugly villages of workmen's houses, over canals and railways, past churches perched high and nobly over the smoke and shadows, through stark, grimy cold little market-places, tilting away in a rush past cinemas and shops down to the hollow where the collieries are, then up again, past a little rural church, under the ash trees, on in a rush to the terminus, the last little ugly place of industry, the cold little town that shivers on the edge of the wild, gloomy country beyond. There the green and creamy coloured tram-car seems to pause and purr with curious satisfaction. But in a few minutes—the clock on the turret of the Co-operative Wholesale Society's Shops gives the time—away it starts once more on the adventure. Again there are the reckless swoops downhill, bouncing the loops: again the chilly wait in the hill-top market-place: again the breathless slithering round the precipitous drop under the church: again the patient halts at the loops, waiting for the outcoming car: so on and on, for two long hours, till at last the city looms beyond the fat gas-works, the narrow factories draw near, we are in the sordid streets of the great town, once more we sidle to a standstill at our terminus, abashed by the great crimson and cream-coloured city cars, but still perky, jaunty, somewhat dare-devil, green as a jaunty sprig of parsley out of a black colliery garden.

To ride on these cars is always an adventure. Since we are in war-time, the drivers are men unfit for active service: cripples and hunchbacks. So they have the spirit of the devil in them. The ride becomes a steeple-chase. Hurray! We have leapt in a clear jump over the canal bridges—now for the four-lane corner. With a shriek and a trail of sparks we are clear again. To be sure, a tram often leaps the rails—but what matter! It sits in a ditch till other trams come to haul it out. It is quite common for a car, packed with one solid mass of living people, to come to a dead halt in the midst of unbroken blackness, the heart of nowhere on a dark night, and for the driver and the girl conductor to call, "All get off—car's on fire!" Instead, however, of rushing out in a panic, the passengers stolidly reply: "Get on—get on! We're not coming out. We're stopping where we are. Push on, George." So till flames actually appear.

The reason for this reluctance to dismount is that the nights are howlingly cold, black, and windswept, and a car is a haven of refuge. From village to village the miners travel, for a change of cinema, of girl, of pub. The trams are desperately packed. Who is going to risk himself in the black gulf outside, to wait perhaps an hour for another tram, then to see the forlorn notice "Depot Only", because there is something wrong! Or to greet a unit of three bright cars all so tight with people that they sail past with a howl of derision. Trams that pass in the night.

This, the most dangerous tram-service in England, as the authorities themselves declare, with pride, is entirely conducted by girls, and driven by rash young men, a little crippled, or by delicate young men, who creep forward in terror. The girls are fearless young hussies. In their ugly blue uniform, skirts up to their knees, shapeless old peaked caps on their heads, they have all the sang-froid of an old non-commissioned officer. With a tram packed with howling colliers, roaring hymns downstairs and a sort of antiphony of obscenities upstairs, the lasses are perfectly at their ease. They pounce on the youths who try to evade their ticket-machine. They push off the men at the end of their distance. They are not going to be done in the eye—not they. They fear nobody—and everybody fears them.

"Hello, Annie!"

"Hello, Ted!"

"Oh, mind my corn, Miss Stone. It's my belief you've got a heart of stone, for you've trod on it again."

"You should keep it in your pocket," replies Miss Stone, and she goes sturdily upstairs in her high boots.

"Tickets, please."

She is peremptory, suspicious, and ready to hit first. She can hold her own against ten thousand. The step of that tram-car is her Thermopylae[①].

Therefore, there is a certain wild romance aboard these cars—and in the sturdy bosom of Annie herself. The time for soft romance is in the morning, between ten o'clock and one, when things are rather slack: that is, except market-day and Saturday. Thus Annie has time to look about her. Then she often hops off her car and into a shop where she has spied something, while the driver chats in the main road. There is very good feeling between the girls and the drivers. Are they not companions in peril, shipments aboard this careering vessel of a tram-car, for ever rocking on the waves of a stormy land?

Then, also, during the easy hours, the inspectors are most in evidence. For some reason, everybody employed in this tram-service is young: there are no grey heads. It would not do.

---

① **Thermopylae**: See the note in "The Isles of Greece".

Therefore the inspectors are of the right age, and one, the chief, is also good-looking. See him stand on a wet, gloomy morning, in his long oil-skin, his peaked cap well down over his eyes, waiting to board a car. His face is ruddy, his small brown moustache is weathered, he has a faint impudent smile. Fairly tall and agile, even in his waterproof, he springs aboard a car and greets Annie.

"Hello, Annie! Keeping the wet out?"

"Trying to."

There are only two people in the car. Inspecting is soon over. Then for a long and impudent chat on the foot-board, a good, easy, twelve-mile chat.

The inspector's name is John Thomas Raynor—always called John Thomas, except sometimes, in malice, Coddy. His face sets in fury when he is addressed, from a distance, with this abbreviation. There is considerable scandal about John Thomas in half a dozen villages. He flirts with the girl conductors in the morning, and walks out with them in the dark night, when they leave their tram-car at the depot. Of course, the girls quit the service frequently. Then he flirts and walks out with the newcomer: always providing she is sufficiently attractive, and that she will consent to walk. It is remarkable, however, that most of the girls are quite comely, they are all young, and this roving life aboard the car gives them a sailor's dash and recklessness. What matter how they behave when the ship is in port. Tomorrow they will be aboard again.

Annie, however, was something of a Tartar①, and her sharp tongue had kept John Thomas at arm's length for many months. Perhaps, therefore, she liked him all the more: for he always came up smiling, with impudence. She watched him vanquish one girl, then another. She could tell by the movement of his mouth and eyes, when he flirted with her in the morning, that he had been walking out with this lass, or the other, the night before. A fine cock-of-the-walk he was. She could sum him up pretty well.

In this subtle antagonism they knew each other like old friends, they were as shrewd with one another almost as man and wife. But Annie had always kept him sufficiently at arm's length. Besides, she had a boy of her own.

The Statutes fair, however, came in November, at Bestwood. It happened that Annie had the Monday night off. It was a drizzling ugly night, yet she dressed herself up and went to the fair ground. She was alone, but she expected soon to find a pal of some sort.

The roundabouts were veering round and grinding out their music, the side shows were making as much commotion as possible. In the coco-nut shies there were no coco-nuts, but artificial war-time substitutes, which the lads declared were fastened into the irons. There was a sad decline in brilliance and luxury. None the less, the ground was muddy as ever, there was the same crush, the press of faces lighted up by the flares and the electric lights, the same smell of naphtha and a few fried potatoes, and of electricity.

Who should be the first to greet Miss Annie on the showground but John Thomas? He had a black overcoat buttoned up to his chin, and a tweed cap pulled down over his brows, his face

---

① **Tartar**: See the note in *The Merchant of Venice*.

between was ruddy and smiling and handy as ever. She knew so well the way his mouth moved.

She was very glad to have a "boy". To be at the Statutes without a fellow was no fun. Instantly, like the gallant he was, he took her on the dragons, grim-toothed, round-about switchbacks. It was not nearly so exciting as a tram-car actually. But, then, to be seated in a shaking, green dragon, uplifted above the sea of bubble faces, careering in a rickety fashion in the lower heavens, whilst John Thomas leaned over her, his cigarette in his mouth, was after all the right style. She was a plump, quick, alive little creature. So she was quite excited and happy.

John Thomas made her stay on for the next round. And therefore she could hardly for shame repulse him when he put his arm round her and drew her a little nearer to him, in a very warm and cuddly manner. Besides, he was fairly discreet, he kept his movement as hidden as possible. She looked down, and saw that his red, clean hand was out of sight of the crowd. And they knew each other so well. So they warmed up to the fair.

After the dragons they went on the horses. John Thomas paid each time, so she could but be complaisant. He, of course, sat astride on the outer horse—named "Black Bess"—and she sat sideways, towards him, on the inner horse—named "Wildfire". But of course John Thomas was not going to sit discreetly on "Black Bess", holding the brass bar. Round they spun and heaved, in the light. And round he swung on his wooden steed, flinging one leg across her mount, and perilously tipping up and down, across the space, half lying back, laughing at her. He was perfectly happy; she was afraid her hat was on one side, but she was excited.

He threw quoits on a table, and won for her two large, pale-blue hat-pins. And then, hearing the noise of the cinemas, announcing another performance, they climbed the boards and went in.

Of course, during these performances pitch darkness falls from time to time, when the machine goes wrong. Then there is a wild whooping, and a loud smacking of simulated kisses. In these moments John Thomas drew Annie towards him. After all, he had a wonderfully warm, cosy way of holding a girl with his arm, he seemed to make such a nice fit. And, after all, it was pleasant to be so held: so very comforting and cosy and nice. He leaned over her and she felt his breath on her hair; she knew he wanted to kiss her on the lips. And, after all, he was so warm and she fitted in to him so softly. After all, she wanted him to touch her lips.

But the light sprang up; she also started electrically, and put her hat straight. He left his arm lying nonchalantly behind her. Well, it was fun, it was exciting to be at the Statutes with John Thomas.

When the cinema was over they went for a walk across the dark, damp fields. He had all the arts of love-making. He was especially good at holding a girl, when he sat with her on a stile in the black, drizzling darkness. He seemed to be holding her in space, against his own warmth and gratification. And his kisses were soft and slow and searching.

So Annie walked out with John Thomas, though she kept her own boy dangling in the distance. Some of the tram-girls chose to be huffy. But there, you must take things as you find them, in this life.

There was no mistake about it, Annie liked John Thomas a good deal. She felt so rich and warm in herself whenever he was near. And John Thomas really liked Annie, more than usual. The soft, melting way in which she could flow into a fellow, as if she melted into his very bones, was something rare and good. He fully appreciated this.

But with a developing acquaintance there began a developing intimacy. Annie wanted to consider him a person, a man; she wanted to take an intelligent interest in him, and to have an intelligent response. She did not want a mere nocturnal presence, which was what he was so far. And she prided herself that he could not leave her.

Here she made a mistake. John Thomas intended to remain a nocturnal presence; he had no idea of becoming an all-round individual to her. When she started to take an intelligent interest in him and his life and his character, he sheered off. He hated intelligent interest. And he knew that the only way to stop it was to avoid it. The possessive female was aroused in Annie. So he left her.

It is no use saying she was not surprised. She was at first startled, thrown out of her count. For she had been so *very* sure of holding him. For a while she was staggered, and everything became uncertain to her. Then she wept with fury, indignation, desolation, and misery. Then she had a spasm of despair. And then, when he came, still impudently, on to her car, still familiar, but letting her see by the movement of his head that he had gone away to somebody else for the time being, and was enjoying pastures new, then she determined to have her own back.

She had a very shrewd idea what girls John Thomas had taken out. She went to Nora Purdy. Nora was a tall, rather pale, but well-built girl, with beautiful yellow hair. She was rather secretive.

"Hey!" said Annie, accosting her; then softly, "Who's John Thomas on with now?"

"I don't know," said Nora.

"Why tha does," said Annie, ironically lapsing into dialect. "Tha knows as well as I do."

"Well, I do, then," said Nora. "It isn't me, so don't bother."

"It's Cissy Meakin, isn't it?"

"It is, for all I know."

"Hasn't he got a face on him!" said Annie. "I don't half like his cheek. I could knock him off the foot-board when he comes round at me."

"He'll get dropped-on one of these days," said Nora.

"Ay, he will, when somebody makes up their mind to drop it on him. I should like to see him taken down a peg or two, shouldn't you?"

"I shouldn't mind," said Nora.

"You've got quite as much cause to as I have," said Annie. "But we'll drop on him one of these days, my girl. What? Don't you want to?"

"I don't mind," said Nora.

But as a matter of fact, Nora was much more vindictive than Annie.

One by one Annie went the round of the old flames. It so happened that Cissy Meakin left the tramway service in quite a short time. Her mother made her leave. Then John Thomas was on the qui-vive. He cast his eyes over his old flock. And his eyes lighted on Annie. He thought she would be safe now. Besides, he liked her.

She arranged to walk home with him on Sunday night. It so happened that her car would be in the depot at half past nine: the last car would come in at 10:15. So John Thomas was to wait for her there.

At the depot the girls had a little waiting-room of their own. It was quite rough, but cosy, with a fire and an oven and a mirror, and table and wooden chairs. The half dozen girls who knew John Thomas only too well had arranged to take service this Sunday afternoon. So, as the cars began to come in, early, the girls dropped into the waiting-room. And instead of hurrying off home, they sat around the fire and had a cup of tea. Outside was the darkness and lawlessness of wartime.

John Thomas came on the car after Annie, at about a quarter to ten. He poked his head easily into the girls' waiting-room.

"Prayer-meeting?" he asked.

"Ay, " said Laura Sharp. "Ladies only."

"That's me!" said John Thomas. It was one of his favourite exclamations.

"Shut the door, boy, " said Muriel Baggaley.

"On which side of me?" said John Thomas.

"Which tha likes, " said Polly Birkin.

He had come in and closed the door behind him. The girls moved in their circle, to make a place for him near the fire. He took off his great-coat and pushed back his hat.

"Who handles the teapot?" he said.

Nora Purdy silently poured him out a cup of tea.

"Want a bit o' my bread and drippin'?" said Muriel Baggaley to him.

"Ay, give us a bit."

And he began to eat his piece of bread.

"There's no place like home, girls, " he said.

They all looked at him as he uttered this piece of impudence. He seemed to be sunning himself in the presence of so many damsels.

"Especially if you're not afraid to go home in the dark, " said Laura Sharp.

"Me! By myself I am."

They sat till they heard the last tram come in. In a few minutes Emma Houselay entered.

"Come on, my old duck!" cried Polly Birkin.

"It is perishing, " said Emma, holding her fingers to the fire.

"But—I'm afraid to, go home in, the dark, " sang Laura Sharp, the tune having got into her mind.

"Who're you going with tonight, John Thomas?" asked Muriel Baggaley, coolly.

"Tonight?" said John Thomas. "Oh, I'm going home by myself tonight—all on my lonely-O."

"That's me!" said Nora Purdy, using his own ejaculation.

The girls laughed shrilly.

"Me as well, Nora," said John Thomas.

"Don't know what you mean," said Laura.

"Yes, I'm toddling," said he, rising and reaching for his overcoat.

"Nay," said Polly. "We're all here waiting for you."

"We've got to be up in good time in the morning," he said, in the benevolent official manner.

They all laughed.

"Nay," said Muriel. "Don't leave us all lonely, John Thomas. Take one!"

"I'll take the lot, if you like," he responded gallantly.

"That you won't either," said Muriel, "Two's company; seven's too much of a good thing."

"Nay—take one," said Laura. "Fair and square, all above board, and say which."

"Ay," cried Annie, speaking for the first time. "Pick, John Thomas; let's hear thee."

"Nay," he said. "I'm going home quiet tonight. Feeling good, for once."

"Whereabouts?" said Annie. "Take a good 'un, then. But tha's got to take one of us!"

"Nay, how can I take one," he said, laughing uneasily. "I don't want to make enemies."

"You'd only make one," said Annie.

"The chosen one," added Laura.

"Oh, my! Who said girls!" exclaimed John Thomas, again turning, as if to escape. "Well—good-night."

"Nay, you've got to make your pick," said Muriel. "Turn your face to the wall, and say which one touches you. Go on—we shall only just touch your back—one of us. Go on—turn your face to the wall, and don't look, and say which one touches you."

He was uneasy, mistrusting them. Yet he had not the courage to break away. They pushed him to a wall and stood him there with his face to it. Behind his back they all grimaced, tittering. He looked so comical. He looked around uneasily.

"Go on!" he cried.

"You're looking—you're looking!" they shouted.

He turned his head away. And suddenly, with a movement like a swift cat, Annie went forward and fetched him a box on the side of the head that sent his cap flying and himself staggering. He started round.

But at Annie's signal they all flew at him, slapping him, pinching him, pulling his hair, though more in fun than in spite or anger. He, however, saw red. His blue eyes flamed with strange fear as well as fury, and he butted through the girls to the door. It was locked. He wrenched at it. Roused, alert, the girls stood round and looked at him. He faced them, at bay. At that moment they were rather horrifying to him, as they stood in their short uniforms. He was distinctly afraid.

"Come on, John Thomas! Come on! Choose!" said Annie.

"What are you after? Open the door," he said.

"We shan't—not till you've chosen!" said Muriel.

"Chosen what?" he said.

"Chosen the one you're going to marry," she replied.

He hesitated a moment.

"Open the blasted door," he said, "and get back to your senses." He spoke with official authority.

"You've got to choose!" cried the girls.

"Come on!" cried Annie, looking him in the eye. "Come on! Come on!"

He went forward, rather vaguely. She had taken off her belt, and swinging it, she fetched him a sharp blow over the head with the buckle end. He sprang and seized her. But immediately the other girls rushed upon him, pulling and tearing and beating him. Their blood was now thoroughly up. He was their sport now. They were going to have their own back, out of him. Strange, wild creatures, they hung on him and rushed at him to bear him down. His tunic was torn right up the back, Nora had hold at the back of his collar, and was actually strangling him. Luckily the button burst. He struggled in a wild frenzy of fury and terror, almost mad terror. His tunic was simply torn off his back, his shirt-sleeves were torn away, his arms were naked. The girls rushed at him, clenched their hands on him and pulled at him: or they rushed at him and pushed him, butted him with all their might: or they struck him wild blows. He ducked and cringed and struck sideways. They became more intense.

At last he was down. They rushed on him, kneeling on him. He had neither breath nor strength to move. His face was bleeding with a long scratch, his brow was bruised.

Annie knelt on him, the other girls knelt and hung on to him. Their faces were flushed, their hair wild, their eyes were all glittering strangely. He lay at last quite still, with face averted, as an animal lies when it is defeated and at the mercy of the captor. Sometimes his eye glanced back at the wild faces of the girls. His breast rose heavily, his wrists were torn.

"Now, then, my fellow!" gasped Annie at length. "Now then—now—"

At the sound of her terrifying, cold triumph, he suddenly started to struggle as an animal might, but the girls threw themselves upon him with unnatural strength and power, forcing him down.

"Yes—now, then!" gasped Annie at length.

And there was a dead silence, in which the thud of heart-beating was to be heard. It was a suspense of pure silence in every soul.

"Now you know where you are," said Annie.

The sight of his white, bare arm maddened the girls. He lay in a kind of trance of fear and antagonism. They felt themselves filled with supernatural strength.

Suddenly Polly started to laugh—to giggle wildly—helplessly—and Emma and Muriel joined in. But Annie and Nora and Laura remained the same, tense, watchful, with gleaming eyes. He winced away from these eyes.

"Yes," said Annie, in a curious low tone, secret and deadly. "Yes! You've got it now! You know what you've done, don't you? You know what you've done."

He made no sound nor sign, but lay with bright, averted eyes, and averted, bleeding face.

"You ought to be killed, that's what you ought," said Annie, tensely. "You ought to be killed. " And there was a terrifying lust in her voice.

Polly was ceasing to laugh, and giving long-drawn Oh-h-hs and sighs as she came to herself.

"He's got to choose, " she said vaguely.

"Oh, yes, he has, " said Laura, with vindictive decision.

"Do you hear—do you hear?" said Annie. And with a sharp movement, that made him wince, she turned his face to her.

"Do you hear?" she repeated, shaking him.

But he was quite dumb. She fetched him a sharp slap on the face. He started, and his eyes widened. Then his face darkened with defiance, after all.

"Do you hear?" she repeated.

He only looked at her with hostile eyes.

"Speak! " she said, putting her face devilishly near his.

"What?" he said, almost overcome.

"You've got to choose! " she cried, as if it were some terrible menace, and as if it hurt her that she could not exact more.

"What?" he said, in fear.

"Choose your girl, Coddy. You've got to choose her now. And you'll get your neck broken if you play any more of your tricks, my boy. You're settled now. "

There was a pause. Again he averted his face. He was cunning in his overthrow. He did not give in to them really—no, not if they tore him to bits.

"All right, then, " he said, "I choose Annie. " His voice was strange and full of malice. Annie let go of him as if he had been a hot coal.

"He's chosen Annie! " said the girls in chorus.

"Me! " cried Annie. She was still kneeling, but away from him. He was still lying prostrate, with averted face. The girls grouped uneasily around.

"Me! " repeated Annie, with a terrible bitter accent.

Then she got up, drawing away from him with strange disgust and bitterness.

"I wouldn't touch him, " she said.

But her face quivered with a kind of agony, she seemed as if she would fall. The other girls turned aside. He remained lying on the floor, with his torn clothes and bleeding, averted face.

"Oh, if he's chosen—" said Polly.

"I don't want him—he can choose again, " said Annie, with the same rather bitter hopelessness.

"Get up, " said Polly, lifting his shoulder. "Get up. "

He rose slowly, a strange, ragged, dazed creature. The girls eyed him from a distance, curiously, furtively, dangerously.

"Who wants him?" cried Laura, roughly.

"Nobody, " they answered, with contempt. Yet each one of them waited for him to look at her, hoped he would look at her. All except Annie, and something was broken in her.

He, however, kept his face closed and averted from them all. There was a silence of the end. He picked up the torn pieces of his tunic, without knowing what to do with them. The girls stood about uneasily, flushed, panting, tidying their hair and their dress unconsciously, and watching him. He looked at none of them. He espied his cap in a corner, and went and picked it up. He put it on his head, and one of the girls burst into a shrill, hysteric laugh at the sight he presented. He, however, took no heed, but went straight to where his overcoat hung on a peg. The girls moved away from contact with him as if he had been an electric wire. He put on his coat and buttoned it down. Then he rolled his tunic-rags into a bundle, and stood before the locked door, dumbly.

"Open the door, somebody," said Laura.

"Annie's got the key," said one.

Annie silently offered the key to the girls. Nora unlocked the door.

"Tit for tat, old man," she said. "Show yourself a man, and don't bear a grudge."

But without a word or sign he had opened the door and gone, his face closed, his head dropped.

"That'll learn him," said Laura.

"Coddy!" said Nora.

"Shut up, for God's sake!" cried Annie fiercely, as if in torture.

"Well, I'm about ready to go, Polly. Look sharp!" said Muriel.

The girls were all anxious to be off. They were tidying themselves hurriedly, with mute, stupefied faces.

Questions

1. What's the author's purpose in giving the reader a detailed description of the tramway line?
2. How do you understand the title of the story?
3. Is there any foreshadowing in the story?
4. Is there any shift of tone in the story? How does the author achieve it?
5. What can we learn about the author's attitude towards industrialization from this story?

Vocabulary

tramway 有轨电车
boldly 大胆地，厚颜无耻地
plunge 突入，冲
dale 谷，溪谷
perch 坐在高处
nobly 高贵地，壮丽地
stark 光秃秃的，空的
grimy 肮脏的
tilt 冲刺
rush 冲，奔
hollow 山谷
colliery 煤矿

terminus 终点
shiver 颤抖，哆嗦
gloomy 阴暗的，令人沮丧的
creamy 奶油色的，米色的
purr （汽车引擎等）发出咕隆声
turret 塔楼，角楼
wholesale 批发
reckless 不注意的，鲁莽的
swoop 飞扑
bounce 撞击
loop （铁路的）让车道，环道
chilly 寒冷的

slither 不稳地滑动
precipitous 仓促的，猛冲的
halt 暂停
loom 隐隐呈现
gas-works 煤气厂
sordid 肮脏的，破烂的
sidle 侧身而行
standstill 停止
abash 使窘迫，使羞愧
crimson 深红色的
cream-coloured = creamy perk 莽撞的

jaunty 洋洋得意的
daredevil 胆大妄为的
sprig 小枝
parsley 香芹菜
cripple 跛子
hunchback 驼背（者）
steeple-chase 越野赛跑，障碍赛跑
hurray 好哇
leap 跳
lane 车道
shriek 象尖叫的声音
trail 一串
spark 火星，火花
ditch 沟，渠
haul 拖，拉
solid 紧密的
panic 惊慌
stolid 不易激动的，执拗的
push on 努力向前
reluctance 不愿，勉强
dismount 下车
howling 极度的
windswept 当风的
haven 避难所
refuge 避难所
gulf 深坑，鸿沟
forlorn 几乎无望的
depot 车站，仓库
derision 嘲笑
rash 急躁的，草率从事的
hussy 粗野女子
sang-froid （临危时的）镇静
hymn 赞歌
antiphony 应答轮唱
obscenity 猥亵的话或行为
pounce 猛扑，攻击
evade 逃避

do sb in the eye 欺骗某人
sturdily 坚强地
peremptory 盛气凌人的
slack 松弛的
hop 单足跳
peril 危险
ruddy 红润的
impudent 厚颜无耻的，无礼的
agile 敏捷的，灵活的
malice 恶意，蓄意
abbreviation 缩短
scandal 丑事，丑闻
flirt 调情
roving 流浪的
vanquish 征服，战胜
antagonism 对抗
shrewd 机灵，精明
pal 伙伴
roundabout 绕道
veer 转向
grind 摩擦的嘎嘎响声
cocoanut 椰子（油）
naphtha 石油
tweed 粗花呢
gallant 对女子献殷勤的人
bubble 像泡的
repulse 严拒
cuddly 令人想搂抱的
discreet 谨慎
complaisant 顺从的
astride 叉开两腿
spin 使旋转
fling 急伸，挥动（手臂、腿等）
perilously 危险地，冒险地
quoit 铁圈
cosy=cozy 舒适的
nonchalantly 冷漠地，若无其事地

gratification 满足
dangle 用（希望）眩惑
huffy 易生气的
intimacy 熟悉，亲密
nocturnal 夜间发生的
spasm （动作、感情）一阵发作
accost 走上前去跟（某人）讲话
drop on 训斥，惩罚
vindictive 恶意的，怀恨的
on the qui vive 警戒着
exclamation 呼喊，惊叫
utter 说，讲，表达
damsel 少女，姑娘
perish 使麻木
ejaculation 惊叹声
toddle 信步走
benevolent 仁慈的
grimace 作怪相，装鬼脸
tunic 紧身短上衣
strangle 勒死
frenzy 疯狂
captor 捕捉者
triumph 胜利
trance 恍惚，发呆
wince （因疼痛）畏缩
devilish 凶暴的，穷凶极恶的
menace 威胁，恐吓
chorus 齐声，一齐
prostrate 俯卧的
disgust 厌恶，憎恶
furtively 偷偷摸摸地
espy 窥探
shrill 尖声叫
hysteric 歇斯底里的
torture 折磨，痛苦
stupefy 使惊呆，使麻木

14.10 "Journey of the Magi[①]" by Eliot

"A cold coming we had of it,
　Just the worst time of the year

---

① **the Magi**: in the New Testament, the three wise men, or kings, who followed the star of Bethlehem, bringing gifts to the newly born Christ Jesus.

For a journey, and such a long journey:
　　　The ways deep and the weather sharp,
5　　The very dead of winter." ①
　　　And the camels galled, sore-footed, refractory,
　　　Lying down in the melting snow.
　　　There were times we regretted
　　　The summer palaces on slopes, the terraces,
10　　And the silken girls bringing sherbet.
　　　Then the camel men cursing and grumbling
　　　And running away, and wanting their liquor and women,
　　　And the night-fires going out, and the lack of shelters,
　　　And the cities hostile and the towns unfriendly
15　　And the villages dirty and charging high prices:
　　　A hard time we had of it.
　　　At the end we preferred to travel all night,
　　　Sleeping in snatches,
　　　With the voices singing in our ears, saying
20　　That this was all folly.

　　　Then at dawn we came down to a temperate valley,
　　　Wet, below the snow line, smelling of vegetation;
　　　With a running stream and a water-mill beating the darkness,
　　　And three trees on the low sky,
25　　And an old white horse galloped away in the meadow.
　　　Then we came to a tavern with vine-leaves over the lintel,
　　　Six hands at an open door dicing for pieces of silver,
　　　And feet kicking the empty wine-skins.
　　　But there was no information, and so we continued
30　　And arrived at evening, not a moment too soon
　　　Finding the place; it was (you may say) satisfactory.

　　　All this was a long time ago, I remember,
　　　And I would do it again, but set down
　　　This set down
35　　This: were we led all that way for
　　　Birth or Death? There was a Birth, certainly,
　　　We had evidence and no doubt. I had seen birth and death,
　　　But had thought they were different; this Birth was
　　　Hard and bitter agony for us, like Death, our death.

---

① These lines are adapted from the sermon preached at Christmas, in 1622, by Bishop Lancelot Andrewes.

40 We returned to our places, these Kingdoms,
  But no longer at ease here, in the old dispensation,
  With an alien people clutching their gods.
  I should be glad of another death.

Questions

1. Can you say something about the Magi? Why are they taking the journey? What is the meaning of "Epiphany"?
2. What is suggested in lines 11-16?
3. How do you understand the last part of the poem?

14.11 "Sweeney among the Nightingales" by Eliot

"Alas, I am struck a mortal blow within" ①

 Apeneck Sweeney spreads his knees
 Letting his arms hang down to laugh,
 The zebra stripes along his jaw
 Swelling to maculate giraffe.

 The circles of the stormy moon
 Slide westward toward the River Plate②,
 Death and the Raven③ drift above
 And Sweeney guards the horned gate④.

 Gloomy Orion and the Dog⑤
 Are veiled; and hushed the shrunken seas;
 The person in the Spanish cape
 Tries to sit on Sweeney's knees

 Slip and pulls the table cloth
 Overturns a coffee-cup,
 Reorganized upon the floor
 She yawns and draws a stocking up;

 The silent man in mocha brown

---

 ① **Alas, I ... within**: a line taken from Aeschylus' *Agamemnon* (Agamemnon's cry from within the palace when he is murdered by his wife, Clytemnestra).
 ② **the River Plate**: an estuary on the coast between Argentina and Uruguay.
 ③ **the Raven**: Corvus (constellation).
 ④ **the horned gate**: the gates of horn in Hades.
 ⑤ **Orion and the Dog**: names of constellations.

Sprawls at the window-sill and gapes;
The waiter brings in oranges
Bananas figs and hothouse grapes;

The silent vertebrate in brown
Contracts and concentrates, withdraws;
Rachel nee Rabinovitch
Tears at the grapes with murderous paws;

She and the lady in the cape
Are suspect, thought to be in league;
Therefore the man with heavy eyes
Declines the gambit, shows fatigue,

Leaves the room and reappears
Outside the window, leaning in,
Branches of wistaria
Circumscribe a golden grin;

The host with someone indistinct
Converses at the door apart,
The nightingales are singing near
The Convent of the Sacred Heart,

And sang within the bloody wood①
When Agamemnon cried aloud
And let their liquid siftings fall
To stain the stiff dishonoured shroud.

Questions

1. Why is Agamemnon mentioned in the poem?
2. What is the theme of the poem?

14.12 *Waiting for Godot* by Beckett (An Excerpt from Act Ⅰ)

Estragon, sitting on a low mound, is trying to take off his boot. He pulls at it with both hands, panting. He gives up, exhausted, rests, tries again. As before. Enter Vladimir.

ESTRAGON: (*Giving up again*) Nothing to be done.

VLADIMIR: (*Advancing with short, stiff strides, legs wide apart*) I'm beginning to

---

① **The bloody wood**: In Greek mythology, Philomela is raped in the wood by Tereus, her sister's husband, who later cuts Philomela's tongue to prevent her from telling the truth. She is later turned into a nightingale by the gods.

come round to that opinion. All my life I've tried to put it from me, saying, Vladimir, be reasonable, you haven't yet tried everything. And I resumed the struggle. (*He broods, musing on the struggle. Turning to Estragon*) So there you are again.

ESTRAGON: Am I?

VLADIMIR: I'm glad to see you back. I thought you were gone forever.

ESTRAGON: Me too.

VLADIMIR: Together again at last! We'll have to celebrate this. But how? (*He reflects*) Get up till I embrace you.

ESTRAGON: (*Irritably*) Not now, not now.

VLADIMIR:

(*Hurt, coldly*) May one inquire where His Highness spent the night?

ESTRAGON: In a ditch.

VLADIMIR: (*Admiringly*) A ditch! Where?

ESTRAGON: (*Without gesture*) Over there.

VLADIMIR: And they didn't beat you?

ESTRAGON: Beat me? Certainly they beat me.

VLADIMIR: The same lot as usual?

ESTRAGON: The same? I don't know.

VLADIMIR: When I think of it... all these years... but for me... where would you be... (*Decisively*) You'd be nothing more than a little heap of bones at the present minute, no doubt about it.

ESTRAGON: And what of it?

VLADIMIR: (*Gloomily*) It's too much for one man. (*Pause. Cheerfully*) On the other hand what's the good of losing heart now, that's what I say. We should have thought of it a million years ago, in the nineties.

ESTRAGON: Ah stop blathering and help me off with this bloody thing.

VLADIMIR: Hand in hand from the top of the Eiffel Tower, among the first. We were respectable in those days. Now it's too late. They wouldn't even let us up. (*Estragon tears at his boot*) What are you doing?

ESTRAGON: Taking off my boot. Did that never happen to you?

VLADIMIR: Boots must be taken off every day, I'm tired telling you that. Why don't you listen to me?

ESTRAGON: (*Feebly*) Help me!

VLADIMIR: It hurts?

ESTRAGON: (*Angrily*) Hurts! He wants to know if it hurts!

VLADIMIR: (*Angrily*) No one ever suffers but you. I don't count. I'd like to hear what you'd say if you had what I have.

ESTRAGON: It hurts?

VLADIMIR: (*Angrily*) Hurts! He wants to know if it hurts!

ESTRAGON: (*Pointing*) You might button it all the same.

VLADIMIR: (*Stooping*) True. (*He buttons his fly*) Never neglect the little things of life.

ESTRAGON: What do you expect, you always wait till the last moment.

VLADIMIR: (*Musingly*) The last moment... (*He meditates*) Hope deferred maketh the something sick, who said that?

ESTRAGON: Why don't you help me?

VLADIMIR: Sometimes I feel it coming all the same. Then I go all queer. (*He takes off his hat, peers inside it, feels about inside it, shakes it, puts it on again*) How shall I say? Relieved and at the same time... (*He searches for the word*) ... appalled. (*With emphasis*) AP-PALLED. (*He takes off his hat again, peers inside it*) Funny. (*He knocks on the crown as though to dislodge a foreign body, peers into it again, puts it on again*) Nothing to be done. (*Estragon with a supreme effort succeeds in pulling off his boot. He peers inside it, feels about inside it, turns it upside down, shakes it, looks on the ground to see if anything has fallen out, finds nothing, feels inside it again, staring sightlessly before him*) Well?

ESTRAGON: Nothing.

VLADIMIR: Show me.

ESTRAGON: There's nothing to show.

VLADIMIR: Try and put it on again.

ESTRAGON: (*Examining his foot*) I'll air it for a bit.

VLADIMIR: There's man all over for you, blaming on his boots the faults of his feet. (*He takes off his hat again, peers inside it, feels about inside it, knocks on the crown, blows into it, puts it on again*) This is getting alarming. (*Silence. Vladimir deep in thought, Estragon pulling at his toes*) One of the thieves was saved. (*Pause*) It's a reasonable percentage. (*Pause*) Gogo.

ESTRAGON: What?

VLADIMIR: Suppose we repented.

ESTRAGON: Repented what?

VLADIMIR: Oh... (*He reflects*) We wouldn't have to go into the details.

ESTRAGON: Our being born?

Vladimir breaks into a hearty laugh which he immediately stifles, his hand pressed to his pubis, his face contorted.

VLADIMIR: One daren't even laugh any more.

ESTRAGON: Dreadful privation.

VLADIMIR: Merely smile. (*He smiles suddenly from ear to ear, keeps smiling, ceases as suddenly*) It's not the same thing. Nothing to be done. (*Pause*) Gogo.

ESTRAGON: (*Irritably*) What is it?

VLADIMIR: Did you ever read the Bible?

ESTRAGON: The Bible... (*He reflects*) I must have taken a look at it.

VLADIMIR: Do you remember the Gospels?

ESTRAGON: I remember the maps of the Holy Land. Coloured they were. Very pretty. The Dead Sea was pale blue. The very look of it made me thirsty. That's where we'll go, I used to say, that's where we'll go for our honeymoon. We'll swim. We'll be happy.

VLADIMIR: You should have been a poet.

ESTRAGON: I was. (*Gesture towards his rags*) Isn't that obvious? (*Silence*)

VLADIMIR: Where was I ... How's your foot?

ESTRAGON: Swelling visibly.

VLADIMIR: Ah yes, the two thieves. Do you remember the story?

ESTRAGON: No.

VLADIMIR: Shall I tell it to you?

ESTRAGON: No.

VLADIMIR: It'll pass the time. (*Pause*) Two thieves, crucified at the same time as our Saviour. One?

ESTRAGON: Our what?

VLADIMIR: Our Saviour. Two thieves. One is supposed to have been saved and the other ... (*He searches for the contrary of saved*) ... damned.

ESTRAGON: Saved from what?

VLADIMIR: Hell.

ESTRAGON: I'm going. (*He does not move*)

VLADIMIR: And yet ... (*Pause*) ... how is it—this is not boring you I hope—how is it that of the four Evangelists[①] only one speaks of a thief being saved. The four of them were there—or thereabouts—and only one speaks of a thief being saved. (*Pause*) Come on, Gogo, return the ball, can't you, once in a way?

ESTRAGON: (*With exaggerated enthusiasm*) I find this really most extraordinarily interesting.

VLADIMIR: One out of four. Of the other three, two don't mention any thieves at all and the third says that both of them abused him.

ESTRAGON: Who?

VLADIMIR: What?

ESTRAGON: What's all this about? Abused who?

VLADIMIR: The Saviour.

ESTRAGON: Why?

VLADIMIR: Because he wouldn't save them.

ESTRAGON: From hell?

VLADIMIR: Imbecile! From death.

ESTRAGON: I thought you said hell.

VLADIMIR: From death, from death.

ESTRAGON: Well what of it?

VLADIMIR: Then the two of them must have been damned.

ESTRAGON: And why not?

VLADIMIR: But one of the four says that one of the two was saved.

ESTRAGON: Well? They don't agree and that's all there is to it.

---

① **The four Evangelists**: the four writers of the Gospels, namely, St Matthew, St Mark, St Luke, and St John.

VLADIMIR: But all four were there. And only one speaks of a thief being saved. Why believe him rather than the others?

ESTRAGON: Who believes him?

VLADIMIR: Everybody. It's the only version they know.

ESTRAGON: People are bloody ignorant apes. (*He rises painfully, goes limping to extreme left, halts, gazes into distance off with his hand screening his eyes, turns, goes to extreme right, gazes into distance. Vladimir watches him, then goes and picks up the boot, peers into it, drops it hastily*)

VLADIMIR: Pah! (*He spits. Estragon moves to center, halts with his back to auditorium*)

ESTRAGON: Charming spot. (*He turns, advances to front, halts facing auditorium*) Inspiring prospects. (*He turns to Vladimir*) Let's go.

VLADIMIR: We can't.

ESTRAGON: Why not?

VLADIMIR: We're waiting for Godot.

ESTRAGON: (*Despairingly*) Ah! (*Pause*) You're sure it was here?

VLADIMIR: What?

ESTRAGON: That we were to wait.

VLADIMIR: He said by the tree. (*They look at the tree*) Do you see any others?

ESTRAGON: What is it?

VLADIMIR: I don't know. A willow.

ESTRAGON: Where are the leaves?

VLADIMIR: It must be dead.

ESTRAGON: No more weeping.

VLADIMIR: Or perhaps it's not the season.

ESTRAGON: Looks to me more like a bush.

VLADIMIR: A shrub.

ESTRAGON: A bush.

VLADIMIR: A? What are you insinuating? That we've come to the wrong place?

ESTRAGON: He should be here.

VLADIMIR: He didn't say for sure he'd come.

ESTRAGON: And if he doesn't come?

VLADIMIR: We'll come back tomorrow.

ESTRAGON: And then the day after tomorrow.

VLADIMIR: Possibly.

ESTRAGON: And so on.

VLADIMIR: The point is?

ESTRAGON: Until he comes.

VLADIMIR: You're merciless.

ESTRAGON: We came here yesterday.

VLADIMIR: Ah no, there you're mistaken.

ESTRAGON: What did we do yesterday?

VLADIMIR: What did we do yesterday?

ESTRAGON: Yes.

VLADIMIR: Why ... (*Angrily*) Nothing is certain when you're about.

ESTRAGON: In my opinion we were here.

VLADIMIR: (*Looking round*) You recognize the place?

ESTRAGON: I didn't say that.

VLADIMIR: Well?

ESTRAGON: That makes no difference.

VLADIMIR: All the same ... that tree ... (*Turning towards auditorium*) that bog ...

ESTRAGON: You're sure it was this evening?

VLADIMIR: What?

ESTRAGON: That we were to wait.

VLADIMIR: He said Saturday. (*Pause*) I think.

ESTRAGON: You think.

VLADIMIR: I must have made a note of it. (*He fumbles in his pockets, bursting with miscellaneous rubbish*)

ESTRAGON: (*Very insidious*) But what Saturday? And is it Saturday? Is it not rather Sunday? (*Pause*) Or Monday? (*Pause*) Or Friday?

VLADIMIR: (*Looking wildly about him, as though the date was inscribed in the landscape*) It's not possible!

ESTRAGON: Or Thursday?

VLADIMIR: What'll we do?

ESTRAGON: If he came yesterday and we weren't here you may be sure he won't come again today.

VLADIMIR: But you say we were here yesterday.

ESTRAGON: I may be mistaken. (*Pause*) Let's stop talking for a minute, do you mind?

VLADIMIR: (*Feebly*) All right. (*Estragon sits down on the mound. Vladimir paces agitatedly to and fro, halting from time to time to gaze into distance off. Estragon falls asleep. Vladimir halts finally before Estragon*) Gogo! ... Gogo! ... Gogo!

Estragon wakes with a start.

ESTRAGON: (*Restored to the horror of his situation*) I was asleep! (*Despairingly*) Why will you never let me sleep?

VLADIMIR: I felt lonely.

ESTRAGON: I had a dream.

VLADIMIR: Don't tell me!

ESTRAGON: I dreamt that?

VLADIMIR: DON'T TELL ME!

ESTRAGON: (*Gesture toward the universe*) This one is enough for you? (*Silence*) It's not nice of you, Didi. Who am I to tell my private nightmares to if I can't tell them to you?

VLADIMIR: Let them remain private. You know I can't bear that.

ESTRAGON: (*Coldly*) There are times when I wonder if it wouldn't be better for us to part.

VLADIMIR: You wouldn't go far.

ESTRAGON: That would be too bad, really too bad. (*Pause*) Wouldn't it, Didi, be really too bad? (*Pause*) When you think of the beauty of the way. (*Pause*) And the goodness of the wayfarers. (*Pause. Wheedling*) Wouldn't it, Didi?

VLADIMIR: Calm yourself.

ESTRAGON: (*Voluptuously*) Calm ... calm ... The English say cawm. (*Pause*) You know the story of the Englishman in the brothel?

VLADIMIR: Yes.

ESTRAGON: Tell it to me.

VLADIMIR: Ah stop it!

ESTRAGON: An Englishman having drunk a little more than usual proceeds to a brothel. The bawd asks him if he wants a fair one, a dark one or a red-haired one. Go on.

VLADIMIR: STOP IT! (*Exit Vladimir hurriedly. Estragon gets up and follows him as far as the limit of the stage. Gestures of Estragon like those of a spectator encouraging a pugilist. Enter Vladimir. He brushes past Estragon, crosses the stage with bowed head. Estragon takes a step towards him, halts*)

ESTRAGON: (*Gently*) You wanted to speak to me? (*Silence. Estragon takes a step forward*) You had something to say to me? (*Silence. Another step forward*) Didi ...

VLADIMIR: (*Without turning*) I've nothing to say to you.

ESTRAGON: (*Step forward*) You're angry? (*Silence. Step forward*) Forgive me. (*Silence. Step forward. Estragon lays his hand on Vladimir's shoulder*) Come, Didi. (*Silence*) Give me your hand. (*Vladimir half turns*) Embrace me! (*Vladimir stiffens*) Don't be stubborn! (*Vladimir softens. They embrace. Estragon recoils*) You stink of garlic!

VLADIMIR: It's for the kidneys. (*Silence. Estragon looks attentively at the tree*) What do we do now?

ESTRAGON: Wait.

VLADIMIR: Yes, but while waiting.

ESTRAGON: What about hanging ourselves?

VLADIMIR: Hmm. It'd give us an erection.

ESTRAGON: (*Highly excited*) An erection!

VLADIMIR: With all that follows. Where it falls mandrakes grow. That's why they shriek when you pull them up. Did you not know that?

ESTRAGON: Let's hang ourselves immediately!

VLADIMIR: From a bough? (*They go towards the tree*) I wouldn't trust it.

ESTRAGON: We can always try.

VLADIMIR: Go ahead.

ESTRAGON: After you.

VLADIMIR: No no, you first.

ESTRAGON: Why me?

VLADIMIR: You're lighter than I am.

ESTRAGON: Just so!

VLADIMIR: I don't understand.

ESTRAGON: Use your intelligence, can't you? (*Vladimir uses his intelligence*)

VLADIMIR: (*Finally*) I remain in the dark.

ESTRAGON: This is how it is. (*He reflects*) The bough ... the bough ... (*Angrily*) Use your head, can't you?

VLADIMIR: You're my only hope.

ESTRAGON: (*With effort*) Gogo light—bough not break—Gogo dead. Didi—heavy—bough—break—Didi alone. Whereas?

VLADIMIR: I hadn't thought of that.

ESTRAGON: If it hangs you it'll hang anything.

VLADIMIR: But am I heavier than you?

ESTRAGON: So you tell me. I don't know. There's an even chance. Or nearly.

VLADIMIR: Well? What do we do?

ESTRAGON: Don't let's do anything. It's safer.

VLADIMIR: Let's wait and see what he says.

ESTRAGON: Who?

VLADIMIR: Godot.

ESTRAGON: Good idea.

VLADIMIR: Let's wait till we know exactly how we stand.

ESTRAGON: On the other hand it might be better to strike the iron before it freezes.

VLADIMIR: I'm curious to hear what he has to offer. Then we'll take it or leave it.

ESTRAGON: What exactly did we ask him for?

VLADIMIR: Were you not there?

ESTRAGON: I can't have been listening.

VLADIMIR: Oh ... Nothing very definite.

ESTRAGON: A kind of prayer.

VLADIMIR: Precisely.

ESTRAGON: A vague supplication.

VLADIMIR: Exactly.

ESTRAGON: And what did he reply?

VLADIMIR: That he'd see.

ESTRAGON: That he couldn't promise anything.

VLADIMIR: That he'd have to think it over.

ESTRAGON: In the quiet of his home.

VLADIMIR: Consult his family.

ESTRAGON: His friends.

VLADIMIR: His agents.

ESTRAGON: His correspondents.

VLADIMIR: His books.

ESTRAGON: His bank account.
VLADIMIR: Before taking a decision.
ESTRAGON: It's the normal thing.
VLADIMIR: Is it not?
ESTRAGON: I think it is.

Questions

1. A play is, generally speaking, made up of logical conversations among characters. Is this excerpt, in your opinion, a logical conversation? Are there any exophoric expressions in it?
2. In this excerpt, Estragon tries to take off his boot to rid something inside while Vladimir tries to clear something from inside his hat. These actions are repeated many times. What does this suggest?
3. Judging from what is mentioned about the Evangelists, the Savior and the two thieves, in this part, what religion is the play about?

14.13 "Who's Who" by Auden

A shilling life will give you all the facts:
How Father beat him, how he ran away,
What were the struggles of his youth, what acts
Made him the greatest figure of his day;
Of how he fought, fished, hunted, worked all night,
Though giddy, climbed new mountains; named a sea;
Some of the last researchers even write
Love made him weep his pints like you and me.

With all his honours on, he sighed for one
Who, say astonished critics, lived at home;
Did little jobs about the house with skill
And nothing else; could whistle; would sit still
Or potter round the garden; answered some
Of his long marvellous letters but kept none.

Questions

1. What can we learn about the poet's attitude towards "the greatest figure" from this poem?
2. Do you think the poet wanted to make a contrast between the life of a great man and that of an ordinary person?
3. What's your understanding of the title of this poem?

14.14 "Their Lonely Betters" by Auden

As I listened from a beach-chair in the shade
To all the noises that my garden made,

It seemed to me only proper that words
Should be withheld from vegetables and birds.

A robin with no Christian name ran through
The Robin-Anthem which was all it knew,
And rustling flowers for some third party waited
To say which pairs, if any, should get mated.

Not one of them was capable of lying,
There was not one which knew that it was dying
Or could have with a rhythm or a rhyme
Assumed responsibility for time.

Let them leave language to their lonely betters
Who count some days and long for certain letters;
We, too, make noises when we laugh or weep:
Words are for those with promises to keep.

Questions

1. What is the poet's purpose in describing the noises made by birds and flowers in the garden?
2. How do plants and animals, according to the poem, communicate? What is your understanding of the title?
3. Why did the poet use words like "words", "language", "letters", "name" and "lying" in the poem? What's your understanding of "noise", "anthem", and "rustling"?

14.15 "In Memory of W. B. Yeats" by Auden

I

He disappeared in the dead of winter:
The brooks were frozen, the air-ports almost deserted,
and snow disfigured the public statues;
The mercury sank in the mouth of the dying day.
O all the instruments agree
The day of his death was a dark cold day.

Far from his illness
The wolves ran on through the evergreen forests,
The peasant river was untempted by the fashionable quays;
By mourning tongues
The death of the poet was kept from his poems.

But for him it was his last afternoon as himself,

An afternoon of nurses and rumours;
The provinces of his body revolted,
The squares of his mind were empty,
Silence invaded the suburbs,
The current of his feeling failed; he became his admirers.

Now he is scattered among a hundred cities
And wholly given over to unfamiliar affections;
To find his happiness in another kind of wood
And be punished under a foreign code of conscience.
The words of a dead man
Are modified in the guts of the living.

But in the importance and noise of to-morrow
When the brokers are roaring like beasts on the floor of the Bourse, ①
And the poor have the sufferings to which they are fairly accustomed,
And each in the cell of himself is almost convinced of his freedom;
A few thousand will think of this day
As one thinks of a day when one did something slightly unusual.

O all the instruments agree
The day of his death was a dark cold day.

II

You were silly like us: your gift survived it all;
The parish of rich women, physical decay,
Yourself; mad Ireland hurt you into poetry.
Now Ireland has her madness and her weather still,
For poetry makes nothing happen: it survives
In the valley of its saying where executives
Would never want to tamper; it flows south
From ranches of isolation and the busy griefs,
Raw towns that we believe and die in; it survives,
A way of happening, a mouth.

III ②

Earth, receive an honoured guest;
William Yeats is laid to rest:
Let the Irish vessel lie
Emptied of its poetry.

---

① **the Bourse**: the French stock exchange.
② Auden omitted the section's second, third, and fourth stanzas in later versions.

Time that is intolerant
Of the brave and innocent,
And indifferent in a week
To a beautiful physique,

Worships language and forgives
Everyone by whom it lives;
Pardons cowardice, conceit,
Lays its honors at their feet.

Time that with this strange excuse
Pardoned Kipling[①] and his views,
And will pardon Paul Claudel,[②]
Pardons him for writing well.

In the nightmare of the dark
All the dogs of Europe bark,
And the living nations wait,
Each sequestered in its hate;

Intellectual disgrace
Stares from every human face,
And the seas of pity lie
Locked and frozen in each eye.

Follow, poet, follow right
To the bottom of the night,
With your unconstraining voice
Still persuade us to rejoice;

With the farming of a verse
Make a vineyard of the curse,
Sing of human unsuccess
In a rapture of distress;

In the deserts of the heart
Let the healing fountain start,

---

① **Kipling**: Rudyard Kipling (1865-1936), a British writer who championed imperialism.
② **Paul Claudel**: French author (1868-1955) with extremely conservative politics.

In the prison of his days
Teach the free man how to praise.

Questions

1. What can we learn about Yeats' position in Irish literature from this elegy?
2. What does the author say about the nature of poetry?
3. Find in the poem examples of the use of figurative language and comment on the effect.

Bibliography

[1] Allison A W, Barrow H, Blake C R, et al. *The Norton Anthology of Poetry* [M]. Revised. New York: Jr. W. W. Norton & Company, 1975.

[2] Barnard R. *A Short History of English Literature* [M]. 2nd ed. Oxford: Oxford University Press, 1994.

[3] Barnouw D. Disorderly Company: From "The Golden Notebook" to "The Four-Gated City" [J]. *Contemporary Literature*, 1974, 14 (4): 491-514.

[4] Brooks C, Warren R P. *Understanding Fiction* [M]. 3rd ed. Beijing: Foreign Language Teaching and Research Press, 2004.

[5] Coote S. *The Penguin Short History of English Literature* [M]. New York: Penguin Books Ltd., 1993.

[6] Corns T N. *The Cambridge Companion to English Poetry—Donne to Marvell* [M]. Shanghai: Cambridge University Press / Shanghai Foreign Language Education Press, 2001.

[7] Drabble M. *The Oxford Companion to English Literature* [M]. 6th ed. Oxford: Oxford University Press, 2000.

[8] Greenblatt S, Abrams M H. *The Norton Anthology of English Literature* [M]. 8th ed. New York: W. W. Norton & Company, 2005.

[9] Hunt D. *The Riverside Anthology of Literature* [M]. 2nd ed. Massachusetts: Houghton Miffin Company, 1991.

[10] Hunter J P. *The Norton Introduction to Poetry* [M]. New York: W. W. Norton & Company, 1975.

[11] Kennedy X J. *Literature: An Introduction to Fiction, Poetry, and Drama* [M]. 5th ed. New York: Harper Collins Publisher, 1991.

[12] Kermode F, Hollander J. *The Oxford Anthology of English Literature: Modern British Literature* [M]. New York: Oxford University Press, 1973.

[13] Ormerod D. In a Derelict Land: The Novels of V. S. Naipaul [J], *Contemporary Literature*, 1968, 9 (1): 74-90.

[14] Ormerod D. Theme and Image in V. S. Naipaul's A House for Mr. Biswas [J], *Texas Studies in Literature and Language*, 1967, 8 (4): 589-602.

[15] Rogers P. *An Outline of English Literature* [M]. Oxford: Oxford University Press, 1998.

[16] Rubinstein A T. *The Great Tradition in English Literature from Shakespeare to Shaw* (Volume I, II) [M]. New York: Modern Reader Paperbacks, 1969.

[17] Sanders A. *The Short Oxford History of English Literature* [M]. New York: Oxford University, 1999.

[18] 约翰·佩克，马丁·科伊尔(英). 英国文学简史[M]. 北京：高等教育出版社，2010.